❖ IN THE SHADOW OF EMERALD FIRE ❖

THE HEIR

To my beautiful little nieces, Ainsley, Maddie,
Holly, Julia, Emily, and Lydia,

And to my handsome little nephews, Caleb and Elias,

Because if you trust Him, God can do amazing things

❖ IN THE SHADOW OF EMERALD FIRE ❖

THE HEIR

A. D. GERMAN

sola Scriptura

sola fide

sola gratia

solus Christus

soli Deo Gloria

Psalm 56:13

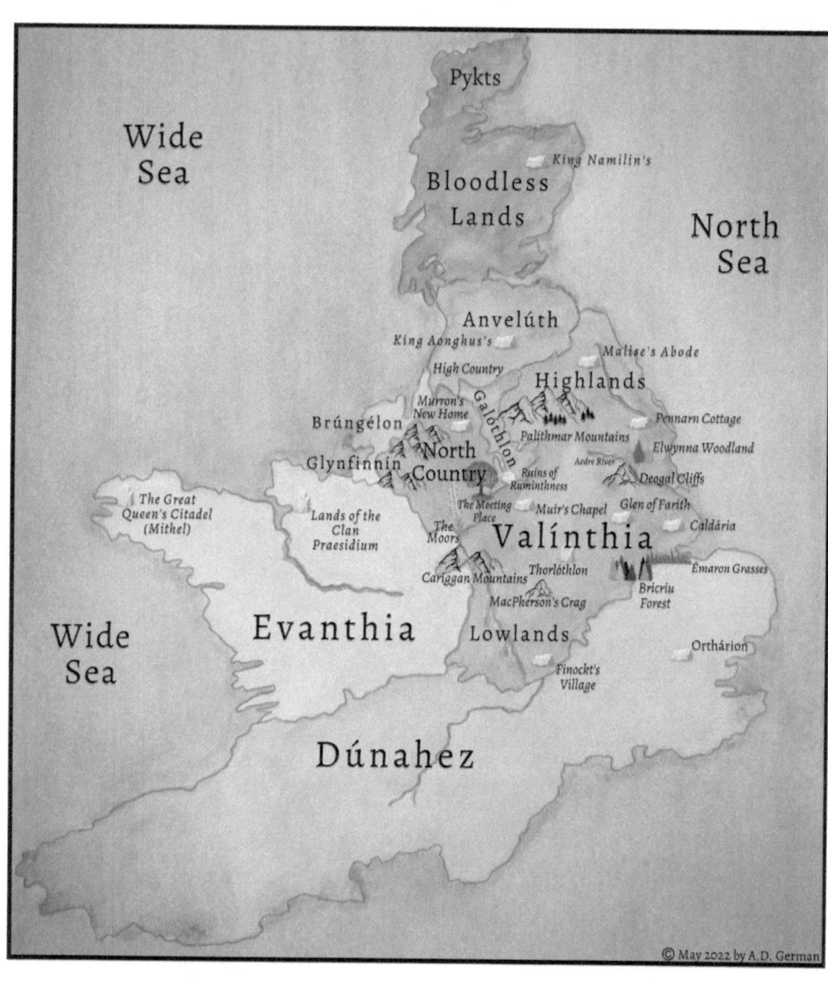

Wide Sea
Pykts
Bloodless Lands
King Namilin's
North Sea
Anvelúth
King Aonghus's
Malise's Abode
High Country
Highlands
Murron's New Home
Galóthlon
Brúngélon
Palithmar Mountains
Pennarn Cottage
Elwynna Woodland
Glynfinnín
North Country
Aedre River
Ruins of Ruminthness
Deogal Cliffs
The Great Queen's Citadel (Mithel)
The Meeting Place
Muir's Chapel
Glen of Farith
Lands of the Clan Praesidium
The Moors
Valínthia
Caldária
Thorlóthlon
Émaron Grasses
Cariggan Mountains
Bricriu Forest
Wide Sea
Evanthia
MacPherson's Crag
Lowlands
Orthárion
Finockt's Village
Dúnahez
© May 2022 by A.D. German

CHAPTER ONE

UST DOWN FROM her bedchamber, Finockt stood at the back stair of her grandfather's cottage and looked over the balustrade at the worn stone steps spiraling out of sight.

No soldiers.

No light.

No noise.

Only silence reverberated in her ears.

This is almost too easy, she told herself. She had not expected to escape Pennarn Cottage without some resistance. The fact that her grandfather's hunting lodge lay so still and so quiet, even at this hour, unnerved her. She gripped the railing harder, and the cold chill of the stone drove the blood from her fingers as she weighed the consequences of moving forward with her plan. All risk in times of war was worth pursuing, was it not? Particularly if it turned the tide for victory from one side to the other?

She chewed her bottom lip and further weighed the success of her plan. Doubt needled its way through her, making her hesitate. *You cannot do this. Your efforts will fail. Pennarn will fall.* Finockt shook the negative thoughts from her mind. This was not the time to second guess herself. Her brow bent with more determination. "Yes, I can," she whispered into the damp, predawn air. Her resolve strengthened with the realization that her thinking was not unlike what the men in her village believed, though they were so few in number against the Dúnarians: the pursuit of freedom was worth any potential risk it incurred.

Her hands tightened a second time around the stone railing. Foolhardy or not, she had little time to convince herself that another means of logic was better. To her right, the shadows had shifted. She glanced up at the wide rectangle of lattice glass cut into the stair's rounded tower wall. Just now the first breaths of white-gold sunlight broke the eastern sky, crept along the contours of the window, and brightened the dusky blue wall behind her. Simultaneously, beyond the stair and around a small bend in the cottage corridor, the soft *tink* of metal reached her ear, reminding her she was not alone after all; her grandfather's guards still kept watch outside his bedchamber. Yet rising above this subtle warning of probable opposition, the gentle, consistent rhythm of her grandfather's snoring allayed her fears: he was in a deep sleep. He would not stop her.

The familiar, light tap of metal again reached her ears—this time softer, fainter. It came at her from her other side and immediately set her in motion. She hastened to the first step, and just as she quietly slipped down the stair into the darkness and shadows below, a soldier gained Pennarn's upper floor and stepped out onto the opposite end of the long hallway. A narrow miss. Had she lingered a moment longer, he would have spotted her. She needed to move more quickly.

Her cloak billowed out behind her as she descended the last few steps of the tightly spiraled stair. To her relief, this lower, much narrower passageway remained dark and unoccupied until she rounded another gentle curve in the cottage wall. Weak candlelight softened the flagstones, its source pooling from a vaulted doorway. No sound came from within, and no shadows loomed against the walls or crossed the flagstones.

Finockt crept up to the doorframe and peeked around its edge. A room no bigger than a deep, wide alcove met her eye. Its side walls were draped with great maps as broad as the hearths. To her left a narrow lattice window looked out upon the rightmost edge of the garden, while straight before her, the middle of the wall was lined with holes cut into the stone: hole upon hole, the entire length of the wall. Therein lay scores of maps, rolled in soft leather and tied with strips of rawhide. And in the midst of all this, bathed in a dimming stream of candlelight, was Deverell, asleep, his head resting on the table, a map of Valínthia for his pillow. Its northern boundaries were anchored by his hands and its southern borders hung free over the table's edge. For all the turmoil that had befallen them, he slept peacefully, his dark hair falling over his chin and cheek. Guilt nipped at her. It was obvious his reasons for being there—to determine their next course of action. For half a moment, she had a fleeting notion to return to her chamber. He would be distressed by her leaving, but, like him, she knew that very soon they would face what she and her people had been avoiding for centuries.

Turning her back on his sleeping form, she hurried through

the cottage to its eastern side. Gradually, the air began to change and the silence to erode. She inhaled its changes first: the warm aroma of scones, the heavy smoked tang of bacon and salmon, and the hot, starchy scent of baked bread; yet above all these mouth-watering smells, a stronger yet more delicate fragrance pervaded the air—the warm, sweet, green, floral scent of clover and open meadow coming from the honey cakes freshly pulled from the oven. She had reached the kitchen. Here, just beyond the wooden planks of the door, the maidservants were already hard at work, making the numerous meals for the day, and for their second journey. Shadows darkened the cracks around the doorframe and traveled over the flagstones, as steaming dishes were carried from the hearth or water was brought in from the outside. And with the dawn had arisen an unusual and most unwelcome guest—fear.

The tangible emotion made its round in the kitchen with every movement of the maidservants, whose voices ebbed and flowed like the turn of the tides and sharpened the atmosphere with the inevitable terror of Tirell's impending presence. Their fear made Finockt all the more determined. She looked to the large, broad window situated at the end of the corridor. Through it, the sky now shone pink and gray. For five long hours she had planned for this moment: her escape from the cottage, her path to the stable, her flight into the unknown. Like the search for the box buried in the depths of Thorlóthlon, she realized she must risk everything yet again to bring them all one step closer to saving Valínthia, to avenging the murders of Gelis and Caslon, and ultimately to freeing herself from this vice.

Suddenly the din of voices that had clamored for so long fell silent, and a sob hiccuped periodically from one of the girls. The gut-wrenching sound further deepened Finockt's convictions and spurred her to action. She reached for the iron hook that held the pane shut and worked to release it. Every so often, she glanced over her shoulder in anticipation of being caught. But, thankfully, the corridor remained empty and silent, save for the low murmurs tumbling now and again from the kitchen behind her. A few minutes later, she found herself still wrestling with the hook. How long had it been since this window was opened?

The chatter from the kitchen suddenly grew clearer and stronger. Glancing back, Finockt saw a young maidservant with honey-blond hair slip out from beyond the kitchen door and close it noiselessly behind her. The girl's eyes were full of trepidation, and her hand trembled when she let go of the latch.

Finockt drew her hood down farther over her face and stepped into a shadowy corner of the hallway. But she did not have to fear being caught. The young girl waited for someone, and Finockt did not have to wonder long who it could be. As if on cue, a young soldier appeared, and the young maid ran toward him.

"Oh, Acair, I thought you wouldn't come," she breathed, clutching his hand.

"I told you I would," he replied. "You must believe what I say."

"Then how long do we have until Tirell comes upon us? The maidservants say there are only a few hours left until he consumes us all!" Her eyes were large and wild.

"Your friends enjoy telling a good story," the young soldier told her. "In truth, we cannot say how long the wait will be. Only God knows that. But the enemy will come, and we will be ready for him. And long before that time comes, you will be far from here. I've seen to that. The king has determined it."

"And you? Will you be alongside me?"

"I am a soldier, Talínnith. My duty is to remain until I am no longer of service to Valínthia's king."

Tears formed fast in her soft green eyes. "Then I shall never see you again," she said, stifling a sob. "Acair, he will leave no one alive!"

"You shall be safe, Talínnith, and that is all that matters to me. Now go, before you get into trouble. I only came to tell you you need not fear."

The young girl shook her head. "No, I cannot leave you. Acair, I won't!" she said with another shake of her head.

"You must."

"I cannot. I don't want this moment to end. I don't want to think of what will happen to us."

"In truth, I do not either." He held her hand more tightly. "Promise me, when you are made to leave, you will do it. You will go. Do not wait for me. Do you promise?"

For a long moment, Talínnith could not look at him.

"Talínnith, do you promise?"

Finally, she looked up at him and nodded. Relief filled his warm brown eyes. "Good. Now go before you are missed. I will see you again."

He kissed her sweetly on the forehead and withdrew.

Stripped of his comforting presence, Talínnith clasped her hands together, and bowing her head, she moved her lips fervently in prayer. Then she quickly cleared her face of the tears she had shed and taking a deep breath, turned back for the kitchen. Finockt held still, hoping she would continue to go unnoticed, concealed as she was amongst the long, thin drapery hanging from the window, but the light had grown too bright; and there were not enough shadows and finely spun linen left in which to hide. At the last moment, the young maid looked up and gasped. Finockt easily read the apprehension in her clear green eyes and heard it in her sharp intake of breath.

"What do you do here?" the young girl demanded, starting toward Finockt. Then she stopped abruptly and spun to call for help when Finockt threw back the hood of her cloak.

"Wait!" she said. "Do not call them to come!"

"My lady," Talínnith gasped, dropping to one knee before her.

"Please," Finockt said, "you need not be alarmed. I mean to help you."

"Help me?" Talínnith echoed, slowly rising. Her brow tensed. "How?"

"I am going to see someone who can help us defeat Tirell."

Disbelief clouded Talínnith's face. "Who, my lady? There is no one around these parts for miles. And there is no army willing to help us defeat this dark lord. Even the servants are wise enough to understand this."

Finockt went back to the window and struggled with the hook. "No, there is someone, not far from here."

I only hope he is willing to help us, she thought.

Talínnith stared at her. "And you are going to see him without escort?" she said. "Of this, I am sure, the king will not approve, Your Highness."

Finockt could see the young girl was ready to retrieve Coinneach. She dropped her hands away from the window. "There are some things that must be done, Talínnith, without the king's command and Thorlóthlon's guard. You want this war to be over, do you not? And you would do anything to keep Acair from having to join the fight, I think?"

Talínnith faltered. "Of course…"

"Then help me open this window, and say nothing to anyone about my leaving."

"By your words, then, I must believe you mean to put an end to the coming war?"

"I will do my best to stop it," Finockt promised, "so that no more lives need be lost." She turned back to her task.

Talínnith watched the princess's continued struggle with the hook while she contemplated Finockt's speech and the difficult choices laid out before her. "All right, I will help you," she determined, her mind focused solely on Acair's safety. She hurried to the window, and taking off her shoe, she smacked its heel against the bottom of the hook. The hook burst free of the ring, and the window pane swung open without a sound. "Go, now, milady! Before someone comes!"

Finockt scrambled over the window casing and dropped to the ground. "Thank you," she whispered.

"Remember your promise. I count on you to spare Acair's life, and therefore, my own. Godspeed," Talínnith returned. Then she swung the window shut, drove the hook back into the ring, and disappeared.

CHAPTER TWO

FINOCKT KEPT CLOSE to the stone wall and followed its length to the side of the cottage. From here she could see the barn through a tiny space the size of a keyhole in the hydrangea bushes; it stood about thirty yards away. Getting to it would require patience and skill. Pennarn's cottage grounds were amply guarded by Coinneach's soldiers. Not far ahead of her, they stood at random intervals and kept watch for any undesirable activity. By the tilt of their heads, she knew they conversed with one another in low tones. And every now and again, they would grow tense and point to something down in the valley. But the moment of fear would pass, and they would stand idly again, bored and yet stiff with the anticipation of what was to come.

Finockt waited until they had their backs to her. Then she ran toward the barn, taking care to hide herself amongst the deep shadows cast by those trees not yet touched by morning's light. The warm, heavy smell of horses and hay tickled her nostrils as she slipped through the unguarded barn door. With haste, she scoured each stall and open aisle for groomsmen or stable hands then felt a lessening of the tension between her shoulders when only a crisp, neat row of well-carved stalls met her eye. Within them stood the strength of Thorlóthlon: stallions, mares, and bays—beautiful horses, sleek and muscled, with coats that shone like polished plates of armor. They eyed her carelessly amidst their leisurely chewing when she first entered then lowered their heads back to their breakfast while she crossed the barn floor in search of a reliable mount. With every step she took, a sudden, unwanted surge of worry rose within her, for she had overlooked one major detail—she did not know how to saddle and bridle a horse. Riding bareback was out of the question. Though she had done it once out of necessity in the hills above her village in order to escape the Dúnarians, she did not trust herself this time to be able to outrun either Dúnarian or Valínthian without falling off. And for certain, in future, only necessity would drive her to risk such again. She bit her lower lip. *Think, think,* she told herself. Had she not seen Caslon saddle and bridle a horse for countless Dúnarian guards from the village fort over the years? Why could she not now remember how it was done?

The only thing of which she was certain was the need for something soft to cover the horse's back prior to swinging the saddle into place. She scanned the room for a thick blanket, retrieved it, and then strode toward the gentle mare she had chosen for her journey; the same one she had ridden from Thorlóthlon. The mare was docile and quiet and would be the easiest to control on this voyage through a foreign land. Lifting the latch on the stall door, she swung it open. Immediately the hinges squealed in protest. Finockt cringed at the unexpected sound and ducked behind the door. The noise was so loud she swore it had announced her presence to the whole of Valínthia. Fixing her eyes on the barn's entrance, she braced herself for the soldiers' rapid approach, but the air remained quiet, aside from the rhythmic crunch of the horses eating their oats and barley. She waited a few seconds longer, and when certain the soldiers were indeed not coming, she rose cautiously and proceeded into the stall.

At Finockt's careful approach, the mare abandoned her carved feeding trough and sniffed the newcomer. Finockt held out her hand, and the horse gently probed her palm with a soft, whiskered nose, her nostrils flaring and her thick lips nibbling Finockt's flesh.

"Haí, Mónwyn." Finockt ran her hand over the mare's forehead. "Will you help me?" She had forgotten a bribe, but to her relief, Mónwyn recognized her and did not flinch at her touch. "I need a favor. A ride. Seemingly to the ends of the earth." Mónwyn lowered her head sharply and blew. "Good girl," Finockt said. "I'll take that as a yes."

Moving painfully slowly to avoid frightening her mount, Finockt spread the thick blanket over the mare's back, then retrieved the heavy saddle hanging over the stall, and swung it into place. Mónwyn sidestepped and nickered softly at its sudden weight, but she did not fight her when Finockt threaded the straps and cinched the buckles tight. With this accomplished, Finockt's face brightened in triumph. The mare was ready for its rider. After all her meticulous planning, it seemed things were finally working to her advantage. She was very nearly free. Already she could taste the mountain mist on her tongue and smell the damp, cloying scent of a new wood.

She reached for Mónwyn's bridle on its peg just outside the stall door when a flicker of morning sunlight washed over the ceiling, and the barn door gently warned of an intruder. Finockt dropped out of sight. But even with the return of silence, she sensed someone was there. She pressed her back against the stall's wooden divider and listened, all the while desperately hoping it was someone other than a soldier who trod the barn's dark, dusty floor. If he knew she was here, unlike Talínnith, he would not let her go, and then she would lose her opportunity to potentially discover a way to defeat Tirell forever.

"Finockt! I know you're here. You can come out now."

Finockt checked herself, madly trying to place the owner of the voice, while Mónwyn fidgeted beside her.

"Finockt?" the voice came again, louder, closer, and more insistent. "I'm here to help you!"

"Eilidh?" Finockt ran to the front of the stall. "Saints above, how did you get past the guards? What are you doing here? You weren't followed, were you?"

"I've come to be your guide," Eilidh said with a winning smile. "And no, of course not! I've been waiting for you since before dawn. I saw in your eyes last night that you had an idea. I came to find out where it was to lead you."

"My guide?" Finockt replied in utter astonishment.

"Aye, you'll never make it where you're going without me."

Finockt stood speechless. *How* did Eilidh know when she had told no one of her plans? "Come with me?" she finally said, stumbling over the phrase. "Impossible," she added with a shake of her head. "No, I'll not have you come. This is something I must do alone."

Hard lines creased Eilidh's brow—a look that did not befit

her. "You know you are risking much in taking such a venture alone."

"Aye, 'tis a risk *I* am willing to take," Finockt replied.

"You'll need my help," Eilidh insisted. "—I know these parts of Valínthia well. I can take you anywhere you want to go!"

Finockt shook her head a second time. "No, I cannot risk it! I'll find my own way, alone. I'm of a mind not to let anyone stop me, not even you."

"Ach, well, there's no reason for you to. I'm going with you!"

Eilidh grabbed a saddle, and Finockt gently stayed her hand. "Don't make this more difficult than it already is. I need you here. Don't you understand? I don't want you to become caught up in this as well. It will be the king's wrath upon us both when Coinneach finds out!"

"That's a risk *I'm* willing to take," Eilidh argued, her bright blue eyes glowing hot. "Although you still haven't told me where you're going, I am certain I can now guess your destination before you even tell it. Why hide it any longer?"

Eilidh was right. Finockt knew her well enough to realize whether she told her or not, her young cousin could easily guess her intentions. It was useless to continue keeping it a secret.

"I'm going to the Highlands to find Malise."

Eilidh's eyes grew big and round with delight. "Ah, you most definitely must let me go with you now!"

"No!" Finockt said more emphatically. "I'll not risk harming you." She sighed. "I told you, I don't want to see you get into trouble, too. This is my own seeking. And if I fail, then it is only I who bear the mark. And if I am by some means captured along the way…" She stopped mid-sentence and cast the unspoken thought from her mind. She did not want to consider what that might entail. Instead, she took Mónwyn by the bit and walked her to the side of the barn closest to the woods. Eilidh watched her steadily, so eager to assist her cousin and so hoping to provide something useful to help save Valínthia and Thorlóthlon. Her people, the House of Eilthárion, had been crucial in turning the tide on events far worse than what they now faced in this search for a wise hermit. Finockt's refusal proved an obstacle she could easily overcome, if only Finockt would give her the chance to conquer it.

"You may prove of better use here, Eilidh," Finockt continued, her mind made up. "This way, if anyone asks where I've gone, you can honestly say you had no part in it."

"*May* be of use?" Eilidh said with disgust, feeling the full sting of her cousin's words, whether Finockt meant it that way or not. She crossed her arms, unable to suppress her rising irritation any longer. "And you know the way, I suppose."

"I will find him. Just as I have found everything else," Finockt snapped, tired of the argument. She looked out the round stable windows. The country was endless and unfamiliar. It would take a miracle really to find him.

"*I* know exactly where he lives," Eilidh said, kicking at the dirt floor of the barn with the toe of her shoe. She raised her eyes to Finockt's retreating figure.

Thorlóthlon's princess stopped so suddenly, Mónwyn pushed against her back. "You know?"

"Yes, I know because…do you want me to help you or not, Finockt? If you don't accept my help you'll be wandering these hills and crags all day and probably never find him… whereas,

I may take you directly to him." She held her breath and hoped this rationale would be enough to persuade her elder cousin to include her on this venture.

Finockt remained silent. The sun was rising fast. There was no time to continue arguing. Her visage softened. Eilidh was right…again. She would arrive at Malise's much faster if she just let her have her way.

At the change in her cousin's countenance, Eilidh's eyes brightened. She knew she was winning. She crept closer to Finockt. "Moreover," she said, "you know I'll follow. And truth be told, we could almost be there and back before Deverell and Coinneach begin the search for us, if I…"

"All right, all right," Finockt sighed, resigning herself. She laughed softly. "You've already won! You needn't add anything more. The sun is already gaining on us. It will peak over the horizon before we know it, and we'll not be any more than a stone's throw from here with all this idle talk—make sure you stay close to me. I'll not have either one of us captured and used as a further threat against my grandfather or against Thorlóthlon. And I'd never forgive myself if they took you alone."

A smile lighted Eilidh's face, and she clapped her hands in delight. Finockt rolled her eyes. "And don't let your victory go to your head," she playfully admonished her young cousin, who rushed to saddle and bridle a stout bay.

"I haven't yet," Eilidh said with another winning smile as she led her horse across the barn toward her cousin.

"Nor will you, I suppose?" Finockt teased.

Eilidh laughed. "Never!"

They mounted their horses in a small clearing behind the barn. Eilidh set her horse into a canter, and Finockt followed.

In the next minute, the two girls were beyond a break in the stone wall and within the safety of the young forest and its crags. To Finockt's utter relief, the worst was behind them. They had successfully and safely escaped. But what future troubles lay on the road ahead could not be easily anticipated.

CHAPTER THREE

N HOUR OR two after Finockt's departure, Coinneach rapped softly on her chamber door. He, too, had been up half the night for reasons other than contemplating Tirell's pending advancement. Not until the wee hours of the morning did he finally drift off to sleep out of sheer exhaustion. When he had woken and dressed, his first thought was to see his granddaughter. It would not be easy to say what he knew needed to be said. He had swallowed much of his pride already just standing before her door. He rapped again, and receiving no answer, he opened it slowly to find the room dark and silent. The curtains were still drawn; only a little light seeped through where someone had pushed them back to peek outside.

"Finockt, my child," Coinneach said again. Passing through the dim light, he crossed the room for her bed, and when he saw it lay empty, his face bore alarm. He strode to

Eilidh's chamber and threw open the door to find her room as empty and silent as Finockt's.

Behind him footsteps pounded down the hallway, and his suspicions mounted. "Milord, milord!" Proinnseas cried, bursting into the room. She slid to an awkward stop before him and curtsied quickly, her small face bright red. "I'm sorry, milord. I cannot find her anywhere," she said, trying to catch her breath.

"You've searched the grounds?" he asked, fearing the worst.

"Aye, milord, and the stable hands found two horses missing from the barn."

His face fell. It was as he thought. "Thank you, Proinnseas. Summon Deverell and bid him meet with me below, immediately," he said, pushing past her for the stair. She bobbed her head and gave his fleeting figure another quick curtsey. Coinneach's mind was ablaze, and his anger soared. He knew where she had gone.

Under a warming sun, several miles from the cottage, Eilidh confidently led the way, taking herself and Finockt through winding, craggy passes and up steeper hills. Their direction carried them north, then west, and then north again before it gradually led them southeast toward the sea. Meeting with a rather steep incline, the girls were forced to dismount and walk their tired horses the rest of the way up the slope.

At the top of the incline, the land leveled and then gently descended toward a small stone roundhouse tucked away in a niche of the grassy crags. Its thatched roof was carefully tended, and thin trails of smoke wound gently from the stone chimney stacked at its side.

Finockt stopped atop the slope, and Eilidh stepped up beside her, grinning madly. "This is it," her cousin said.

Finockt looked again. It was not what she had expected for a hermit's hideaway. Tiny round windows were cut into the stone for evening's light to pass through, and the doorway was larger than most and made from the same heavy wood Finockt had seen at Thorlóthlon. Around the cottage, the area was very clean and well cared for and boasted a small pen for animals, while at its back, was a well-laid, simple garden. Beyond this, the land stretched up a graded slope populated with dense evergreens.

The wind ran free over this desolate countryside and bullied the long, dry grasses covering the gentle rise and fall of the knolls and crags surrounding the little cottage. Even the evergreens in the distance shivered and cowered at its presence. The only things that did not seem disturbed by its ferocity were the green mountain peaks slowly changing in color as summer transitioned to autumn.

Eilidh led her mount by the bit and began descending the slope to more level ground. "I haven't set foot here for what seems like ages," she said, nimbly finding her way down the rocky, shaggy hill face.

Finockt followed close behind her cousin, then she stopped midway and gazed again with uncertainty upon the humble abode. "You've been here before?" she asked, her voice tinted with surprise and her eyes now trained on Eilidh's back.

"Aye. I shall wait for you here," Eilidh said. She led her horse to a soft shady spot beneath a random bower of young aspen trees that seemed completely out of place next to the grassy crags, unending knolls, and the narrow brook, trickling down from the far green mountains. "You'll probably want to speak with Malise alone."

"How is it that you know him so well?" Finockt asked, again following her cousin's lead.

"He has been a dear friend of mine for a very long time," Eilidh replied with a deep sense of satisfaction as they tethered their steeds to an aspen's white trunk. Finockt stared intently at the humble cottage and absently gave Mónwyn a pat on her long, firm neck. Eilidh finished tying her horse's reins into a knot and then ducked under his head. "The sun gains on us. It's best you hurry," she said, unusually vigilant about the time.

"You're waiting here?"

"Aye. I've kept my desired end of the bargain. I've brought you here, but I'll meddle no further. I understand there are certain things which should only be discussed within the presence of Malise. Now hurry! I'll keep my eye to danger, but in the meantime, you must be quick, for the sun is already halfway up into the eastern sky. Midday is nigh upon us."

Finockt leaped over the brook and headed across the crags and knolls for Malise's door. It seemed a long space between the trees and the cottage. The land was wide and open. Never before had she felt so small, vulnerable, and unnerved. Now she stood before the broad oak door, and as she reached up to knock lightly on its smoothly finished surface, a sudden pang of fear caught at her. She withdrew her hand. Perhaps this would be like the necklace. Perhaps she did not really want to know who Malise was and what connection he had with her father. Maybe she would regret learning more about the past just as she now regretted the consequences of the emerald necklace falling into her possession. Her conscience pricked at her, countering her misgivings; she could not leave this place without inquiring. Her father had trusted this man and had sought his counsel, had he not? The entry from Anwyl's diary confirmed that. It was that very entry that led her to this moment. Surely then Malise knew truths and carried a wisdom uncommon to most men. And it was Coinneach who had described her father as a lover of knowledge and a frequent visitor to Trythwyn's study. It made sense then that Anwyl would seek the highest form of human counsel to determine his next steps. And undoubtedly, she herself must recall to mind the inevitable truth that in these circumstances, with the giving or receiving of counsel, there almost always precedes a revelation of dark secrets, moral dilemmas, and the unending need for carefully crafted decisions—decisions that, if made unwisely, could ultimately end up destroying lives rather than preserving them. She must find the courage then to move forward in hopes of finding answers to a past no one else knew—in order to help her people and herself—, or else her heart could never truly lie at peace.

Mustering up her courage, she again raised her hand to rap on the door, but before she ever had a chance to, it abruptly opened. She gasped and stumbled away from the threshold, while the old man in front of her stiffened and leaned back into the shadows of the doorway. His lowly appearance did not erase his carriage as one born of a higher station, and he studied her from head to toe with a calculating gaze—thoughtful yet wary—though his placid facial expression did not betray his reservations.

"You've come from afar," he said in a kind voice when his shock had passed.

Finockt regarded his sharp gray-blue eyes still scrutinizing her and swallowed hard. "Aye, 'tis true, sir. I have come a little ways," she said, regaining her composure.

"And what is it then you have come for?" he asked, shifting his stance. "It's not often a young lady of royal blood visits these parts of Valínthia. Be you then in trouble?"

He gave a glance past her for a military escort, and when he saw Eilidh sitting under the aspens, his heart started within him, quieting his suspicions about the young girl before him and raising a fragile hope in their place.

"Of sorts," Finockt answered him, "but it is not what you would believe. My troubles are of a different kind."

"So you have come for answers to riddles, have you?" the old man replied. He waved off her partial attempt at protest. "Haí, I am an old man, child, and I've lived long enough to know one expression from another, to read it even better, even down to the subtle change of the eye. You want something, but can it be that I am the one who can help you?"

"You distrust me, I see, and doubt the sincerity of my coming."

"By all accounts, lass," the old man replied, leaning now against the door frame. "It takes a skilled man—or woman—to find this place. I live in the wilds by my own choosing and have yet to see a soul stumble upon it by accident. Your presence here is purposeful. Clearly, you seek something."

"I have come for counsel."

"From me?"

"From a man by the name of Malise. Do you know him?"

"Malise? Aye, milady, I know him very well," the old man said mischievously, but Finockt did not detect the teasing coloring his voice.

"Will you take me to him?"

The highlander shifted uncomfortably. "He is a private man…"

Finockt kept her gaze steady. "I know he must be. On my honor, this intrusion of his privacy stems only from necessity."

The highlander crossed his arms and tucked his chin, as if he needed more time to consider her proposal. "You may very well be wasting your time," he said, locking eyes with her again.

"Please sir. You can be sure I'll not leave this place until he gives me audience. In truth, my time is short, and I cannot be sure I have not been followed by someone. I need to speak with him immediately. Many lives depend on it, including my own."

The old man sobered. "Enter then, and be brisk," he said, stepping back and gesturing her in.

Finockt readily passed beneath the lintel. As she entered, a young man quickly departed by means of a rear entrance. The sunlight caught his golden hair for an instant before the door closed, and Finockt's heart quickened. *"Gwri!"* she said, under her breath.

"Be you all right, child?" the old highlander asked, somewhere between curiosity and humor. "'Tis only the back of the house. It hasn't changed for almost fifteen years." He pressed the door closed against the wind and slipped past her for the hearth.

"I thought I saw someone…a young man."

"Young man?" the highlander asked with a grunt, adding another log to the fire.

"Aye," Finockt answered, studying him. "One not much older than myself."

"Ah, that was most likely Uisdean," he said, casting another glance toward the back door. "He helps me out with work around the place and visits me every now and again. Though

God in His glory surrounds me in nature's fairest form, even an old man can hunger for the sight of human company. Your company is most unusual. I would sooner think you were desperately lost, had you not said you have come on a specific errand." He shifted two finely crafted oak chairs closer to the small, deep-set hearth; the inlaid designs along the chair backs were also reminiscent of those at Thorlóthlon. "Now come, seat yourself beside the fire," the highlander said, motioning Finockt away from the door and to one of the chairs. "Though it is late summer, the mountain air is still cool enough to chill one's bones."

"Will I meet with him?" she asked, crossing the tiny, sparsely furnished abode to join him by the fire. "Will he come?"

"Aye, he will come," the old man said. "But his coming depends on the nature of your inquiry."

Finockt untied the laces on her cloak. "If you please, I wish to say only in his presence."

The old man dusted his hands off on his tunic and crossed the dirt floor for the other side of the barren cottage. "I see," was all he said; he ventured nothing more.

Finockt added, "I have come a long way, sir, and my duty is of haste…"

"Gone against your guardian's wishes, have you?" the old man smirked.

"I have."

Malise's playfulness suddenly faded at the seriousness of her countenance, and a dark pall fell over him. He could no longer avoid the truth of her coming. Though his stoic expression left him fully unreadable to any other observer, he could not conceal from Finockt the deep, visible sadness that crept into his blue eyes: a sadness so morose, it was as if what he was about to say pained him and he was not wont to reveal it.

Finockt grew more troubled and looked at him expectantly, hoping against all odds she had not now just lost everything she had hoped to gain. *Please let him meet with me,* she silently prayed. The highlander briefly absorbed her inquiring gaze, then he quietly said, "This charade has gone on long enough then. Speak now, for the man you so seek stands before you."

CHAPTER FOUR

INOCKT EXAMINED THE highlander carefully, skeptical of his revelation. "You are he?" she said incredulously. She did not know what she had expected, but it did not occur to her to expect this. His apparel, though clean, suggested he was nothing more than a lowly shepherd, and yet there was something about him. A deep familiarity resided in the suntanned, wrinkled face, capped with snow-white hair flecked with thick streaks of sable gray. A feeling of home.

"Is it so hard to believe, child?" he asked. "Or was it that you were expecting a grand lord?"

Finockt blushed. "Yes…no, it's just…I suppose I was. Forgive me. This meeting has begun so differently than I imagined. And you…you appear so familiar to me somehow, as if I already know you and have for a very long time."

"Hm," Malise said, taking a bucket full of water and pouring a bit into an iron pot. "And so, will you speak? Now that you know I am the one for whom you were searching?"

Finockt braced herself. This was the exact moment she had been preparing for. She took a deep breath to settle her nerves. "Word has been given that you knew Anwyl well," she said, closely watching him for his reaction to her father's name.

Having securely hung the pot on an iron hook over the fire, Malise looked up sharply. "Aye, I knew him well. I knew him very well. But 'tis a name I have not heard mentioned for many years." Grievous memories filled his mind and brought a sheen of tears to his eyes.

"Can you help me then?" Finockt asked. "For you are a man he highly trusted. As such you must know everything about him?"

The highlander remained silent—the same response she received every time she hoped to learn something more about her hidden past.

"Please! Will you not speak with me?" Finockt cried, desperate for answers in her race against time. "What I ask of you is not solely for myself as I have told you. I have coin to compensate you for your trouble, would you take it."

Malise sat on the smooth wooden chair. "I don't want your money, and I could never claim to know everything about Anwyl."

"Perhaps not," Finockt replied, straining to control her eagerness, "but what little knowledge you hold I long to possess. Was he long a friend of yours?"

Malise looked upon her intently for a moment. "I've known him since the time he was about your age," he finally said. "He was like a son to me, the closest that a man can get without being of the same blood—but he is dead now and has been dead for more years than I care to count." Sadness filled his voice, and he poked the fiery cinders in the small hearth with a thin sheath of iron, breaking the glowing forms into smaller pieces. A bit of home entered her mind.

"I know he is dead," Finockt said, filling the silence.

Malise looked at her keenly. "'Tis news that was widely spread, I imagine. The death of Valínthia's Lost King. But 'twas not he alone that was taken, 'twas my daughter as well. Thus, you now know the full connection between us."

Finockt caught her breath. At the sound, Malise's blood ran cold, and her look, somewhere between horror and surprise, aroused suspicions festering since he had first opened his door to this strange lass. His eyes grew hard as ice, and his demeanor quickly transitioned from wary to defensive. "Why have you come here?" he suddenly demanded. "It seems you know your subject well enough without my aide. Why then does this man mean so much to you? Anwyl's name was buried alongside him all those years ago—why have you come to ask about him now?" His hardened stance did not change as he attempted to sort her out. "Be you a friend of Finain?"

Finockt's eyes brightened with intrigue as Malise's vague clues now fell into place; she tipped forward on the edge of her seat. "You speak of Tirell, don't you? When you speak of Finain you speak of the same man who was supposed to rule Thorlóthlon and yet was not meant to?"

"I demean myself to speak of a man with a heart as cold as stone and eyes as menacing and full of hate as no natural man's ever should be." His anger now spent, Malise resettled himself into his chair, as if a great fatigue overwhelmed him.

"I am no friend to Finain," Finockt said, "if that is what you fear. Although, in truth, I have rarely heard him called by such a name. Rather, I am one of his most hated enemies. I fight for my father."

"Your father? Is it he from whom you have flown? 'Tis dangerous for a lass to ride alone. 'Twould have been wiser for you to bring him along. Perhaps it would have been better."

"Aye, perhaps, if he were not bound from the living by the grave."

Malise looked upon her in surprise, his hopes rising another inch. "Were you very young when it happened?" he managed to ask, curiosity pressing the words to his lips.

"I was told I was little more than a very young child when he passed, along with my mother."

"You were told? So you do not remember."

Finockt gave a slight shake of her head.

The water was at a rolling boil now; some of it leaped over the side and sizzled in the fire. Malise quickly turned his attention to it. This lass was becoming stranger by the moment, and he was glad of the diversion. She sat quietly while he attended the wooden mugs. Cinnamon and cloves and some spices she could not recollect rose strongly from them.

"Sometimes I wonder what it would have been like, had he lived," Malise said quietly, his words softly shattering the small but comfortable silence.

"You mean if Anwyl had returned as king as he should have?"

Malise looked back at her and smiled, as if he knew he should not have spoken his thoughts out loud. "A lot of things would be different could they be done again. It's not good to dwell on what might have been."

"And yet one must, if he is to change the future."

"You really believe that?"

Finockt regarded his demeanor and his face. He did not seem a mere shepherd. "Were you once a knight?"

"No, a noble, favored at one time by the king," Malise said matter-of-factly. He sat back from the fire. "But I suppose you would not believe such from my appearance this day."

"What happened that you should be thus disgraced?" Finockt asked, then blushed again, for the words came faster than she could stop them.

"No, save yourself, lass, it is naught but a question of curiosity," he said, brushing off her embarrassment. "'Twas an end I saw coming. If it weren't for my wife, I would have died long ago."

"You are married?"

"I am a widower, and have been for nearly twenty years—ah, they are ready." He picked up his mug and extended the other to Finockt. She cupped it between her hands, relishing the heat seeping into her palms and the distraction of holding something. She was at a loss. Obtaining information about her father from this old man did not prove easy—no easier than plying the truth from Deverell and her grandfather at Thorlóthlon. And what was worse, she did not know exactly what to ask him. Instead, she waited in hopes Malise would release some valued information of his own. But she had already been here long and had gained little more than she already knew. And even stranger was the living link between them—something more than she had ever hoped to imagine. She knew he suspected the kinship between them as much as she did, but fear and doubt cast a shadow over its complete revelation. She had to keep unearthing the facts until he confirmed what she already knew had to be truth, and she was able to give him solid proof that he was indeed her grandfather. Her mother's father.

"Do you miss them?" Malise asked her, believing her silence was due to a sudden reflection on her parents.

Finockt gave him a sad smile. "Such I cannot say…I think I miss the idea of them, but my years were too few, and I was bereft of them too early to know what it was like to have had them with me. However, I have been told my father bestowed this on me just before his death." She pulled the cross up from where it hung amongst the lace of her embroidered neckline.

Malise angled the pendant toward the firelight. It caught the flames and sparkled intensely where it lay in his palm. With his other hand, he fingered it gently, and tears suddenly surfaced in his eyes.

Finockt's breath quickened. "You've seen this before, haven't you? You recognize it! Like all the others! Your connection to me is deeper than you would have me think. You were more than just a counselor to Anwyl. And by such a tale, you have left me only to believe that it is true." Malise slowly raised his eyes to her own. "You are my mother's father."

"You are, are you not?" Finockt persisted. She intently searched his gray-blue eyes, her brow crinkled with expectation and sadness. "You must see the link between us, same as I?"

Malise dropped the cross and pulled back from her, almost as if her words were too much to bear. The look in her eyes, the color of her hair, all fit a familiar memory that had always haunted him. And the fact she was with Eilidh made the lost pieces to the broken puzzle fit all the more perfectly. But how could it be? She had been lost all those years ago. He could not bear it should his hopes be shattered once again.

"By what means would you have reason to call me by this name?" he asked, unsuccessfully blinking back more tears.

"By means of the words you've just rendered to my ears," Finockt replied. "Did you not say you lost your daughter and your son by marriage to an early death only a few years ago? Is this not what you told me?—How many years mark the day?"

Malise looked at her sadly and wrapped thick hands around his mug. "Fifteen *long* years, my child..."

"'Tis the same number of years that marks the death of my parents..."

"Aye, lassie, but this could all just be nothing more than a coincidence," Malise broke in. "Death claims too many young people's lives too early."

"But you recognized my necklace, and there are very few who have ever laid eyes on it. Yet you knew of it. I can see it in your eyes. And there is one other thing that unlocks the mystery altogether." Malise looked upon her, his gaze curious and hopeful. "Anwyl *is* my father..."

The old man fell weak in his chair. "Could it be that my prayers have finally been answered?" he whispered in disbelief. "Ah, it cannot be, the Lost King's daughter come back to me... Finockt?"

She nodded. "Aye, 'tis my name, and 'twas my father himself who said you could be trusted. 'Tis why I have come, little knowing you were indeed of any relation."

"Ah, child," Malise cried, his face damp with tears. "My little Finockt. How many years have I prayed for this day?" She leaned forward and caught one of his worn hands in her own. His heart nearly broke at the gesture, and he pressed tired fingers against her cheek. "How did you find me, child?"

"By means of a letter, written in my father's own hand. He spoke of your name and how you were to be trusted. I thought if I could only speak with you, then I could learn more of the truth that has been buried far too long. I never dreamed you were actually my grandfather."

"I'd almost given up hope of ever seeing you alive," Malise said. Hesitantly, he held out his arms. The warmth of his smile crushed her, for deep in the recesses of her mind it awoke another heartrendingly familiar memory, so weakened and faded by time that it forever remained elusive, no matter how hard she tried to envision it. But here and now she could not mistake this gesture; he was welcoming her home. She fell into his embrace, and he held her close while lightly kissing the top of her head. Eyes closed, she breathed deeply, her face pressed gently against his chest, and his scent filled her nostrils: sun and woodsmoke and a sweetness she could not rightly place. A new and sudden sorrow bloomed in her heart: a deep longing for past years and memories that could have been made, the years in which she could have known him. How much she had missed! Yet amidst this sorrow burst a desperate yearning to know more—a desire to know everything about herself, her parents, her brother, and the dark history surrounding them that everyone else was either too afraid or too reluctant to share.

Malise gently released her. "There is more then that you would be wanting to know, isn't there? I can see it in your eyes," he said, reading the immense confusion, pain, and hurt emanating there.

Finockt could not prevent her flow of tears; she could taste them on her lips. "If you were here, if you knew, why did you not come for me?" she asked from where she now knelt on the dirt floor in front of him. "Did you not know I was still alive?"

"You don't remember anything about the night they died?" He sighed and turned his face toward the fire. "But I should not ask such a question. You were much too young to remember."

Finockt gently took him by the arm. "Malise, what *happened* to them?"

He shook his head mournfully.

"Please, Malise," Finockt said, trying to meet his eyes. "Do not hide the truth from me as do all the others at Thorlóthlon. If you know it, let me partake of it as well."

He patted her hand between his dusky, dark ones. "It's not a question of hiding it, lassie. It's a question of keeping it in the past where it belongs. Greater sorrows arise from revisiting the past, and more pain than good comes of it."

Finockt lowered her gaze, and a lump of unshed tears grew in her throat; like all those she knew, he, too, had closed the door to her learning more about her past, right on the very cusp of her actual attainment of some new fragment of information or a solid clue as to what had really happened all those years ago. She felt the aching pain of disappointment welling up inside her, but then, in the same moment, before that disappointment could blossom into something uglier and darker than she cared to entertain, she heard his voice again, rumbling soft and light above the gentle whistling hiss of the hearth fire: an unexpected, comforting tone that left her startled and anxious and left her ears straining to capture the sound, while she held onto his every word with growing anticipation and a renewed hope for the truth of her lost story…

CHAPTER FIVE

"Y OU COULD ALMOST say I knew it would come to pass," Malise said softly, his memories unfolding, taking him back to a time and place he did not care to remember. "Your father had been quite on edge those last few weeks though he tried not to show it, and in your mother's face there was always a…a great sense of foreboding…" The memory drew sharp lines of grief over her grandfather's visage, and he snuffled into a handkerchief. "I cannot tell you the whole of it because that exact truth is hidden from me as well. I was told it was an ambush, that Finain had their caravan followed, and that he attacked when they were helpless and mired in mud after a storm. I don't know the rest. I've no thorough knowledge of what befell them, and I cannot say I am wholly unhappy not knowing it."

"Was I with them when Finain attacked?" Finockt asked after a time.

"Yes, you and your brother. Deverell, too. There was much

fighting. It was a miracle the three of you made it out alive. The Lord was with you that day. No one else from the caravan survived."

Finockt started, as if coming out of a deep sleep. Deverell? What had he been doing there? And what long connection did he have to her family? Her mind throbbed in a web of confusion, and she slumped, defeated, beside her grandfather. What more did she not know about this ever-mysterious Northerner? Furthermore, what other secrets did he withhold?

Malise rose and stepped around her to rearrange the logs in the hearth; it was then Finockt realized the room had fallen under a thick silence.

"How was it that I made it out alive?" she asked, not wanting the story to end there.

Malise retook his seat. "Deverell brought you and your brother to me. By then, I had already lost everything and had only a few possessions left—what I had on my body and deep in my pockets. I took a small cottage and worked with my hands at what tasks I could find within the village, but I was given to a noble's tasks: governing the land granted me by the king and paying homage to him through military service. Thus, I possessed none of the experience needed to work a skilled man's labor, and I was too old to apprentice. They knew of my lineage and my fate, and they would not help. With two small children, I could not make enough to feed you all and pay the king's rent exacted from me. Deverell helped out as much as he could, but in the end, he had not the means to save us either. He was naught but a young lad then, yet he left to seek aid elsewhere. Then she took you, and the decision to let you go ripped my heart right out of my chest. I can still hear your cries from that day."

"I was taken?" Finockt said, her eyes mirroring his deeply felt sorrow. Her hands grew cold. "By whom? Who took me?" she demanded when he hesitated to voice the words.

"The Dúnarians knew you lived still. Finain knew. He was looking for you and your brother." Malise took her cold hand between his warm ones. "Ah, lassie, too many are willing to exchange a friend for a few coins. It was a desperate time. Despite fierce opposition by Valínthia and her allies, the Dúnarians had just gained control of several of the border villages in the south, their victory the start of a relentless tug of war between the northern and southern kingdoms that lasted for more than a decade, until the years of peace, which had remained steady until recently. But at the time of Tirell's first major advancement, like Deverell, you and your brother were naught but a wee lad and lass. The Dúnarians had the upper hand, Valínthia was staggering back to her feet to fight another offensive, and the uncertainty of the future kept everyone on edge. Even the most uneducated man knew it was better to find favor with the new rulers than fight against them. The people were willing to make their mark, and they did. They had already given us up to the enemy. That was the reason I let you go. How could we escape with a wee lass, such as you were? It was Deverell, smart lad, who found the solution in a childless widow from Evanthia—one of the last of the Great Queen's remnant and clan praesidium. She promised to care for you and protect you. Losing you to her was worth it to keep you alive. And separating you from me gave you a chance. Your brother kept the hope alive in me that someday we'd get you back…"

Finockt collapsed onto her heels, and all the blood drained from her face. The dark pieces of her memory slowly snapped together and brought to life images she had wrestled with so many times before. Now she realized they were truth. She remembered. She knew. The young boy who shifted her on his hip as he trudged through the wood was Deverell. The damp log in the middle of a green and healthy forest was the meeting place where she was found by young hands who had hoped for so long to hold a child of her own. It was Gelis who had come, in the middle of the wood, who had taken over where Deverell had left off in caring for her. She remembered the tears that burned her eyes and the tiny child's fear that enveloped her heart at the appearance of this stranger. But when the kind eyes and loving arms had embraced her, and the gentle hands had wiped away her tears, the fear had ebbed, too. Exhausted, she had laid her head on Gelis's shoulder and fallen asleep. When she had awoken, she was in the village she had always known, just north of the Dúnahez.

The finality of her story left her grieved and hurting. She had wanted to know the truth for so long, and now it was over. There was nothing more to tell. Its revelation was almost darker than the images she had harbored in her imagination over the years.

"It's not easy—the truth," Malise said.

"And my brother?" Finockt asked, desperate to distract herself from the torture of constantly turning over in her mind her real story. "What of his fate? Did Deverell save him as well?"

"Aye, of sorts," he said, his heart aching for her. "To hide his identity, your older brother ended up working in a Dúnarian noble's fields. But one day, he found me on the edge of an obscure village. I thought I had seen his spirit, he had changed so much. He'd become a miniature man in those few short years. When he told me he had come home for good, I didn't believe him and bade him return before things grew more gravely worse. It was then he told me he had gained favor in the noble's eyes." At this, Malise laughed aloud. "Gained favor! Could you believe it! He's a wily one, your brother—'twas the very man he had served that kept him on, nearly as his own son. He learned much: horsemanship, the art of war, sword play. It was only after your brother begged return to his family that the nobleman let him go. So you see, Finockt, not all Dúnarians are bad."

"Yet only one of so many, Malise? For myself, I cannot believe this to be so. I have only ever known fear and cruelty under their hand. No," Finockt said, shaking her head. "I cannot believe the same until I have better proof of such kindness—"

Malise leaned back in his chair. "So we must wait and hope then that God allows you the opportunity to see it," he said gently.

Finockt chose to ignore this statement. The pain of the Dúnarians' reign was still too fresh in her heart to consider them anything other than what they were: evil. "Did my brother stay then?" she asked, hoping for more information regarding this sibling she previously never knew existed.

Her grandfather nodded. "Aye, he stayed, but I could not manage to pay off my own debts. I was growing old and weary, and I had no strength left to work. So we left for the upper Highlands, where no man wished to venture. It seemed then that we were free, and all was well. All save one thing—we didn't have you."

"Did you not search for me, when it was safe to do so?" Finockt asked, her voice catching on the words.

"Aye, lassie, we searched high and low for you—for months. Yet it was as we had planned. The widow had hidden you well to avoid your discovery by the Dúnarians. It was as if you had disappeared. There was no trace of a young girl with a cross of gold. We once held hope that perhaps the cross alone had been discovered by the Dúnarian nobles, or that the widow had sold it to further protect you, and that the Dúnarians had, in turn, either sold it or kept it for themselves, but no one knew of your existence or that of the cross's. And though we met with many a young child with various shades of red hair in the villages we visited, not a one of them was you.

"So it was that we settled here with heavy hearts, trusting you were somewhere safe, alive and well in the world alongside Gelis. And now here you are!" Malise laughed again. "I can scarce believe my aging eyes. My own beloved granddaughter! I never thought I would say the word again. How I've missed you!"

Finockt smiled warmly at his laughter, for it brought into remembrance still another buried memory. "And I you," she said, "for now I know that the kind old gentleman who told me stories atop a green sloping hill with a loch at our feet and the wind plying through the trees at our back—that man was you."

"So you do remember!" Malise cried, his eyes shining. "Ah, you were so very young then. How I miss those blessed days…"

"I wish I could remember more about them," Finockt said wistfully. "It's odd to me that I am even here, with you, in this moment. It's as if…" She paused and then shook her head, dismissing the nearly implausible notion, and stared into the fire.

"As if something were guiding you?" Malise asked, pulling out his pipe and lighting it.

"Aye," Finockt answered in surprise, her eyes momentarily flickering with hope and then all at the same time losing it. "But what power exists save that which has been fashioned by mortals? The songs of the elders speak of naught but that. There is none other."

Malise smiled gently. "So have others said before you."

"So it is as it was told to those who heard it spoken. It is true then?"

Malise rose stiffly and walked to the fireside. Reaching over the mantle, he pulled a thick book from the shelf and gently ran a hand over its smooth, decorative wooden cover. Its pages were worn, and a magnitude of rich colors flashed from within as he flipped through the ornate pages.

"It is more than that. It is yet alive and well and as unchanged now as it ever was. The account is told here," he said, "of a great Power, more terrifying and more wonderful than you can imagine."

"Aye, I recognize it. Such has also been told by the lords of old," Finockt said. She glanced up at him. "It is an old and familiar line of legend, well-known to all. But the Power of which you speak was a myth. The men in my village told me."

"Is it?" Malise asked her.

"You believe it exists?"

"Don't you?"

"I don't know if *it* exists. I only know what I *feel* inside cannot be mistaken. It is something I cannot lay way even if I wanted—it comes as a voiceless heeding, a prompting, a warning felt without words." Malise watched her keenly, and

Finockt dropped her gaze. "And yet there are times when it is not always there. I do not always *feel* it guiding me."

"Do you always have to feel something in order for it to be aiding you?" Malise questioned. "Do not be misled by the same songs of the elders, who dealt with things that had to be felt and understood in order to be real. Sometimes it is the things we do not fully understand that are the most real."

"And yet, as I tell it to you, what I sense is more than *just* a feeling, Malise. It is a guiding force I cannot explain, a force that remains with me for as long as I allow it or follow its given course. If I choose to ignore it, then it departs. But I have only once chosen to do so. And in listening to it, it has never led me astray."

"Perhaps then it is God Himself who speaks to you through His Spirit."

Finockt's brow wrinkled. "You believe it is possible for Him to speak to us?"

"Aye, for those who believe it," Malise returned. "God speaks to us in many ways: through His Spirit, through His Word," —at this he held up the thick, richly ornamented book—"and through the counsel of others who follow Him closely. You must understand, child, whatever you were told, these are not mere stories. It is God Himself speaking to us. The words written therein pierce the soul and bring life to the one who reads them. There is power in them, Finockt, a power the entire world fears and rejects because the very words contained within foretell the heart of man and decipher his utmost thoughts." He blew out a thin trail of smoke from his pipe and looked at her thoughtfully. "By the look on your face, you believe in Him still, though others, and perhaps your circumstances, may have, at times, shaken your faith. True faith withstands the test. It cannot be broken."

Finockt looked up at him, startled. "And yet I haven't believed in Him for a long time."

The fib struck heat across her cheeks and dampened her hands with moisture. Twice at least she had prayed for deliverance. Both times it was not a flippant request for God to save her from the Dúnarians; she truly relied on Him to do so.

Malise detected the stain of red deepening the rosy hue of her cheeks. "Ah, so you say," he said. "But I've seen a man who's turned his back on God, and this is not what he looks like. You still believe even now."

"Once I did. With everything in me."

"What changed that?"

"He didn't save me." She gnawed the inside of her cheek. "He didn't save me from the enemy. I prayed and prayed, and still they came. They took over our way of life. Subjected us to all kinds of horrors and cruelty. Could I trust Him after all that? When He didn't answer my prayers?"

"But He did."

Finockt shook her head in disbelief. "Were you not listening, Malise? The Dúnarians ruled my village. They killed Gelis because of me. They killed Caslon. They murdered them!"

"And yet here you are, alive and well. His purpose for your life prevails still, despite the enemy's attempts to thwart it. He's calling you, lass. Why do you think you survived? He hasn't given up on you. He knows your heart. Let go of all the past, and trust Him."

Tears filled her eyes. "How can I when I've lost everything? When I didn't want Him anymore? He's punished my sin by taking away those most dear to me. I deserve this."

"No, lass. He's waiting for you to release all that to Him. God is merciful and gracious. If you ask it of Him, He will forgive you."

"But what answer have I for Gelis's death and Caslon's murder?"

"Did they know Him?"

"Aye, for certain. Their hearts were pure before God. Gelis often spoke of Him and His will, but I didn't understand it. And Caslon and Murron were always kind and gentle, the truest of friends by all accounts." She looked up at her grandfather, her heart stricken and her face pale. "Why wouldn't He spare a friend who sacrificed himself for me? Why wouldn't He spare the only mother I've ever known? He allowed them to die. Why? He allowed my parents to die, too, Malise! Why were they not spared? I was just a child. I needed them. I needed them!" Sobs caught in her throat and wracked her body.

Malise pulled Finockt onto her knees before him and embraced her. "The Lord didn't promise us an easy life, where pain and suffering cease to exist," he said, his cheek upon her head. "The inner workings of God can never be fully understood here on earth, but that doesn't mean God in His infinite wisdom has chosen wrongly. For some, He chooses to intervene and physically save a man or woman from death. For others, He chooses for His children to live with Him in Heaven. Such is the way I believe for your mother and father. For a purpose you, or I, may not be able to see. It was His choice, Finockt. We cannot question it, and we should not because we will never comprehend why. Anger festers when we don't have the answers we believe are right, and it grows to construct a useless barrier that only prevents us from healing and moving on with our lives. The truth is we *do* go on living. We cannot alter that, and we waste a life we can use for good if we mire ourselves in what we cannot change. We allow all the dark forces of this world to win. Our life here on earth is a constant battle against sin and evil and against men like Finain or others of his caliber. The painful circumstances surrounding your parents' death I still feel keenly to this day, but I know I will see them again. Nothing can alter that either. My path is secure. My hope is eternal. God promised these blessings through the sacrifice made by His Son. To this I hold, knowing another life exists in which the imperfections of this world will no longer hold sway over any of us. God knows the pain of your past, dear lassie. He wants only to help you heal. He's waiting for you with open arms."

"You're so certain He will take me back."

"If you repent, yes, lass, without a doubt."

She buried her head in her hands. "I carry so much guilt. How could He love me when I no longer wanted to love Him? I was so angry with Him."

"Read this." Malise opened the book from the mantle to John 17. Then he handed her the Scripture and pointed out the verses he wanted her to read: John 17: 6, 9, and 20-21.

Her eyes increasingly glassy with tears, she read the beautifully sculpted letters in succession, treasuring each soul-affirming word.

"*...I have manifested Your name to the men whom You gave Me out of the world; they were Yours and You gave them to Me, and they have kept Your word...I ask on their behalf; I do not ask on behalf of the world, but of those whom You have given Me; for they are Yours...I do not ask on behalf of these alone, but for those also who believe in Me through their word; that they may all be* *one; even as You, Father, are in Me, and I in You, that they also may be in Us, so that the world may believe that You sent Me."*

"Christ did this for you," Malise said, cupping her chin in his hand. "He prayed for your strength and protection, just as He prayed the same for those closest to Him on that dark night so long ago. Before He died in your stead, Finockt, He prayed for you to cling to Him and the Father, and that your faith might be strengthened as it should. And read this to give your heart greater comfort."

Taking the heavy book into his hands, he deftly flipped back a few pages to John 15. Finockt watched his finger slide along the verses he pointed out for her: John 15:1-6.

"I am the true vine, and My Father is the vinedresser. Every branch in Me that does not bear fruit, He takes away; and every branch that bears much fruit, He prunes it so that it may bear more fruit. You are already clean because of the word which I have spoken to you. Abide in Me, and I in you. As the branch cannot bear fruit of itself unless it abides in the vine, so neither can you unless you abide in Me. I am the vine, you are the branches; he who abides in Me and I in him, he bears much fruit, for apart from Me you can do nothing."

"And lastly," Malise said, "read these." He brought her gaze to verse 7 and then verses 9-11.

"If you abide in Me, and My words abide in you, ask whatever you wish, and it will be done for you…Just as the Father has loved Me, I have also loved you; abide in My love. If you keep My commandments, you will abide in My love, just as I have kept My Father's commandments and abide in His love. These things I have spoken to you so that My joy may be in you, and that your joy may be made full."

"May I borrow this?" Finockt whispered, her tears spilling over.

"You may keep it."

Finockt closed the fine wooden cover and tucked the Scripture close to her heart. "Thank you."

Malise smiled. "God promises renewed life, child. His gift is freedom from this world and a future unattainable on earth: Light rather than Darkness. It is only in the light that we can truly see. Don't let the darkness of the past mar your future. Step into the light, and embrace the freedom only Christ can give. You have only to repent and believe in Him, and it will be so. Faith is all that is required. His promises do not fail us. You may read of every one of them here." He tapped the thick book.

Finockt choked back another sob. With all that had come to pass, she had not expected the added burden of such words. In essence, as Deverell had all those many months ago, Malise was asking her to make a life-altering decision. One she desperately wanted to make and yet did not rightly feel she could. With all her heart, she wanted to commit herself—wholeheartedly, without reservation—to God, but could she? Everything in her told her she must, but she was scared. This frustrated her, and she hated herself for her hesitation. Why would she delay? She knew the answer. She had already hastily committed herself to the quest of the cross in order to preserve it, a commitment that had changed her life so drastically and permanently. She must think before she hastily committed herself to something so infinitely more important, a faith and way of life she might not be able to sustain. She could only hope and pray the Lord would understand her need for more time and help her reach that level of commitment that never looked back for what was but trusted unwaveringly, no matter the cost.

Malise rose and gently emptied the ashes from his pipe into the fire. "It is best you be on your way now," he said, breaking the silence. "Your guardian will be wondering where you have been."

Finockt rose and followed him to the door. There, he helped her with her cloak and pulled her hood up over her head as if she were a small child.

"You'd best hurry," he said. "Highland weather can be unpredictable, especially this time of year."

"Aye," Finockt said, tears welling again in her eyes. She did not want to leave him.

"It has been good for my old eyes to see you, lass. Should you need aid, my hand is always ready to lend it." He opened the door for her, and the wind that had been shuddering against it and whistling around the house swept in and encircled them both. "What is it, child?" Malise then asked at the tears and worry clouding her bright eyes.

She sniffed and dried her cheeks with the back of her hand. "You have been so kind and so helpful already," she said, "and if I'm honest, everything you've said about my past troubles me...and yet, strangely, it all the same gives me hope...that perhaps I am not so very lost after all."

"Then He is already working in your life," Malise replied, laying a heavy hand on her shoulder. "Leave yourself open to the Lord, lass, and He will show you what you must do. Both for your life and every unknown step you take."

"And my father?"

"What about him?"

"Did my father..."

"Your father's one wish was for his children to know the Truth, which you have known through Gelis's gentle teaching, and you still know. My prayer for you now is that you will let the Lord work in your heart, however He may, unto full repentance. He never forces us to choose Him, Finockt. He freely offers His gift of salvation, but He leaves the decision up to you." He regarded the additional tears filling her eyes and pulled her to him, embracing her. "There, child," he said, stroking her head. "Trust Him, lass. Unless you make the decision to cut yourself off from Him forever, He will never leave you. You may count on that."

She choked back a sob and clung to her grandfather. "I have felt alone most of my life."

"Haí, you need not feel that way any longer. God is with you, as am I, for as long as God grants me life." He hugged her tightly then released her.

"I shall miss you."

"Ah, there now, lassie," he said, tears springing to his own eyes. "This isn't the end. We'll meet again soon. Do you know your way back? I would never forgive myself if you fell into the hands of Finain."

Finockt nodded. "My way is sure. Eilidh is my guide. But I must ask of you, have you some safe place to which we may flee? We've no safe haven to speak of, and I know I've already jeopardized my guardian and his men by coming to see you."

"Ah, then the hour grows very late," her grandfather said. "They will be combing the mountainsides searching for you. It will be worse for them to do so, for it will only bring more unwanted attention. You believe there are not many who dwell in these parts of the Highlands, but you'd be wrong. You must return quickly for it is not safe here anymore, and it looks as if another storm will pass over."

"But you will come, won't you, Malise? You will come and help us?" Finockt asked, thrusting away more stray tears. "The mountain pass is blocked, and we don't know another direction in which to flee."

"Aye, dear girl," Malise said, patting her shoulder. "Rest assured, I will help you and your kin, but you must return first. And I must gather some things before I depart." He kissed her gently on the forehead and then ushered her out the open door and into the wind. "Now go! I'll keep watch until you make it safely to Eilidh."

Even then, as they had been deep in conversation and ignorant of the quickly changing Highland weather, fierce clouds rolled in and filtered the sunlight. The earth now cowered under an odd shade of yellow-green haze, its ominous color a cursory warning to the severity of the approaching storm.

Across the knolls, Eilidh stroked the horses' necks to calm their growing agitation and cast another worried glance to the darkening sky. Finockt had been gone a long time. They must leave soon, or else there might be trouble. But, unbeknownst to Eilidh, it was too late. For back at the cottage, the frenzied search for Finockt had already begun hours earlier.

CHAPTER SIX

"Gone?" Deverell exclaimed, alarm knocking the last remnants of sleep from his mind. "For how long?"

"Since before dawn, it seems," Coinneach said. He swiftly trod the length of the Main Hall a second time. "How could she do this to us?" he growled. His question addressed no one in particular, and his anger intensified like the summer storm building in the northwest. "She knows the folly of conducting herself in such a manner!"

"Acair?" Deverell shouted.

"Aye, my lord." The young man bolted into the room from his post just outside the Main Hall. He gave Deverell a slight bow.

"Gather Strahan, Cronan, and Boynton. We leave immediately."

"Aye, my lord," he replied with a rapid nod before hastily retreating.

Coinneach strode back toward Deverell from the opposite side of the room. His hands shook, and his visage demanded both action and answers. For the second or third time in his life, he did not know what to say. He looked expectantly at Deverell for some sense of reassurance.

"I shall set out with a small party, Sire. We must act quickly. Everything counts upon it. Continue with everything else as planned. We must leave tonight!" Deverell said, now racing for the door. "And do not fear, my lord, I shall return with her," he added.

"I know, Deverell. You are my most trusted man. Godspeed to you, and be safe." Tears glistened in the corners of Coinneach's eyes, and his heart lay greatly troubled at Finockt's absence. Though he hardly wanted to admit it to himself, he was afraid of losing her.

Deverell gave him a short, hurried bow then departed quickly for the barn. His heart thudded against his chest. He only hoped and prayed Finockt had not been captured.

Back in the Highlands, Finockt started making her way over the knolls to Eilidh when she suddenly hesitated and looked back at Malise's solitary form lingering in the shadows of the doorway. There was something else she needed to know from him. Something perhaps only he could answer well enough to quiet her curious heart. Carefully, she retraced her steps over the coarse grass battered by the harsh, Highland winds, which sent her hood fluttering around her face and the long, flowing edges of her cloak swirling about her, like a bird too afraid to take flight. She pushed on until she reached her grandfather.

"What keeps you?" he asked gently, sensing her angst.

"Did my mother really love my father?" She pulled her hair away from her eyes, the strands driven there by the wind. Coinneach's vindictive and heartless words concerning her mother replayed in her ears, and the memory wounded her all over again. She needed answers, and she needed to hear it from him.

"Aye, she loved him, child—I'd never seen her happier," Malise answered her. "Why do you ask?"

"Some say it was my mother who took my father's title away from him because he fell in love with her, and her title did not equal his own."

Malise was silent a moment. "I suppose that could be construed as partially true," he said slowly. "She was not born of royal blood as was your father. But in marrying him, your mother did not take anything away from your father. The king's laws grant marriage openly between nobility and royalty, should the noble's family—and his daughter—find favor with the king and the king's son."

Finockt's eyes widened, and relief flooded over her. "Then she could never have taken the crown from him?"

Malise shook his head. "The crown was always your father's to hold. No one could take it away from him—man or woman—except through death. Then, by law, the crown returned to Coinneach to reign until Anwyl's heir was of age."

Shock distorted her face. "Then why? Why would he blame my mother for something she could never have manipulated? He deceived me," she murmured under her breath. "He led me to believe it was her fault, but all this time it was a falsehood. It was never the truth. And all of this goes beyond my mother. He only despised her because Anwyl wouldn't heed his every word! He used her to avoid the truth about himself!"

This realization now troubled her even more than the first time she had heard Coinneach's accusation, and it fueled an even deeper passion to find her brother: Thorlóthlon's *rightful* heir. Sadly, Coinneach's selfishness and his ambition had gone too far.

"You'd best leave now, lass," Malise said, reaching for her arm. "We've tarried far too long. Every moment you stay increases your chances of being caught."

Finockt tucked a stray lock of hair behind her ear. "I know, but please, I cannot leave until I hear this last truth from you: you must tell me about my brother. Is he still alive?"

"Perhaps this telling should be kept for another time?" Malise suggested.

"He is alive then."

"Aye, he's alive," Malise finally said, weighing the resolution in Finockt's face. "Your brother is…" Finockt searched his face eagerly for the answer. "Your brother is…Uisdean."

"Uisdean?" Finockt repeated, blinking back a sudden rush of tears. "The same lad who works the land with you?"

Malise gave her a short nod.

"Is he here?" Finockt asked, grappling for the words. "May I meet him?"

"Of course, lassie, of course," Malise said.

She ran forward into the roundhouse when Malise gently stopped her. "Haí, lassie, before you grow too keen on meeting him this day, understand I do not know if he abides here still. I saw him just this morning, but most times he is away in the woods near the Lowlands, hunting and scouting and living free for months at a time. If he has already left, I know not when I shall see him next."

Finockt buried her bitter disappointment. Once she had

believed herself alone; now her family grew by the hour. Suddenly she did not want to leave Malise's small abode. She wanted to stay, where a security and comfort she had never known within Thorlóthlon, or the village, expanded by the minute. But the choice was not hers.

"Soon then," she said with a grim smile. "I must meet him when first he returns."

Her grandfather nodded. She turned to leave when a tumble of logs against the back of the house startled her. Her eyes locked on Malise, and he read her thoughts.

"Wait here. I shall go and see," he said and pushed past her to the back door.

Her brother. Excitement threaded through her at the very word. Always she had wondered what it would be like to have an elder brother: a protector, a counselor. She no longer need harbor any subtle feelings of jealousy toward Eilidh, for she, too, possessed a sibling and a tie to her past and her parents. But what she would say when she first saw him, she did not know. In the back of her mind, she hoped he would be most like Malise, but it was her second thought—that perhaps he may be bent more like Coinneach—that disturbed her more.

Presently, a quiet, steady voice interrupted her musings and drew her more fully into the cottage. Was she hearing things? Again the soft, melodical sound came to her ears. Finockt followed it to the back door and appeared upon its threshold seconds before a tall, blond-haired young man vanished up the tree-lined slope that led farther into the mountains.

"Gwri," Finockt whispered, drawing her hand to her lips in surprise. But was it really him? Each glimpse of him was so brief; his presence could have been nothing more than the hope of seeing him here.

"Are you all right, Finockt?" Malise asked at the change in her face.

She leaned against the doorjamb. "Aye," she said, her tongue thick and her mouth suddenly dry. Her gaze flicked over the wooded slope. "He has gone then?" she asked in reference to her brother, but her mind was still bent on the possibility of who the young, blond-haired man was.

"Haí, do not worry yourself. You haven't missed him. That was only Gwri. He seldom comes this way with Deverell, but something or the other brought him this way only a short while ago." Malise looked in the direction Gwri had taken, but the slope was empty. He turned back now to Finockt. "He was very downtrodden when he first arrived, poor lad, but it seems he's a bit better now. It appears it was a matter of the heart that brought him low."

The color fully drained from Finockt's face, and her legs grew weak. She sank onto the wooden bench situated near Malise's neatly stacked wood pile.

"Are you sure you're all right, lassie?" he asked.

"No, I'm sorry, Malise. I suddenly feel unwell." She rested her head in her hands.

"Steady yourself."

He hurried inside then returned with a fresh cup of cool water, which she sipped gratefully.

"Better now?"

"Aye, a bit," she whispered.

"Do you know the young man?" Malise asked, trying to suppress a wry smile.

"Aye, I do…" she answered, avoiding his gaze and looking to the slope, which still stood green and empty. "It is a long tale." Sadness lingered in her voice. "But more importantly, do you think my brother will come?"

"Aye, Gwri has gone for him. It seems he has taken a ride."

Just then the muffled thud of hooves played against the grass, and a young man rode down the steep slope toward the pair. Finockt sat up straighter at his approach. Somehow she remembered this man, and it struck her suddenly why: he closely resembled the descriptions of Prince Anwyl that Gelis had shared with her as a child. Her guardian had painted such a vivid picture; she could not mistake it.

His hair was a rich brown, as dark as the ripe, broken bellies of walnuts freshly fallen from the tree in autumn. And his brown eyes were bright and clear from the mountain air. He was tall, too, and slender, reaching almost a head above that of Malise. And from his long bouts under the summer sun, the paleness of his skin had turned dark, almost a smoky color, even darker perhaps than Malise's suntanned complexion.

The young man dismounted quickly before them with a grace that matched that of Finockt's father, Malise mused for the hundredth time. "I had word that you sent for me, Grandfather," he said. His voice was kind like Malise's and deep.

"Aye, there is someone I want you to meet," the old man said happily and stepped aside to introduce Finockt. She set aside her half-empty cup and rose from the rough bench as the handsome, young man came forward to greet her.

"How do you do, milady?" Uisdean said with grace and courtesy. He bent and kissed her hand. Rising, he faced his grandfather, and a troubled look passed over his face. "Is there something else to which you have called me?" he asked.

"Does she not appear somewhat familiar to you, Uisdean?" Malise asked him.

He flushed. "Aye, perhaps a little. Forgive me, milady, I cannot make the connection."

Finockt smiled. "Aye, that's to be expected," she said. "'Twas long ago we knew each other, and time has undoubtedly changed us."

Uisdean looked even more confused at her answer. Malise chuckled. "Uisdean, my dear lad, I would like you to meet your sister, Finockt."

"Finockt?" Uisdean said, stupefied. "It cannot be!" he cried, looking her up and down. "You were just a wee bairn when last I saw you. We've been looking all over the place for you since that day. We thought you'd been lost forever!" He laughed aloud and spontaneously clasped her tightly in a quick, strong hug, which surprised her and left her stiff and awkward. Releasing her, he stepped back and looked at his grandfather again in disbelief. "How did you find her?"

"*She* found us," Malise returned. "Came to us in search of information about your father. They are seeking the next successor to the kingdom," Malise added, raising an eyebrow.

"They?" Uisdean asked.

"Aye," Finockt answered, now free of her insecurities. "Perhaps you have the items for which we search. Do you know anything, Uisdean, about Father and what he left behind? Did he leave you any instructions or parchments—any proof at all that *you* are the true heir to Thorlóthlon's throne?"

Uisdean exchanged a subtle, knowing look with Malise. "I fear not, milady. I was too young for Father to tell me anything of the future before he died, and I inherited no written documents legitimizing my ascent to the throne. Why?"

"And Father never told you anything about a box?"

Uisdean's brow wrinkled. "You're looking for a box?" he said, his interest piqued.

Dark clouds slid over the sun, abruptly ending their conversation and giving warning to his sister's perpetual lingering.

"We do not have time to discuss this any further. Finockt, you must return before the rain falls," Malise said more sternly, catching her gently by the arm. "Quickly now!"

Finockt tossed a cursory glance at her brother and then looked up at her grandfather. "You will come tonight won't you?" she pressed as he began to lead her away.

"Aye, I will, but perhaps your brother would be more effective at finding a safe haven for you and your friends. Could you help them, Uisdean?"

"Aye, I know these woods and mountains well. There are several places where they could find shelter depending on the number. But why all the urgency?" he asked, growing more perplexed by the minute.

"I will explain it later, my son," Malise said. "But for now, Finockt must ride."

Her grandfather guided her farther down the slight gradient toward the front of the house when Uisdean said, "I'll see you soon then, Finockt."

She hung back a step, then suddenly she turned around and, rushing up to her brother, threw her arms around him. He held back an instant in surprise but then hugged her tightly in return.

"Still the impulsive little sister I remember," he laughed. "It seems time has not changed so many things."

"I'm so glad to have found you, Uisdean," Finockt said earnestly.

"You're safe now, little sister. We're together again," he said jovially, giving her shoulder a gentle shake.

Finockt smiled and turned to join Eilidh when a rider burst up the hill from below. All three turned quickly at the sound of hoof beats and the urgent voice that followed: "There are riders down below carrying the colors of the Dúnahez, and this man is hurt—!"

The young man stopped speaking upon sight of Finockt and sharply reined in his horse. It whinnied and tore at the ground with its hooves. Its rider's head was deeply hooded, and his body was cloaked in a long mantle. An odd lump hung wearily behind him and slumped against his back like a sack of freshly ground wheat. Uisdean and Malise rushed forward to help the wounded man down from the horse, but Finockt's eyes were more closely tied to the rider's horse. Its familiar black coat gleamed; its eyes were ablaze. She would recognize him anywhere.

"Tohr," she murmured.

"He's wounded in the left shoulder," the rider said as he gently handed the man down from behind him.

Malise and Uisdean caught the injured scout under the arms and carefully lowered him the rest of the way.

"How did this happen?" Malise asked.

"We were on the lookout for Finain when they came upon us unexpectedly," the rider answered, his voice tense with urgency. "They attacked from the southwest. We barely had enough time to get away. It took us a while to lose them, and I fear it will not be long before they find us again."

"They are searching for the young lady of whom you spoke who has no name?" Uisdean asked.

"Aye, they are," the other said slowly. He shifted his eyes

upon Finockt, and though he wore a hood, she felt the full impact of his gaze burn her skin.

"Will he be all right?" Finockt now asked Malise, turning her eyes upon the affected man. He did not look like one of the king's soldiers or scouts.

"Aye, he'll be fine, but we must get him into the house quickly," Malise answered after inspecting the open wound. He turned to Finockt while Uisdean helped the injured man to the roundhouse. "And now, Finockt, you *must* return. It is no longer safe here. Be sure to take the northwestern route. Eilidh will know it," he said, squeezing her shoulders gently. "Go, and hurry, lass. I do not want to tell you again."

Not waiting for her answer, he hastened to assist Uisdean, and together they brought their wounded comrade into the house with undo haste. Finockt watched until all three were inside, and when the door had shut securely behind them, she retrained her eyes on both horse and rider. It was undeniable. He had been found! He tore at the ground and strained to draw near her, but his rider checked his efforts.

"You're a long way from home," the young man said.

"And you," Finockt returned.

"Draw near," the rider added, "for he cannot be held back for long."

He alighted from the saddle, and she hurried toward them with unbound joy.

"Ah, Tohr," Finockt said, stroking his forehead and planting a kiss upon his downy nose.

He tossed his head and whinnied, and she rubbed his face while he nuzzled her shoulder and hit her arm with his nose. Reuniting with him was like connecting her to a piece of home, and seeing him made her feel as though Caslon might appear at her elbow at any minute. Sorrow rose unannounced in her heart, and she choked back the bitter sting of a sob.

"He's yours," the rider said and extended the reins.

But Finockt did not take them. Rather, she kept her attentions on Tohr. "Where did you find him, sir?"

The young man made no immediate answer, only drew close to Finockt. "Roaming the woods," he said quietly, "like a wild king." He put a hand on Tohr's nose. "I think it's clear he missed you."

Finockt laughed. "He was never really mine to miss, but I am glad to see him. All those months ago when he left me, I didn't think I'd ever really see him again."

The rider watched her stroke Tohr's neck. "Haí, you should heed your grandfather and go."

"I know. I know I must go back, but it won't ever be the same," she said. She rested her face against Tohr's.

"Never forget, you are Thorlóthlon's hope. You must return, and the faster the better. Tohr will get you there much more quickly than that gentle mare you are riding."

The familiarity of the rider's voice left her in no doubt now of who he was. That, and his reference to her as Thorlóthlon's hope.

"Gwri," she said, her heart breaking. She looked up into his face for the first time since he had dismounted. His hood was still drawn low over his forehead, but he was so close to her now his unmistakable blue eyes seemed to glow in the shadows of it. She inhaled sharply at the sudden warmth of her hand in his and started to pull away, but his grip gently tightened.

"Finockt!" a voice called above the wind.

Finockt severed her gaze with Gwri and focused on Eilidh as she came around the side of Malise's house. At her approach,

Gwri released Finockt's hand, but he was not fast enough to escape Eilidh's quick observations. She easily noted the intimate gesture and averted her eyes.

"Milady," she entreated. "The hour has grown very late, it must be midafternoon. We need return."

"Aye, Eilidh, I come now," Finockt called back to her. "I promise."

Eilidh bobbed her head in affirmation then disappeared beyond the roundhouse wall once more, but not before she tossed the two another quick, curious glance.

When Eilidh had gone, Finockt laid hold of Gwri's arm and looked earnestly into his face. "Meet me at Pennarn Cottage," she said, "when the shadows fall thick and lie heavy beyond the garden. I'll be waiting for you. Be sure to bring Tohr."

Then she left him, looking back only once before following after Eilidh.

CHAPTER SEVEN

"H! I thought you'd never come!" Eilidh exclaimed when Finockt drew near. "Your grandfather is going to be angrier than ever with us when we get back!"

"Haí, I shall worry about that when the time comes," Finockt returned, her eyes bright and fearless. She swiftly mounted the gentle mare, and Eilidh tossed her the reins.

"Were you successful then? Did you find out what you needed?" Eilidh scrutinized Finockt's face for her answer before her cousin had a chance to verbalize it.

Finockt gathered the mare's reins and quickly adjusted the thick leather straps in her hands. "Come on then. I'll tell you on the way," she said, a slip of a smile pressing her lips.

The light was changing rapidly ahead of the late summer storm. Already it had faded to a pale and sickly yellow-gray color when Eilidh and Finockt cantered down between the trees onto the open, level track leading to Pennarn. Rain fell heavily in the distance behind them, making the dark cloud cover a thick trailing mist, and thunder rumbled overhead, low and long, and gave warning of an imminent downpour. Both girls slowed their horses to a walk when they were within sight of Pennarn's gated entrance. Soldiers drew back the locks and pulled open the doors to admit them, and just as Eilidh and Finockt passed between the gate's wide pillars, the first fat drops of rain began to fall. Once they were safe in the courtyard, Thorlóthlon's soldiers rushed forward and secured their horses by the bit. Finockt and Eilidh dismounted quickly, taking care to avoid the guards' heated glances as much as possible, and made their way toward the cottage. Terror filled Eilidh's heart-shaped face more and more the closer they came to actually entering the cottage, but this was not the first time Finockt had met with trouble; nor would it be the last time she was sure. She was sorrier now that Eilidh had been a part of her travels. She knew Coinneach's consequences would be severe. For her part, she anticipated it and expected it. For Eilidh, practically a child still, the consequences of what they had done would hit her harder. She must find a way to protect her.

Finockt looked back at her cousin, and reaching out a hand, she briefly caught Eilidh's in her own and squeezed it reassuringly. Then lifting her gaze to the cottage entrance, she saw one of Coinneach's most trusted soldiers standing at the top of the steps and understood, before he had even spoken, that he waited there for her. "The king wishes to see you, milady," he firmly announced, confirming her suspicions. "Follow me."

Finockt automatically started after him then stopped in

the middle of the causeway when Eilidh bounded up the steps after her. "No, Eilidh, not this time," she said. "It is my doing, not yours, that brought me to Malise's door. I will not have you partake of a punishment solely meant for me."

"Aye, so you say," Eilidh protested, "but it was a risk I was willing to take, remember?" Her eyes were more radiant than Finockt had ever seen them. "And it was of my own free will that I brought you to Malise. You did not force me into it. In truth, if it had not been for me, you would have never found him. Therefore, I am to be counted as guilty as you."

"Haí, you are a good friend, Eilidh," Finockt said, "more than just a cousin. But hear me in this, I believe it best if I speak with the king alone."

Over Finockt's shoulder, Eilidh caught the head soldier's steely gaze. Her eyes widened a touch, and she nodded, her laugh short and grim. "Aye, milady, do not believe me so thickheaded. I understand there are some things in which one would never win with you—for the better. May all go well…"

"Milady, the king is waiting," the soldier said impatiently.

Finockt gave Eilidh's hand another squeeze and then turned and followed her guide the few steps it took to quit the corridor. They passed along a dimly-lighted passage, past an ornate vase of overflowing flowers, and so arrived near the eastern side of the cottage. Here the soldier opened the heavy wooden door to the Main Hall and bowed low.

Finockt looked into the room. From this angle, she could not see her grandfather. Dread filled her. It would not be easy to face him. During her journey back to Pennarn, she had hoped that her account of her meeting with Malise would somehow break forth into something simply accepted by him. Now that she had arrived, she knew there was no way she would escape unscathed. But neither could she face the loathsome thought of cowardice. Taking a deep breath, she braced herself and entered.

"Thank Heaven you're all right," Coinneach said with joyful relief when she stood within the open room. He briskly crossed the flagstones toward her as though he would embrace her, then he stayed himself. Finockt saw the rapid shift in his temperament before she heard it in his voice. "And where have you been?" His tone and manner overtly bristled with anger, almost as if all forms of outrage were allowed now that he knew she was safe. Ultimately, she did not blame him, considering his responsibilities and her seemingly reckless behavior. But this was a risk she had been willing to take. Now she must face the consequences of her decisions.

Her grandfather paced the Main Hall then stopped again before the hearth. "Don't you know Deverell has…" Unable to finish his sentence, he shook his head in disgust. It was obvious he was using as much self-control as he could muster to speak this civilly to her.

Finockt's own frayed nerves manifested themselves in a repetitive twisting of the gold, inlaid ring on her finger. "Forgive me, my lord," she said. "I know I have wronged you in this, but you would never have allowed me leave if…"

"No, I wouldn't have!" Coinneach shot back at her, his dark eyes savage with rage. "'Tis the reason you stand before me now. By your actions, you needlessly risked the lives of my men. Even now they comb the countryside for you, as does Deverell. And only God Himself knows where Tirell and his men might be! The fact you know you have done wrong makes your actions all the more despicable!"

"Aye, I do not justify it as right," Finockt returned, "but

I am also not ignorant of the fact that in battle the actions of one man may turn the tide toward victory. Given the chance, would you not have taken the risk to see that it was so?"

She unwaveringly returned her grandfather's stare as he approached her yet again.

"Aye, one man! Not a woman!" he thundered. Beside himself, he strode away from her, and quickly passing over the length of the stone floor, he turned sharply at the end of the hearth and locked eyes with her. Finockt imperceptibly shifted her stance beneath the growing oppression of that uncomfortable gaze, and she clenched her fists tightly to maintain her own composure. Anger seethed and smoked behind her grandfather's eyes more vehemently than ever before. Finockt could see him visibly shaking.

"So you would not take the chance, even if you knew it would stem the tide?" she asked him.

"No!" The simple word filled the whole hall.

Finockt's brow furrowed. "Then you misspeak, for I, myself, know that you would."

"If we had needed your counsel, lass, you would have been summoned!" Coinneach barked. "You have nothing to contribute to this effort but staying alive and keeping the cross out of the enemy's hands. Your utter disregard for your place within this pending war is at the very least incomprehensible!"

At this rebuke, Finockt felt her strength falter. Unlike Coinneach, if she had stopped to consider every possible disappointment that might arise from each journey she had made up to this point, she would most likely never have carried on. In her heart, she already knew what her rebuttal would be to these doubts creeping in after her grandfather's heavy tongue lashing—each decision she had independently made had been worth the sacrifice, scorn, and derision she endured from him at the end of every journey's return because she always came home with hands full, not empty. She would not discredit her own impetuous actions, even though others did not share the same perspective, and she would not shame herself into owning it. Everything she did, she did for the good of all those involved, not self-interest.

"Where did you go?" Coinneach now demanded in a softer tone, already knowing but not wanting to hear her reply. And yet he wanted the truth from her.

"I went in search of answers," Finockt said quietly, her voice like tempered steel. "Answers you felt were unimportant, though our very lives may depend upon the man who gave them." She suffered herself to take a deep breath. "I rode to the Highlands to see Malise."

"After I specifically bade you leave him out of this?" Coinneach asked, his manner strangely calm.

Finockt began to protest, but Coinneach cut her off.

"I told you, Finockt, that man bears no relevance to Thorlóthlon. 'Tis shameful that you have gone to see him at all, and most notably after I bade you not to interfere. I cannot believe you would be so foolish, so selfish, so…so outrightly defiant as to sabotage our entire plan by seeing a man who bears no worth to Thorlóthlon or her cause!" Like usual, his voice grew louder with each spoken sentiment.

Finockt worked to steady herself against the frustration and anger welling within. She knew Coinneach bore no interest in summoning Malise for help. That understanding had already been established for her the previous evening when Deverell encouraged her to disclose her father's parchment. It hurt that Coinneach would refer to her kin with such disdain, and even more distressing was the fact that Coinneach would allow his pride and resentment to determine their course of action rather than skilled strategy and common sense. How could he willfully refuse the aid of one man who could bring closure to the inevitable war against the Dúnahez? His decision to withhold potential aid to Thorlóthlon, and thus Valínthia, for the sake of proving a point, baffled her. The injustices of it made her anger soar.

"*You* would be wise to hold your tongue, my lord," she said, "when you know of his relation to me."

Coinneach leveled on her a burning gaze. "And you would be wiser to hold your own. You are lucky I do not consider it well to have you flogged for your behavior this day!"

As soon as she had uttered the words, she knew she should not have, but there was no taking them back. The words kept coming, as if she could not stem the flow of them.

"It is well then that you do not. The cross disappeared once before. Do not doubt it could happen again," she said calmly, wielding in two strokes all the power she had against him.

Coinneach raised a thick eyebrow. Inwardly he fumed, yet outwardly his only betrayal of his emotion was that of disbelief, which shone brightly in his eyes. Her speech reminded him too much of her father and his bold, spirited ways; he knew her words were more than a threat. Anwyl had already taught him that.

He flung another steeled gaze upon her. "And did you glean your answers?"

Finockt's skin flushed hot, and her face reddened beneath the intensity of so severe a look. "Yes, I did," she said, trying to remain calm, "more than I thought possible."

Coinneach shook his head, and Finockt averted her eyes as

she battled with herself to swallow her own pride and say what was right. She inhaled deeply and prepared herself to concede, but what rose to the surface was not what she expected, even of herself.

"My father counted on Malise for counsel."

"Did he?" Coinneach's voice couched disgruntled sorrow.

"I sought him out for the same. I held hope he might have something of value to share with me concerning Anwyl's heir. But I knew nothing more about him. I swear it."

Coinneach held his head high and clasped his arms resolutely behind his back. He refused to look at her, and his silence grew nearly palpable in the quiet room. The tension between them nearly drove Finockt mad.

"Have I no right to know the truth of a past about which I know nothing?" she asked him. A muscle twitched in Coinneach's jaw, and tears welled in his eyes though Finockt could not see them since his back was to her.

"Why do you hate him so?" Finockt persisted.

"That's none of your concern," Coinneach answered, trying to mask the bevy of emotions building within him.

With sinking spirit, Finockt regarded her grandfather. Communicating with him was impossible. He would never see reason, no matter how hard she tried to convey it. And perpetuating his anger served no purpose either. It bothered her, even though she was herself still unhappy with her grandfather's opinion of Malise.

"Forgive me, Sire. I shouldn't have…" She shook her head, searching for the right words, but she could not find them. "Please do not be angry with me," she began again, drawing a step closer to him. "I know you cannot approve of what I've done, but…in my heart I *knew* I had to see this man. I know

I do not have to share with you the rest because you know the truth of this tale more fully than I. But, I beg of you, Sire, why, when you knew Malise was my mother's father, why did you keep this from me? Why did you not tell me the truth? I have no past to recollect regarding my family. But you! You have the power to disclose a history I will never fully know or understand without you. He is a good man, Sire, as are you—what else can I do to prove I am not against you?"

"Obey me!" Coinneach bellowed. "Promise me that you will never seek another way to solve the unknown without my authority! And promise me that you will stay out of harm's way!"

Finockt stubbornly shook her head. "I cannot! You know that. I cannot stand by and watch Thorlóthlon fall to Tirell when there may be an unconventional means of defeating him! Even if it meant risking your wrath all over again to see Malise, you know I would."

For an instant, Coinneach's brow briefly loosened, then his frown settled back in, deeper than the first, its presence agitating her. She watched as he glowered at her as if he would strike her on the spot if he could. By such looks Finockt grew more defeated.

"Does this infraction mean I have erred so wrongly for the sake of Thorlóthlon?" she entreated. "In truth, I have not betrayed you, my lord, though my actions this day might suggest it."

Coinneach remained silent and sullen.

"I know my duty," Finockt continued. "My allegiance is to Thorlóthlon. But know this, as well, Thorlóthlon's quest will not bear triumph over those with whom life can be regained. You are not the only one who has lost. There is much that

I have suffered, and much I suffer yet because of what has come to pass. If there are things I may salvage and piece back together to create that which I lost so long ago, then, so help me, I will risk everything to see that I get it!"

Her words had little effect on him, and she grew more desperate as the gulf widened between them, one which she saw no hope of ever spanning.

"Is there no way, Sire," she begged, "in which we may find the means to see eye to eye? Must we always be torn apart by a past neither one of us can help?"

Coinneach kept morosely silent, leaving Finockt to voice more of her feelings aloud. "Will you *never* see reason?"

The king glared at her. "I have already shared my sentiments, and *you* have willfully chosen to cast them aside, to draw excuses for your behavior and your misdeeds. You have disappointed me beyond comprehension."

Finockt reeled in disbelief. "Has my father wounded you so deeply that you will never be able to accept me for who *I* am? Do not punish me for something over which I have no control. I am Anwyl's daughter, not Anwyl himself!"

Coinneach glowered at her again. "You are more like him than you realize."

Tears shone in her eyes, and Finockt shook her head, each of his remarks wounding her more deeply than the first. "I had hoped time would change us," she said, her voice catching, "but it is clear you will not let it go. I can only assure you of this, my lord. My sentiment still holds—I will never be able to stand by and watch Thorlóthlon fall when there may be a means to save her. Even if that means taking a path which Thorlóthlon's king does not approve."

Coinneach remained unmoved. Her heart wrenched.

The delicate framework she had built since her arrival at Thorlóthlon had come crashing down in one fell stroke, and the fragile alliance she had once forged with this complete stranger had shattered. She ached to mend their relationship. He was not Malise, but he was still her kin and the first to accept her as Anwyl's daughter. She could not forget his speech in the Great Hall and how he had defended her—whether for his own purposes or not—against Egan when Egan had accused her of being an imposter. He stuck by her, and now she must do the same for him.

Drawing near, she reached a hand out to touch his arm then stopped, afraid she would somehow anger him further. At the same time, Coinneach sensed her approach and tucked his arm closer to his body.

"I know what you must think of me, my lord," she said. "I know I must appear untrustworthy, but I do not seek to defy you. I have never sought to." She let her hands fall to her sides in defeat, as he stood firm and unyielding. "Even now is your pride so deep you will not allow us the hope of moving forward?"

"Are you finished?" Coinneach asked. He stared at the crest mounted above the fireplace. His lips were pinched nearly white, and his jaw was locked, the muscle bulging where he tightly clenched his teeth.

Finockt gave him no answer. She could not. She had said too much. She had voiced her own feelings too well without thought to how this would affect either their relationship or their connection as king and princess of Thorlóthlon. A deep sense of utter failure overwhelmed her, as well as disappointment at her own lack of self-restraint. At last he looked upon her, his gaze hard and implacable. Finockt held her head high before him, but inwardly she crumbled.

"Then go to your room," he said stiffly, "and I shall call you when arrangements have been made to further our journey."

He turned his back on her and stared into the fire as she hurried from the room. His brow knit tightly, and an angry scowl turned the corners of his mouth down farther. He kicked the logs that slowly fell to ash, the act sending up a multitude of sparks and causing an eruption of hissing and popping to fall over the now silent room. He coughed and sputtered at the effort and grasped his chest in pain. The tie was breaking. It would soon be over, but how would he last until the end? What would happen to the kingdom he fought so hard to save? He knew his fate. It would only be a matter of time before the others knew it, too. But he could not let go of the anger that habitually choked him. For him, the pain of this life would not cease soon enough.

CHAPTER EIGHT

INOCKT BURST INTO her chamber and slammed the door shut behind her so forcefully the panels shuddered and the latch rattled in its niche. Her mind raced in a thousand different directions, and her emotions boiled over, culminating in a thick, desperate ache that caught in her throat and stifled her ability to breathe. Her eyes were wild with grief and indignation, and she scanned her bedchamber for something—anything—to give her hope and clear her mind. But nothing met her tortured gaze. Enraged, she clenched her fists tightly at her sides, and her breath came short and fast, until suddenly, she closed her eyes and whispered a prayer. Immediately the unbearable impulse subsided, simultaneously releasing her pent-up wrath. Slowly, surely, she felt herself returning to some semblance of normalcy, despite the immeasurable depths of her lingering anger. Grief now overtook her. Breathing more evenly, she choked back a rush of hot tears and furiously paced the floor, unable to stop, her footsteps clipping sharply over the painted tiles. "Ah!" she cried. How foolish could she be? Of course Coinneach would not embrace her for jeopardizing his men and seeing a man with whom he was obviously at odds, even if that purpose was to save Thorlóthlon, Valínthia, her people, and her kin. It was a false hope. She realized that now. Her expectations were too high. And her flagrant speech had all but obliterated the alliance between them. It now hung by nothing more than the thinning thread of kinship.

She paced again, tears now streaming freely down her face. Whether they fell from a place of anger or despair or a combination of both, she could not stop them. The argument between herself and Coinneach was yet another painful reminder of their continuing struggle to reconcile. She told him she would only ever act according to what she believed was best for Thorlóthlon, but how could she abide by this when what she truly believed was right consistently went against her grandfather's authority? Justifying her actions was easy, but was it moral? The two seemed impossible to balance.

Thunder rolled outside the cottage, and rain slashed steadily at the thick stone walls. Slowly, Eilidh approached the threshold of the doorway connecting her chamber to Finockt's and looked in on her cousin with sad eyes and a wistful smile. "Was he so very angry then?" she ventured.

"Angry?" Finockt repeated, finally standing still for a moment. Her hands took over where her movement had stopped, and with nimble fingers, she furiously began unwinding her thick, damp braid. "I think at one point he would have killed me were I not his relation and somehow the key to..." She sighed and sank against the bed. "I was wrong to have seen Malise, I suppose. At least that's what my grandfather wants me to think."

Her cousin kept silent.

"I went believing only good would come of it. That I would have something to carry back to Coinneach that would safely turn the tide of war." She laughed bitterly. "Ha, a fool's hope that Malise would have something invaluable to use against Tirell to defeat him!" She pulled her hair over her shoulder and snaked her fingers through her tired, tangled curls. "I knew Coinneach would be angry with me," she continued, "but there was more than anger in his eyes…there was very nearly hate. And all of it is my fault."

"At least his intentions for not wanting you to go are good," Eilidh said, seeking the positives in their dilemma.

"Were they?" Finockt asked. She stepped away from the bed. "Or was he only trying to hide more of the past? I want to believe only well of him as you do, but when he does *nothing* to salvage the bits of truth that come to us and scorns efforts made to seek that which we so desperately need, I cannot help but believe it is the opposite of our hope. Were it Deverell who…"

She trailed off, her mind returning to the fact that even he had not spoken completely honestly with her. She dropped into a chair beside the hearth, and her thoughts fell pensively on her paternal grandfather. "By his actions, it is almost as if he doesn't want to vanquish Tirell—" She tossed her hair back from her face and stared into the hearth. "You know there will be no peaceable end to this, Eilidh. There cannot be. Tirell is not a peaceable man." She shook her head miserably. "War and bloodshed are inevitable. Oh, Eilidh," she said into her hands, "my worst fears are evolving before my very eyes. I had hoped to be vital in stopping it, and now, now I have proved useless to both Thorlóthlon and those I have learned to care about most!" She shook her head again. "And why, why do I feel so responsible to fight in a war about which I knew nothing until four months ago?"

Eilidh settled herself at Finockt's feet and laid her hand on her cousin's knee. "Haí, do not burden yourself with such thoughts, dear cousin. I know your grandfather must be a hard man with which to converse, but you must learn to place your trust and your hope in God, not man. God will never fail us, but even the most fragile hope in mankind leads to failure and disappointment. You seek your own way to victory, but it is God Himself who determines the victor. It is to Him we should go to determine our thoughts and our next steps in order to prevail against Tirell. You are never alone, Finockt. You must know this."

Finockt rested her head back against the chair and looked upon her beloved little cousin, her eyes heavy, their depths exuding a deep sadness Eilidh could not understand. "With all my heart, I want to believe it," she said. "But I'm not ready, Eilidh. I can't explain it. I'm just not ready."

The young girl nodded and smiled broadly. "Then I pray someday you are free, as I am." She squeezed Finockt's hand and stood, shivering. The air had suddenly grown chilly and the room dark. Lighting a thin piece of wood from the fire, she shared its flame with several candles, and the room gradually lost its dim, morose appearance. Eilidh shivered again and huddled closer to the fire, its warmth a growing comfort against the return of night.

"What, what is it, Finockt?" she asked, watching her cousin suddenly rise and gain the window. A nightingale cut across the sky, and dark shadows that had long since begun to hang over the garden, now crept in toward the heart of the cottage. Finockt hesitated and then turned to find Eilidh already holding a fresh cloak out to her.

"Am I doing the right thing?" she asked her.

"Only your heart can tell you that," Eilidh replied, smiling gently. "And I think you already know the answer."

Finockt reached for the garment. "I'll be back as soon as I can."

"I know. Be careful. The way only grows more dangerous."

"Aye," Finockt said, flinging the heavy cloak over her shoulders. "Keep vigilant, Eilidh."

"And God be with you."

Finockt nodded, and in the midst of bolting for the door, she spied a scrap of parchment on her dressing table. She looked back at Eilidh who shrugged her shoulders.

"Did you see who delivered this?" Finockt asked her.

"No. I didn't even know it was there. Is it bad news?"

Finockt took it up and scanned Deverell's roughly written print. "No," she said. "It's nothing important."

"Then go, before it's too late."

"Aye." Finockt ran across the room and embraced her cousin. "Thank you, Eilidh. Thank you for everything."

Eilidh clung to her and suppressed a sob. "Godspeed, Finockt."

Finockt embraced her warmly a second time, then she hurried from her chamber and down the narrow, spiral staircase. On Pennarn's lower level, she tossed her hood up over her head and made her way past the alcove in which she had seen Deverell sleeping just that morning. She paused only a moment before the open door and observed that the map he had used for a pillow lay in a heap on the floor next to his chair, as if he had left in a hurry. A sharp pang of guilt ensnared her. With difficulty, she assuaged her conscience by pushing the awful feeling aside and hastened toward a small side corridor near the kitchen, in hopes of leaving unnoticed through a door at the rear of the cottage. But she was one step too late. As she crossed the flagstones, one of Coinneach's messengers ran up to her.

"Milady, I was just about to come for you."

"Aye, Rognvaldr, what is it?" she asked him, without slowing down.

"The king has sent me to tell you we are to leave immediately," he said, keeping pace with her.

Finockt stopped dead in her tracks. "Immediately?"

"Aye, king's orders, milady."

"Has Deverell returned?"

"Not yet. But seeing as it seems you are already prepared to leave, shall I escort you to the king?"

"No," Finockt said, her mind racing again. "It's too soon." She gazed through the lattice window overlooking the garden's farthest edge. Through the tiny baubles and waves marring its panes, she saw a pink summer rose in full bloom. Somewhere out there, beyond the rose and the carefully laid paths of Pennarn's garden, Gwri waited for her. Rognvaldr's sudden message from her grandfather was inconvenient at best. Her brow creased, and she battled herself for the decision she should make. Either way she chose, she sensed she was making the wrong choice. She clutched Deverell's note in her hand. "I need *him,*" she mumbled. "The king will never approve of what I have to say on my own."

"Milady?" Rognvaldr pressed. "What shall I tell the king? Will you come?"

"Tell His Majesty we are not to leave until Deverell has

given his word." She handed him the parchment. "For your sake, give him this note as proof it is as I say."

Rognvaldr accepted the bit of parchment with overt disappointment. "Aye, milady, as you so wish."

With a nod, Finockt dismissed him, and Rognvaldr, unhappy with his errand, ran down the corridor to the Main Hall. Nearing the rear of the cottage, Finockt continued down several angled passageways and then eased her way out into the cool, late summer night to meet Gwri.

CHAPTER NINE

WHILE FINOCKT EASILY dodged the restless guards roaming the garden, Rognvaldr entered the Main Hall. Coinneach turned expecting Finockt, and his small smile was displaced by a raging scowl when he saw the young man standing before him alone.

"Have you forgotten your duty?" he fumed under raised eyebrows.

"She told me to deliver this to you, Sire." Rognvaldr bowed low and handed Coinneach the crumpled note. In quickly releasing the scrap of parchment into the king's grasp, he only hoped the king did not notice his trembling fingers.

Coinneach glanced over the hastily scrawled message, and a hot flush of anger passed over his face. "What is this?" he growled, holding the parchment up between his fingers.

"Forgive me, my lord, I was told by the princess we are not to depart until Deverell has given word."

Coinneach leaned heavily on the dining table with both

hands. "How dare she defy me yet again!" His anger soared with every intake of breath, and he trained his gaze on the poor lad standing before him. "Where is she now?"

"I know not, Sire. I think she was headed in the direction of the garden." His limbs shook like a newborn lamb's.

"Find her! And bring her here at once! We leave as soon as she is found. Now get out!"

"Aye, Sire," Rognvaldr said with a rapid bow. Then he flew from the room, as if chased by wild boars.

Under a veiled night sky, Finockt picked her way carefully along the perimeter of the garden. So far, so good. No one followed her or obstructed her path. With one last glance over her shoulder, she wended her way between the saplings and entered the forest itself. Within a few minutes, she found herself at the serpentine wall dividing the outer woods from the king's cottage grounds. The night air was damp and chilly after the summer storm, and her breath hung in faint silver trails that rose and vanished faster than pipe smoke. She wrapped her cloak more tightly around herself and restlessly scanned the wood for any sign of her visitor.

But he had not yet come.

Kneading her hands together once or twice, she glanced back over her shoulder to the cottage. Torchlight twinkled and winked between the trees, and the soft scrape of metal or jostle of mail drifted across the garden now and again, as the soldiers made their continuous rounds. But the wood itself remained breathless and still, aside from rainwater dripping lightly from the branches and thick foliage overhead.

Finockt gleaned the wet wood a second time for Gwri's tall,

familiar figure, but clouds had again occluded the moonlight, deepened the dark, and obscured her sight. Seconds later, the moon's white rays reemerged to reveal a strange individual standing in the midst of the wood, where just before only trees and darkness had been. The stone wall was the only thing separating them from each other. At first Finockt dared not breathe for fear it was the enemy who stood no more than six feet away from her. His slightly shorter height and slimmer build—though close—did not match Gwri's, and for a moment, she did not know what to do.

"Finockt, are you here? 'Tis Uisdean."

Her blood initially ran cold at the sound of her own name, but the soft, comforting depth of her brother's voice and the assurance of his identity drove all fear from her heart. She stepped out of the shadows and ran into the moonlight that was now beginning to disappear behind more passing clouds.

"Uisdean?" she said.

"Haí, don't sound so displeased," he said with a laugh. "'Twas Gwri's wish that I come in his stead. He has gone to find Deverell and did not want you out on a fool's errand—I now know all that is upon us. Malise has told me everything."

"Then you know how vital you are to saving Thorlóthlon?" she said, hastening to the wall. "As king and rightful heir to the crown, you can stop the coming bloodshed and claim victory for Valínthia and her people. Our worries are behind us! We have only to reveal our good fortune to Deverell!"

"King? Ha, 'tis a strange word on the lips of one who has never born such a title. Even that of Prince seems so very strange to me."

"Aye, and the title of Princess is equally strange to me. But we are safe now. I need no longer dread what will come, for you will become king as is your right, and the fear we face will gladly be behind us. We will have won! And the obligation to fight will no longer be necessary!"

"I fear not, little sister. Finain is not the type to be reckoned with, and as we are reckoning with him, I fear we will have no rest until he has obtained what he so desires."

"And yet what say can he have, now that you will be king?"

"This is not the place in which to discuss such matters," Uisdean said suddenly, his eyes narrowing. "May we withdraw into the house?"

The flicker of torchlight from the front of the cottage captured both brother and sister's attention.

"That will most likely be Deverell," Finockt whispered. "Come with me. I must discuss all with him. Are you able to scale the wall?"

"Aye, easily," her brother replied.

"Then come, we shan't have much time."

Side by side, they strode toward the cottage with Finockt intensely relating her desire to speak to Deverell and her grandfather alone.

Scattered close behind them, men, darkly clothed and prepared for battle, hid in the darker parts of the garden and the forest, and as Uisdean and Finockt retreated, the enemy moved in toward the house.

CHAPTER TEN

"I T IS BEST this way, Uisdean," Finockt reiterated once they had gained the cottage. "The king has been very ill in spirit the past few days. He's even worse today, for I have set him quite out of sorts with my seeing Malise. It is best if I speak to them first."

She flung open a side door for him.

Uisdean glanced into the small chamber that faced the courtyard of the cottage. Rich rugs, wolfskins, heavy ornamental wood, and fine wax candles met his eye. Such opulence he had never seen in all his life; every detail indicated the delicate manner in which he needed to address its owner. He turned back to his sister.

"I believe it would be more prudent if I escorted you to the Main Hall. We do not have time for idle measures. There is naught but great danger upon us."

But his words fell upon deaf ears.

"He doesn't even know you're alive, Uisdean! No one's told

him anything about you. Give me leave to set in his mind the hope you are still with us. He will take it better, I'm sure. You will be quite a shock to him otherwise. Please, let me have my way in this. I'll be back shortly. I promise."

In the same instant Finockt made for the door, an almost imperceptible sound caught at her brother's ear. Alarm filled his face. Taking care to conceal himself, he crept alongside the wall toward the window and peered into the darkness outside. But the noise had died.

"Finockt, stay back," he said, motioning to her. "Finockt?" he repeated, half over his shoulder. He spun to face her when she did not answer him, but to his chagrin, he found the room empty. "Haí, Finockt!" he cried, his voice hoarse. He sprang for the door, but his sister did not reappear; and Uisdean was left staring down a shifting set of corridors, alone. Worry clenched his features. No one in the cottage was safe.

They had come.

Finockt slipped down the passage. With every step, she glanced sharply behind her. Something was not right. Everything was strangely silent and empty, except for the heated flare of speech that grew in volume as she approached the Main Hall. She did not wait to beg entrance, for the eerie silence of the cottage bode ill; and in her mind, she had brought them hope, a hope that could not wait. She lifted the latch amidst an intense and divisive conversation between Coinneach and Deverell.

"He's practically at our doorstep—" Coinneach cried.

"Aye, so he may be," Deverell interjected, "but such knowledge does not change the course of action we must take!" He shook his head in frustration, then his eye leveled upon her.

"Ah, thank God you're safe," he said, his whole countenance brightening, though he looked exhausted. His hair was damp and disheveled, and his clothing had hardly dried from the rainfall earlier that afternoon.

Coinneach balled his hand into a fist and jammed a stern finger in her direction. "You are not to be here," he said with barely a glance toward her, contradicting his earlier command.

"You told me to come," Finockt replied. She shut the door firmly behind her. "And now I'm here, with aid."

"Where did you go, Finockt?" Deverell asked.

"Deverell, I gave you an order. Take her out," Coinneach spat. "This discourse need not be brought anew."

Finockt shook her head. "I refuse to believe you so simple, Deverell," she said, her gaze resting solely on him. "Are you so afraid of the connection that even now you will not speak of it?"

"I won't say it again, Deverell," Coinneach said, his voice rising. "Take her to her chamber. We are on the brink of war and do not have time to give fancy to whims."

"Then 'twould be better you allow me leave to speak, my lord," Finockt said, finally addressing her grandfather.

Coinneach fumed, and Deverell pulled her off to the side before anything more could be exchanged between the two. "Is your leave this morning not enough? Do not incite him to anger," he said brusquely.

"You knew where I'd go, Deverell," Finockt returned. "Do not believe me unaware. Why did you not come for me straight away if you were so worried?" Her eyes flashed her increasing wrath at his close and hidden friendship with Malise. "You wanted me to go, to find out. Why do you hide it? Tell me. How is it you knew of Malise, and yet you would not give answers? You cannot leave all to fate! You must give aid!"

He stood unmoved.

"Will you not admit it, even now?" Finockt practically begged. *How could he lie to her still when he knew of Malise all along?* "Why, Deverell? Why do you of all people hide the truth from me?" She searched his face. "I'm a part of this. It was told me months ago, and yet the longer I am with you, the more you distance yourself from me. You leave me to fight my own battles!"

"And why do you argue with me every chance you can?" Deverell returned, his bright eyes glowing hot.

"Because you hide the truth!" Finockt cried with equal fervor.

A look of exasperation passed over Deverell's face, and reading the disappointment that shone therein, Finockt's heart turned in remorse. Of all those she knew, she could bear his ire the least. It always pained her more deeply when she found she had not met with his approval. It pained her now.

"He is here, Deverell," Finockt said quietly, absorbing his gaze. "My brother is here. I only seek a way to divulge his presence to Coinneach. Will you at least help me in this?"

"Uisdean is here?" Deverell said in surprise.

Yet before any one of them could draw another breath, a shrill scream cut the air. Its echo pierced the heart of each one of them and resounded with deafening clarity throughout the cottage. Finockt's gaze flew to the door. "My God, my God, Eilidh!" she cried, her whole body falling weak for an instant before she ran toward the door.

"No, Finockt!" Deverell cried, gently holding her back from crossing the room. He looked at the tiles beneath the door and glanced at the windows. No shadows moved against them. Then he turned his gaze back upon Finockt.

"Stay here," he ordered, his heart pounding fiercely in his chest. "And do not leave this room until your grandfather and I return. Promise me!"

Finockt wavered on her feet, her eyes still fixed on the thick oaken slabs separating them from the open corridor. Her face was whiter than the sheer, silken veil she typically wore since coming to Thorlóthlon.

"Finockt," Deverell urged, grabbing her by the shoulders and stooping until she looked now into his troubled blue eyes. "Promise me," he repeated.

Her hands fell away from his arms. "Aye, aye, I promise," she whispered.

"Good," he said gently. "Stay put. I'll come back for you." He squeezed her shoulders then sprinted across the open room. "And bolt the door!" he called over his shoulder as he and Coinneach slipped out into the hallway.

Finockt ran and pressed the door shut behind them and threw the bolt into place. Then she stepped back from the sealed entrance and did something she had never done before. She sank before the hearth and bowed her head, committing herself to the God she had never thoroughly known before now and still did not fully know. But the prompting called to her. *He* called to her. She knew it. She understood it. And she answered. And in the wake of her steadfast commitment, she prayed over and over, "Oh, please God, please, do not allow anything to have happened to Eilidh. For it's all my fault."

CHAPTER ELEVEN

ER SCREAM STILL echoing in his mind, Deverell raced down the familiar corridor. Never had its length seemed so long or its width so narrow. Only now did the dread that had been slowly building within him since they had first come to Pennarn Cottage amplify itself in his heart. He was the first to see her, curled up on the cold flagstones, her slender white hand clutching her tiny waist. Moans and soft whimpers escaped her lips, and she shuddered every now and again as if she were cold.

At the Northerner's abrupt halt, Coinneach also stopped short and peered past Deverell's shoulder to determine the reason for their delay. "My God in heaven! The poor lass!" he whispered, his face crumpling in agony at the sight of the young woman covered in her own blood. With his spirit no longer able to bear up against the tide of evil, deep waves of anguish and regret washed over him.

"Eilidh!" Deverell exclaimed, his heart breaking even more

at her mortal condition. The horror he foresaw and attempted to prevent was now a reality. Even without examining it, he knew her wound was fatal. Intense sorrow filled his blue eyes. He slumped to his knees beside her and took her hand, slick with blood, in his own. She clung to him for comfort as her breath filtered into tight gasps. To ease her passing, he stroked her dark hair back from her face and spoke gently to her—so gently Coinneach could not make out his words. Then he strove to draw her from the floor.

"No, don't move me," she cried out. "Leave me where I lie. Please. Please. I know I am fading."

"Eilidh," Deverell said. Fresh tears brightened his eyes.

"They're here," she said, interrupting him, her speech barely audible now.

He looked over his shoulder at Coinneach then back to Eilidh.

"Who's here, Eilidh?" he whispered.

"They are…"

"Who?" Coinneach gently urged. "Who is in the cottage?"

"I have done…my part…haven't I, my lord?" She looked at Deverell and clutched her waist and his hand more tightly. "Ah," she cried, tears muddling her vibrant blue eyes under another paroxysm of pain. "Finockt…is…safe…"

"Aye, aye, you've seen it to be so. No lass could be braver," Deverell answered her, his heart breaking. "You've aided Thorlóthlon. You shall be remembered forever, Eilidh. God waits for you."

"Then…I am…free…" she murmured, another tear sliding down her cheek.

Deverell nodded. "You are home."

She smiled up at him. "Do not…weep for me," she said.

Then the light fell from her eyes, her hand went limp in his, and she was gone.

"Who are *they?*" Coinneach pressed.

But his answer slept with her in death, and when Coinneach saw Eilidh no longer breathed, he stepped away and hung his head in his hand. Nearly beside himself with grief, Deverell closed Eilidh's bright eyes and laid the soft white hand at her side. Ever so gently he took her in his arms and crossed the corridor into the dark confines of a front room. There, he laid her upon a divan, and after saying a prayer over her in the language of old, he then kissed her forehead before rising to his feet. A smile lay sweetly upon her waxen lips, and her face was pure and untroubled. It was in fact as if she rested in a deep, comforting sleep rather than death.

Coinneach stood before the couch, his shoulders slumped under the heavy weight of his own intensifying anguish, his face downcast, and his heart trembling, while beside him Deverell listened intently.

"Where are all the soldiers?" he now asked in a low voice.

"I don't know," Coinneach replied, irritated by the question. He endeavored to keep himself from showing any outward emotion over Eilidh's death. To lose one so young… she did not deserve such a fate at so tender an age. The House of Eilthárion had always served him well, but their daughter did not deserve to have her life taken so suddenly and with such open deceit and cruelty. His heart clenched.

"Sire," Deverell said.

Coinneach looked up from Eilidh's pure white face, himself still disgruntled by his own battered emotions over her early death and all the mistakes he had already made. It was his fault Eilidh was dead. If he had acted sooner, she might still be alive. He had known Finockt would not be satisfied to leave her father's relationship with Malise alone. He had seen as much in her eyes the night before, though he denied himself the comprehension of it at the time, and yet he had not wholly believed she would be so bold as to depart for the Highlands without the surety of a military escort. Now, because of his own inaction, two lives may be forfeit. He feared for his granddaughter and was anxious to return to her.

"Sire," Deverell exhorted him. "The soldiers. Did you give new orders?"

"The soldiers are gone," someone said in a low whisper behind them.

Coinneach and Deverell whirled to face Uisdean, whose sword was drawn and ready for defense.

"Who are you?" Coinneach demanded. His fury unleashed tenfold, as he grappled for control over something; the brunt of it revealed itself in the ever-reddening hue of his face.

"Introductions can be made later, Sire. For now, you may know, I am a friend and ally to Thorlóthlon and her cause. Come, let us speak in here." Uisdean pointed to a small benched alcove away from the windows and with a strategic viewpoint of both ends of the corridor; they gathered grave and silent within it.

"Where are all the soldiers?" Coinneach barked, not waiting for the lad to speak. He would have paced, but there was no room for it.

"They have gone to save us, but the enemy is too powerful," Uisdean said quietly. "You will find most of them slain, though a few have escaped with Deverell's men to the woods where they are rallying for a renewed attack upon our signal." He read the disbelief in Coinneach's face. "The cottage is surrounded, my lord. Believe me when I say there are none left to give aid, and my own coming fell too short of late," he added with a nod toward Eilidh.

"And how was she murdered?" Coinneach cried.

Uisdean lowered his voice another notch. "Sire, please. We are not alone. We must keep quiet."

"But how was she killed?" Coinneach repeated, his tone somewhat less sonorous.

"By one of Tirell's men of course. I slew him for his gutless act—though I regret it now. But it is done, and we must leave immediately. There is nothing left here but death. Is there another way out?" Uisdean now asked Deverell.

"Aye, there is," Deverell replied.

"And what about Finockt?" Coinneach interjected. "If they killed this girl without second thought, Anwyl's daughter will surely be next. We must return to her!"

He quickly hobbled toward the hallway, but Uisdean stayed him and shook his head. "No, Sire, there are too many of them. They are lurking, lying in wait. It is folly to wander the corridors now. Finockt will be safe…it is we who need to be quick and silent." He looked over at Deverell in full confidence. "Will you show us the way out?"

"Aye, follow me," Deverell said with a sharp nod.

In the meantime, behind locked doors, Finockt prayed continually for her cousin and tried to keep the hope alive that Eilidh was well, but a dark, helpless feeling that evil had befallen her overrode any faint glimmer of hope stored within. Restless agitation sent her pacing back and forth in front of the hearth, her mind completely overwhelmed by countless depictions of what may have happened. Twice she had stopped mid-step and listened, hopeful for any sound at all of her grandfather and Deverell's return with Eilidh safe and unharmed, but the cottage remained eerily and persistently silent. The minutes ticked past, the sand in the hour glass slowly slipping away, collecting the slow, tortuous minutes into nearly a solid half hour. Not knowing what kept all three of them from returning gnawed at her, and ceaseless action was the only thing that kept her racing heart satisfied. Twice she moved to the door then resisted the temptation to look beyond it. Deverell's wrath at such folly would be unbearable. So she resumed her endless pacing.

At this point, she could no longer reject the truth of what her heart told her—her cousin was dead. But as soon as she acknowledged this truth to herself, she dismissed it. Denial kept her moving forward; it preserved her sanity and dampened the horrible reality until she was in a better state to handle it. She rubbed her arms to warmth, even though there was no need to—the blazing fire radiated plenty of heat. She stared at it, willing herself to think of anything other than what her mind constantly returned to: Eilidh. Regret filled her. Over and over again, the thought ran around in her mind— she should have heeded her cousin. In her attempt to protect her, she had unwittingly thrown her in harm's way, and the responsibility for whatever had befallen her sweet cousin was too much to bear. She closed her eyes and kneaded her hands together, but this did nothing to ease her inner torment.

Suddenly, the thick, eerie silence thinned. Finockt stiffened when she first noticed the change and listened harder. The faint scuffle of more than one pair of footsteps scraped the corridor just outside the door. Initially, she believed it signaled the return of Deverell and her grandfather. But the longer she waited with bated breath for Deverell to bid her unlock the door, the more she realized it was not he, but someone else who had come. She scanned the space under the door for additional light and shadows only to discover nothing. All remained dreadfully silent, and the long wait ensued. She could feel the tension in the air, growing sharper with every passing second. Then something in the atmosphere changed, and she knew that change involved Tirell. The whole cottage bristled with his presence. He was here, searching every room and walking every corridor in Pennarn. He was looking for her. And he would find her. He would take the cross, and he would win. She had to get out.

She hurried along the walls, trailing her fingers over the length and breadth of the tapestries hanging here and there, inspecting them for some secret passage, but the cottage gave up neither a clandestine corridor nor a hidden doorway to make her escape.

She was trapped.

The silence returned, much heavier, darker, and eerier than before. Finockt quit fumbling with the edge of an intricately woven tapestry and listened. Maybe they had left? Maybe they had found a new quest? One that did not involve the cross.

Barely a second later, her heart hit her throat. *Bang!* The piercing cry of metal resounded with terrifying fervor down the long corridor outside the Main Hall, as every few seconds doors were knocked off their hinges or set awry upon them. The warning struck her like a thunderclap. It would not be long before they reached her. She pressed her hand against her stomach to quell her rising fear.

Suddenly the Main Hall seemed amplified in both noise

and size. It caught every whisper, down to the smallest strain of human sound, the walls loomed impossibly skyward, and the large, rectangular stretches of lattice glass overlooking the garden never seemed so wide or so openly vulnerable.

Finockt knelt on the cold tile flooring. Voices leaked under the door, low and rough in tone. Then an inescapable silence spread over the whole cottage, worse than the first two—one that could be felt everywhere and closed in on Finockt like a vice. The depths of such silence was almost murderous and infinitely worse than her growing fear of doors being caved in. She strained her ears to capture any sound of the intruders. However, nothing but the eeriness of the silence prevailed; and only the quick popping and crackling of the fire dared break the mounting tension.

Finockt stood and scanned the hall, her eyes flitting from the long, flowing lattice windows on either side of the great fireplace, to the wide, heavy tapestry on the other side of the room, then to the thick walnut beams holding up the roof, and back to the door. But there was no sign of any disturbance. Torchlight twisted its way from the outside through the wavy glass panes, yet nothing moved in the darkness beyond. Time seemed to inadvertently stand still.

Then she felt it. A violent *thud!* that filtered through her chest and made the thick door to the Main Hall shudder. The hinges sighed, and the bolt creaked and groaned, as the heavy oaken planks resisted the entrance of those on the outside. Finockt smothered a scream and frantically scanned the hall. There was nowhere to go and nothing with which to defend herself. The Main Hall was not replete with swords and crossbows as had been the Great Hall of Thorlóthlon. The only thing within it was Coinneach's silver drinking cup left upon the table. Finockt took it up. It was heavy in her hand, but it would serve its duty, ridiculous as it was.

The pounding continued, and the bolt and hinges now squeaked like crying mice, the agitating sound boring itself into her mind and fraying every nerve. Her blood ran hot. She braced herself for what would come next when suddenly a soft *crack* behind her made her sidestep. To her horror, she whirled to see the wall opening before her very eyes. They were advancing from everywhere!

Her heart sank like a stone, her breath grew shallow, and she vainly tried to control her emotions, as a deep shadow stepped out of the darkness and into the room.

CHAPTER TWELVE

INOCKT DID NOT wait to see the man's face. Pulling back her arm, she let Coinneach's drinking cup sail across the room. The figure ducked, and the cup smacked against the wall. Now defenseless, Finockt hastily unclasped the cross from around her neck, and clutching its length in her fist, she held it partway over the flames and stood all but trembling before the fire. If the man before her advanced, she would release it into the flames to keep him from having it. Even if he were successful in pulling it out, the fire would have done its duty: the cross's face would be unreadable and its length even more disfigured than it already was. Or so she hoped.

But she did not have to release it.

At the sight of her holding the cross over the fire, the man held up his hands and stepped farther out from the darkness into the flame-light; the bright yellow glow reflected off a strong frame, keen blue eyes, and a grim smile.

"I wouldn't give that up just yet."

Finockt's whole body collapsed with relief. Springing forward, she threw herself into Gwri's arms, and he held her tightly. Beside them another heavy *thud!* resounded against the door to the Main Hall, the deafening noise driving them apart. Slowly, the wood began to give and splinter, as the enemy broke through.

"We don't have much time. Let's go," Gwri said.

Finockt's hand found his, and he pulled her behind him into the secret passageway. The secret door swung toward them, and just before it sealed shut, Finockt let out a cry, her eyes fastened on a short granite shelf built into a corner of the stone wall adjacent to her. Filling the entire length of its dull rough surface was a box, highly polished, its frame reflecting a plethora of exquisite colors.

Gwri followed her gaze, and Finockt began to brush past him when he stopped her.

"Finockt, we don't have time," he said, his gaze quickly shifting between the quiet windows and the splintering door.

"I have to get it," she protested, attempting to push past him once again. "If I don't, they will!"

He held her more firmly. "Finockt, it's just a box. Leave it be. It's not worth your life."

"Gwri, you don't understand! It's been under our noses this entire time. I can't leave it!"

He sighed. There was no time to argue. Reluctantly, he let her slip through his arms. Hurrying to its side, she hastily examined the box while running her hands over its elaborately carved face.

She cast a triumphant smile at Gwri. "This is it! It's everything we've been looking for."

"Finockt! Hurry up, lass! Come on!" Gwri hissed from the passageway, beckoning to her with a violent stroke of his hand.

At that very moment, the lattice windowpanes on either side of the fireplace exploded and the high-pitched shattering of glass enveloped the entire room. In the same instant the glass gave way, the Dúnarians appeared, brusquely swinging their way inside on ropes secured to Pennarn's roof.

"Finockt!" Gwri cried with a violent sweep of his arm.

Racing across the room, she jumped into the passage beside him, and he reached out and pulled the secret door toward them, just as the second wave of soldiers broke down the door to the Main Hall. With barely a sound, the leaf of the secret passage snicked closed, shielding them from the enemy.

Now, from behind the thin door, crashes and swearing could be heard as the soldiers threw furniture, toppled tables, broke vases, and ripped the ornate tapestries from the walls. Then the cursing grew louder and harsher.

"She's not here…nor's the box!" a voice scowled.

"Keep searching," another growled. "They have to be here somewhere."

"They'll be searching the walls next," Gwri said. "Their leader isn't stupid."

"Tirell is here?"

Suppressed images of the rider at the market and in the woods so many months ago came flooding back more real than before. What was worse, she could not keep those cold silver-gray eyes at bay. They pierced her soul, like the same otherworldly silver-gray eyes hidden in the oak tree off her balcony the same night Darce made an attempt on her life.

She shuddered and swallowed hard.

"No, not Tirell," Gwri said, alleviating her fears a little.

"Only his right-hand man, Maegowan. He betrayed his king and country with Tirell all those many years ago when they fled Valínthia. He considers himself to be a Dúnarian now, though he keeps the name he was born with. Com'on, we'd best get going."

Grabbing her by the hand, he jerked her down the extremely narrow corridors. Each was black as pitch and covered in a fine dust with soft cobwebbing hanging in thick threads here and there: another dismal, unchartered path of darkness. Finockt was glad she was not alone this time. Their only light spilled from a pudgy, tallow candle Gwri held in his hand. Yet it appeared he was not in need of it, for he trod the passageway with great haste and seemed to know his way quite well through the maze of tunnels.

With distance, the savagery of Tirell's men had faded, but Finockt swore she heard the dampened echo of footsteps behind them. In the end, it was only her imagination.

"Why all the urgency for the box?" Gwri asked in a hushed voice, tearing her mind now from the worry of who followed them.

"It most closely resembles the one my father described in much detail on a map." Finockt smiled softly to herself, grateful for the distraction. She tucked the box more securely onto her hip, and the cross swung freely from her hand; in her haste, she had forgotten to fasten it back around her neck.

"On a map?" Gwri asked.

"Aye, one my father made not so very long ago based on the steady nature of his penmanship. I found it in Trythwyn's study—ah, well, I too easily forget you were not there for its discovery, nor were you there when I found the first box hidden in the depths of Thorlóthlon. My father laid emphasis on the box's importance. In truth, there is too much for me to tell you now. I may only tell you that I believe it has something to do with the kingdom. Perhaps its purpose is to reveal the next successor, whom I already know."

Gwri glanced back at her in surprise. "You know who is to rule Valínthia?"

"Aye, I've only just met him. He can only be my brother, Uisdean."

Gwri stopped abruptly. "Uisdean?" he said. "He is your brother?" Finockt nodded, and Gwri gave a slight humph and shook his head in amazement. "I've known Uisdean for a great many years now. Had I only known he was your brother, this whole thing might have been avoided."

Finockt studied his intense blue eyes. "And yet if you had known, it may have been that I would never have met you."

He stopped her from touching his face.

"What? What is it?" she asked him.

"You so openly show your affection now, but what of Caslon?"

At mention of her friend, Finockt pulled her hand from his grasp. Her face flushed, and her throat constricted. "I loved him, Gwri, I did," she admitted. "But not in the way you think." She worked hard to constrain her emotions, but while her voice remained effectually steady, she could not waylay the tear sliding down her cheek. "A part of me will always love him," she confessed. "I would not wish to change that...I don't want to change that," she said, partially in afterthought.

Gwri nodded and looked up at the ceiling, as if he was considering something. Then he looked back at her and said, "You give me hope then, that I, too, will be remembered."

Confusion creased Finockt's brow.

"I've come for you, Finockt, but that's as far as it must go."

"What do you mean?" Her voice was sharper than she meant it to be.

"You will not see me after this," he said, wishing he did not have to say it.

"Because of Coinneach?"

Gwri forced himself to look at her. "No, in truth, this is something I should have done long ago."

Finockt shook her head. "What are you saying?"

"Deverell was right—I'm sorry, Finockt."

"Deverell?…This is because of him?"

Gwri sighed. He wanted her to hate Deverell, but he was not capable of it, and for that he was rightly glad. It would be low of him to encourage such feelings, even out of anger.

"Ah, Finockt, 'tis your grandfather who's more so in the right of it—" He paused, his words becoming ever more hesitant and restrained. It was too much for him; he could bear it no longer. Even this simple task of rescuing her was too much. He hardened his stance, and his blue eyes grew cold. "It is my duty to protect you, and that only. Even the bonds of friendship wound that pledge." His shoulders wilted under the confession, and he walked on, leaving Finockt standing frozen in the corridor.

She was stunned. Only the candlelight washing farther and farther away woke her from her stupor. With no other option at hand, she hurried down the corridor after him.

Gwri did not slow his pace. "Please, Finockt, no questions," he said as she drew near. "You have only to take my word as truth. There is nothing more I can do—"

His words pierced her, even more than her now aching heart. She did not understand it. Only three nights ago in the tower, she was certain he would not have rejected her so adamantly. He would not have rejected her at all.

"That's it then?" she said in frustration, her eyes fixed on his shoulders since he would not turn to face her. "You refuse me even your friendship without explanation?"

"Don't be a child, Finockt!" Gwri responded, bracing himself as the tunnel shifted downwards.

A child? He sounded like Deverell more than ever.

"Do I have any other choice?" he continued. "You know as well as I, there is nothing I can do to reverse the past! There are some things that cannot be helped."

Finockt's brow bent. "Aye, so others have said."

They hurried on in silence. Finockt tried to bury her feelings with every step, but the pain was too great. It was more lies, all of it. She felt as though something inside of her had snapped. Her mind was seething, but the shock and puzzlement of Gwri's words bound any further speech and left her so weary with wondering how she should truly respond, she did not have the energy to argue.

Gwri increased his gait, and Finockt almost had to jog to keep up with him. After many twists and turns they came to a dead end where a ladder was built against the cool earth and stretched upwards into darkness.

"This is it," Gwri said, locking eyes with Finockt. "When you get to the top, open the hatch, get out as fast as you can, and then run for it. I'll follow. Don't look back, and don't wait for me. Keep running until I say. Do you understand? Finockt!"

Finockt looked up quickly, dissolving her troubled thoughts.

"Do you understand?" he asked again.

"Aye," she said.

"You'd better fasten the cross around your neck. I'll help you."

"I don't need help," Finockt said, wanting to avoid the utter humiliation of his assisting her out of duty. "I only need you to hold the box."

After she had fastened the cross into place, Gwri passed the box back to her, helped her mount the ladder, and then started after her. Their ascent was slow as Finockt could only climb awkwardly with one hand. The other she used to move the precious box up a rung with each laborious step she took and to steady herself somewhat, though the hole dug in the earth was so snug, she could almost lean her back against the dirt wall in the event she grew tired; and yet it was wide enough to easily accommodate a soldier with armor or any broad-shouldered man. When they finally reached the top, Finockt unlatched the trap door by the light of Gwri's candle, then she waited until he blew it out and dropped it into the darkness below before she opened the roof a crack. The tight ring of wooded growth in front of her was silent. Nothing stirred. From what little she could see, the secret passage had let them out in the middle of the woodland, not far from the cottage. If she strained her eyes, she could see the cottage, barely visible against the dense screen of trees on her left. It glowed a strange color: orange and red. And the air smelled faintly of smoke. Their only enemy present was the moon, whose light fell in full beams over the earth and threatened to betray their every move.

"Do you see anyone?" Gwri asked.

"No."

"Stay in the shadows as best you can. When I tell you, go,

and don't stop! Remember, don't stop!" Gwri said urgently from his rung on the ladder beneath her.

"Aye, aye, I understand," Finockt said, nodding her head in affirmation though Gwri could not see her.

He listened a moment. "Is the way clear?" he asked again in a whisper.

Finockt carefully scoured the wood. No glint of metal shimmered between the trees or amongst the bracken. "Aye," she whispered back.

He listened intently a moment longer and waited for the moon to sink behind more cloud cover before giving the command. "Go! Now!" he cried.

CHAPTER THIRTEEN

O SOONER HAD Gwri's order escaped his lips than Finockt threw back the hatch and scampered up the last three rungs of the ladder, simultaneously tossing the box out in front of her as she rose out of the earth. The long, thick folds of her gown and her cloak restricted much of her movement, but this did little to impede her progress. With her hands flat on the sparse grass before her, she wiggled and pulled her body the rest of the way out of the secret passage. Such strenuous effort expended more of her energy than she anticipated, and when she was finally free to stand erect on the damp forest floor, she instinctively hesitated despite Gwri's frequent admonitions. Fatigue led her to falter. She stooped, her hands on her knees and her labored breaths heavy in the night air. Above her head, the moon swept free of the cloud cover and illuminated her position.

"Go, Finockt, go!" Gwri hissed. He swiftly climbed the

few remaining rungs of the ladder and sprang out into the open air behind her.

She snatched up the box and took off at a run, ducking under low hanging branches and dashing through shrubs. Their sharp edges bit her skin and whipped her face. No footpath rose to guide her, and the denseness of the wood forced her to forge her own way, a task that further slowed her escape. A few yards ahead, the wood cleared to the right, and a meager path formed between the trees. Unhindered now, Finockt increased her pace. Gwri was nowhere to be seen.

The farther into the forest she went, the blacker the night became; the leafy canopy overhead shut out nearly all the moon's majestic light. Every so often, she fell still and listened, trying to glean some insight into where she should flee. But no disruption of the forest floor gave her any indication of where either Gwri or a potential enemy could be, and her eyes were useless. She could see no more than six feet in front of her. The only thing acutely visible was her breath trailing into the cold night air, identifying her presence to anyone or anything that could penetrate the dark better than she now could. She stopped briefly again, but the wood provided no direction; thus she plunged down the uncharted path with renewed vigor.

Her nerves were starting to get the better of her. She could feel panic setting in. *Where was Gwri?* She counted on his directive to guide her, to tell her how far to run. A foreign feeling reminded her that not long ago she would never have considered it an obligation to follow Gwri's or any other person's instruction, but now, now as she floundered through the wood, not knowing how far or in which direction she should flee, it struck her how much of her fiery independence she had lost since leaving the village. Bit by bit, she was changing. She succumbed even now, and she was not certain it was a good thing.

Distracted by a sudden flurry of wings overhead, she stumbled forward, barely scaling the large, undulating root of a tree. Eroding earth gave way under her foot on the other side, throwing her off balance, and her back foot caught under the arch of another half-exposed tree root, the snare pitching her forward and sending her sprawling chin first onto a balding patch of grass. The box flew from her grasp, and she watched as it finally skidded to a stop under a blanket of dirt and early fallen leaves.

Dazed, Finockt slowly worked her way back to her feet. She caught a hand to her jaw to stop the sharp, throbbing pain in her head, only to realize the pain she sought to quench emanated from her left temple. Cautiously, she raised her hand and dabbed at the affected area, then sucked her breath in sharply at the burning sting of touching an open wound. Though it was a small abrasion, a volume of bright red blood trickled across her fingers. Gradually, the throbbing pain spread, until her head ached with a growing ferocity. For a moment, she forgot where she was and what had brought her this far into the wood. Then, somewhere in the swirling mist of her mind, it came to her. The box!

Dropping to her knees, she groped the forest floor for the precious chest. It was harder to see now. Moonlight lay in thin, watery patches over the forest floor, and her vision, jarred by her fall, faded in and out of an even deeper darkness, creating more havoc. Touch rather than sight led her. Her hands flew over the ground, frantically searching its surface for the lost possession, and her breath hung in great sweeping trails of smoke in the growing cold. She had to find it, for it would not be long before—

She stopped suddenly, her trembling hands hovering over a pair of tall mail-covered boots. They winked in the faded moonlight, like a snake's deceptive eyes.

"Looking for this?" an unpleasant voice remarked. Finockt scampered back from his feet. The clouds again parted, and she gasped as she looked up into the scarred face of the enemy. The box glittered in the pale moonlight from its nook in his huge hand.

"Stand up, you little wretch," he said, placing an iron grip around a thick wad of her hair and pulling her to her feet.

"Ah!" Finockt cried out. She clutched at his hand, and his fingers tightened, twisting the fine strands of hair at the nape of her neck. She winced and gasped.

"Quiet!" he growled. "We've been waiting for you, *Princess.* Waiting a long time. You've had us on quite a chase, but the wait is over now. I don't think I need to thank you for bringing the box, but Lord Tirell sends you his thanks in advance, I'm sure!" He laughed—an obnoxious, grating sound—and held the heavily ornamented wood up under her nose. "It is quite beautiful to behold, is it not?"

Set close to her face, the box's pearly craftsmanship shimmered almost painfully in her eyes. A second later, the Dúnarian's mirth ended, silenced by the feathered shaft that clipped his ear before sinking into the tree behind him. He dropped the box and unsheathed his sword.

"Let her go, or I'll send another, and I'll be sure it does not stray."

Finockt worked against the Dúnarian as he searched the perimeter of the clearing for his adversary, but he did not relinquish his hold on her. When Gwri advanced into the patches of moonlight dappling the forest floor, his quiver of arrows in place over his back and another arrow attached to his bowstring, the Dúnarian's bitter smile slipped back into place. He jerked Finockt forward. "Thorlóthlon's second." He sniffed. "So, it seems the Lord of Mithel has come to claim the prize has he?"

He thrust Finockt aside. She hit the ground hard and immediately snatched a hand to the nape of her neck to quiet the pain pulsating there. Then she crept back from the clearing, while the soldier tossed his long sword from one hand to the other and whipped it through the air. Across from him, Gwri flung aside his bow and removed his own sword from its scabbard. The blade sang, cold and high, as it left its sheath. Tension wreathed the air as each man circled, waiting for the other to strike—Anwyl's box the common ground between them. Seconds later, the harsh melody of sword fighting broke the still and empty night and sent Finockt scrambling for safety behind a massive oak.

"Finockt, get the box, and get out of here!" Gwri shouted between blows.

She lunged forward, but the clash of their blades drove her back. She dug her fingertips into the tree's grooved bark and watched helplessly as the two men advanced, spun, and parried with intensifying force. Her insides coiled. What Gwri asked of her was impossible! Unless there was a break in the fighting, she would never be able to reach the box unharmed.

"Finockt!" Gwri said a second time, jumping out of reach of the Dúnarian's sword point. "The *box!*"

The Dúnarian struck at Gwri with more fervor. His blade flashed white in the moonlight. Once. Twice. As it came down a third time, Finockt ducked and simultaneously threw her arms up in front of her face to shield her eyes. Fragments of bark erupted from the oak and pelted her skin and cloak. Another sweep of the soldier's blade buffeted the air close to her ear. She clung to the oak and half ducked, involuntarily cringing at the intensity and strength of the Dúnarian's determination to eliminate them both. Gwri maintained the offensive, but the Dúnarian was quickly gaining ground. His strokes grew more powerful and unpredictable, and by slow measures, he took the upper hand. Now Gwri struggled to maintain his defensive stance parallel to the oak. Their positions faltered a second time. Gwri knocked the box out of his way with his foot, then lunged forward in small steps, struck hard right then left, and the offensive was his once again. Knowing he had lost his advantage, the Dúnarian snarled, his eyes hardened even more, and the violent arc of his blade caught the clear sheen of the reemerging moon, the movement casting a brilliant spark of light across the woods before his sword sank into the side of the oak just above Finockt's head. Too close to the tree, the Dúnarian had miscalculated his intended angle, leaving his blade deeply lodged within the oak's stout trunk and the tip of his sword stretched out toward Finockt. Scrunched down and cowering near the oak's ancient base, Finockt stared up at the sharp bit of iron wedged two inches above her.

On the opposite side of the oak, three feet away from her, the Dúnarian grasped the hilt of his sword with both hands and wrenched the blade back and forth, his violent efforts slowly working its edge loose. Across from him, Gwri stood poised, trying to catch his breath while waiting for a renewed attack. Thin beads of sweat framed Gwri's face, and determination glowed hot in his eyes. The Dúnarian had nearly drawn his blade free. The muscles in Gwri's forearm tightened, as he gripped his sword, and for the fleeting moment his gaze locked with Finockt's, he flicked his chin toward the box and urgently mouthed the word *go!* Then he retrained his eyes on the Dúnarian, who braced his foot up against the oak's base and yanked his sword out of the tree into the open air.

At the same time, Finockt ran into the middle of the clearing in pursuit of the box. Behind her the heavy clash and clang of metal rang out with an even greater ferocity. She fell to her knees on the damp forest floor, madly sweeping aside leaves and dirt until she uncovered her father's box. Instantly, a long, black arrow forced her hands back, the feathered shaft drawing a line between her and the precious chest. Her breath fell shallow in her throat, and she stared at the tri-barbed arrowhead lodged in the center of the lid. It had split the wood and fractured the grain.

Fear gave way to fury, and Finockt wrenched the arrow tip from the top of the lid. Another streak of black whistled through the air, imperceptible at first until it embedded itself into a tree to her left.

Go! Go now! The simple words sprang alive within her, urging her escape, and she stood to find Gwri and the Dúnarian locked in the heat of their fight.

"Go, Finockt, *go!*" Gwri cried between parries and cross blows with the sword.

She did not want to leave him, and yet she had no choice. Bolting free of the clearing, she plunged blindly around another massive white oak and directly into the arms of a soldier. She gasped when she hit his breastplate. His arms enclosed her before she could even turn on her heel, and he swiped the box from her grasp.

"Ahh, let me go!" she screeched, wrestling his grip and trying to pull his muscular forearm from around her shoulders.

Distracted by her cry, Gwri barely missed being impaled by his opponent's long sword. He struck back, knocking the Dúnarian off balance. Following another quick succession of strikes, he aimed for the soldier's heart. But at the last moment, the Dúnarian managed to block his blow. Gwri's blade pierced the soldier's sword arm instead, and the enemy, defeated and damaged, sank to the earth, his gloved hand wrapped tightly around his wound. Released from fighting, Gwri raced across the clearing for Finockt. He made it halfway before he slid to a stop, his path countered by a secondary figure—a tall, broad-shouldered, heavyset soldier with a sinister smile; his sword tip wavered just beneath Gwri's chin.

"Well done, lad," Maegowan said. He struck Gwri's hand with the flat of his blade, and Gwri's sword hit the forest floor. "You fought well. But, remember, you're outnumbered."

His smile sickened Finockt. Dragged closer to the confrontation by her captor, she had no other choice but to face head-on the cruelty and revolting nature of Tirell's second-in-command. Her stomach churned in disgust, and the sharpening feeling of powerlessness overwhelmed her, bristling her insides. In its wake, she found herself loathing the enemy more than ever before.

Gwri's brow drew low over his eyes. He stepped forward to challenge Maegowan when he was struck across the back of the head and crumpled to the ground unconscious. One of Maegowan's foot soldiers stood behind him, smirking.

"Gwri! *Gwri!"* Finockt screamed and again fruitlessly attempted to break free.

More soldiers ran up from between the bushes and through

the bracken. Soon they were completely surrounded. Finockt slumped with defeat in the enemy's arms only to immediately stiffen, as the scar-faced soldier Gwri had wounded sifted through the crowd and eased the point of his blade between Gwri's neck and shoulder.

"Shall I finish him off, my lord?" he asked Maegowan.

In the partial moonlight, Finockt now saw the Dúnarian's face and arms were more heavily scarred from battle than what she had previously beheld, and the look of long service and bloodlust was in his eyes. Vainly, she scuffled with the soldier holding her fast, but he would not release her; and all her efforts did nothing to save Gwri. Defeated, she stopped her useless attempts at freeing herself and instead waited with bated breath for Maegowan's answer. He held her terrified gaze while he spoke, and a glimmer of a smile touched his lips, for he read in her eyes the fear she tried hard to conceal. "No. Leave him. Tirell requested them both."

A heavy wave of relief filled her, yet it faded as rapidly as it had come when she noticed Maegowan staring at her, malice narrowing his dark eyes. For a brief moment, the air between them thinned, and the silence bent and shifted beneath a lengthening tension, which crackled strangely in her ears, almost like the breaking of a brittle sheet of ice. The weight of what Finockt knew was coming nearly stopped her heart.

"And the cross?" he asked.

Finockt's captor slipped gloved fingers between her neck and the gold chain she wore and brought the broken, cross-shaped pendant to light.

Maegowan nodded, an even uglier smile parting his lips. "Lord Tirell sends his many thanks, Princess, for keeping it safe." He then shouted to his men, "Let's go!"

Immediately, Finockt lost sight of Gwri, and a new fear filled her. "No!" she cried. She dug her heels into the earth as her guard pushed her toward a group of dark-colored horses, all as sinister in appearance as their riders. They restlessly stamped the ground, eager to run. Finockt tried anything to slow the Dúnarians. The hope that Deverell and the others could not be far away kept her fighting. They only needed a few moments' time, she was sure. Her thoughts were frantic. Once she was before the horses, however, and they had not arrived, all prospects of rescue dimmed, and she lost her will to fight.

She stood defeated. Within seconds, her hands were tightly bound, and she was astride a horse, charging away into the night. Her only budding comfort was the fact that it was still possible for Deverell and her brother and those who remained of Thorlóthlon's soldiers to intercept their flight. She looked back once more for any sign of them, although she knew they would not be there, and her heart grew heavier at the strengthening scent of fire blowing in the wind. Above the tree line to the northwest, she now discerned the sky was tinted an angry red and thick trails of smoke blanketed the stars. An utterly sinking feeling ensnared her. Anxiety quickened her breathing, her eyes widened, and her heart beat with increasing force at her predicament. She scanned the knot of soldiers encircling her for Gwri, but there was no sign of him either.

Dark, fear-filled thoughts she could no longer suppress invaded her mind. Their path took them to Tirell. There was no way to protect the cross. And in an uncertain number of hours or perhaps days, she would stand before the very man who had started all this nightmarish horror. And when that happened, she could not prevent him from taking what did not belong to him, no matter how hard she tried.

CHAPTER FOURTEEN

DEVERELL DONNED HIS cloak before the towering flames consuming the cottage. Somewhere in the conflagration, glass broke, the panes no longer able to withstand the intense heat from the fire, and the heavy walnut beams holding up the roof inevitably followed suit, crumbling and caving inward with a creaking, thunderous roar, as the flames gnawed through the dry timber the way fire shrivels a blade of grass. The endless burning licked fiercely into the cold night sky amidst an upward trail of dense, billowing smoke, so thick and black and heavy, it dampened the stars and rendered the wild black of night a shade lighter—a strange but striking juxtaposition that seemed unnaturally beautiful and out of place given the gravity of their circumstances. It was as if the world had turned on its head. The weight and shame of having failed the ones they were meant to protect became an even heavier burden for Deverell and his men to bear. With Finockt captive, the way now seemed lost. Losing her was what

Deverell had feared most and what he had come to dread these past few months. Now, like Eilidh's death, it had happened.

"You're certain they won't show?" Boynton asked, approaching him.

"They would have been here by now if they had managed to escape," Deverell replied, drawing his sword from the battered ground.

"What now then?" Boynton asked.

The Northerner cleaned his blade and sheathed it, then turned his back on the burning remains of the cottage. "We head for the Deogal Cliffs as planned."

"Deverell, watch yourself!" Boynton stepped in front of him, an arrow ready on his bowstring, his eye trained on an almost imperceptible tremor of movement in the wood next to them.

Deverell looked in the same direction, his eyes narrowed, his gaze following the same line of movement about which Boynton was concerned. A moment later, Boynton drew the arrow's fletching back another inch to the hollow of his cheek, until the bowstring stretched taut and creaked under the pressure.

The movement in the wood grew more pronounced. Further tightening his hold on the fletching to steady his aim, Boynton kept his lower fingers level, a smooth guide for the arrow's chosen path. Beside him Deverell monitored both the wood and his comrade at the same time, then he threw out his hand and firmly grasped Boynton by the shoulder. "Wait!" he said.

The saplings, underbrush, and bracken trembled and shook, though neither one of them could hear it, silent as it was under the constant roar of the fire devouring the burning cottage beside them. Deverell's hand instinctively gained the hilt of his sword. Beside him Boynton remained ever steady, his arrowhead unwavering, its path still pointed northeast into the wood.

Finally, the underbrush and bracken parted, and Uisdean appeared, panting for breath, his chest heaving from his dead run. Immediately Deverell exhaled a pent-up sigh of relief. He had yet half expected a Dúnarian soldier to burst free of the forest, but now he looked eagerly to Uisdean, hopeful his friend's rapid approach was a precursor to the news he so desired to hear regarding Finockt and Gwri.

Boynton breathed out his own sigh of relief and lowered his weapon. "Were it not for Deverell, lad, I might have skewered you," he said, slinging his arrow back into his quiver. "It's about time you showed up."

"Aye," Uisdean replied, coughing. He placed his hands on his knees, his mouth pinched in a tight circle, as he steadily breathed through the pain and worked to settle his racing heart and rest his burning lungs.

"Did you find their trail?" Deverell asked, his eyes bright with urgency and hope.

Uisdean shook his head. Slowly, he moved his hands from his knees to his hips. Soon his breathing returned to a more normal rhythm. "No." He winced suddenly and clutched his side to staunch the pain catching there. "They took care to cover their tracks well," he said. "It's a new tactic. They're never this careful."

"There's no trail at all?" Deverell pressed, his brow lowering in disbelief.

"I found vestiges of one. There must have been a fight of some length at one point. The grass was flattened, the dirt disturbed, and I found a couple of random bootprints here and there. And one of the great oaks had gouges out of its trunk where a sword may have fallen. Other than that, despite a vigilant search, I found no other mark. It's as if they disappeared."

"You're right," Deverell said, disgruntled. "The Dúnarians are never that careful. If you take me as far back into the wood as you can, I may be able to find their path, resurface their whereabouts."

"No, Deverell," Uisdean admonished, catching his friend by the arm. "I'm as good a pathfinder as you are any day, and you know it. I was taught by the best," he added, acknowledging the Northerner with a sharp nod. "You must face the truth of it. My sister and Gwri are gone. We need to get my grandfather and the wounded to safety. We only waste time the longer we stand here. You know I speak truth. Let us move on and make a plan, then we'll act. Heed me in this, I beg of you."

Reluctantly, Deverell nodded.

"Shall we move then, my lord?" Boynton asked, his eyes trained on the Northerner.

Deverell nodded again, evermore slowly, reluctantly.

Uisdean cuffed him on the shoulder. "I'll see to the king."

Together Boynton and Uisdean returned to the others and roused them to their feet.

"Let's go!" Boynton ordered, his voice low and urgent. "Come on, up! We move south!"

"Sire," Uisdean said, extending his right hand to the king. "We move to safety. You may lean on me for the journey."

Coinneach hooked his hand in Uisdean's, little knowing the wiry, young man before him was indeed his grandson. Under Uisdean's guidance, he rose with ease and steadied himself. "Thank you, lad."

"My pleasure, Sire."

The wicked tongues of firelight from the cottage relentlessly flickered and washed over the small group as they continued to help each other up and then assisted their comrades at Boynton's command. Hardly any of Thorlóthlon's men remained. The majority had been killed by the Dúnarians, and those who did remain of Coinneach's royal company were weak and wounded; even the Northerner's companions had not escaped unscathed. With hunched backs and drooping heads, they fell in line behind Deverell and departed in pursuit of what mattered most: Finockt and the cross.

The Northerner walked up the steep incline in silence. Masked in the confines of a thick cloak, Malise came alongside him. "This is not defeat," Malise whispered sternly. "There is still hope left. As long as Finockt is alive, hope remains."

Deverell grunted. "Hope is fading, my friend. The enemy closes in." Then he hastened his pace and strode on ahead of the others.

CHAPTER FIFTEEN

B y midnight, Pennarn's forlorn group had entered the Elwynna woodland—a thick forest of steepled firs several miles southeast of the Palíthmar Mountains and south of Coinneach's cottage. Above these dense evergreens, a wider portion of the starlit night could be glimpsed, only when the chilling, early autumnal night wind purred through their branches. Its raspy, haunting whisper teased and unsettled the minds of those men with weak hearts.

Presently, Deverell stopped forging a path between the trees, as the sound of water singing softly in the night floated toward them. By one upward glance, he saw they had reached the Deogal Cliffs, a jagged fortress of stone rising up out of the Elwynna woodland. Before the cliffs ran the Aedre, a small, crystal clear river, which flowed decisively along its given course and cascaded with a low, pleasant murmur off a deep ridge below. Along its far side, another heavy covering of firs grew by the water's edge—a mirror image of Deverell's side of the Aedre. He let his gaze drift downward from the myriad of clefts and crevices in the rock above to the tightly woven firs guarding the entrance to the cavern: a small cleft in the cliff, not easily seen except by those who knew its purpose and design. No sign of life met his fervent search, whether in the rock above or amongst the firs beneath. But he knew that did not mean the men he sought were not there, watching.

He stepped toward the edge of the forest where the silent, needle-padded floor met the coursing river's gentle song. For a moment, he stayed close inside the firs' deep shadows and motioned for those who followed to slacken their pace. Then he advanced into the silken moonlight and waited patiently beneath its white glow, his keen eyes carefully scanning the clefts a second time. Coinneach, too, regarded the cliffs with a wary, expectant eye. However, all remained still. No movement was detected on the southern border. Only the flow of the Aedre drew the eye.

Deverell waited a few seconds longer, then stooped beside the sandy riverbank, and pulled up from beneath the neck of his tunic a small, flat, oval stone: a reflecting stone, one of the last of its kind from the white-silver halls of Evanthia. It was smooth and dark, and its surface shone and rippled a glossy liquid black, as it caught glints and winks of moonlight. Now slipping the cord over his head, he cupped the odd stone between his hands and angled it into the moon's radiant light. The river surged beneath it. Soon white fire grew from its heart, faint at first, then gradually, with prolonged exposure to the moon's radiant beams, the stone magnified in brilliance until Deverell's hands were bathed in a hazy ring of vibrant white light. In the next instance, there arose from the middle of the glowing stone a great four-pointed star. At first glance, it fired deep blue and green like the waves that broke the faraway shores of old Evanthia, then it faded to a bright and limpid purple only to deepen once again to a refulgent blue that rivaled the clearest morning sky in spring. Its beauty burst forth upon the range of cliffs before them and for an instant reflected in magnificent, haunting gleams off the river's flowing silver tresses. Then, as suddenly as it appeared, the brilliant light was gone, and night encroached dark and bleak upon the small group yet again.

With the signal thus given that all lay clear below, Deverell waited for the sign that all was safe within. Soon the thin line of a man filled the shadowed edge of one of the dark hollows that littered the cragged face of the cliffs, and a sharp streak of silver glanced off the side of his blade into the night. Deverell waved his arms in two great sweeps, and the man disappeared.

Thankfully, the night was clear, the signal received.

The Northerner walked back toward the middle of the embankment. Instantly, a round arched wooden bridge swept down from the trees on the opposite side and slid into place over the narrow river. It was made of the clean wood of an ash: cut, hewn, and linked together with much skill and craftsmanship. Delicate undulations of carved wood created a fancy railing on either side of the bridge, and the bark still clinging in places to its surfaces lay mottled with silver-green lichen and the soft plush of silver moss; and here and there was carved the emblem of its makers—the delicate weave of trisceles and interlacing.

One by one, they traversed the river by aid of the secret ingress. Deverell helped Coinneach, who struggled against the gradient. He held his chest and briefly stopped midway across the bridge to rest before Deverell urged him forward and they safely descended onto dry land. Now they walked single file, following a short, gritty stone path up a narrow incline, straight into the tight, open arms of a stone cleft. Here, a keeper of the entrance to the Deogal Cliffs helped them squeeze and maneuver their way through the confined entryway. Entering was hardest on Coinneach and the wounded. Once inside, they braced themselves against the tunnel or sat in the dust to rest. Deverell was last to angle his lithe body between the rocks. As soon as he entered, the beautifully constructed bridge silently receded into the heights of the surrounding firs behind him.

Inside the cliffs, all lay still and dark and emanated a dry cold that rivaled the damp chill of most of Valínthia's stone fortresses. A narrow passage awaited them, at the end of which ran a hewn stone stair. Deverell took it readily. In mounting, they passed several keyholes on the right—arched entrances chiseled into the cliffs' wall—that branched off from the endless curve of the staircase. Each led to a circular stone room at the end of which stood a wide aperture that spanned the full height of the room from floor to ceiling and provided ample views of the land below. Pale splashes of moonlight soaked the far end of the flinty cavern floor, allowing the newcomers unobstructed glimpses of the dark wood without, and yet at the same time, the nocturnal light seemed to steer clear of the two watchmen crouched near the very edge of every lookout, each man, on guard, with a bow and arrow at the ready on his knees. At first, Thorlóthlon's company did not see them, blinded as the weary group was by the contrast between the bright moonlight and the otherwise pitch-black of the hollows. But as the forlorn company trudged upward, they saw that they in turn were watched. The whites of the Cliffs' keepers' eyes gleamed faintly in the dark and were in fact the only telltale sign giving surety to their presence there.

All this remained consistent to the right of the Deogal Cliffs' interior stair. Keyhole upon keyhole, strategically placed throughout the Cliffs, preserved and protected its keepers. In stark contrast, to the left of the Cliffs' stair, Coinneach's men noted shallow alcoves held what resembled modified armories, replete with neatly bundled rows of arrows, an abundance of short and long swords, and along its back a single row of broad shields, stacked two deep. In similar fashion to those on the right side of the stair, additional keyholes were present on the left. However, unlike the cavernous, gaping mouths of the lookouts on the right side of their journey, these keyholes on the left were naught but long, narrow corridors that delved deeper within the mountainside and whisked men away into the unknown. Only Deverell was familiar enough with the Deogal Cliffs to know these carved tunnels, which receded into an unnatural darkness, either eventually led down to more mysterious dwellings or broke forth on the opposite side of the mountain, the latter of which offered a quick route of escape when under siege.

They kept mounting until their legs burned and they grew light-headed and dizzy from the endless climb. Three times Coinneach forced his retinue to stop. He breathed hard, and perspiration dampened his temples despite the frigid chill of the dry stone. He rested his hand against the stone wall's face, where wolfsbanes, Old Northern circles, neverns, and emblems of the forest were painted in bright and ferocious colors. Some of their fierce forms reflected vivid color and mesmerized Thorlóthlon's soldiers. Others rippled in fickle shadow, dancing between light and darkness and keeping time with the flickering glow emanating from tallow candles found at foot level; each candle dimly illuminated every fourth step from a rounded nook chiseled into the left-hand side of the stone wall.

Farther up, more alcoved armories on the left expanded to house an overflow of provisions and excess weapons, and just when the survivors of Pennarn Cottage thought they should collapse from fatigue, their wounds, and the effort of their ascent to safety, the stair gently widened, finally allowing its visitors a greater space to breathe and the hope of rest. They had reached the top. To their relief, the relentless monotony of the staircase was now behind them, and the gentle echoing thrum of hushed voices and battle preparations ushered them into a spacious domed room with a rough stone floor. Smooth, round projections of rock rose idly here and there to give respite to Pennarn's weary travelers and their fainting, wounded comrades, while further to the left, three separate stairways rose to join in a tight, interlacing pattern in the rock above and led to additional strategic overlooks, various rooms, and doubtless, more interconnecting tunnels and stairways. In this particular section of the Cliffs, the sharp chill of stone and damp earth hung thick in the air, and water ran in faint trickles down the sides of the burrowed fortress.

At their sudden presence in the room, the small group of men who were gathered there stopped their whisperings and ceased their work of mending bows and sharpening swords; a heavy, awkward silence fell over the open space. All eyes drifted to Deverell, who slowly advanced into the room, trailed by his remaining company of weary friends. The keepers' leader, Morvan, lumbered to his feet and strode toward him.

"Greetings! *Mond a ra mat, ar bed ganeoc'h! Go that does well the world with ye?* Ha, ha, lad, we've been expecting you for some time now!" he exclaimed in a deep, booming voice.

He gave Deverell's shoulder a rough shake. "Ah, it is good to see you alive, boy!"

Deverell smiled wearily. *"Mond a ra. Ha c'hwi, ma breur? It goes. And you, my brother?"* he returned, clasping Morvan's forearm. "You received my message then?"

"Aye," Morvan answered, nodding at Cronan, who sat amongst Morvan's men. Cronan grinned and nodded in turn, then bent back to repairing the arrow set between his nimble fingers. "All is well," Morvan continued. "Nothing has changed since you left Pennarn. The way remains clear, and the woods have been searched. No one follows your path."

"And the message to the clan nobles and the northern kingdoms?" Deverell then asked.

"Sent out just before you arrived. It will not take many days to assemble them all."

"Good. We need all the time we can spare. Have your men see to the wounded. Then follow me. There is much to discuss."

"Like the absence of Darce and Banain?" Morvan asked, meeting Deverell's gaze after a quick inventory of Pennarn Cottage's forlorn group. He studied the angst on his friend's face at his pointed question. "Come on, lad. Out with it then. What happened there? They weren't killed, were they?"

Deverell shook his head. "Darce we haven't seen since he made an attempt on Finockt's life at Thorlóthlon, and Banain… well, Banain lives still, under guard of the last trusted souls living at Thorlóthlon—a faithful remnant of Thorlóthlon's soldiers who await further orders. It wasn't possible for me to take all those who *hadn't* defected to Pennarn. It would have given our position away more readily than has already been done."

Morvan ignored this latter information, his mind transfixed

on the Northerner's initial report. "Banain?" he said incredulously. "Under guard? Whew, lad. To what end has that been made?"

Deverell's eyes narrowed at the doubt and skepticism in his friend's face. "I had no choice, Morvan," he said, his voice low. "He helped his brother escape."

"Helped him?" Morvan considered this thoughtfully. "Doesn't sound like Banain to me. His loyalty was always to the quest and Thorlóthlon, despite his heritage. He only ever sought to prove himself."

"That may be, but, as I told you, I had no choice. He'll remain at Thorlóthlon until I can sort out the truth of it for myself."

Morvan laid a heavy hand on Deverell's shoulder. "I'm sorry, laddie."

"As am I. He was my best swordsman."

"He still is."

Deverell gave Morvan a grim smile. "So Banain informed me."

"Then give him leave to explain himself. I'm sure when you discover the truth, it won't be what you believe it 'tis." He wrested Deverell again by the shoulder. "Rest now, lad. I'll see to the others."

Deverell nodded. *"Trugarez, ma breur. Thank you, my brother."*

At Morvan's command, the cave burst to life, and those wounded were whisked away to unknown rooms where they would be carefully tended. In the small chaos, Malise and Uisdean stole up one of the stairs to the left and disappeared into the rise of rock, leaving Coinneach and Deverell alone.

Deverell, too, took a small, hewn stairway, which rose to

meet another natural cavern, slightly more elevated than the first and of a size grand enough to comfortably accommodate half a dozen grown men. So close to the wood, it was devoid of light and enveloped in shadow, as were all the other rooms of similar build. Coinneach followed him and then collapsed upon one of the hewn boulders to fight off a spasm of violent coughs. Deverell remained silent. He stood before the hollow's wide-open mouth and gazed absently over the land.

"And what do you propose we do now? Have you a plan?" Coinneach asked, holding his hand to his chest after the spell had passed. He grimaced at the deep, rattling pain of it, then he shook off a mounting chill and wrapped his ornate cloak more closely around himself. A scowl marked his visage, and he looked around the moist cavern, glaring at his surroundings and hating his reduced circumstances and all the mishaps that had brought him to this point. His nephew's victory irritated him, as did the fact the traitor had caught them unawares much sooner than he ever expected; he thought they would have had more time.

"I thought she was safe," Coinneach mumbled, maddened by Tirell's sudden attack and the loss of both his granddaughter and the necklace. Agitated, he rubbed his forehead with his hand, slowly, deliberately, the act a nervous, useless habit.

"She will be," Deverell encouraged. "Gwri is yet with her, Sire."

"That lad?" Coinneach scoffed. "'Twas that boy that nearly got her killed in the first place!"

"You cannot blame him, my lord," Deverell protested, turning desperately toward the king. "It was an event purely unforeseen!"

"Ah," Coinneach said, glowering at Deverell's remark. He

sighed in frustration then waved the Northerner off. His attitude steadily worsened, and in an instant, he grew morbidly quiet and reflective. "What good am I any longer?" he asked aloud, more to himself than to Deverell, while he glanced around the damp stone room. "What good is Thorlóthlon? Once I was the most powerful king in all of Valínthia… and now…now I've not even the strength to protect my own granddaughter!" His anger escalated with each uttered syllable. "A mighty king now resolved to besting Tirell within the dank quarters of a cavern! This cannot have happened. Why was there not someone with her?"

"Because they were all dead!" Deverell suddenly cried. "We must count ourselves lucky that Gwri made it to her in time, or else she would be as dead as the rest, and we would be—"

He caught himself as Coinneach started, the severity of his outburst surprising them both. His patience had slowly been wearing thin under the stress and pressure of losing Finockt. He stroked his jaw twice, and then his shoulders sagged. He had foreseen this, just as he had foreseen everything else. Despite all the caution in the world, he knew he was powerless to change what came to pass; it was out of his control. Save now. Now he must meet Tirell on his own soil and arrange some way of getting Finockt back, if Tirell had not killed her already. The thought sickened him, and turmoil wrung his heart. He needed solace.

"Forgive me, Sire," he said.

He bowed stiffly then crossed the cavern and ascended into a more intrinsic darkness, this time with an even heavier heart.

CHAPTER SIXTEEN

LOWLY, DEVERELL WANDERED into a small cavern, several feet above the one he had departed, and sighed, eager to shed his fears, his worries, and his feelings. He hoped they would slip away, as he now longed to do.

Moonlight flowed through the large aperture at the far end of the stone room, its glow drenching the flinty, gritty stone floor. Keeping himself just shy of the slow moving circle of light, he slumped down upon a flat stone shelf jutting out from the cavern wall. Sorrow distorted his visage and reflected bitterly in his bright eyes. He hung his head between his hands then removed from his cloak an intricate round gold brooch. He looked upon it long and ran his thumb over the flawless face of the smooth jade stone. What hope did he have left? What could possibly be done to save his friends? To save Finockt?

He stood now at the cavern's mouth and gazed over the

land. From this height, he was able to look down upon the firs and the miniature waterfall that plied its course from one cragged outcropping to another. From there, it tumbled peacefully into a deep pool, where it gathered strength before fighting its way amongst rock and branch to seek the ways of the river once more. The setting moon drizzled bountiful ribbons of resplendent light over the pool's surface, and where the fall foamed and writhed below, the firs rippled gently in broken reflection.

"I remember the day your father gave you that," Malise said, taking a seat at the back of the cavern. His pipe glowed brightly for an instant, and its sweet scent filled the air.

"I try to forget that day," Deverell said, without turning around. Tears of shame welled fiercely in his eyes. *Ne oan ket gouest da skoazellañ ma zud.* I failed them, Malise, and with my failing goes all hope. I wasn't able to help shoulder the burden of my people. Tirell fells me yet again," he said and pounded a white-knuckled fist against the sheet of rock beside him.

"All men feel the same way at one time or another, lad."

"God forgive me, but it shames me to say it."

"There is no shame in it, my son. You did what you had to do."

"Played the part of a coward is what you mean," Deverell returned with disgust.

"You were no coward," the old man answered gruffly. Defense for the lad he had nearly raised as his own emanated in his voice. "If anything, you were a brave lad. The bravest. Cowardice cannot be given to a man who was betrayed by his own."

"Is there no punishment for being so gullible, Malise?" Deverell replied mournfully.

Regret weakened his resolve, and he pressed his thumb

over the brooch's face, as if by one sweep of his hand he hoped to erase the sour memory it contained. "My father would flush red with the shame I have brought upon his good name. He was a fighter, Malise, the strongest and the bravest. He backed down to nothing!"

"And he died for it!" Malise rejoined, his pipe idle in his hand. "Haí, Deverell, wise and just your father was and a fighter for all things good, but he was also brash and hot-headed. He taught his son wisdom and trust, to discern between the wayward makings of men. He taught you to use your head. But do not forget you have also been taught to use your mother's gift of patience. This quality your father lacked, and that brought him more harm than good… he did not want you to live the life that he did, my dear boy. Remember the words of Solomon the Wise I made you recite as a child: *Better a patient man than a warrior, a man who controls his temper than one who takes a city.*

"Because you fight with wisdom does not give you leave to merit the title of a coward. The spirit you have reflects the ultimate character of a man, one of which your father would have been most proud."

"Yet he would not have been so taken by Tirell, as I was all those years ago, nor would he have let things pass, as I so did this night. Is that using the wisdom of my fathers?" Deverell retorted.

"Ah, Deverell. Forget the past."

Deverell stood stone-faced, his arms crossed over his chest.

Inwardly Malise sighed. To move forward, they both had to supplant the old memories shared between them. "Did you allow Maegowan safe leave when he turned hide against the king?" Malise now asked him.

"No, I did not," Deverell replied. "You know it well. Once Tirell knew I understood the conspiracy, he foiled the plans to make it look as if it was I who was the loathsome traitor and Maegowan loyal servant to the king. Thus, I was arrested and Maegowan let free to join Tirell. By the time the wrong had been righted, Maegowan was already lost beyond the Dúnarian border."

"And did you pursue him?" Malise asked gently, sucking another draught from his pipe then slowly releasing it in curls and thin wisps toward the cavern's high ceiling.

"Aye, to the further humiliation of my character. I followed alongside Coinneach with my fellow brothers and fought him in the Dúnahez. But it was all in vain. Maegowan escaped, and my only reward was the loss of one of my dearest friends." The tragedy of the scene played out before him in pitiless recollection. He looked at Malise, his eyes moist. "For that, there is no hope of absolution. It is a cursed memory I must bear for the rest of my life."

"You must forget the past, Deverell! You did not have the power to keep evil men from spreading violence then, nor did you have the ability to spare the innocent from the evil intent borne of those without conscience and good will," Malise said firmly. "And you do not have that power now. Only God wields that strength. You were no more than seventeen then. Not yet a man, but even then you lived and acted well beyond your years. Haí, shore yourself up, lad. There is no reliving the past. It is done. But you can change the future. Finockt and Gwri need you now. You must turn your thoughts to Valínthia and the saving of its kingdom. There are many that need you now. Your men still trust you. They ride by your side in faith. The king still trusts you. They *believe* in you, as do I, wholeheartedly.

"Anwyl would not bear such markings of pride for you should he have known that you would give up. He, too, loved you, like a son. And most of all, *he* believed in you. Would you mar his memory by refusing to be the man that you are? Mark my words, lad, you *will* fail, if you do not follow the path that has now been laid out for you. Trust your heart, for it will tell you the inner workings of your spirit. And remember what Anwyl said, *all is not lost, should God be by your side, for He is watching over you.*"

Deverell straightened, and hope returned to his countenance. With growing confidence, he looked out into the glittering night sky.

Malise joined him by the mouth of the cave. "We fight Tirell on his ground now. He has the upper hand. You must act swiftly if you are to counter him."

"Aye," Deverell said quietly, glancing over his shoulder at his mentor. "He will take them south to the Dúnahez. But to where I do not know."

"Are you sure?" Malise asked.

Behind them torchlight grew, until it flooded the cavern, and Morvan suddenly entered after it. "Everyone stands ready, my lord. What shall you have us do?"

Deverell straightened to his full height, pushed aside his lingering doubts, and reassumed his role as leader once again. "Send out riders to Thorlóthlon to summon the remainder of her greatest army, and make camp in the Glen of Farith. Give word to Mithel that her aid is most sought after. Further instruction will be sent as needed. Leave only eight here to guard the Cliffs. Send the rest to protect the king and his company in safe passage to Farith. And gather what men we can spare. We leave at dawn for the Dùnahez."

"It's good to be with you again!" Morvan said with a wry smile. He bobbed his head and retreated with haste.

Deverell looked out over the Aedre. "Will you join the fight, Malise?" he asked after a time.

"No. My hour has not yet come. I am still needed here," he answered. "I will see to the king."

"And Uisdean?"

"He has his own mission. He will join us at the Glen of Farith when he is able."

Deverell's brow crinkled. "His own mission?"

"Aye, a personal one," Malise said quietly.

"And you let him go?"

"Easy, Deverell. The lad knows what he's doing. He's a man now. Not the half-grown lad you remember even from a few months ago."

Deverell held his peace and reluctantly nodded, his eyes still focused on the scene outside the cavern. "It is best he remains out of the fight as long as he can. I understand more rides on his shoulders than being king."

Malise murmured his agreement then looked up at Deverell, who kept his back to the old man. Malise easily perceived the tension mounting in Deverell's heart by the rigid way he moved and carried himself. The old highlander smiled wistfully, though Deverell did not see it. "Take heart, lad," he said solemnly. "Gwri and Finockt lay out of danger for now, for they do not hold the whole of Thorlóthlon's power in their hands. He will not harm them yet."

"Aye," Deverell said more confidently. "It is only by the hand of God that we have escaped the clutches of Tirell so many times before. The man's wrath will be great for such dealings. My only hope is that there be some other way the world may return to peace without the shedding of blood. But, in my heart, I know this cannot be so." He felt his whole being fall heavier, and he turned to look upon the stature of wisdom by his side. "Farewell to you, Malise," he said, safely stowing his father's brooch inside his tunic and then grabbing the old man in a rough hug. "You have been as a father to me. And for that, I thank you."

"It is an honor to be called such," Malise returned warmly. "Farewell to you, lad. May the strength of God be with you!"

"And you, my dear friend!"

CHAPTER SEVENTEEN

LOST IN THE night, miles away from Deverell, Finockt gave up trying to mark the terrain. It was too dark for that, and they rode too hard. As they flew over the land, she turned her attention instead to her tightly bound hands, working her wrists this way and that, discreetly trying in vain to loosen the ropes. After a while, she gave up. The ropes were expertly woven and tied fast. They would not give no matter how hard she tried, and all her heroic efforts left her with nothing more than a gnawing pain, as the tightly wound cords chafed away more of her skin.

She lifted her gaze skyward and prayed silently as they galloped further into the night. *God protect me and guide me. Give me Your Strength and Wisdom, for I cannot do this alone.* Instantly, her prayer was answered. A warmth and peace she could not mistake as anything other than coming from another realm blossomed in her heart and flooded her with the simple assurance that she only need listen and follow when the time came to act.

For hours they rode through the dark, as if some other force was at their heels. The night seemed to last forever when finally the first pale rays of dawn lighted the eastern sky. With the light, the land grew more distinct and delineated in form and was no longer the eerie shadowed outline backed by a star-studded sky that her eyes had grown accustomed to.

Finockt searched her surroundings, but the result was disappointing. Nothing was familiar. The only thing consistently visible to either side of them was an endless line of dark green forest. The mountains, still tall and proud, were now a quiet, shrinking scene in the distance. She did not know where they were going and could only guess their course took them in a southeasterly direction, since they had been descending for quite some time, and since the sun rose blinding and beautiful in its glittering array to their left.

They traveled all that day and night. Sleep was impossible, and by dawn the next day, Finockt was exhausted. Her whole body ached from steadying herself in the saddle for so long, and she shivered from the flux in temperature. The nights were cold, but the days grew warm. She sweated to the point that her clothes were damp, and when night fell, the cold bit her flesh and left her feverish.

This day, like the day before, the air had begun to warm with the rising sun, except this time its warmth did not penetrate her. She still felt cold, and her fingers were numb. The muscles in her legs cramped, sending waves of pain up and down her thighs, and her toes had all but lost their sensation. Tremors of exhaustion followed every muscle in her back, making her cringe. She was desperate for relief, but there was none. They did not slow for rest of any kind, aside from a quick change of horses.

Once, not long after they had switched mounts, her head grew heavy, and she slipped into sleep. Instantly, the soldier next to her jerked her awake to prevent her from falling, an act for which she was surprisingly grateful. Now struggling against intense waves of sleep and fatigue, she wondered if Gwri had ever regained consciousness, and if he suffered as much as she did. She had not seen one glimpse of him since they had left the Highlands. She only hoped he was still alive.

More hours passed, the sun marking their agonizing time spent in the saddle. Toward midafternoon, the land began to change. At first, it sloped steeply downward to the left, and then the path whittled itself away until it was only wide enough for one horse at a time. They fell in line quickly and quietly, the soldiers ever careful to guard their prisoner well. In this manner they steadily descended the narrow winding pathway at a slow, mind-numbing pace.

Glints of light sparkled between gaps in the trees. Soon Finockt realized these glints of light were actually sunstruck patches of clear water. The path's descent now brought them to the bank of a wide loch that stretched from one end of the forest to the other. Across the water stood a foreboding castle. The blood red and gray and black banners of the Dúnarians flew high above its turrets and hung like a snake's forked tongue over the pointed arch of the portcullis. On the whole, the castle was only a third the size of Coinneach's, but nevertheless it was large, menacing, and very much intact. Soldiers stood guard atop every tower, landing, and wall walk, their weapons gleaming brightly in the late afternoon sun. And great trees, almost as old as the land, surrounded the castle, ensconcing it in a green, leafy nest. Their giant boughs hung low over the water's edge and cradled large portions of the dark gray castle within their arms.

All of Finockt's fears returned, sharper than before. She looked behind her for Gwri and finally found him, pinned near the back amongst a heavy entourage of soldiers. He caught her eye and gave her an encouraging look, but she could not absorb its comfort.

Beside the loch, the soldiers immediately dismounted, amassing into a moving pool of gray tunics, silver armor, and tired horses lathered in sweat. Each man milled back and forth, removing bundles and small weapons from his saddle then carrying them to the loch's edge where several boats awaited.

Water lapped gently against the embankment. The air was much cooler here, and a soothing breeze swept up from the loch. But Finockt, finding no comfort in it, shivered at its passing. Her eyes locked on the castle, and apprehension made her shudder. In moments she would be within the power of Tirell. Escape was impossible. And though a well-planned distraction might give Gwri time to flee, neither one of them would get very far. There were too many Dúnarians.

She looked again at her wrists. Dried blood mixed with fresh, and what blood the ropes had soaked up from her raw skin only served to fatten those woven lengths of cord and shrink what little space was left between them and her flesh. Her mind grew weary. Even if she were successful and could disencumber her aching hands, she did not know what steps she would then take.

She scanned the soldiers for Gwri. He had already slid down from the saddle and was in the process of being shoved toward the water's edge. She ached to dismount and cross the water with him, but with her hands bound and her long gown encumbering her feet, she was held captive. No one came near her. It was as if, for the time being, she did not exist.

"You! Get her off that horse!" the scarred soldier with the wounded arm barked.

Finockt started at the sound of his voice.

Across the way, a tall, fierce-looking soldier threw down his supplies and turned in her direction. Finockt paled. His gaze was cold and brutal at best, as if all depth of feeling had somehow died within him. She tensed in the saddle and held her breath, inwardly praying for deliverance, but to her rising dread he kept his pace, marched up to her horse, plucked her from the saddle, and slammed her feet on solid ground. She fell against her mount when he let go of her.

"Walk!" he ordered with a jerk of his head.

She lifted her face and moved to follow him, but the ground was too unstable. The Dúnarian locked an iron grip around her arm and yanked her forward. *"Walk!"* he repeated.

Land and sky heaved in loose, undulating waves. Another step and she caught herself on her horse's saddle to keep from falling. A mind-altering weakness pooled over her. She could not open her eyes, and she could not move forward no matter how much she wanted to. The only thing she could do was rest her head upon her bound hands and pray for fortitude.

"Get her going," Maegowan yelled over the mass of men and horses while he supervised Gwri's placement into one of the boats. He kept his menacing stance at the loch's edge, his shrewd, dark eyes watching to ensure his orders were carried out.

Infuriated by her weakness, the soldier attending her snagged a passing comrade, snapping him backwards and shoving him toward Finockt. "You! Take her to the boats!" he spat. Then he bent, refilled his arms with blankets and bundles of arrows, and lumbered toward the loch.

Finockt might have sighed with relief had she been aware, but it was all she could do to hang on to that last, fading glimmer of consciousness.

"Com'on, lass," her new guard said gently. He took her lightly by the arm and patiently drew her away from the saddle.

"Will you release me?" Finockt asked, her eyes briefly closing.

He analyzed her, as if weighing the possibility of her escape.

When he hesitated, she added, "You can be sure I haven't the strength to run."

He delayed a moment longer then removed his dagger and slipped its point under one of the rope strands. The first few fibers twisted away from the dagger's edge, but further progress was stopped by the wounded Dúnarian, who clapped a hand on the soldier's wrist.

"She'll stay as she is," he snarled, then turned for the boats.

Her captor sheathed his dagger.

"Thank you," Finockt whispered, her tongue sticking to the roof of her mouth. She was so thirsty she could barely talk.

The soldier gave her a grim smile. "They wait, lass," he said. She nodded. He helped her forward, but the effort was too much. She collapsed into darkness at his feet. Immediately, he bent to one knee, gathered her in his arms, and carried her to one of the boats. Gwri watched with growing concern until she was safely stowed inside. The men shoved off, and together they settled into the rhythmic chore of rowing, each dip and glide of the oar swift and strong and nearly hypnotic.

Water sloshed gently against the sides of the boat as it cut its way to the opposite end of the loch. Just before reaching the other side, the soldiers pulled up their oars, and the prow rammed into the embankment, the jolt bringing Finockt back to consciousness. Her head felt light and empty when she woke, and she looked around in bewilderment until she saw the Dúnarians seated around her rise and empty the vessel. Her heart constricted anew. She had not been dreaming. The same soldier who carried her to the boats rose to help her disembark. He set her on her feet, then pulled his dagger and, with a swift tug, cut her bonds. "They'll not have much to say now that you're here."

He leaped over the side to dry land and gave her a small, sheepish smile when she grasped his outstretched hand to steady herself against the rocking boat. Though his intent was only to help her, she felt discomforted. Or perhaps it was the endless pairs of eyes fixed upon her?

A flush crept over her cheek, and she snatched her hand away once she set foot on stable ground. The rebuff caught the Dúnarian by surprise, leaving him an easy target for his comrades, and the increasing snickering amongst them dissolved his hesitant smile into a scowl. His cheeks flushed bright red, and closing his hand around the hilt of his sword, he strode up the embankment and disappeared into the crowd. Almost Finockt was sorry she had done it. With his absence came the understanding that she was now without even the remotest form of protection. Fear mixed with dread, and the one phrase that pushed through the mire of her churning thoughts was: *find Gwri.* She spied him amidst the other soldiers not far to her right, where the empty boats, now pulled ashore, plied a deep row in the damp earth.

"Keep yourself over here, lass." Maegowan's deep voice checked her pace.

She stopped, and Gwri saw she wavered on the verge of tears, though she tried hard to conceal it. He stepped forward to save her. "We'll not run," he said, his gaze locked on Maegowan's, "and I believe your men are too well-equipped to fear our escape. Surely it won't harm your plans if she walks with me?"

Realizing he was right, Maegowan let her go with a growl. "See to it," he said to a soldier standing near Finockt.

"Are you all right?" Gwri asked when she stood beside him. Genuine concern troubled his features. She looked as though she were about to collapse again. Panic engulfed her, the intense emotion testing every ounce of her fortitude. They were running out of time. How could she get it into his hands? Gwri studied her face. "What is it?" he asked her, but Finockt did not have time to answer. At Maegowan's order, they were both shoved forward, and the soldiers, hemming them in on all sides, led them up the embankment, across the bridge, and under the great ironshod jaws of the main gate. Once inside the courtyard, the portcullis dropped ominously behind them, and the soldiers dispersed, save three, one to guard Finockt and two to handle Gwri.

"Take her to the tower," Maegowan said. "And him, to the dungeon."

His order given, Maegowan turned his back on them and began to retreat toward the castle. Gwri looked at Finockt. She could not sever her gaze from his own. She felt the enemy's hand wrap around her arm and turn her in the direction of the tower at the same time the soldiers thrust Gwri toward the opposite side of the castle. She was losing ground fast. Full-blown panic surged within her, somehow renewing her strength.

"Wait!" she heard herself calling out. She pulled against her captor for Maegowan's attention, and miraculously, he stemmed his gait at her entreaty. "Please, allow me a moment with him…alone," she begged.

The soldiers stopped tussling with their prisoners and looked to their captain. Maegowan hesitated, and by that one stoic glance, Finockt could tell nothing. Was it even working? She had to try harder.

"Or have the Dúnarian customs changed since last Royd Annar dwelt in the old halls of Evanthia?"

At this, Maegowan glared at her, and anger flickered hotly in his eyes. "Many things have changed since that reign, Princess," he spat. "My only instruction was to bring you before Tirell, unharmed." His look made Finockt's skin crawl, and when he abruptly released a sudden burst of raucous laughter, she felt as though every nerve inside her had snapped all at the same time.

"You women," he scoffed, "sentimental to the end. I'll leave your request to Creighton."

He started up the stairs again. Then, as if on second thought, he turned back and said, "As to being alone…whatever you have to say can be said in front of my men."

This he said more to inform Creighton than to warn Finockt. A disgusted smile curled the corners of his mouth. He mounted the stairs and was gone.

Finockt turned a pleading eye upon Creighton. He was her last chance. His face was stern and unyielding, and he seemed to enjoy his newfound authority.

"Please," Finockt said. "Only a brief moment."

Creighton looked upon her long but said nothing, and after a time, he gave her a rough, irritated nod of his head and a shove. The other two soldiers released their prisoner and stepped back a few paces.

Finockt drew close to Gwri, but she could not immediately look him in the eye.

"It doesn't end here, Finockt," he said.

She looked up at him, distress filling her eyes. "There is little hope for us." She shook her head. "If Tirell gets out of me what he wants…the kingdom…"

"Don't," Gwri said. "We'll make it out—together. I won't abandon you."

She smiled weakly. "Together? Is your sense of duty so easily tossed aside now that we face the enemy? Would you now do anything and everything in your power and more to aid me?" Her eyes flicked back and forth across his own.

"Aye, even before now. You know I would," he answered her.

Discreetly, she pulled her cloak down from around her throat with one hand, and with the other, in one deft motion, she broke the gold chain holding the cross. It fell free and unnoticed into her palm. She drew closer to Gwri, and raising up on her tiptoes, she folded her arms around him, holding him close, her cloak forming a curtain around them both.

Creighton eyed them warily.

"Take this," she whispered urgently in Gwri's ear. "They may search me, and they must not find it. Do not let them have it. Promise me!"

She brushed his cheek with her lips.

"All right, that's enough!" Creighton spat, his face twisted with disgust. He flung his hand up.

The soldiers rushed forward, and just before their captors ripped them apart, Finockt dropped the cross into Gwri's bound hands. She gave him a subtle, knowing nod. He said nothing but simply exchanged one last look with her as they were dragged in opposite directions across the courtyard. Then Creighton pushed Finockt ahead of him, and she could no longer see what happened to Gwri. She suspected his captors escorted him as rapidly to the right as she was escorted to the left. And as he disappeared somewhere on the opposite side of the castle, Finockt found herself pushed another twenty paces to the left, where the castle wall protruded against dense forest. Here she and her guard ducked through a small door and mounted a flight and a half of stairs. At the first landing, he opened a heavy door to a small, circular room. In one glance, Finockt surveyed its interior: roughly built cot, small table with a pitcher and wash basin, a small stool, and a single arched window surrounded by endless rising walls of stone.

For certain, the room was cold and cheerless, and the cot was old. The ropes strung between the bed frames sagged, and the mattress was filled with nothing more than a pallet of old, half-molding straw. Ratty, woolen blankets had been thrown at its foot, and there was no pillow for her head. Across the arched window stretched thick iron bars that created five large, open squares vertically and three large, open squares horizontally. Well, it was a cell after all, was it not?

The soldier stood back to let her pass. She ducked her head and stepped inside. Immediately, the door slammed shut behind her, startling her despite her anticipation of it, and she jumped. The key rattled and scraped the lock, then she heard it fall against all the others on her jailer's key ring as he shuffled quickly down the staircase. The soft scuff of his boots and the quiet jangle of the keys faded with him into the distance. What followed was a thick, monstrously heavy silence.

Finockt half expected herself to cry, and perhaps under any other circumstances she would have, except she felt different somehow. She felt stronger, and the fears she originally harbored were gone. In their stead, the undying feeling that she would be saved coursed her veins, and without understanding how or why, she knew deep within her heart she would not meet with death. Not here.

Wanting to get her bearings and scout out the terrain, she drew the three-legged stool over to the barred window and stood upon it. From here, she noted thick forest shaded most of the land, creating a warm canopy over the sloping green hills that receded to the water's edge. A giant wisteria grew near her window, its thin wispy branches almost drooping inwards through the bars. Its presence reminded her of the village and of Murron and how they would sit and talk under a bower of pale purple petals every spring. Her heart churned at the thought. How very long it had been since that day when she had first escaped on Tohr! She missed the quiet peacefulness of the time she had known before Thorlóthlon, the acres of damp forest surrounding the village, and the dry, sweet smell of the meadow's grasses at summer's end. And as it often did, her mind wandered still to Gelis. Wearisome memories of the burning roundhouse filled her mind, and she questioned yet again whether Gelis could have made it out alive. If she had, contrary to everything Finockt truly believed, what must she be doing this very day? Did she somehow know what had become of the child she had raised? Perhaps, in her way, she did know Finockt had finally won her chance at freedom. Or perhaps she was in a place where it did not matter.

With the sun drawing its arch across the sky, the air in her cell grew warm and stuffy. Stepping down from the stool,

Finockt removed her cloak and, with a flick of her wrists, spread the heavy garment over the bed. The burgundy hue of dried, flaking blood caught her eye, and the stiff catch in her wrists alerted her to her injuries. She headed for the pitcher on the small table near the entrance to her cell, took it up, and hastily poured out its contents, alternating its tepid flow between each injured wrist. The clear water splashed over her skin into the bottom of a deep, oversized bowl. When she had drained the pitcher dry, she soaked her hands and wrists for a while before gently massaging her skin clean.

Ever numb to her task, she watched the stretch of wall above her head darken with evening shadows and felt tension thread its way back into every fiber of her being. She hated the helpless, oppressive feeling of being trapped. It made her angry. But there was nothing that could be done. She dried her hands on her gown and, driven by fatigue, settled herself on the bed. The silence nearly drove her mad. And what was worse, she could not rest. Sleep evaded her, as if it knew she needed to use every minute she had left to plan for what was to come. But did it even matter? Sleeping or scheming, Finockt did not hold hope she had what it took to best Tirell. This she must leave up to God. With this thought, she relaxed a little and felt some of her anxiety wane. Tilting her head back against the wall, she closed her eyes and attempted to doze.

CHAPTER EIGHTEEN

O VISITORS ARRIVED until midevening, when someone, most likely a soldier, brought her water to drink. Finockt did not see his face, only his hands, as he lowered the stone pitcher and cup onto the cell floor through a trap door. Then, without a word, he disappeared. For a moment, she contemplated the possibility of the water being poisoned. But then her thirst got the better of her, and she drank the cool, clear liquid greedily.

With her thirst slated, she struggled to ignore the fact that her stomach was empty. An hour or so later, there was still no sign of food. Her hunger pains intensified. Relief came only through fitful bursts of sleep that were broken by the patter of feet on the stairwell just outside her cell. Each time she heard it, she jerked awake and sat upright, listening and waiting in terror for a soldier to unlock the cell door and take her to Tirell. But no one came. The feet passed by, disappearing down some adjacent corridor or carrying themselves farther up into other reaches of the hoary castle, and she would be left alone again with her choice of either pointless sleep or restless wandering.

Soon restless agitation won out, and she settled for dividing her time equally between pacing the floor and staring out the ironclad window. In her mind, she tried to visualize her meeting with Tirell and rehearse what might take place between her and the enemy. Countless scenarios ran through her head, devouring time but never altering reality. Ever so slowly, evening changed to night, and the heat of the day began to die with the lengthening shadows. In concurrence with this diurnal change, the sharp click of boots that Finockt had continuously anticipated since her imprisonment echoed off the stone walls outside her cell. This time she knew the footsteps were headed for her. Accompanying the authoritative sound was the softer, unexpected, hurried gait of a woman or a young child.

As the key scraped through the lock for only the second time that day, Finockt slipped down from the window where she had been sitting with her knees drawn up under her chin. A soldier entered then stepped back to admit an agitated young maiden. Tall and thin with hair fairer than a golden sun, she carried a large tray laid with food and drink. Her face was sour, and her mouth pulled into a tight scowl, almost as if it had been pinned that way. She kept her eyes down as she performed her duty. For all purposes, it was clear she did not want to be there. Finockt studied her more closely as the girl crossed the small cell. Before she even saw her light blue eyes, Finockt recognized her. "Annwn?"

The young maiden seemed to brighten at the sound of her name, but when her eyes locked with Finockt's, she grew cold and steely, a coldness Finockt could only identify as typically Dúnarian.

"Your memory seems to have misled you, my *lady*," Annwn said. She set the tray down hard on the small table.

"Has it?" Finockt returned.

Annwn kept her gaze steeled and her stance cold.

"Are you not the same maiden who placed yourself under the protection and authority of Thorlóthlon?" Finockt closed the distance between them. "Annwn, you may trust me. We can get out of here, together," she said, her voice nearly a whisper.

Annwn remained cold and unyielding.

With everything in her, Finockt wanted to believe Annwn had been taken captive and was yet Tirell's prisoner, as she now was. But her heart warned her about Annwn's betrayal before any of the young girl's words could have. Still, Finockt found she could not help but ask the question. "Have they taken you prisoner as well?" Intently, she searched Annwn's countenance, hoping she would find therein some glimmer of denial regarding her blatant presumption that Annwn was indeed a spy. A traitor. But her misfortune deepened when she detected a growing disdain in Annwn's facial expression that could not be mistaken as anything other than the broadest form of hate.

"I have free reign, milady," Annwn said matter-of-factly, her glare strengthening. She tipped up her nose and settled her hands on her hips. "I may come and go as I please, if that's what you're questioning."

Color flooded Finockt's face, and her brow narrowed at the young girl's confession. For certain Annwn could never be an ally in this war against Tirell. "You *willfully* consort with the enemy then?" Finockt asked her.

The soldier eyed them briefly, and Annwn shot him a nervous glance.

"That all depends on *who* you determine the enemy to be," she replied, her voice lower. "Some of us have no choice in the matter."

"Then you were working for him all along?" Finockt said. "You weren't taken, as you wished me to believe?"

"No," she answered. "And it is a sorry thing indeed you interfered. Then you wouldn't have to be here!"

"It's good I did interfere, Annwn," Finockt replied. "You would never have made it out alive, had *you* gone on alone."

At this, Annwn laughed. "Ha," she said. "You don't give me enough credit, *Princess*. You endangered your life for nothing. I, too, knew the box you found wasn't the one for which we were looking. You missed one very important detail."

Finockt's eyes widened in surprise. "That's why you left the box in the depths of Thorlóthlon, because you knew? You had the final page of my father's map, didn't you? Did you share it with Tirell?"

Annwn rolled her eyes. "All this fighting," she said. "Don't you get tired of it? Every day hammering out the same rhetoric, the same ideas, all the while knowing you will have to give it up? This war cannot be over until we are united."

"You mean subdued!" Finockt interjected.

Annwn rolled her eyes again. "Ah, Finockt, he is not the tyrant you believe him to be. With all others, there is no help to be found, but there is hope yet left—in Tirell."

"And yet you fear him," Finockt said, studying her face. "There cannot be hope in that."

"No, he promises peace—a better life. Can you not see it,

too?" Her voice grew sharper. "I beseech you, give him what he wants!"

"Peace?" Finockt cried. Her heart roiled at such incredible blindness. "Peace at whose expense? *His?* It was by your hand, Annwn, that he found us. By your use! Are you thus so blind? 'Twas not he who plowed the path to find the cottage! How can you not see what you have done? Once he has his power, you'll be gone, useless, nothing! He won't *need* you anymore. And where then will you be?"

Annwn's eyes hardened. "No!" The word came out like a hiss. "He promised me—a better life, a grander one. The life I now lead will no longer be mine. I will be equal to you. Wear fine clothes and jewels in my hair. Work will be done by my will. And those lands viciously subjected to and broken by Thorlóthlon's kings will have a chance at life again. They will become their own masters. They will be given freedom from people like *you!*" She shook her head violently in disgust. "You squabble over a kingdom that rightfully belongs to another. Your battle lies thick with words and blade, yet the true battle stands before you in the fields and granaries! What of those who work the land and give you every fine thing to both eat and wear? Do their lives and their wants mean nothing?"

Finockt looked upon the maid in shock and dismay. "How blind you are! How painfully blind! You have to know it's not like that, Annwn. You have to know you're wrong. Without them we would be lost. Every person of means knows that. They do not ignore the difficulties of those with lower stations. Wealth and title are tools used by those like Tirell to manipulate you. Only true men and women understand the role and responsibility that wealth and title require. You've been told and you readily believe money and prestige may alleviate the struggle somewhat, but truly it is only the king himself who lives without the burdens of life; and he, too, only to some degree. And to how many is such a privilege applied? Can every man be king? You cannot make everyone the same, Annwn! It's impossible—a lie meant to use your weakness against you!

"And those lands of which you speak that lie fallow and desolate are the lands of *my* people, lost amongst your borders, while the Dúnarians thieve and lie, hoarding the prosperity of land and river and sea for themselves. They live well while *my* people, who were once free, are now slaves, slaves to a tyrant. I grew up with them, Annwn, shackled and chained to a Dúnarian lord, every ounce of their sweat and blood poured out for his will, their freedom vanquished, nearly every coin they made snatched from their hand, their children left on the brink of starvation, their families nearly destitute. I've seen the Dúnarian power kill countless innocent men and women to keep the people in terror and under their control. And now, now they waste into nothing, with no hope, no freedom to be had. Their children have no future! All this because of Tirell! You mistake yourself in thinking you know everything about me. I was once a commoner, like you. I was. I know what it's like to live under the hand of the Dúnarians. Under *Tirell.*"

Annwn clenched her hands into fists. Her heart seethed. She believed him and would still. The promises he made were real. She had tasted a glimmer of all that she would have, and she was determined to do what she must to receive the rest.

"So only *you* would say, *Lady* Finockt. Only you would lay blame upon the people who kept you alive for all these years. It's not only the Dúnarians who thieve and lie. 'Tis your wretched grandfather as well. Everyone knows he, too, treats his people like worthless chattel!"

Finockt's eyes blazed. "If that is what you believe, then lies you have willfully been told and lies you have willfully accepted!"

Though Coinneach was harsh, Finockt could never imagine him culpable of such atrocities. And what angered her more was the fact that Annwn fully acknowledged the Dúnarians' own intolerable deceit and cruelty in the matter.

"Ha, do not believe everything you hear!" Annwn cried. "Tirell has sworn to me he would never have ruled the kingdom so harshly had he been placed as king. 'Tis your grandfather who is the tyrant. He rules with an iron fist making life a misery for those who have no other choice than to serve him. I believe Tirell…I *must.*" She said this almost as if attempting to further convince herself. "No one has ever cared for me the way he has. No one!"

She stood, almost shaking. Whether from anger, fear, despair, or all three, Finockt did not know. The girl's words had escaped her lips in nearly a whisper, and her eyes focused on something far away, as if her mind and her thoughts carried her to scenes and feelings only she herself knew and understood.

No longer pleading, Finockt shook her head. "Your life will waste away, like his, in an endless pursuit of something you'll never attain. God cannot honor a man or a woman whose life is bent on nothing more than building wealth and power through conceit and greed. If Tirell cared for you as he said, would you be here now, in this cell, with me?" Annwn studied her, contemplating her words, her anger growing, while Finockt's voice continued to fill her head. "You'll see before it's over. He'll use every ounce of everything you have to offer, and when he's done with you, Annwn, he'll discard you, like chaff from the threshing floor."

"Enough!" Annwn screeched, pressing her hands against her ears. Anguish swept through her. She felt so lost, like a blind man, groping through an unending darkness for a light that can never be attained. She glared at Finockt. "He told me you would say such things! He has been right all along! And he isn't using me, as you so suggest. I have free reign to come and go as I please as I told you before! And do not choose to forget, it was of my own free will that I brought him to the cottage. I wanted you to suffer!"

As soon as the words fell from her lips, Annwn wished a thousand times over to recall them. Such cruelty seemed too much, even for her. She could not believe herself capable of willfully inflicting injury and pain. But now she had done it. She had crossed the threshold, had gone too far. She had promised herself she would never stoop that low. In an attempt to hide her utter misery, she maintained a cool and indifferent stare.

"I had hoped to trust you," Finockt said. "Does such confidence mean nothing?"

The accusation hotly branded her. Inwardly Annwn squirmed under Finockt's scrutiny, but she could not restrain herself. "Only to those who believe in it," she said, her bitterness mounting. She turned on her heel.

"If you suffered, he didn't know it," Finockt said after her, "because if he had, my grandfather would not have stood by and seen it done. And yet, what 'ere may come, I hope for your sake, that it be nothing but blessings, so that one day you may see the truth and embrace it as your own."

Annwn narrowed her eyes. "Smooth as silk and sweet as honey to the ear, but all your carefully spun words won't save you. You had your chance to be free. An awkward choice lies before you, Princess!"

"Could *you* give me freedom from all this, Annwn?"

Annwn stared at her. Her mouth went dry, and wrenching her gaze from Finockt's, she said, "Just remember. Give him the cross, and you'll live."

She turned sharply and left, and as the door slammed shut for the second time that day, Finockt could have sworn she saw Annwn wipe away a tear from her eye.

CHAPTER NINETEEN

OT LONG AFTER Annwn left, a soldier summoned Finockt. The light was gone from the day, and the castle was filled with a deep darkness softened only by the cold, bright moonglow streaming through her cell window. The striking juxtaposition between light and darkness blurred the lines in her mind between reality and the more dismal illusions her mind conjured up, encouraged as they were by her constant fears.

Before the soldier's arrival, she had nodded off twice, her body no longer able to sustain the mental anguish of what was inevitably to come, and only when she felt herself rapidly falling through space and time, had she twice snapped back awake. The powerful sensation jerked her back to her senses and a renewed awareness of her circumstances.

She tilted her head back against the stones and struggled even now with the lingering effects of it. Everything around her spun, moved, and swayed before her eyes until she had no other choice but to close them against the whirling chaos. Even then, behind the blackness of her closed lids, the spinning, moving, and swaying did not cease. She felt that if she did not lay her head down on the cot, she would tumble off its side onto the floor out of nothing more than sheer exhaustion and dizziness.

But now the soldier had come, and she no longer knew whether she was awake or asleep. Her every action appeared slower than it would have been in reality. Perhaps it was true. Perhaps reality was not what she actually faced. Perhaps what she witnessed was nothing more than a fearsome figment of her imagination. Had she considered the possibility, she might have attempted to test her surroundings in some way, in order to determine whether she truly dreamed what she was seeing, or she actually walked in obedience to the soldier's command, as she sensed she did, one foot in front of the other, following her captor without question through many corridors and up and down countless stairways, until they finally stopped before a broad wooden door fitted with thick brass hinges and bolts. Here, the soldier opened the heavy door for her, ushered her in, and then shut and locked the door behind her. Within, the room was dark as pitch, save for a sheen of light emanating from the hearth. She squinted, trying to make sense of the darkness spinning shadowy patterns over the room, particularly in the corners where the firelight did not reach. Soon her eyes grew accustomed to the dim lighting, and a man sitting quietly in a chair in front of the hearth came to her attention.

His tunic she immediately recognized, and it did not take her long to distinguish his features. "Gwri!" she cried, her mind now clear. She ran to his side and fell to her knees before him. Firelight and shadows flickered gloomily over him, and the severity of his injuries, once observed, made her stomach turn. His face was badly bruised and bore the bloodied lines of many cuts and scrapes. "Oh, Gwri," she cried, tears distorting her vision. She gently touched his face and smoothed his hair. "Forgive me."

No sooner had she spoken the words than additional light bloomed in the chamber, and Finockt stood to see a candle's open flame reflecting off a dark and sinister face.

"Tirell!" she gasped.

He strode forward, accompanied by Maegowan. "So I finally meet the illustrious Finockt. I've heard so very much about you my dear," he said in a loud voice. Too loud. It hurt her ears.

Finockt made no reply, but moved closer to Gwri and placed a hand on his shoulder to comfort herself.

"And you brought me the box," Tirell continued. "You shouldn't make my job so easy. I might have to take over more kingdoms if you keep this up." He laughed sharply—a high, irritating sound. "Now where is the necklace?"

"I don't know what you're talking about," Finockt said, hoping her voice sounded convincing.

"Come, child." Tirell motioned to her. "You're a clever girl and know very well what I'm referring to."

"I don't have it," Finockt protested.

Tirell gave Maegowan a nod and then asked Finockt again, "You test my patience, my lady. Where is the cross?"

"I don't know," Finockt insisted.

"Quit wasting time, lass, and hand it over!" Tirell ordered, his voice rising.

Maegowan advanced to Gwri and roughly pulled him to his feet. Finockt fell back from them and watched helplessly as Gwri wobbled back and forth and his head lulled.

"I haven't got it," Finockt pleaded, her gaze fixed on Tirell. "On my honor!"

Maegowan pulled a dagger from his hilt, and a wicked smile replaced his habitual frown.

Across from him, Tirell tucked his hands behind his back. "Finockt, this is the last time. Where is it? You know I'm not a man with whom to play games. Annwn told you that. I suggest you choose your words wisely. Now *where* is it!"

"I swear to you! I don't have it! Search me if you like! Please, I beg of you!" she cried, her eyes locked on Maegowan's dagger.

"Ah, Finockt," Tirell said. He rubbed his fingers over his forehead in mock misery. "I'm afraid you've quite insulted me with your trivial games. I believed you more artful than that. But fortunately for you," he said, wagging a finger at her, "you will live to see the consequences of a very poor answer."

Finockt braced herself for Maegowan's advance, but as Tirell had promised, Maegowan did not move in her direction. Instead, he kept his thick hand clamped on Gwri's shoulder and looked to her cousin, who nodded once. Maegowan raised his dagger. Eyes wide and filled with terror, Finockt heard herself gasp. In the next instant, his dagger swung down hard toward Gwri. Finockt's heart leaped to her throat, and then wakefulness rushed upon her. She sprang upright on her thin pallet, her heart pounding. Deep, shaking sobs overwhelmed her, and she slumped against the frigid stones. *It was only a dream.* She whispered the words over and over to comfort herself, but she could find no comfort in them, nor could she bear the thought of what might have occurred had the whole scene not been just a wicked trick of her mind, nor could she stop shivering, despite the fact her body was drenched in sweat. She pulled her mud-stained cloak up close around her and hugged her knees.

Further heightened by the darkness of her cell, the painful, nightmarish images kept flooding her consciousness. She sobbed and sobbed until she had no more reserve, and there was nothing left for her but to sleep.

CHAPTER TWENTY

EVERELL HELD IVAR back by the bit, and the others riding with him checked their mounts as well. After two days of endless riding, the tracks leading from the cottage suddenly disappeared. He nudged Ivar forward a few paces and stopped a second time, his eyes and ears attuned to every blade of grass wavering in the breeze before him and every audible and nearly inaudible sound.

Ivar shifted his weight, as Deverell stiffly dismounted and searched the ground in earnest. Then he knelt upon it and thoroughly examined the whole of the land stretching out before him both by sight and by ear. Its breadth lay mantled in eastern shadows, and a light wind blew in from the west.

Ivar nuzzled Deverell's shoulder.

"Haí, Ivar, good boy." Deverell patted his horse's neck then rose quickly and looked over his weary group of faithful followers. "We rest here for a time," he said, "When the shadows grow deep and long, we ride again. Take your ease, gentlemen, for we shall not rest again 'til neither starlight nor moonlight may define the way before us."

At this, the forlorn group hastily dismounted, and finding themselves a quiet place to rest amongst the cool moss-laden trees and gray-green lichened rocks, they greedily delved into their sacks and devoured what little food they had left. When they had eaten, they sought sleep or stretched out their aching legs or sat and massaged their knotted backs.

"Which direction do we head now, lad?" asked Morvan, taking a seat beside Deverell, who lifted his waterskin to his lips for a quick drink before answering him.

"Their tracks are lost along the plain here," he said, looking out over the long, whispering grasses. "It will be slow going. The Émaron grasses are thick and buoyant. Tirell has picked his passage well. I believe he is taking them south to Orthárion. That road is not easily traveled."

"Orthárion? Is it not folly, lad, to follow such a passage? There are more than a hundred black paths that lead down to the Dúnahez."

"Aye, but we must hope and pray, for it is only by the grace of God that we should find them—tell the men to pack up. Daylight fastly wanes while we linger here."

Continuing southward, they pressed on through the monotonous sea of thick grassland, but no sign was given that Maegowan and his men had passed there. Around late evening, they halted at the threshold of a black, dark wood. Deverell mentally weighed the consequences of entering such a place. It was rumored that a band of nomadic peoples had settled there—a fierce and wild race of men, who welcomed no stranger and dealt with foul magic and black spells. Those who wandered its acreage were ne'er seen again. But black magic or not, it was the path that led to Finockt.

Deverell moved forward. "Keep your eyes open, lads," he warned. "These woods welcome no sane man."

His friends grew visibly uneasy at his words. With vigor, they searched the black markings of the wood for any sign of movement and strained their ears for the slightest footfall or stretch of bowstring as they slowly entered the morbid realm.

Darkness closed in about them, and the sharp, acrid odor of decaying leaf and limb filled the forest. Giant twisted tree boughs labored to uphold an impenetrable covering of silver-green foliage that choked the light and weakened the men's ability to see throughout the wood. Moss crept over every tree root and rock, and the forest floor was strewn with a damp, rotting carpet of brown leaves. The wood lay so thick, no breath of air could wander through and render it anew.

Now alongside them and stretching out in an ever-widening ring ahead of them rested great fragments of rock. These broken monoliths poked their smooth granite faces through the leaves and forest growth, while perfect mounds of massive boulders lay randomly over the wood—some close together, others scattered abroad—each strange and ominous in form and height. More moss and leaves blanketed their bases and clung to every uneven slip of space. Here, amongst this strange collection of rock, the horses' tread lay muffled and dull upon the earthen floor, and all lay strangely—almost deathly—quiet.

Suddenly, Deverell stemmed his horse and signaled for all to remain silent. From the west, the distant murmur of an approaching rider sounded stiffly upon the earth, the noise dampened by the dense woodland. Ever so carefully, Deverell unleashed his sword, its blade making little noise as it left its sheath. Behind him Morvan and the others whipped arrows from their quivers and pulled them taut on their bowstrings; the stretch of the string lingered eerily in the air. All sounds seemed caught and caged in this listening, watching wood.

Unaware, the rider continued his fearsome flight, racing straight for them. Tense with anticipation, Deverell's men rose up in the saddle and leaned forward in readiness, but the rider descending upon them abruptly pulled back on the reins. His horse reared at the sudden command, and a look of surprise befell Deverell and the others when they found it was not a man seated before them, but a young woman, clad in a gray-lavender cloak with a silver silken veil covering her hair and face. She looked upon them in alarm. Then her features softened when her gaze fell upon Deverell. His horse danced eagerly beneath him as he gently worked to hold him in check.

"Who are you?" he demanded.

The young maiden urged her horse forward, angling the beast between rock and tree, where pale rays of white moonlight struggled to reach the forest floor. Reaching up, she tossed back her silver veil.

Deverell's eyes widened in disbelief. "Annwn?"

CHAPTER TWENTY-ONE

INOCKT STIRRED STIFFLY in her sleep then woke with a start. Her cell was so pitch-black she could barely see her hand in front of her face. Now she knew why. The moon was gone. It had drifted behind a thick copse of trees, whose robust foliage had extinguished its bright flare for the time being. She pressed her back against the stone wall and shivered. The air was cold and grew colder still when a draught of it filtered in through the barred window. The painful need for sleep crept in behind her eyes and dragged at her aching lids; however, such encouragement to rest did not last long. It lifted quickly, replaced by a paralyzing fear: how to survive. She now could not give in to sleep's command even if she tried.

Tilting her head back against the stones, she looked up at the sky. One bright, lonely star stood out from the rest, its frosted point of light always constant, never changing. She sighed, and her thoughts settled on Gwri. But she could not reflect on him without remembering the cowardice of her dreams. Did he suffer at the hands of the Dúnarians for her sake and that of the cross? Or did they extend to him the same respect she received? What worried her most was the uncertainty of whether or not she would defend him, if her nightmare came true. Her lack of conviction bothered her. But was it truly conviction she lacked? Upon further reflection, she knew it could not be that. Rather, it was her own lack of faith that weakened her and left her feeling more vulnerable than ever.

She hung her head in her hand. If only she knew Deverell was close, she could hold on until then and devise some plan to stall Tirell and protect the cross from falling into his hands. Her mind grew more hopeful and eager at the thought of Deverell's coming. Perhaps even now he and the others followed in pursuit of them both? In the next moment, she shook her head in dismay. A fool's hope. He could not possibly determine their whereabouts. No one had witnessed their departure, and the rough and wild lands through which they traveled were enough to lose the well-trained for days.

Finockt buried her troubled thoughts and shifted her gaze toward the cell door. Weak torchlight slowly brightened the stairwell outside her prison room. She sat up straighter as the light bloomed stronger, making the cracks around her cell door glow. In the next instant, a soldier unlocked the door and threw it open. She was not dreaming this time. Rising, she threw her cloak around her shoulders and waited for the Dúnarian to enter.

"Go," he mumbled, his voice gruff. He tipped his spear toward the corridor and then pushed her to the left.

Outside her cell, they climbed a long train of stairs to a small landing that let out onto a wide corridor. Torchlight bounced uneasily in the dark passages, brightly illuminating the way before them and beating back the darkness one minute, and then the next, obscuring everything in eerie shadows. Nothing of interest drew the eye. All was solid stone and sealed doors. And ever more peculiar was the mournful song that seemed to exude from the very stones themselves, a tune that both thrilled and terrified her with its melancholy melody overshadowed by tones of death.

Finockt glanced at the soldier. He did not appear to hear any part of the song she did, nor did he appear bothered by his duty or his role in securing another man's throne for a madman. Though he was the enemy, Finockt stayed close at his heels until he grabbed her roughly by the arm and pushed her ahead of him.

At the end of this wide, empty corridor, he directed her down another stone hallway slightly larger than the first and as gaudy in color and ornament as the other was plain. Well-lighted and teeming with rich décor, its entire length was filled with luxurious tapestries, tables, vases, and long embroidered rugs. Here and there badger, mink, and otter, similar to those she had seen at Pennarn Cottage, stood stuffed and mounted on wide bases like statues, with a little wooden tray secured in their outstretched arms. The wild light in the animals' eyes and the fierce boldness in their tiny faces made Finockt's skin crawl. Almost she believed if she proceeded too closely to their snarling heads, a sharp claw might happily remind her they were in fact very much alive. She took an extra step to the side.

More stairs. More corridors. More sealed doors to either side. Finockt tried to determine a pattern in their journey, but the layout was too complex. The thought was disheartening. Even if she found some means of escape, the castle would give her up before she ever made it to Gwri.

Suddenly, her guard stopped before a large, broad door that resembled the very one in her dream. She fought off a rising chill when he moved to open it and braced herself for what would surely follow, but as soon as he had thrown open the door, she did not feel the need to be so alarmed. The room within was well-lighted, and much to her relief, upon immediate inspection, there was no sign of Gwri sitting before the fireplace.

Exhaling gently, she entered of her own accord. No sooner had she crossed the threshold than the soldier jerked the door shut behind her and locked it. Finockt barely noticed. She could not. She stood spellbound. To be in the lair of the enemy, all was favorably arranged. A fire roared in the open hearth, and over a dark, wide table, a lighted chandelier burned low. It was then that she saw him, sitting at the head of the table in a sable, high back chair. His appearance was even darker and more sinister up close, and all at once her feelings regarding her surroundings changed. He looked up from his cup of wine and dismissed the servant who poured it with a flip of his hand. His eyes were even colder and brighter and more mesmerizing than she remembered. He rose slowly, confidently.

"Greetings Princess," he said, bowing cordially before her and giving her a sardonic smile. "My dear little second cousin. Welcome to Caldária!" His tone was light and teasing—despite his mockery—and his voice set her so much at ease she almost forgot he had been hunting her all these years. "I pray your journey wasn't too arduous and you found your accommodations not in too much disrepair."

Finockt gave him no reply, only watched him keenly, trying to anticipate him. His steely gray eyes left her with a terribly vulnerable feeling, and his every movement aggravated her; it took everything in her power to keep her roiling emotions under control.

"Quite the young lady, aren't we?" he continued. "But then, perhaps not quite as clever as Deverell should have hoped. For it was you, milady, who reminded us of the cottage. Otherwise, I might have had a far more difficult time discovering your hiding places. Annwn proved quite useful to me as well. I didn't think she could do it at first. But she has held up her end of the bargain without flinching." Finockt clenched her jaw at this remark. "It was quite generous on your part, too, to bring the box with you. Had you not, I might have had to spend quite some time looking for it, the effort of which is sometimes exhausting." He took a sip of wine. "Ah, don't look so frightened, child," he said glibly. "If you do not displease me, I promise, I will let you go. But I need something from you first of course." He set his wine cup back upon the table.

"Do you honestly believe I brought it with me?" Finockt said, her voice quivering lightly. "I am well aware you covet it."

Tirell looked over at her in surprise. "You've wounded me, Finockt," he said, feigning hurt. Finockt tensed, as he joined her near the opposite end of the table. "But," he added, "perhaps you have not wounded me quite so much as I can wound you."

"You would never really kill me. I'm too valuable to you."

"Yes, yes, you *are* right," he said quickly, as if he had thought the situation over a long while before she arrived. "I still need you. However…"

He looked over at a shadowy corner of the room, where the outline of a side door could just be made out. An ominous figure, invisible until that moment, opened the door wide enough to allow someone to enter. Finockt followed Tirell's gaze, the anticipation of the unexpected gathering within her like clouds before a fierce storm.

"However, my dear—" he repeated, easing himself down on the edge of the table. "I do not need your friend, and yet, it would seem that you do."

At that moment, Maegowan strode forward from the shadows, pushing Gwri in front of him; the box lay cradled in the palm of Maegowan's other hand. Finockt gasped and started toward Gwri, but he stayed her movement by a subtle shake of his head. Maegowan handed the miniature chest over to Tirell. Horrified, Finockt looked at Gwri in dismay then followed his gaze back to Tirell, who sat grinning, a wicked smile twitching the corners of his mouth, for his ever-watchful eyes had not failed to catch even the slightest hint of interaction between herself and Gwri. It was as Tirell had hoped. She cared for Gwri, quite deeply. Tirell held the box protectively upon his knee, and all at once, Finockt felt her heart inexplicably harden. Words rushed to her tongue, but Gwri intervened before she said something she should not.

"You have the box. Now let us go," he said.

"Not just yet," Tirell said, his eyes fixed on his young cousin. "There is one last thing I need from you, my dear."

Finockt stared back at him coldly, anticipating his request. "Do you believe I lie?"

Tirell's brow lifted, and his lips pressed into a thin, hard line. "I hardly think I need ask for what is mine," he said matter-of-factly.

Finockt's eyes narrowed, vexing him. "I told you, I will give up nothing."

At her stubbornness, her older cousin's gaze flashed impatient surprise. Deliberately, he set the box aside and folded his hands in his lap. "Finockt, I suggest that if you want to leave this place alive, you give me what I ask of you."

"Threaten me if you like," Finockt boldly returned. "But you cannot harm me. You know you cannot. You have no power over me and when Thorlóthlon's regent arrives…"

Tirell laughed boisterously, cutting her off and agitating her. "Ha! They were right about you! You are full of spirit, even for a lass of your age. However, you've outwitted even yourself this time. Surely you know by now Coinneach no longer legally rules Valínthia. He's done, and so are you. You are in the middle of nowhere. Deep forest encompasses you on every side, making the land a miserable, hidden pathway. Therefore your friends will undoubtedly believe that you lie entombed within the Dúnahez, *not* on the edge of Valínthia. So cease this childish façade, Finockt. Your boldness gives you no hope here. They'll never reach you in time, even if they knew where you were, and that's exactly how I intended it."

"Are you so sure?" Finockt asked, the high arch of her brow betraying her defiance. "Deverell knows the whole of Valínthia better than you know your own castle. He will find you."

"Don't delude yourself, lass," Tirell snapped, before tipping back another drink from his cup. "Deverell is weak of heart. He did not have the courage to stop me years ago when he might have had the chance. I am more powerful now than I was then. Even if he could find you, he is no match this day. And your grandfather is nothing. Powerless and ancient. An easy foe to overtake. The one for whom you should have fear is not Coinneach or Deverell but yourself, for you will die much sooner than they."

His eyes were cold and penetrating, and yet within them, there also shone the faintest glimmer of uncertainty.

Finockt saw it and clung to that one emerging flaw. "I will not fear you," she said, her voice low, her gaze fixed on his.

"Your brazenness betrays your lack of wisdom, my dear cousin," Tirell fumed, his bright eyes glowing hot.

"And your overconfidence loses you the crown. For all your cruelty, you have nothing to show for it. That which you seek evades you yet again and will so forevermore!"

"Silence!" Tirell roared, yanking his dagger from its sheath and driving it deep into the table.

Gwri set his gaze on Finockt. Worry for her cast its hand over his countenance, and at Finockt's recognition of it, she grew frightened; she had pushed her cousin too far. Now, as Tirell enclosed his fist around the hilt of his dagger, a new evil seemed to overtake him and an ominous light gleamed in his silver-gray eyes, one she had never seen there before. The same subtle doubt she had read in his gaze now overtly reflected in her own. He knew he had broken her. She was afraid of him.

"It isn't wise to play games with me, lass. My patience wears thin. Do not mistake me for Deverell. I am not a man who tolerates imprudent actions. Now I ask you again, where is the necklace?"

"In truth?" Finockt replied, her gaze never wavering from his face, though her voice faltered.

Tirell's eyes narrowed. "Where is it?" he cried, bringing his fist down hard on the table.

Finockt jumped, and her heart constricted. She looked him in the eye and prayed he could not perceive the intense fear she felt inside. "I don't have it," she confessed.

Tirell advanced towards her, wrenching his dagger from the table as he closed the space between them. Finockt resisted his sudden approach until she found herself pinned against the door. He slammed a heavy hand against the wooden planks and eyed her viciously. Finockt started at this abrupt act of violence and swallowed hard. "I swear to you, I do not have it in my possession," she repeated. She shrank against the door and scanned the coldness of his light gray eyes inches from her own. Solemn dread rose within her, and her dream came floating back to her like a devilish curse.

"I'm giving you *one* last chance," Tirell said, his patience nearly spent.

Finockt pressed herself harder against the wooden boards, but there was nowhere else for her to go. His dagger caught the firelight. Gwri tensed, waiting for what would come next, and he stepped forward to stop Tirell when Maegowan slapped his huge hand on Gwri's shoulder and held him in check. Finockt's mind raced. If she told Tirell the true location of the necklace, she failed not only her grandfather, Deverell, and her brother, she failed the whole kingdom and would bring down upon their heads a curse far worse than the one which plagued the Dúnarians. Thorlóthlon and all the other kingdoms would be at the mercy of Tirell, and the thought that pervaded her mind was the fact that he would not let any of them live. She shivered involuntarily and looked with dread past her cousin to Gwri. She could not do it.

Tirell sensed her dilemma. "I guess there's no further need to threaten you," he said, eyeing the thin line of freshly knitted skin on her neck. "It looks as though somebody's already done my work for me. But I warn you, Princess, that wound will resemble nothing more than a scratch when I'm finished."

Finockt was strangely quiet, her silence both unnerving and irritating him.

"Where's the necklace?" he spat.

Finockt steadily returned Gwri's gaze and struggled to release the words pent up within her when Tirell's dagger beneath her chin reverted her attention to the mesmerizing glow of his silver-gray eyes.

"Tell me…" her cousin pushed, "or I swear he will die."

"I told you the truth," Finockt said faintly. Her heart beat a frenzied rhythm in her chest. "I told you."

"Maegowan," Tirell said, not taking his eyes off her.

Maegowan unsheathed his sword, and Gwri closed his eyes against the press of Maegowan's blade against his flesh. The threat was real. Finockt's blood rushed hard through her veins. The length of Maegowan's blade glistened in the firelight. Tirell held her, pinned still against the door, his dagger still tight beneath her chin, while Maegowan balanced Gwri's life in his hands. One mistake, one ill-timed word, and they would both be dead. At her silence, Maegowan dug his sword tip into Gwri's back, its edge slicing his skin and drawing blood. Gwri grimaced, and Finockt paled.

"I let it go," she blurted, a tear slipping down her cheek. "I wanted it safe…so I gave it to someone else to keep for me." Her breathing fell shallow as she waited for the fatal cut, but none was delivered to either her or Gwri.

Tirell's eyes now flamed fire. His hand was like a vice around her neck, and Finockt stiffened at the rage burning in his smoldering gray gaze. "Who has it?" he demanded.

Finockt kept silent. No matter what happened now, Thorlóthlon's betrayals must stop with her. What she had already shared was as far as she could go. At her continued silence, Tirell's anger grew more visceral, and he shook her violently twice so that her teeth rattled in her head. "*Who* has the necklace?" he repeated. "Who? Answer me!"

But Finockt only stared back at him, trembling with fear, her lips pressed firmly together, intent on holding to her promise.

Tirell's grip tightened on her neck until darkness clouded her vision. "Who has it, lass? Who?" he shouted. "Tell me, or I'll…"

"I have it!" Gwri exclaimed.

Finockt looked at him, terrified. "Gwri, no!" she choked out, tears springing to her eyes.

"I won't let him kill you, Finockt," Gwri returned with a haggard look, his voice gripped with sadness. "The necklace is not worth your life. It was not meant to be this way."

Finockt slumped in her ruthless cousin's grasp, and her mind began to play out the details of her horrible dream all over again. "Oh, please, no," she whispered to herself.

"Give it to me," Tirell demanded, his vicious gaze now resting upon Gwri. He threw Finockt aside into a small table, and she barely caught herself upon it.

"It's here, in my hand." Gwri let the gold chain dangle between his fingers and extended the cross out as far as his bound hands would let him. Maegowan snatched up the thin rope of gold and triumphantly delivered the pendant to Tirell.

Every bit of the golden chain sparkled in the firelight, and he stared at the cross's face. It was finally his. After all these years, the kingdom would return to its rightful heir. But all was not right. Barely a second later, a deep-set frown replaced his jubilant smile for he realized half of the cross was missing. The situation did not look promising. Finockt shot Gwri a worried glance. To her distress, he returned the same. A sinking feeling came over her, and despite all her earlier convictions, she felt the end drew very near. For them both.

CHAPTER TWENTY-TWO

NNWN DREW HER horse closer to Deverell's and looked upon him and his men with a cold but elegant grace. "There is no need to fear. It is no sorceress who is before you," she said calmly, her jaw slightly set and a pout settling over her lips.

"Lower your weapons," Deverell ordered. As she reined her horse in before his, he looked at her intently, his features masked in shock. She fit Finockt's description perfectly.

"You do well, Lord Deverell. I am Annwn, but do not ask me to explain my wanderings, for this is not the time or the place," she urged and cast an apprehensive glance to her side. "We do not have much time if we are to save your friends. I fear that it is too late already."

Deverell looked at her, flummoxed. Whispers ran scattered throughout the wood, and his companions looked about themselves with great trepidation.

"Be you friend or foe, lass?" Morvan inquired with

unbridled anger, while ignoring the restless stance and growing fears of the men around him.

"You can be sure I am now no foe." She shifted uncomfortably in the saddle. "In truth, I have been searching for you. I know the whereabouts of your friends, who hold the necklace you so seek to recover. Their very lives hang by a thread. I may take you to them, but we must not tarry. Every second determines whether your friends live or die."

The men looked at her skeptically.

"Please," Annwn begged, looking upon Deverell. "Tirell's wrath cannot be kept at bay for much longer."

"Where are they being held?" he asked.

"He holds them prisoner at Caldária. It is a secret place, a stone dwelling, on the edge of Valínthia, to which few dare wander, for Tirell's forces abide even there with much strength. But you may yet save your friends by my aid."

"Be you a traitor? How is it that you know so much about Tirell and his keepings?" Morvan asked through clenched teeth. "It behooves us not to trust the likes of such a maid," he muttered under his breath.

"I would be yet such as you say," Annwn answered, her blue eyes welling with tears, "but honest words from your lady brought an otherwise callused heart back to its senses." She sat silent on her steed while Deverell examined her closely, and she returned his gaze without waver.

"Show us the way," he told her.

Annwn nodded willingly. "We move northeast."

Turning her steed back into the heart of the rotting woodland, Annwn rapidly escorted her allies through the black workings of the Bricriu Forest, and only when they traveled at an even pace side by side did she then dare to converse quietly with Deverell.

"How is it that you found us?" he asked. "If Caldária lies northeast, we must be far from its setting?"

"The ground rises high west and south of Caldária, and from such a point can one see far and wide. But great forests guard its dwelling, much like Thorlóthlon. 'Twas an arduous journey, which brought me to its summit, and upon reaching it I knew not in which direction to flee. It was at that moment that I first saw it." She fell silent, her memory bringing it all back to her in vivid recollection.

"First saw what?" Deverell gently probed. Both riders leaned forward, as their horses lurched over the craggy terrain.

Annwn regarded him with a steady eye. "The light. It was so distant at first. Yet it grew in brilliance, illuminating the whole of the southwest before it gradually shifted eastward. A white light so brilliant and bedazzling, I thought myself dreaming. I felt strangely drawn to it, and so followed it."

"And where is it now?" Morvan cut in. "Where is this white light you so saw?"

Annwn looked about her in wonder and strained her eyes to see between leaf and limb the dull patches of night sky above them. "I know not," she said. "How strange! It has diminished. What could it have been?"

"It was an answer to prayer, Annwn," Deverell said softly.

She held his gaze with uncertain astonishment. Then the wonder faded from her face, and she remembered her mission. "Caldária is not so far as you would believe, my lord."

At this, Deverell looked up to find they had left the wood to enter a much different part of the land: a wide green valley spotted with tufts of long, blowing grasses and domed, thatched huts and marked on its far side by sheepfolds.

"The Halvarnathness," Annwn informed them, "shepherds of the East and border guards of the Dúnahez. But do not fear them. They will not harm us, for their watch sleeps this night." She nodded to the few dark, slumbering forms, which lay scattered here and there amongst the huts. "Come. We must move quickly."

Deverell and his men looked warily at the black-clothed figures then pulled their horses away to follow Annwn. Now galloping down the outskirts of the valley, they thundered across it and up a small hill without slowing their pace. When they had gained ground on its other side, they spurred their faithful horses on toward a distant tree-lined rise to the northeast, which glimmered in the moonlight. Time was against them, and the hope that Finockt and Gwri still lived waned slowly from Deverell's thoughts.

CHAPTER TWENTY-THREE

"WHERE'S THE OTHER half to this?" Tirell demanded. He glared at Finockt from across the room and gripped the broken pendant so tightly in his fist that his knuckles turned bright red and white.

Finockt looked at him in surprise. Did he not now have what he had always desired? She clutched the edge of the round table to hold herself up and felt a triumphant glimmer of hope fill her. They still had time.

"The other half? Where *is* it?" Tirell repeated, his fair skin beginning to flame red with anger.

"What other half?" Finockt asked him.

"Don't get wise with me, lass, where *is* it?" His eyes followed her every move.

"I don't know what you're talking about," she replied in earnest, while progressively easing herself away from his slow, steady advancement. "There is no other half."

"Don't lie to me!" Tirell cried. With one sweep of his arm,

he sent his silver wine cup sprawling across the floor with a loud clatter. At this violent outburst, Finockt slinked back against the wall. "Where is it? Where's the real necklace?" he cried. "Where's Arnorylja's cross? Where's the other half to the cross? Tell me!" he screamed, dangling the disfigured pendant in front of her face.

"I'm telling you no lies!" Finockt protested. "The pendant has always been that way…ever since I can remember!"

The scrutiny of his eyes terrified her, and then a sudden twinge of relief washed over her, as the unimaginable occurred: he believed her. "Useless," he mumbled. Turning away from her, he cast the necklace to the floor and placed a hand to his head. "It won't work. This isn't the real necklace." Disgruntled, he lodged his dagger into the wood table and then leaned both hands heavily upon its surface. He would have to regroup and find another way to reclaim his losses.

Meanwhile, Finockt's mind wreaked havoc with her thoughts. Not the real necklace? The phrase stung. Had her father not trusted her either? If Tirell was right, then perhaps she was not really the one prophesied to free her people? But Malise had recognized her and the cross…and Coinneach knew it instantly. Even Deverell spoke of its disfigurement. Had they all been duped? Did Tirell know something they did not? Was there more to the story?

An uncomfortable silence spread over the room, and the terrible eeriness that encroached upon Finockt was quickly interrupted by Tirell's exasperated voice: "Maegowan, open the box. Now!"

Finockt felt her heart catch. Instinctively, she stepped forward to stop them when she caught Gwri's eye and realized the foolishness of what she was doing. She stopped herself just in time.

For a brief moment, the room went deadly silent again, until Maegowan jammed his dagger through the narrow slit between box frame and lid. What followed was a horrible cracking that exploded across the room, as Maegowan wrenched his blade to the right and then thrust it upwards. Finockt cringed, seeing the beautiful woodwork splinter beneath his knifepoint and some of the jewels break free from the box.

His task complete, Maegowan stepped back quickly, and Tirell bent to lift the box's broken lid. He whispered, almost like a crazy man, speaking of the kingdom, the crown, and his title finally redeemed. Finockt was repulsed by his behavior, and yet almost, she felt sorry for him.

Anxiety and anticipation fell over them all, and Finockt's impatience soared as she awaited what would inevitably come. The seconds seemed unending. Her cousin's face wore a mask of pure greed, and his eyes shone with a diabolical gleam as he traced ever so carefully the remaining jewels lining the front of the small chest.

"For so long," he muttered. "So long have I waited for this day!"

His declaration incited protest within Finockt, but she dared not betray her feelings. He was about to open the box. More dreadful silence encompassed the room, followed by a sharpening tension. Then he threw back the lid, and for several minutes, he stood motionless and stared into the box's velvet-lined interior. From her position across the room, Finockt could not see what the small chest contained; Tirell blocked her view. And yet she feared the worst had come upon them—the quest was finished and all their work to protect the kingdom was vanquished—when Tirell began to shake uncontrollably. Whether he shook from laughter or tears, Finockt could not tell, and the inability to discern his state of mind irritated her, for there was no predicting what he would do next.

Deepening waves of fear pressed down upon her. She eyed her cousin with uncertainty and inched her way along the wall in hopes of gaining a better view of the box and Tirell. Another step and her fingers suddenly brushed across something she did not expect to find. Something smooth and cool. Something that in no way resembled stone. It could not be! She kept her eyes fixed on Tirell, while her fingertips skimmed a metal orb, and then her hand enclosed a ribbed handle. A sword! She gasped in surprise and looked down to find it was indeed so. It stood blade down in the corner. She glanced up at Tirell then gripped the hilt with surety. She had only gripped the hilt of a sword once before, and the thought that washed across her mind was the fact that she did not believe herself capable of wielding it now, as she was not wont to do then. She had seen blood spilt, but could she spill it herself?

Tirell shook even harder. It was obvious now he was not amused but angry. And then Finockt saw the reason why. A flicker of a smile brushed her lips. There was nothing, absolutely nothing, bound within the box's velvet contours! Finockt's hope rose on swift wings, and yet in the next breath, her joy vanished. Like an ill-contented child, Tirell shoved the box off the table with such force that one of the fragile hinges broke when it hit the flagstones. The once gorgeous chest now lay crudely open on the floor near the fireplace and revealed the same green velvet lining that had covered the interior of the first box.

Finockt inhaled softly. Firelight yellowed the flagstones before the hearth, and it seemed as if the box began to glow, gently highlighting a bulky object hidden behind the velvet-lined lid. It was smooth and straight and appeared to be folded several times. Another piece of parchment!

Finockt stepped toward the box when she was arrested by the fury in Tirell's voice. "Where's the real box? And where's the real cross? I want answers, or I'll kill you both right here on the spot!"

Finockt fell numb at his words. She looked helplessly at Gwri, who stood calm and cool, his head held high, indifferent to Tirell's crazed behavior. The Dúnarians' confident lord did not look so confident any more. Once again, he did not have what he sought, and the power of a kingdom he had pursued for so long eluded him yet again. His defeat reflected in his eyes as nothing more than a dull flicker in the room, a subtle change that only Finockt witnessed. She watched, suspended in time, as he scrutinized Gwri and herself then held her gaze for what seemed an eternity. For five precious seconds, she feared he knew of the sword. But he made no move, and those steel gray eyes revealed nothing. Then suddenly his mood shifted. Anger built swiftly within him, and he leveled a raging scowl on Gwri. It was as if it were the first time he had ever laid eyes on him, and his look swore that Gwri, not Finockt, held all the answers.

"Is it housed at Mithel now?" he asked. "Kept safe by the great clan of the Gwrithlís?"

"You're wasting your time, Tirell," Gwri replied. "You know I would never tell you."

"No, you won't," he said with a smirk, "but perhaps she will." His gaze came back to Finockt, and she froze, her hand still clutching the sword behind her back.

"She doesn't know the location of the real box any more

than you do. No one does. It's as great a mystery to us as it is to you."

What was Gwri saying? How could he tell him such? The man was mad. It was useless to divulge such information. Doing so left them weaker than when they had started this insane dialogue, and it brought them both that much closer to death.

"Ha!" Tirell laughed. "The Prince of Mithel spills all does he? This grand lord with whom I wage a battle of words. The very one who was to take the kingdom upon Coinneach's death, if no successor was to be found?" he said in a maddened rage. "Take the kingdom that was taken from me! Everyone seems to forget that part. And even after all these years, it still goes to another. But not anymore. No. Soon, soon, it will be my own again when the king is dead."

"It surprises me, Tirell, that you actually believe you'll outlive the king," Gwri replied, his voice harsh and strong. Finockt looked at him in surprise. "Is Thorlóthlon really worth dying for when you already have wealth, land, and title? You know it well yourself, Tirell. You'll never win." Gwri smiled defiantly. "The curse binds you to its will." Slowly, he worked his hands around, trying to loosen the rawhide strips.

"Bold words from one so young," Tirell said with a surprising calmness back in his voice. "You have more pluck than I presumed." He walked over to Finockt, and she stepped back from him to find the wall pushing her forward. "Anwyl's child. Eideann's bane. She bears the beauty of her mother as the stories foretold, does she not?" He wrapped a stray curl around his finger and absently studied its color.

Gwri set his jaw. "Do you think Valínthia would mourn

her?" he asked in an attempt to save her. "Do you think her people would care?"

"No, perhaps not," Tirell answered. "You may be right. Perhaps they would not mourn her. But would you, Gwri? Would you be able to bear her loss?"

Tirell's breath was hot against her face and smelled sickly of wine. Finockt stood frozen against the wall, one hand grasping the rough slabs of stone for useless support, the other weighted down by the sword and too weak and pathetic to wield it. She wanted him away from her. One strike and it would be over. But for the second torturous time she could not do it. Her head began to swim, and she felt as if she were going to faint when Gwri spoke, reviving her. "Leave her, Tirell," he said.

Tirell straightened, his eyes still locked on Finockt. "Don't worry, Gwri, I won't harm her…for now. She is my cousin after all, and I still need her. But I do believe it's time I brought my dealings down a notch or two. And this one, this one I do myself."

He left her, and Finockt's whole being sighed with relief. However, his absence now only served to transform her relief into horror. He rapidly descended upon Gwri, punching him hard in the stomach and sending him to his knees. Gwri wheezed, and Finockt cringed at the sound, helpless to give aid. Tears seeped to the edges of her eyes, and she cursed her weakness.

"No, enough!" she said, as Tirell drew his dagger from the table top. But her words trickled out in a whisper.

Her cousin chuckled softly, all his attention absorbed in his prisoner. "A pretty broken present you'll make for Deverell," he said, "and a warning."

Gwri looked up into Tirell's face by force, Maegowan's massive hand tilting his head back. Her cousin's eyes hardened.

"If he wants Finockt, he'd better bring me the real box and the real necklace. No more games." He held the blade across Gwri's throat. "The wound I give you now, lad, will leave you only enough time to make it to your precious Deverell and give him the message. You'll not last beyond that. I suggest you keep your errand swift."

Every second he waited for the cut, Gwri regarded Tirell with more anger than fear in his eyes. Finockt's blood surged. She had only a moment to act, and yet hours seemed to pass. She clenched her hand, and the hilt of the sword awakened her to what she *had* to do. There would be no forgiving herself if Gwri died. This realization gave her courage. She sprang away from the wall.

"Drop the knife!" she said, her borrowed blade resting firmly against her cousin's neck.

Tirell's visage spelled alarm, and he glanced at her out of the tail of his eye. What happened next, unnerved her completely. He smiled, slow and steady, as if trying to ignore the whims of some cantankerous child. "Where did you find that?" he asked, slowly turning to face her.

"Release him," Finockt repeated, her heart hammering in her ears. She eyed both Tirell and Maegowan with a scalding gaze despite the fact that her insides trembled, raw with fear. The room was morbidly quiet and rank with deceit and hatred, even the air seemed to be poisoned and to work against her. Her gaze shifted back and forth between them, and to her relief, the blade wavered but a little in her hand. But deadlier than the act of standing there between them was the endless waiting to see who would move and who would take her words to heart. Then, ever so gradually, Maegowan raised his sword. Finockt saw it.

"Stay your hand," she said. "Stay it, or I will run him through. I mean it!"

Strangely, Maegowan obeyed.

"I honestly didn't think you capable of it, Cousin," Tirell said, crossing his arms. "You have more tenacity than I gave you credit for."

Just then Maegowan feigned a leap forward. Finockt turned to take him when movement caught her eye. She was too late.

She dropped her sword and fell back against the thick, ebony table, her hand clamped around the weapon. Her face blanched white, and her blood flowed hot. But she could no longer stand. The impact was too much. She drew her breath sharply and sank to the floor in a heap, her brow knit in pain. Huddled on the flagstones, she felt the warm flow of her own blood run down her arm and watched it seep through the sleeve of her gown. She shuddered. Her arm felt heavy, skewered as it was, and her wound burned and left her dazed and sick.

Tirell knelt before her. "You're not protected here, Finockt," he half whispered. "Even being of kin will not save you." Then he laid hold of the hilt and drew the dagger free.

Finockt cried out and clutched her arm more tightly with her free hand. Tirell looked on with delight and, pulling out a white handkerchief, held the dagger's bloodied blade upon it.

"It's been told," he said, "that the sight of blood can weaken or strengthen a person depending on whom it affects."

He now wiped the blade clean, but Finockt could barely see what he was doing. The pain of her wound blinded her and threatened her courage all the more.

"Best stay out of this, lass," Tirell said, letting the dagger hang lazily in his hand. "Take it that you've been warned. Your father would still be alive today if he had." Then he rose, smiling, and tucked the bloodstained kerchief into the belt of his tunic.

Her mind fogged with anger, Finockt struggled to her feet when she was seized roughly from behind by Maegowan, who clutched each arm in his iron grasp. Blood flowed anew. Finockt moaned. "Leave it be, lassie. All's over now." Maegowan's deep voice rumbled in her ear as he watched Tirell cross the room and level Gwri in the stomach a second time.

"No! Leave him!" Finockt cried, openly shedding tears. "Leave him!"

Though drained by her fight with Tirell, she tried frantically to get away, but Maegowan held her fast; and to her distress, her urgent attempts to attack her merciless cousin only increased his mirth and brought about another outburst of laughter from him as well as waves of agonizing pain for her attempts.

Amused, he watched her, only three steps away from Gwri's hunched frame. "You're quite the fighter, Cousin, but such efforts win you nothing here."

Maegowan smirked, thoroughly enjoying the reign of evil.

His blood rising hot within, Gwri looked up at Tirell with clenched teeth and flaming eyes. But there was little he could do, bound as he was.

"Ra Doue ho pardono evit an droug ho-peus gwraet!" Finockt cried. *"May God forgive you for the evil you have done!"*

As soon as the words left her mouth, she felt the stinging slap of Tirell's hand across her face, and blood moistened her lips. His eyes screamed hatred, and his every word cut into her, like a knife. "Don't ever speak that name before me again," he said, his eyes like ice. His dagger was poised for death, but the act was faltered by something more than himself. "More men have died for lesser offenses than this," he added and again sank his dagger into the table beside him.

"My lord!" Maegowan cried, but not quickly enough. Gwri was already on his feet and had lodged the toe of his boot in the back of Tirell's knee. Instantly, Tirell hit the stones and clutched at his leg. Then he curled pitifully on the floor, his arms wrapped around his stomach. He now fought his own battle for air as Gwri stumbled back on one foot to save his balance after his well-aimed kick.

"Fiend," Maegowan cried, thrusting Finockt to the flagstones and drawing his sword.

Just then the door burst open, and a Dúnarian soldier stood before them, sword in hand.

"Get him!" Tirell cried, his voice hoarse and the veins in his neck threatening to burst.

But to Tirell's surprise, the soldier ignored Mithel's lord. Instead, he pulled Tirell sharply to his feet and held his blade against Tirell's throat. Tirell danced on one foot and cringed at the pain shooting through the back of his knee.

"Throw down your sword," the soldier said gruffly to Maegowan, "or he dies!"

Maegowan looked at Tirell. His lord's face was one twisted portrait of pain. Unable to give a response, Tirell cringed and hobbled on one foot again. The soldier angled his blade more fully into Tirell's flesh, drawing blood. "Drop it!" he cried. Maegowan's sword hit the floor with a clatter. "Now keep your hands where I can see them!" the soldier added.

Meanwhile, beside them, Gwri freed his hands by Tirell's dagger, still stuck upright in the table. Then he moved to aid Finockt, who sat motionless upon the flagstones, her face blanched white. But the Dúnarian soldier stopped him.

"Leave her now," he cautioned. "There's some rope in the hall. Grab it and tie them up."

"You'll die for this, traitor!" Tirell spat through clenched teeth. He set an unforgiving eye on the helmeted face just above his, but the soldier just laughed.

"I doubt that," he said, "for I am not one of you!"

CHAPTER TWENTY-FOUR

AEGOWAN, NOW WELL bound and gagged, sat in a chair beside Tirell, who was similarly held prisoner in his own stronghold. The armed traitor yanked the last knot tightly around Tirell's wrist then looked up at Gwri. "Come," he said. "We go now."

He charged toward the door and held watch, while Gwri knelt before Finockt. "Are you all right?" he asked her. "Finockt." He held her face in his hands, and she looked up at him, as if coming out of a dream. "Come on," he said, gently helping her to her feet. She moved mechanically.

"Come, we've not much time," the Dúnarian said urgently, looking back at them. Gwri swiftly took up Maegowan's sword, but the soldier shook his head. "Leave that one. It's too heavy. Take this one instead!" He tossed a second sword to Gwri, who caught it by the cross bar. Half a glance at the details covering the weapon's hilt and sheath revealed its fine Evanthian heritage: it was his own sword. He quickly belted it around his waist, and then led the way, racing for the door. Finockt followed blindly at first, but something was not right. Something was missing. Memory flooded her consciousness, her surroundings grew clearer, and the farther she fled down the corridor with Gwri, the more the parchment beseeched her return.

"Wait!" she cried, pulling her hand free from Gwri's. Before he could stop her, she had reached the end of the corridor and rushed back into the room where Tirell and Maegowan viciously worked at the ropes binding them to their chairs with the hope of eventually freeing themselves.

"Stay your retreat!" Gwri called after their rescuer.

"Madness and folly!" the soldier cried when he turned around and saw Gwri reenter the room after Finockt. He glanced down each corridor, his heart racing.

"Finockt!" Gwri said impatiently. "We've no time for this! Forget the box, there's nothing in it anyway!"

But Finockt had already stooped beside the broken chest. Tirell's eyes flashed anger at her every movement. "No, Gwri," she said. "There's something here."

She reached for the lid when the clatter of a latch and a soft creak enveloped the room. Finockt looked up to see a servant enter through a side door. He froze when he saw Tirell and Maegowan tied up and Gwri standing free with a naked sword in his hand, then he vanished back through the door, sounding the alarm as he ran. Tirell's eyes sparked both fury and triumph.

"Let's go, Finockt!" Gwri commanded. He locked his hand securely under her elbow, and in helping her to her feet, the glint of gold caught his eye. In one deft motion, he snatched her necklace off the flagstones and stuffed it into his pocket, while Finockt slammed the box shut. Together they bolted for the door.

The soldier who rescued them met them in the doorway. "They're coming up the side corridor! We have to get out now! Follow me!"

Running through corridors and up and down stairways, they dodged sleeping guards that had not yet been roused to the chase until finally they came to a very dark part of the castle. Bypassing the stair that led down to Finockt's cell, they continued their ascent, climbing yet another large flight of tower stairs before turning down a dark passageway toward a dimly lighted corridor that curved to the left and branched to the right. At the sound of footsteps, they flung themselves against the shadowed protection of the castle wall.

"Ahhh!" Finockt cried out, as she hit the wall hard. Sliding to the floor, she dropped the box into her lap. Gwri quickly pulled her to him and clapped his hand over her mouth. Pain seared her left arm and blinded her eyes with fresh tears.

Their rescuer whipped around in alarm. "Keep her quiet!" he hissed.

Gwri scanned every inch of the corridor behind and before him, and all his muscles tensed as he waited for an attack. None came. The Dúnarian traitor motioned for them to keep still, then he crept toward the lighted corridor. For several minutes, he listened to all the sounds in the castle, but the soft *clink* of the approaching soldier's armor and the trudge of his footsteps had disappeared into silence. Now only a soft ring of voices floated down the hall toward them. Farther away, beyond the hall and the thick castle walls, the distant, internal search for them could be heard. Outside, a similar commotion erupted, but within, on this one wing of the castle, all was still, except for another almost imperceptible *clink* of metal.

Their rescuer pressed himself against the opposite wall of the dark corridor and motioned for Gwri and Finockt to stay put. He listened a moment longer then slipped around the corner. Gwri rose and strained his ears against the silence. At his release, Finockt clamped her hand over her burning wound.

Suddenly there was a suppressed yelp, a shuffle, and the high, clear clinking of armor. The small struggle ensued for several seconds, after which a muffled groan was heard along with the light scraping of metal against the flagstones. Then all was silent.

Presently, their protector returned, stopping a moment in the middle of the well-lighted corridor to glance down its length a second time to ensure they had not been detected. Gwri relaxed upon seeing him and quickly knelt next to Finockt.

"What's the matter with her?" their rescuer demanded, looking back at them both. He cast one more wary glance down the bronze-lighted corridor then strode over to them.

"Tirell's malicious nature," Gwri answered with disgust. Gently, he pulled Finockt's cloak away from her wound, and with care, he peeled away the pieces of her dress sleeve to examine it. Finockt winced and sucked her breath in sharply, as the inch long cut reopened, oozing more blood.

"It could be much worse," Gwri said, lightly maneuvering his fingers around the stab wound. "Your cloak sustained most of the injury."

Finockt bit her lip to prevent herself from saying anything against the pain as he swiftly picked up the edge of her gown, ripped off a long strip of cloth, and wrapped it tightly around her upper arm.

"Are you all right now?" the soldier asked, his tone of voice edged with concern. He took off his helmet and knelt in front of her.

"Aye, I'm fine," Finockt replied, barely glancing at his shadowed face. She was grateful for the darkness, for then he could not see the flush of shame that spread over her cheeks at her clumsy outburst.

"Good," the young man said, standing.

"May I ask who you are?" Gwri asked. "We owe you much."

Before their guide could answer, a harsh ring of voices echoed loudly off the walls. Several enemy soldiers advanced down the main hallway toward them. The closer they came, the softer their voices turned, until their speech trickled into nothing more than mere whispers of sound.

"I think that's best saved for later," their rescuer quickly responded. "This way, and make haste!"

Crouching down, he ambled through the semi-darkness toward the well-lighted main corridor—and the enemy. Across from them, a continuation of the passageway they were on led into further darkness. After a few moments' hesitation, their guide motioned Finockt and Gwri closer. They crept up behind him and stopped just short of the torchlight's full reach. Visually, their rescuer searched that portion of the hallway closest to them, but thankfully, the Dúnarians were yet a good distance aways. They still had time.

Finockt held her breath, agitation building within her at the danger awaiting them. Beside her Gwri pressed his lips tightly together and narrowed his brow, the only two outward signs giving evidence of the anxiety churning within him. She had never seen him this nervous, which only served to heighten her own fears. Both looked expectantly at their guide, who, after surveying the main corridor one last time, turned around and faced them.

CHAPTER TWENTY-FIVE

"When I give the signal, go as fast as you can past the corridor," the young man urged. "I'll meet you when all is safe."

Gwri and Finockt nodded in affirmation. Ahead of them the guards' voices grew louder, and their shadows loomed long and dark over the castle wall.

"They have to be around here somewhere," one said.

"Aye! We'll find them soon enough," another replied.

All three fugitives kept a firm gaze on the lighted corridor, with Gwri and Finockt restlessly awaiting their rescuer's cue to move. In the precious seconds of silence and inaction, Finockt studied their leader's face and hair with an impatient eye, sifting through the darkness and flitting shadows for some sort of recognition. Who was he? Mentally, she scanned the faces of all of Coinneach's soldiers who had been their military escort to the cottage. This one was perplexing. His features did not match the others and yet were increasingly familiar. In the next instance, Finockt shed her bewilderment when their rescuer shifted forward and his face and bright hair briefly caught a dim stream of light from the torches.

Shock flooded over her in that one fleeting moment. "Gawain!" Her voice traveled in a loud, joyous whisper down the hall. She placed her hand over her mouth a moment too late. Gawain cringed and pressed himself flat against the wall, while Gwri and Finockt leaned back in the shadows; neither of the three moved a muscle. The guards went silent and drew their swords.

"What was that?" one finally asked, his voice low.

"I don't know."

"Steady lads," said a third. "I think it may be we've found our prey."

Knowing their presence was no longer a secret, Gawain signaled violently to Gwri and Finockt. "Never mind, go, go, go, go, go!" he hissed.

They vaulted past the well-lighted corridor as fast as they could, but they were not fast enough to escape the trio of soldiers who crept down the hallway toward them.

"There they are!" one shouted, taking off at a run. Another followed, while the third turned back to rally the others.

"Hurry!" Gawain cried. He flew down the dimly lighted corridor, Gwri and Finockt close on his heels.

Passing through an open archway, Gawain turned back to receive Finockt and help hasten her down the narrow stone steps. They moved quickly, hugging the exterior wall of the tower and staying as far away as possible from the stair's outside edge, which sported no railing or interior wall and dropped off into nothing but thin air. Gwri followed suit behind them.

"We'll never escape this," Finockt said, her eyes wide with fear.

"Yes, we will," Gawain assured her, but his voice was tight. He pulled her faster down the steps.

Gwri's silence unnerved Finockt even more and convinced her their circumstances were far more dire than they seemed, even to her, despite Gawain's reassurance.

Not far ahead, the long, curving stairway quickly leveled off at a small landing, where a large, broad, deep-set window stood a few feet above the flagstone floor. By one glance, Finockt surmised the window was wide enough and tall enough for them to crouch down and sneak through, with a little space left to spare over their heads. Its dusty window well mirrored the dimensions of the window itself. It was deep and wide and led down to a thick wooden shutter, which hung from its hinges at a hideous angle, like a broken arm. Past this landing, the staircase continued but rose and disappeared onto a higher level of the tower.

But Gawain did not take it. Instead, he halted abruptly on the landing. Finockt reeled back in shock and surprise, righting herself at the last second. Behind them the Dúnarians maintained their rapid, noisy pursuit. Finockt gasped. Her eyes widened with fear and panic, and her grip tightened around the box. In front of her, Gwri unleashed his sword. She shrank back.

"Haí!" Gawain snapped. In a flash, he shrugged from his shoulder the thick rope he carried and threw the heavy coil into Finockt's trembling arms. She blinked at the unexpected toss and only half caught it. Her focus now turned to the box, which she struggled to balance in one hand while also maintaining control of the long length of rope in the other. She failed. One heavy corded end dropped free of her grasp and fell in a messy heap over her feet.

Meanwhile, behind them, Gwri anchored himself on the stair, ready for the onslaught of the two soldiers, who barreled down the steps toward them, their swords drawn and prepped for action. Sword play soon clashed in a cacophony of harsh, grating sounds as Gwri fought heartily, lunging back and forth on the steps to fend them off as best as he could.

"Forgive me, Gawain," Finockt begged, "but you were the last person I ever hoped to set foot here."

"Time falls short for weak excuses, but that can't be helped now." He heaved himself up into the window well, worked his way to the end, and kicked the shutter off its crooked hinges.

"Hurry!" Gwri yelled above the strike of metal. "I can't hold them off forever!"

Gawain looked at Finockt. "Take off your cloak," he ordered, hopping down from the window onto the landing. He snatched the thick rope from her hands, recoiled it in seconds, and threw it back over his shoulder.

Just then a groan filtered up to the tower roof; one of the soldiers had fallen. His comrade leaped over him, grunting as he wielded his sword. Gwri winced under his opponent's blows, each one becoming stronger and harder.

Gawain's hand clamped down on Finockt's wrist, and she jumped. "Your cloak, Finockt," he said; his eyes were harsh. He need not say more. Her fingers flew to her neck, and she fumbled with her tassels with one hand, while she juggled the jeweled box in the other. He pulled the small chest from her grasp.

"What are you going to do?" she asked as she yanked the tassels free from each other and tossed her cloak aside. The wound in her arm pinched with every movement of her muscles, and her brow furrowed with pain. But she kept her eyes focused on Gawain, who opened his mouth to answer her when suddenly the Dúnarian's sword flew through the air and landed at their feet with a loud *clang* and a clatter. Finockt jumped aside. At the same time, both she and Gawain swung their attention to the stairway. The Dúnarian soldier now stood weaponless, his hands raised in surrender, while Gwri held him at bay with his sword.

"Hurry! There'll be more of them coming," Gwri said over his shoulder.

Their surrendered foe slowly backed up the stairs.

"Aye!" Gawain handed the box back to Finockt and began his ascent onto the window's stone ledge.

Finockt kept an anxious eye on both Gwri and Gawain while awaiting her next order. "Gwri, look out!" she suddenly cried.

But it was too late! The Dúnarian had already armed himself with his fallen comrade's sword and lunged toward him. Gwri jumped to the right and simultaneously drew his sword down to block the soldier's blow, but he was not fast enough. The Dúnarian's blade slid past his own. Gwri fell against the wall and clutched at his waist. Pain weakened him for an instant, his legs gave out, and he shuffled down a few steps toward Finockt and Gawain. Seizing his opportunity, the Dúnarian moved forward, his sword arched and ready to plunge into Gwri's chest, when Gawain unsheathed his own sword like lightning, bounded up the stair, and drove his blade hard through the soldier. The Dúnarian halted mid-descent and dropped his weapon. It clattered to the floor before slipping over the edge of the stair and disappearing into the dark, inner void of the tower. There, it remained silent, even as its owner crumpled to the ground. Bloodstained sword in hand, Gawain stared down at the soldier to ensure he would not rise again.

Finockt collapsed beside Gwri. "Gwri!" she cried, her voice quaking and her face even paler than before.

"I'm all right," he murmured, gulping short breaths.

"Can you make it?" Gawain asked. He, too, knelt beside him.

"Aye, it's not that bad. You go first. I'll follow after Finockt."

His face twisted even as he said it. Blood seeped around his hand and soaked through his tunic in dark red lines.

"Aye," Gawain answered grimly, eying Gwri's wound. Finockt watched while Gawain cleaned his blade on the Dúnarian's tunic, thrust it back into its scabbard, and then nimbly reassumed his position in the window well. "Com'on," he said, pivoting back to Finockt and extending his hand.

She faced Gwri. His color had changed, and his eyes were lowered, midway between pain and fatigue. "We have to find another way out," she said, her eyes never leaving Gwri's face.

Gawain dropped his outstretched hand, his mouth hard set in astonishment. Finockt looked him in the eye. "We have to find another way out, Gawain," she repeated.

"There is no other way. This is it," Gawain said.

"There *has* to be another way—"

"I'll be fine, Finockt," Gwri interjected, his voice faint and breathless.

Finockt looked back at him sharply, her hand still resting on his shoulder. "No, you won't," she said.

"You have to get the box to safety," Gwri argued. "You're Thorlóthlon's only hope now. Deverell and the others are counting on you. Do not make the others share this fate."

Finockt fingered the brightly ornamented box on the floor beside her. Above her head, Gawain crouched impatiently within the window well. Perspiration beaded on his temples and trickled down his cheek.

"For Thorlóthlon, Finockt," Gwri said. He took her hand and squeezed it. She held his gaze then rose reluctantly.

Gawain glanced up the stairs and out at the rampart below. He shifted his stance, and his feet ground across the window well's gritty surface. Then he looked back for Finockt. "Com'on, lass! Com'on!" he said.

She lifted the colorful box from the floor. "Take the box," she whispered and tossed it to him.

He reached for it and caught it with one hand, but the weight of it was more than he anticipated. His balance lost, he tilted dangerously out the window. The box plunged from his grasp, and Finockt watched in horror while Gawain groped wildly for something to support himself and regain his balance. His fingers brushed stone and slipped. Finockt gasped and reached for him as he flailed once more and then caught a sweaty hand in the smooth, tight grooves of mortar above his head. His breath came quickly, and he looked down with dismay upon the box, which lay in smattered bits on the rampart. Finockt heard it hit the stone pavement moments before, but there was no time to think of its loss. Because of it they had almost lost Gawain.

"Never mind, Gawain," Finockt said. "Help me up!"

Wedging her toe against the stones, she attempted to ascend into the window. But even with Gawain's aid, their efforts were futile. Her long gown, shorter stature, and the height needed to reach the window thwarted any success.

"It's not working!" she cried, her voice echoing off the tower walls. "I can't do it!"

"Yes, you can, Finockt," Gawain urged her. "Use the rope!"

He flung one end toward her. She grasped it with both hands, and he awkwardly pulled her into the window well; Finockt clenched her teeth against the pain such effort inflicted on her wound. With both of them now set close to either end of the window's open edge, Gawain looked down upon the rampart, one leg dangling over the window's side, the other tucked up close to his chest. Finockt sat rumpled about three feet away from him and teetered on the gritty ledge of the window. Her right leg dangled off its interior side, and her left she kept half bent, with her toes braced against the interior seam of the wall. She gripped the stones with force, half praying the window would not tip her back out, then she drew both legs in quickly as Gwri thrust himself into the window well to join them. Finockt did her best to pull him to safety and squirmed aside to make more room for him. He crawled up close beside her and leaned heavily against the curved interior portion of the wall, his back hunched, his hand still glued to his side. His face was ashen. Finockt's heart churned. She pressed her head back against the stones and fought tears. She no longer believed they would make it out alive…and what would happen to the others if they did not? What would happen to Gwri? She could not leave him, not like this.

Gawain laid a hand on her shoulder. She looked up at him quickly to find his gaze had softened. "We can only save him if we hurry." Then he put a finger to his lips, signaling for her to keep quiet, and jumped from the window onto the rampart below. He landed on the stones, rolling as he hit them.

Finockt stared down at him in disbelief. It was so high! There was no way she could jump! He motioned to her again. "I'll catch you!"

She tilted her head back against the stones and closed her eyes.

"You can do it, Finockt," Gwri said, his breathing shallow and faint.

"I don't think I can. Gwri, there must be some other way down. 'Tis murder to jump from such a height!"

"You have to, Finockt. I can only follow after you've…" He grimaced, sucked in a quick, short breath, and held his side. His tunic was nearly black with blood. "Please…Finockt."

She looked down once more. Her hands broke out in a sweat, her heart pounded in her ears, and she felt the temperature suddenly rise in her face. Gawain beckoned her again. "Remember to tuck your legs!" Her eyes widened. She could not believe she was doing this. She took a deep breath, closed her eyes, and jumped. The next thing she knew, she landed roughly in Gawain's arms. He let her down, and they both looked up expectantly for Gwri.

From the far side of the castle, soldiers spotted them on the wall walk and raced toward them, shouting orders to those below as they ran. Torchlight flooded the inner courtyard and filled all the towers and ramparts around them, and the sound of the soldiers' feet grew more thunderous with every second.

"He'll never make it, Gawain!" Finockt cried. "The height will kill him, wounded as he is."

"He'll make it," Gawain said. Then with a nervous glance toward the courtyard below, he whispered, "Com'on Gwri. We don't have much time!"

Just then the heavy thud of spears struck the rampart door, and the Dúnarians' threats drifted between the wooden boards.

"The door!" Finockt cried. Her terrified gaze rested on the

narrow entrance nestled between the base of the tower and the rampart.

"There's no need to worry about that. I secured it before I came after you. It should hold them…for a while anyway," Gawain said, taking up the bow and quiver he had laid by. He shot a worried glance at the still empty window. In the next instant, horror filled his face. "Finockt, get down!" he shouted. He pulled her to the ground and used his body to shield her.

A barrage of arrows flew up from the courtyard, pinging off the stones and flying over the castle wall to land in the wooden hoarding behind them and the empty space beyond it. "Stay down!" Gawain commanded, his eyes wild. He breathed quickly, his lips pursed, as he mustered up the courage to launch his own full scale attack. Beside him Finockt crouched at the foot of the retaining wall that overlooked the castle's open courtyard and waited out another heavy barrage of arrows. Gawain tensed. He looked at Finockt, who returned his fear-filled stare. It was now or never. In the seconds before the Dúnarians released their third strike, Gawain jerked his bow from around his body and whipping arrow after arrow from his quiver, he leaned over the retaining wall and fired with terrible accuracy upon the onslaught of soldiers beneath him. At his feet, Finockt covered her head and huddled close to the stones. She felt like a coward, but there was nothing else for her to do. Beside her Gawain continued to offer protection and prayed Gwri would make the leap before the worst happened—leaving him behind. He knew this would never set well with Finockt and would make his task of bringing her to safety that much more difficult.

To Finockt, time seemed to creep ever more slowly when finally Gwri could be seen—a dark shadow in the smooth contour of the window. He waited while Gawain and Finockt dodged yet another rain of arrows. The Dúnarians had already made it to the tower at the other end of the rampart and were rushing toward them, while those in the courtyard dispersed to join the chase.

"Gwri, com'on!" Finockt called up to him. "Oh, God, please let him make it!" she whispered under her breath.

Half a blink later, he dropped from the window and landed hard on the pavement, grunting as he hit the stones. Finockt was sure he had been felled by an arrow. But, ever so slowly, he half stood, crouching low on the ground, one hand still clamped to his side. In seconds, Finockt was beside him.

Meanwhile, Gawain threw the rope off his shoulder, and wrapping one end of the thick rope around one of the rampart's merlons, he tied it off. He tugged the knot tightly and shot a glance toward the advancing soldiers. They were almost on top of them. Several drew their bows while others awoke their slumbering blades.

"Finockt!" Gawain's eyes flashed bright with urgency, and he beckoned her to him with stiff, rapid strokes of his hand. With haste, she grabbed Gwri's arm and helped him limp across the rampart to Gawain. Once there, Gawain took over, guiding Gwri past the brazier and into the hoarding. Finockt followed them then stopped, her gaze invariably drawn to the broken box. The soldiers' cries seemed but a distant clamor in her ears as she stooped to look at the shattered pieces of its once beautiful form. Jewels were scattered everywhere. Her eyes glossed over with tears, and she slipped rough fingers over the interior's velvet-lined lid. It was there, just beyond this coverlet. The whole succession to the kingdom. Everything. The mystery would soon come to an end, and life would become new again.

Gawain had already made it into the hoarding with Gwri when he realized Finockt was still on the rampart. He leaped around the brazier and raced to her side. "We have no time." He pulled her by the arm, but she resisted.

"It's all here, Gawain," she said. "All the answers we've ever needed."

"Then it's best you grab it, and we go," he urged.

Ripping aside the green velvet lining, she snatched the parchment from its hiding place. Arrows whistled over their heads, pinging with greater intensity off the rampart and tower walls as they missed their targets. Finockt stuffed the parchment down between the layers of her dress, then scampered past the brazier and disappeared into the hoarding.

Now it was Gawain who lingered in harm's way. Behind him a torch burned just above the small flight of steps to the tower door. He grabbed it, and just before a set of arrows flew past and sank into the door, he jumped around the brazier after Finockt and landed inside the hoarding also. There he found Gwri had already thrown the rope down the murder hole—a large round opening carved out of the floorboards on one side of the hoarding. Even now Gwri had begun descending. Finockt held her breath against the dizzying height and the rank, oily smell of the small fort and hastily made her way down after him. As soon as the top of her head disappeared down the hole, Gawain set fire to the hoarding and slid down after her. It caught quickly, and soon hot flames were licking up the dry wood he had doused in oil earlier, the blaze rising high into the night air and providing a small form of protection from the soldiers who now covered the rampart. They glared through choking black smoke and intense flames, blindly searching for their prey, and fired aimlessly in hopes of wounding or felling their escaped prisoners. Gwri, Finockt, and Gawain lowered themselves as fast as they were able amidst a twisted hail of black and orange, while burning bits of hoarding and tongues of fire showered down over all three of them.

"Faster!" Gawain said, his hands black with soot.

They were halfway to the bottom when Gawain saw the rope had caught fire and was burning quickly. Below him Finockt stopped her descent to get a better grip on the swaying weave of cords when Gawain yelled down to her, "Keep moving! The rope is breaking! Slide! Slide!"

Shock filled her face. She let go and slid as best she could, gritting her teeth in pain as the rope bit into her hands like fangs and scorched her flesh. Six feet from the ground, the rope gave them a jolt and swung them side to side, then suddenly it snapped, dropping both Finockt and Gawain to the ground in a heap.

He scrambled off Finockt as fast as he could and jerked her to her feet. Head throbbing, she rubbed her injured shoulder as he yanked her across the castle grounds toward the loch. A great mist hung thick over its surface and crept into the surrounding hills and crags. Catching up with Gwri, together they ran for the boats moored beneath the giant trees down by the loch's edge.

Arrows shrieked past them in the night, and the horrible, complacent thumps diving into the soft earth all around them sickened Finockt. She cringed, her heart pounding out a furious rhythm. Every second, she awaited death by those screaming, feathered shafts. But as their distance from the castle slowly increased and their every step drew them closer to the boats, unscathed, the higher she allowed her spirits to rise. They had almost reached the protection of the boats and the softly rising veil of mist when Finockt felt herself pushed violently to the ground. She yelped and covered her head; another rain of arrows whistled past.

"Finockt, run!" Gawain cried, staving off the burning pain in his thigh. He stumbled to his feet.

Ahead two guards, with swords brandished, ran up from the loch. The clash of the blade cut the night amidst the roar of flames and the cry of the enemy pursuing their prey. Gwri ducked under a second strike and then struck back with a steady hand, slaying the enemy.

Finockt kept running when Gawain cried out. She skidded to a stop in the wet grass and then screamed when she saw him lying motionless upon the mist-laden earth, his fatal wound not by the sword but by arrows. They pierced his back in multiple places.

"Gawain! Gawain! No!" Finockt screamed. Beside herself with grief, she strove to reach him when Gwri caught her and pulled her back. In the next instant, he was forced to release her. With one dodge and a cut, he felled the Dúnarian who charged them.

"Gawain, Gawain!" Finockt cried, half crazed with horror. She ran toward him, stumbling and slipping in the wet grass.

Their friend inched forward on his stomach.

"No, Finockt!" Gwri cried. He caught her by the arm with a bloodstained hand. "The die has been cast."

Gawain looked up at them, his face bearing a hallow, haunted expression, and he read in Gwri's face what he did not want to admit to himself: he was dying. "Leave me! Leave me! Get out of here! It's too late!" he then cried with labored breath and waved for them to depart. "Oh God!"

"No!" Finockt shrieked. "No! Gawain!"

Even as Gwri wrestled with her, soldiers poured from the dark doors of the castle like wild beasts and charged over the drawbridge and down the wet hills toward them.

"Go, Finockt!" Gawain said, his voice hoarse. "Remember me, and tell Liusaidh, tell her…I love her."

Finockt looked back, even as Gwri shoved her into the boat. With a sinking spirit, she sat down hard on the thwart closest to her, her heart breaking, and she watched motionless as the boat pulled away from the embankment. For what seemed an eternity, she kept a vigilant eye on Gawain until she saw him pull breath one last time. Then she buried her face in her hands.

The boat continued to roll out over the calm, glassy surface of the lake, and the mist pulled in tightly around them like a dense, wet curtain. Now only the orange-yellow glow of distant fire burned through the fog and created a fuzzy, flickering light on the dark, silent lake. Gwri said nothing as he rowed rapidly toward safety, but Finockt could see the sorrow emanating in his blue eyes. A shade had been drawn across them, and the brightness she had seen that first day she had met him had been extinguished.

She looked up at the sky, its expanse a bitter reflection of her own mournful sobbing. Even now, the moon, as if out of respect, hung wreathed in clouds, the stars burned faintly in the night sky, and thankfully, with each thrust of the oar, the shouts of the soldiers waned.

CHAPTER TWENTY-SIX

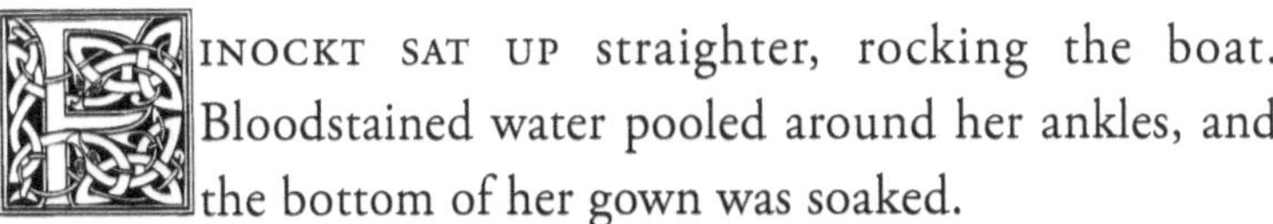

INOCKT SAT UP straighter, rocking the boat. Bloodstained water pooled around her ankles, and the bottom of her gown was soaked.

"Gwri, we're sinking!" she cried, cupping her hands and shoveling water out as fast as she could.

Alarmed, Gwri rowed harder, but it was no use; he was too weak. Pain burst anew with each stroke he made, and his blood loss mounted. The boat continued to fill despite Finockt's frantic attempts to save them.

"It'll be all right, Finockt, we're almost to shore. Can you swim?" Gwri asked, closing his eyes every now and again against the agonizing waves of pain that matched the push and pull required to row.

Finockt gave a shuddered breath. *This is it,* she thought miserably. *We've cheated danger, sword, and ultimately death, only to meet it another way.*

"I need an answer from you," Gwri said.

"Aye, I believe that I can." Her voice cracked, and she bit her lip hard. Gwri was in too much agony for her to continue panicking or to remind herself how much she feared the water after her experience in the pool of Thorlóthlon's underground.

Gwri smiled very faintly now. "What's that look? Do you think we've come this far to give in now?"

Finockt forced a doubtful smile. She braced her hands against the boat's side and the thwart on which she sat and calculated the distance to shore. Their prospect was grim. Gwri could now row with only one hand. His attempts to keep them moving paved a useless, jagged path across the loch, turned the craft sideways, and undermined their progress. The shore was still far away, and the boat barely glided through the water. Despite his dismal service, Gwri continued to row until Finockt sprang up and took to the oars herself. Slowly, he inched his way into the stern so he could rest. The water was so high now it nearly covered his wound.

Finockt dipped the oars and pulled. The first time she sliced through the loch's surface and tried to maneuver the boat, she smothered an anguished cry. Never did she imagine the weight of the water to be so heavy or so difficult to push against. Every thrust of the oar wrenched even the tiniest muscle, and the painful exertion clawed at her knife wound with a fearsome delight.

Digging her heels against the bottom of the boat, she heaved on the oars. The water hovered just under the center thwart now and almost reached the back of her knees. If she had wanted to, she could have reached out and dipped her hand into the loch with minimal effort.

She pulled again on the oars and clenched her lip between her teeth to staunch the recurrent pain and her growing fears.

She rowed on a diagonal now. One oar hardly skimmed the loch's surface, the other was covered halfway up the shaft. On her second pathetic pass with the oars, the boat rolled up on its side and tumbled them both into the water. It was icy cold. Finockt broke the loch's surface with a loud gasp and took in labored breaths, as the lake's frigid temperatures tightened her chest and drove the air from her lungs. She moved her arms and legs as best she could, but she kept sinking. Her dress weighed heavy over her body like a millstone, dragging her downward, and the cold left her disoriented. Soon her strength faded. It was nigh impossible to breathe. The more she focused on keeping her lungs open, the harder she found the task.

"Stay afloat, Finockt! We're almost to shore," Gwri encouraged, although with his raw wound he had as much trouble swimming as she did.

Finockt glanced toward the land, a dark mass beneath the night sky. It looked far. Too far. She kicked beneath the loch's surface and broke free from the lake's depths once more, spitting water as she reemerged. Her arms were like lead. She looked for Gwri. Was he still moving? Yes, she could see him, but he was barely stirring now. She made two more attempts to reach him and dry land when she saw him sink beneath the loch's black surface.

"Gwri!" Finockt cried, floundering and gasping for air. "Gwri!" Desperately, she extended her hand, but the distance between them was too great. She looked up into the dimming night sky. *Lord, help us!* she silently cried.

She fought hard, but she could not remain afloat. Cold lake water sloshed around her ears. Then it rose to cover her nose and mouth, and though she willed them to continue moving, her legs fell numb and useless. The mist hovering over the loch drifted skyward, and soon the black, star-studded paths of night could not be determined from the lapping dark green tongues of the loch. Finockt felt the icy water close over her head and slide past her body as the loch slowly drew her to the bottom. She could see nothing in the darkness, and just as her lungs gave out, a strong hand suddenly drew her to the surface, pulled her free of the water, and dragged her headfirst into a boat. Secure against its floor boards, Finockt quickly revived, gulping air and shaking with cold. Two darkly clothed figures sat in the boat with her, one at the bow and one directly behind her on the center thwart. Alarmed, she scrambled upright, and frantically searched the water and the length of the boat for Gwri. There was no sign of him any-where. Fresh fear enveloped her. Vulnerable and alone, she looked up at the two figures hemming her in and tried to determine if she had once again fallen into the hands of the enemy when the stranger seated before her spoke.

"He's all right, Finockt."

Deverell's familiar voice immediately stabilized her, its gentle cadence restoring her sanity and squelching her fears. She watched him point to another boat that came up alongside them, showing Gwri safely stowed therein, and felt another powerful wave of relief wash over her. She looked back at the Northerner, and tears of joy and gratitude filled her eyes; God had answered her prayer.

"Aye, lass, it's me," Deverell said.

She leaped forward and threw her arms about his neck, half sobbing and half laughing. He hugged her close and stroked her sopping wet head, while Strahan rowed them to shore. "You're safe now," he whispered gently.

She squeezed her arms more tightly around him then let

go. "Once again, you've saved my life. I fear I owe you too much." Her voice cracked with emotion.

"You owe me nothing, as I've told you before. To see you safe is my reward enough."

Gently, he pressed her hand before wrapping his cloak around her and tucking the laces up close under her chin. Finockt smiled gratefully, the boat hit shore, and they rapidly disembarked. Once on solid ground, both he and Strahan hurried to assist the boat drawing in beside them. Finockt shivered and shook on the embankment where Deverell had left her, and amidst the frenzied activity circulating under the dark night sky, she kept a vigilant eye on Gwri as he was carried, unconscious from a great loss of blood, from the boat moored nearby.

Seconds later, Deverell returned to her side and hastened her trembling form to the base of the hill ahead of them. They swiftly climbed its steeply winding path, the men still carrying Gwri between them. At its summit, they set themselves astride waiting horses and rode off into the night, Finockt holding tightly to Deverell's waist as they galloped hard for the northwest.

CHAPTER TWENTY-SEVEN

Hours later, Finockt awoke to a soft green light illuminating everything around her and the sound of fabric lightly snapping in a passing breeze. At first, she could not determine what made the world such a strange color or altered its sound. Then, little by little, her eyes cleared, and she realized she lay inside a brightly colored pavilion. She forced herself to sit up and then winced as a sharp pain pounded her temples. Her heart throbbed gently in her chest. The tent was humid, warm, and unguarded. It was hard to remember how she arrived here, obstructed as her comprehension was by her aching head. But, slowly, deliberately, her racing thoughts arranged in perfect order every memory she held, until she had relived in vivid detail the whole barbaric scene of the previous evening. Such recollection only succeeded in turning her stomach.

She looked around the sparsely furnished tent. No weapons. No healer. No watch maid. However, in looking at her arm, she observed her wound had been cleaned, mended, and newly dressed. She lifted her wrists. No fetters encumbered her. But she would not believe herself completely free of Tirell's clutches until she saw it for herself. Limbs stiff and aching, she made her way to the pavilion's flap. Beyond the thin green fabric, the tumult of a great many men could be heard. Their voices were tense but lacked the hostile edge the Dúnarians loved to employ. Pulling back the tent flap, she stepped into the midmorning light and squinted against the sun's bright rays and the crowded glen bursting with color.

She was free.

Pavilions of every bright shade stood at rapt attention all over the clearing. And at the top of each pavilion, a bright pennant of contrasting color fluttered in the breeze. Great trees with stout arms and broad foliaged hands grew strong and vast around the perimeter of the camp and made the silken tents appear small. Soldiers milled in thick groups before and behind her, and the glint of metal flashed in the sunlight.

Finockt stumbled along, wincing with every step. Her entire body felt beaten, bruised, and sore. Now that she walked the grounds, she vaguely remembered entering the camp the night before, but the scene touched only the frayed edges of her memory. Then, under that heavily bejeweled night sky, the domed frames of the tents appeared like sleeping giants. Now, under the light of day, the world was left reeling from the strong flood of color. Finockt shook the mental image from her mind. Her next thought to surface was to find Deverell so she could find Gwri. The key to finding him in this juxtaposition of bright color and warfare was to find her grandfather. Once she found Coinneach, undoubtedly, she would find Deverell.

Slipping around the sides of the tents, she made her way to

the outer edge of the encampment and gleaned its crowded, inner grounds for some sign of her grandfather or of Deverell. A young boy brushed past her on his way to a white pavilion edged in blue that was noticeably bigger and broader in size than were all the others. Above it, a soft blue pennant whipped gently in the breeze.

"Eoin!" Finockt gasped, recognizing his limpid brown eyes and dirty blond hair.

The young lad ground his jog to a halt. "Aye, milady?"

"Is it really you?"

"Aye, milady, it 'tis. May I help you?"

Relief encircled her at the sight of a familiar face and drove away the last lingering wisps of self-doubt and uncertainty. It was true then. She had escaped. Inwardly, she crumbled, the emotion of it too strong to withstand. Yet outwardly, she managed to maintain a semblance of weary impassivity.

"Have you heard from Liusaidh? Does everything fare well with her?"

"Aye, milady, she fares well enough, although her mother has worsened. They say it will not be long until she dies."

At Finockt's ensuing silence, Eoin lifted his brow. "Is there anything more I can do for you, milady?"

She passed a hand over her face. She was weary. So, so weary. And this news only added to it. "Aye," she said. "Will you take me to the king?"

He smiled. "Certainly, milady. Follow me."

Leading her up to the large white pavilion that was the central focus of the camp, Eoin approached its open entrance and ushered her in. She smiled. "Thank you for your help." He ducked his head in reply, and released from his duty, he scurried off to attend to some of the soldiers who waved to him from across the camp.

Coinneach looked up as she entered. Seeing his granddaughter alive and well and walking around overwhelmed him. He hurried across the tent and embraced her warmly; his slight limp, however, did not escape Finockt's notice. "Ah, lass," he said. "I was afraid I'd lost you forever." He rested his cheek against her soft curls and kissed her often on the top of the head.

"I as well, Grandfather," Finockt replied.

Gently releasing her, he gave her a tap under the chin. Finockt felt he was about to say something more, but he remained quiet. His eyes were on her, and yet in the same moment they were not. Events outside the tent caught his attention instead. She shifted her gaze over her shoulder, then left his side and approached the tent's open entrance just as a small troop of armed soldiers trotted by.

"What's happening?" she asked, gazing after their retreating figures. She already knew in her heart the answer to such an obvious question, but it was as if she needed to hear the words out loud.

"We are making ready for war. Finain will not stop until he has attained the kingdom," Coinneach said. "Our scouts have brought word they have already crossed the loch and are making their way toward us. I fear the battle will strike soon." He ended his sentence by coughing harder than usual.

Finockt knit her brow and hastened to him. "Grandfather, are you all right?"

"Aye, child. I just need some rest. I'm growing old too fast is all. Now, I had better lie down," he said, short of breath and distant. He lay down upon his cot, his movements slow and labored, as if even this simple effort was too much for him to bear. "But do not wander, Finockt, promise me…" he whispered. His voice trailed off, and he lay quiet, breathing gently.

Finockt wanted to say she was sorry, to beg forgiveness for all that had passed, to have someone blame her for what evil had befallen them and for the loss of Gawain and Eilidh. But the words would not come; they lodged in her throat—cold, lifeless, and empty.

"Rest well, Grandfather," she said instead. She kissed his forehead and pressed his hand. "All will be well with time." But at that moment it was difficult to say whether she truly believed it.

Once outside the tent, Finockt hurried through the encampment. There were so many soldiers and blacksmiths and swordsmiths and the like she felt she would never find Deverell. She had been so certain he would have been right beside Coinneach. Now she was not sure where to search for him.

She wove between a tight clump of soldiers. They regarded her briefly before returning to their work. Soon the clatter of armor, clang of hammer and anvil, and the piercing grind of the whetting stone against metal calmed the farther she wound around the encampment. Not too far ahead, she found him, on the camp's farthest edge, inspecting the men's weapons and giving them orders. He looked up as she approached and came forward to meet her.

"Has your strength returned?" he asked with a slight bow. He searched her face carefully.

"Aye, a little."

"Come," he said. "A short walk should further renew you then."

With Deverell leading the way, they took to the wood and separated themselves from the camp's perimeter.

"You prepare for battle," Finockt said as they wandered along. "There's no stopping it, is there?"

Deverell shook his head.

"And will there be much bloodshed?" she asked, ever aware of the ordered chaos within the camp behind them.

Deverell nodded. "Aye," he said. "But this is war. We do what me must in order to survive. The loss of life is inevitable. One cannot change fate."

They stopped beneath the wide canopy of a white oak, and Finockt pondered his reply with crescent helplessness. He had grown progressively grimmer as each new day dawned, and the transformation distressed her. Standing before him now, she was sure this was the dourest she had ever seen him. Such a change ensured evil to come. And the sudden realization that Deverell would be set within the battle itself smote her.

"You will promise me, won't you?" she said suddenly, prematurely feeling the effects of his potential loss. "You will promise me, whatever happens, you will guard yourself and keep yourself safe."

His gaze intensified, and heat unexpectedly fanned her face. The awkwardness of such an abrupt confession exacerbated the uncomfortable silence enfolding them, as if what she had voiced went against the tie between them. Finockt felt it keenly, and for lack of better wording, she added, "In truth, should all of Thorlóthlon and I give our lives, such a gesture would pale in the face of what you have done. You are a gifted counselor and leader. If we lost you, I fear what would become of Thorlóthlon and our people. We stand unbalanced as is. Without you, I believe it would all come crashing down."

The words did not feel right on her tongue, but there was no taking them back. And the tension between them sharpened. She blushed harder.

"I am deeply honored, Finockt," Deverell said. His words seemed hesitant, and the care dampening his eyes escaped Finockt's attention when he respectfully bowed his head before her. "For your sake, I will try my best not to fail."

Finockt nodded, pleased she had his full agreement to her request. A fraction of her burden lifted, and the awkwardness soon melted as did the mounting tension between them. They walked on. Bit by bit, the surrounding wood engulfed them, and they ventured farther within it until the din of the camp was low in their ears. Here a small stream gushed through the vibrant forest, repeating a calming lull that eased Finockt's tense nerves. She sat down beside it on the flat, ridged face of a small boulder. Deverell sat beside her.

"How did you find us? How did you know to come to the lake?" Finockt asked him. She watched the stream roll and twist as it swept over submerged rocks and around broken tree branches.

"It was Annwn who brought us to you," he said. He studied her countenance with unusual scrutiny.

Finockt looked up at him in disbelief. "Annwn!" she cried. "And you trusted her? She, who willfully consorted with the enemy?" Unable to comprehend Deverell's speech, she paused, her mind racing. "How can you be sure she won't betray us again?" she then asked. "She may only be seeking our position so she can report our weaknesses, our every plan of attack, to Tirell."

"She is not the same girl you met at Thorlóthlon, I think."

Finockt set her jaw and looked away.

"Haí," Deverell said gently. "It is not man who rules the order of earth, but God. And though the run of justice and the fall of mercy fail in the hands of some, you do not have to follow in their footsteps and help lead such foolishness to the forefront. If you allow their injustices to rule your mind, they will rule your heart as well and blind you to what you know is right. You must be discerning and choose then how to act."

Finockt absorbed his words in silence, her heart fraught with confusion and disquiet. His counsel challenged her, and she did not like it because she did not want to forgive Annwn for her betrayal and, ultimately, for her part in Gawain's death. He watched the sharp tapping of her foot against the boulder and sensed her aversion smoldering beneath the surface.

"Without Annwn," he said, "we would never have found the castle. You would have died last night in the loch."

Finockt released a nearly inaudible sigh, and tears stung her eyes.

"I'm sorry—about Gawain," Deverell added. "He was a good lad."

Tears coursed her cheeks. "Aye," she answered. She sniffed and wiped at her eyes and nose.

Deverell remained quiet.

"We found my father's box," she said when she had recovered herself a little. Just mentioning the box seemed to require much of her strength; its loss also brought a burden too hard to bear.

Deverell's blue eyes sparked life.

"It was broken during our escape from Caldária, but I retrieved these documents from it before we escaped the castle—"

She pulled the waterlogged parchments free from between

her shift and her dress. They were still damp, their corners crumpled and curled from the lake water.

Deverell's eyes brightened a second time upon sight of the packet. "You mean the box was at one point in Tirell's possession?" he asked.

"Aye, my breath stilled when I saw him open it, but he did not know the parchments were there in the lid, like the other."

She handed the folded papers to him, and he opened them carefully then let out a short sigh while stroking the dark stubble along his cheeks and chin.

"Unfortunately the writing has been smeared," he said, leafing through the wrinkled pages. "I fear it is incomprehensible."

He handed the parchments back to her, and she quickly scanned the water-stained letters. Indeed, the bold black ink had run together, leaving bleeding pools and blurred, ashen smudges, all of which prevented even the most learned reader from distinguishing anything important.

"There's nothing we can do. I fear the kingdom is lost now. We needed that box," Deverell said.

Fatigue suddenly filled his face, making him appear older, and his eyes reflected a trodden spirit. With no hope before him save that of hand-to-hand victory against Tirell, he rose and made his way past her for the encampment.

Finockt watched his retreat. "How is it that you knew of me, yet still believed I had died alongside my parents that day so long ago?" she inquired before he was out of earshot. She knew she risked much by asking him such a question, especially at a time like this.

He turned back to her and swallowed with a dry throat. "That's a hefty accusation you've just leveled at me. Did I ever say such a thing? You ought to know me better than that by now."

She looked down at her hands and the parchments. "Malise said it was you who saved me and my brother in the wood the day my parents died. How is it that you know of such things yet you do not act upon such knowledge?"

At her question, Deverell grew more visibly cross, and a great agitation filled him. He drew his brows down low over eyes of deep blue flint. "There are some things that cannot be told…secrets sworn to be kept…"

Finockt averted her gaze, but not before Deverell caught the mistrust and abounding hurt rooted in that one brief moment. The effects of his retort distressed him, and he immediately softened his mood and extended his hand toward her.

"Come, I'll take you to see Gwri." His voice had returned to its usual, gentle cadence.

Finockt looked up at him quickly. "I may see him?"

Deverell half smiled and jerked his chin toward the center of camp. "Aye, come with me."

Just before bounding up from beside the stream, Finockt glanced down at the next to last sheet of parchment rumpled in her hand and read there the only portion that was legible. *Uisdean.* Her heart jumped. The letters were faint, but there was no mistaking it. Pulling her gown up from around her feet, she hurried to join Deverell. She had to see her brother… before it was too late. But first she would see Gwri.

CHAPTER TWENTY-EIGHT

EVERELL THREADED HIS way past several pavilions before stopping at a red one trimmed in yellow-gold with a pennant of the same color flying high above it. He drew back the flap. Finockt ducked her head and stepped into the humid warmth of the enclosed space. It smelled of old blood and wine and lake water. Deverell entered after her and let the tent flap fall back into place behind him. Now with the light of day securely barred from view, her eyes swam in a reddened darkness, groping the strange color for something familiar. Not long after, her vision adjusted and inanimate objects appeared—a cot, a washbasin littered with scraps of bloodstained cloth, and a darkly colored bottle, half full; the cork lay in the grass beside it.

Deverell slipped past her. Finockt visually followed his path, her eyes finally landing on Gwri's sleeping form stretched out on the flimsy, makeshift bed. She looked to Deverell, and he motioned for her to approach. Slowly, she advanced until she stood beside him, and they both looked down in silence upon their friend. His eyes were closed, but his breathing was soft and regular; and his side was bandaged tightly, wound with white cloth.

Finockt knelt next to the cot.

"He has lost a lot of blood," Deverell said.

She bit her lower lip. "Will he live?"

"Aye, he should get better in time. He just needs rest now. I'll leave you two alone."

"Wait, Deverell." She grasped the sleeve of his tunic to prevent his departure, and at the solemn look on her face, he knelt beside her. "Will you take these for me?" she asked, holding the parchments out to him. "There may yet be something important hidden in them, and I know with you they shall be safe."

He gave her a grim smile. "I'll do my best." Rising, he patted her on the shoulder and made his way to the tent flap. Before he exited, he tossed one last glance at Thorlóthlon's princess, huddled on the ground at Gwri's side. Then he stepped forward into the heart of the encampment and set his mind on everything that was to come.

An hour later, Finockt still knelt on the ground beside Gwri with her arms folded and resting on the edge of his bed. Worry and fatigue had taken their toll, and she had fallen asleep with her head nestled in the crook of her arm. Now he shifted, and his movement on the tiny cot shook her awake. Raising her head, she smiled and brushed his hair back from his eyes as he gathered his bearings. His face pinched with misery, and he put a hand to his side. "Finockt," he said in surprise when he saw her. Grimacing, he gave another shuddered breath as he moved and pain racked him.

"Lie still," she gently ordered. "You need to rest. Everything's taken care of. We're free."

"Ahh," he said, wincing. "I think I'll take your advice on that part. This must look a pretty picture," he added, laughing a little.

Finockt brightened at this more jovial remark. "Aye, it does," she said. She drew a freshly placed water basin toward her, wrung the water out of the clean cloth sitting in it, and gently wiped the sweat from his brow. "I'm just glad you're safe and well. I thought so many times I was going to lose you, but seeing you now…I'm just so glad you're here."

She took his hand in hers, but he solemnly withdrew it, his heart filling with a sudden, guilt-ridden sadness.

"How did we get here?" he asked, looking around in confusion.

Finockt shifted back on her heels. Color fanned her cheeks, and inwardly she reeled at the subtlety of his rebuff. The bitter sting of it pierced her heart, and the groaning question repeated itself in her mind: *why the sudden change? Why the growing indifference?*

Pushing aside her flustered thoughts, she struggled to answer him. "Deverell rescued us from the water and brought us here last night. You were unconscious when they took you from the boat."

Gwri rubbed the back of his neck. "Ah, now I remember the loch."

Had she been so wrong about everything? She looked down at her hands, still trying to sort her thoughts, when the sudden thrum of the bódhran broke the silence, followed by the frenzied hum of chaos. Gwri bolted upright with difficulty, his face bearing alarm, his hand glued to his side. He drew his boots on, using two hands only when necessary.

"The battle has begun," he said and struggled to his feet.

Finockt's eyes widened with fear. "Where do you think you are going? Gwri!" she cried in disbelief.

Ignoring her protests, he proceeded to the tent flap and flung it back. The whole camp was a buzzing mayhem. Soldiers ran here and there, shouting orders to one another while snatching up swords, spears, and bows. At the sight, a dark change overcame Gwri's countenance, and his features appeared turned to stone.

Finockt's heart tightened. "Gwri. Please," she said. "You have to rest. They say you have lost too much blood. Please. Leave the fighting to those who are strong enough to endure it."

He kept his back to her. "I cannot ignore my duty."

Duty! Always duty! Finockt thought. *Was common sense always subject to duty?*

Gwri dropped the tent flap and hastily retraced his steps. His face was deathly pale, and his lips pursed tightly when he breathed. Beside the cot, he threw on his tunic and belted his sword around his waist, grimacing slightly as he tugged it into place. Then he marched to the foot of the cot and snatched up his bow and his quiver brought earlier by Deverell.

Finockt looked on in helpless dismay. "Are you mad, Gwri? They'll kill you. You're not well enough to fight! Please, Gwri. Won't you listen to me? You can't do this. Not after all that's happened—I couldn't bear it if you were killed, too!"

Gwri stopped adjusting his quiver and looked at her over his shoulder. "I swore allegiance to Thorlóthlon and her king as well as my own countrymen. Were I to promise you even the hope of my safe return, such a pledge would be borne from naught but lying lips and a deceitful heart." His gaze hardened, his heart and mind set. "In truth, I cannot promise you anything, for I am not free to do so. I am bound, Finockt, by word and by faith."

He reached into his tunic pocket and withdrew her necklace. Finockt looked at it lying in the palm of his hand and felt her heart twist anew with unbearable pain.

"My heart's yours in amity, Finockt. I think you know that." He lifted his hand, quieting her protest. "That time between us is gone. Let us not say things we will later regret, and stay your mind on this, should I die in battle, it shall be God's will. Yet should I live, it is only for reasons of God's design and purpose—His will for things not yet known to me. He must decide for us."

Enclosing the emerald cross in her palm, he looked upon her long, searching her face for something. Something Finockt did not understand nor could she give. An agreement with him perhaps?

"To you should the cross return for safekeeping," he said. "We both know the truth of it. Guard it well, Finockt."

The turmoil outside the tent's thin walls dwindled. Soon they would be gone, and still Finockt could say nothing. With one last parting gesture, he pressed her hand to his lips. Then seizing his bow, he jogged from the tent and vanished amongst the pavilions. He never looked back.

CHAPTER TWENTY-NINE

INOCKT WATCHED GWRI disappear amongst the final mass of organizing soldiers and cavalry until the tongue of the tent slipped, swinging down over the entrance and cutting off her view. In a sudden helpless fit of rage, she turned and kicked the water basin to the side, hurting her foot and dousing the back of the pavilion and everything near it in a miniature flood. Tears sprang to her eyes, and she covered her mouth with her hands amidst a torrent of sobs. He would have no chance at war. They would cut him down before he had even delivered the first strike. Fool! He fled to his own death without regard for how she or anyone else felt.

She clenched her hands into fists, and her heart throbbed in her chest, as a surge of panic warned her she had lost all control. She could not direct the future any more than she could Gwri's actions. No matter how hard she pleaded with him to stay, he had chosen his own path: one that did not include her.

Let him go then! Let him die a hero's death for all his

senselessness. To think he would last five minutes against the Dúnarians! What a fool. What a *fool!* She had already seen one friend die, must she also lose another?

Her heart ached at the possibility, and the one grave thought that grew heavier and more oppressive with time was the fact she could not make Gwri return her growing affection. His declaration of amity moments ago meant nothing more than absolute friendship, if even that. The realization deepened her anguish. After all they had endured together and everything he had said and everything he had *not had* to say, that one little word stung. Why did he so abruptly deny how he felt? His sudden allegiance to his duty was a newly adopted anthem that made him act more strangely by the day. He had become a worse version of Deverell overnight—even she understood the Northerner well enough to know he would never toy with her affections. Gwri's transformation frustrated and confused her, especially since she had never heard him voice such sentiments before. Did he not feel more deeply than that? The night of Coinneach's banquet surely justified her own feelings and unequivocally confirmed the truth: he did care, *had* cared for her, had he not? What could have changed between then and now? A more dire thought crossed her mind: or had his feelings really changed at all? If the latter were true, why then had he done it? Why did he try to convince her in the beginning he was sincere when his intentions were untrue?

She slumped onto the cot and clenched the grass beneath it between her bare toes. She had not been ready to handle the emotion of losing Gawain. To lose Gwri to friendship or even death or both all at once was too much. She gripped the cot's bony edges with a determined hand until the effort made the wound in her arm throb and her fingers numb; still she gripped it harder, welcoming the painful distraction. It gave her an outlet for everything she could not or would not do because her own conscience forbade it. Try as she might, she could not upend the tumult of emotions torturing her soul. What had she done wrong? The bitter sting of Gwri's rejection hurt, and in its wake, anger festered and fueled an underlying doubt she had harbored since her arrival at Thorlóthlon. What other lies had she sold herself? Only this? She was so convinced Gwri cared for her she could not surmise his reasons for rejecting her now. Was it Caslon? If so, she could not help but think it was petty of him to hold this against her. Did he not see she had been so afraid of her own feelings at the time? Being with Gwri scared her; she had never met anyone like him. Caslon was reserved and quiet, patient and kind, a protector and friend. He had sacrificed his own life for hers. Aside from Christ, nothing could match that. Caslon was a precious soul, providing clarity amidst the darkness of the evil surrounding her.

A sob filled her throat, making it ache with more unshed tears. Gelis. Carynton. Caslon. Eilidh. Gawain. Now Gwri. An ever-increasing number of casualties for Thorlóthlon. For the cross. She contemplated Gwri's inevitable loss. Though death lay imminent for all, she could not imagine life without his bold and easy manner. He made her feel important and every inch the King's Daughter that she was. He never doubted her, even when all the others had. Perhaps she had waited too long? How could she expect Gwri to hang on forever? She had wounded his pride. Though she did not consider herself anything extraordinary to look at, she had to admit it had still taken courage for him to express himself—twice—once in the tower and once in the garden, though each attempt had been thwarted, whether by her own methods or those of fate. Any man could vouch for another regarding the vulnerability of laying open the inward places of the heart. Why should she have thought it would be any different for a Prince of Mithel?

She lowered her head into her hand. Carefully prescribed caution measured her steps all her life in the village, and her fiery independence held in check by her Dúnarian rulers waned even further once she escaped their clutches—her path dictated in part by Coinneach. Despite all her daring, she was not used to risking everything for matters of the heart. Her heart was what she guarded most from destruction at the hands of those who only too gladly sought to inflict pain. Whereas others left themselves open, she put up a wall, intent on protecting herself from the unpredictable run of emotions that easily unhinged the heart of even the most cautious individual. Experience had left her wary.

Now she was caught at a crossroads—teetering between heartbreak and heartache. She could no more save Gwri than she could any of her people. She could neither fight nor lift a finger to protect anyone, and she had not the skills to best Tirell, even if she wanted to. Striking out on her own nearly always proved a disaster and a much heavier burden to bear. To do so again invited folly, and now without Gwri to watch over, Finockt felt even more useless. Her blood boiled, and a growing disdain for herself, her feelings for Gwri, and her own ineffectual ability to help her people defeat Tirell gnawed at her. Her current worth was intrinsically linked to the cross. At present, it hung in her hand an uncertain symbol of Thorlóthlon, with no accurate prediction of its continuing role in establishing the next successor to the throne. Was it possible that even now its role had already been accomplished and its future use and importance to both Thorlóthlon and Valínthia had become as empty of purpose as she now was? Her heart sank, and she tightened her grip on the cross. She did not want to think this precious bit of metal no longer held sway in determining Thorlóthlon's future.

Bathed in a thickening silence, her mind quieted. The army had gone. She sat, absorbing the warmth of the tent for a long moment, and sighed, feeling more useless now than at the outset of her own tortuous musings. Gwri's march toward death only enhanced such feelings of worthlessness. To make things worse, should Deverell let him fight, and he perish, the blame would lie full well upon the Northerner's shoulders. Deep down Finockt knew Deverell would never be able to bear that. He should stay. Keep Gwri here, where it was safe. Where they were both safe.

She fought another rising flood of tears and frustration when the thunder of horses' hooves preceded an increasing clamor of male voices that arose on the far side of the encampment. A tremor of fear shot through her. She jumped up from the cot and ran to the door of the tent. Once there, however, she paused, her hand clamped around the brightly colored fabric. The sudden uproar without made her hesitate. For, in drawing back the crimson fold, she feared what she would find, but for the third or fourth time in these many months, something more profound than herself told her she must. She took a deep breath to steady herself. Outside the tent, the morbid sounds escalated, a pandemonium that could not be Thorlóthlon's men. Hate and animosity permeated every heinous deed and vibrated along every cursed word that fell from their lips. She swept the fabric aside, and her gaze instantly locked on a wash of faded gray and blood red uniforms. They poured into the camp on horseback, like a rush of unleashed water. Ahead of them Thorlóthlon's remaining guard sprang to arms to keep off the advancing enemy.

"The king! The king! Guard the king!" several shouted, while positioning themselves before the white pavilion. The rest threw themselves into combat, as the small, contending cavalry charged them, yelling and swinging their weapons with a ferocity that was hard to comprehend. Finockt even recognized some of Thorlóthlon's defectors amongst them.

One by one, Valínthia's soldiers began to fall.

Finockt let the tent flap slip back into place. It had been no more than a half hour since Deverell had left with Thorlóthlon's eager army! Her gaze fell to the emerald necklace cradled in her palm, and she clasped her hand more fully around it. So Tirell had realized his mistake after all. They would soon be after it. She now knew its worth was far more valuable than she had originally believed. The quest was not over. For Tirell to seek it out a second time when he already had it once in his possession indicated it must reveal something even more powerful than she anticipated. She must not let them find it. Once it was in their hand, it would be no easy feat to get it back again, as it had been at Caldária.

She maneuvered out into the bright sunshine. Across the encampment, the enemy encircled her grandfather's tent. It would not be much longer before they reached him.

Finockt skimmed the glen for aid. Within seconds, she found both her escape and the one diversion to save the king: horses from Thorlóthlon. Tied to posts near the edge of camp, several had been left behind to carry the king to safety should the need arise. For Coinneach, it was too late. But for her, their potential use was a Godsend. They were close, but not close enough.

She looked once more across the encampment, her heart beating fiercely in her chest, and in the preceding moments before she acted, she heard a still, small voice within her, as if it had set a small flame aglow. She knew she was doing the right thing, but she was not sure she would make it in time.

The Dúnarians surrounding her grandfather's tent regrouped and attacked with renewed vigor, their tactics merely a farce meant to play with the men's minds. Finockt only hoped Coinneach's guard could hold them a short while longer. She had but one chance to orchestrate her escape correctly. She could not fail, and there could not be any turning back. With every second she formulated her escape, her plan cemented itself more fully in her mind, giving her surety. She reexamined the horses, counting their number and measuring each one's use in turn, when her heart suddenly leaped into her throat. There, amongst the orderly row of tall, polished steeds, was Tohr! Finockt blinked back tears of joy. For all her anger with Gwri, she could not help but thank him for bringing Tohr back to her. Agile and swift, he would be her best chance to escape with the cross and hopefully save her grandfather.

Crouching low, she kept a firm watch on the confusion and began to cross the wide-open space to a frantic Tohr when a small hand arrested her advancement. She gasped and twisted away from the touch, the movement landing her on her backside.

Eoin cringed when she hit the grass.

"Saints above!" Finockt whispered loudly when she saw him. "That was not the best way to get my attention, right?"

She scrambled to her feet.

"Haí, shhh," Eoin said, his finger on his lips. "You're sure to get yourself killed if you go that way, milady. Follow me. Quickly!"

He pulled her back amongst the montage of colored tents to the outskirts of the camp—on the western side where the wood grew thick. There, he jumped over the large, bony root of a tree and pulled Finockt down beside him. The two tossed another glance at the small battle raging within the encampment, then Finockt sank against the oak.

"How is my grandfather?"

"I don't know, milady," Eoin replied, his great brown eyes drowning his little face. "It looks hopeless."

Finockt peered around the tree's broad base once more. Even as Eoin spoke, she saw the Dúnarians' opposition to reaching the king had lessened. They had already fanned out, viciously ransacking every tent they came to. Each step drew them closer to her and Eoin; they had already entered the pavilion Finockt had just left.

Finockt slumped once more against the oak's trunk, her mind racing, her face troubled. She took a deep breath while trying to stem her own nerves. She could not let Eoin see her worry. Though he was a brave lad, she could tell even now he hung on by nothing more than a thread of hope. She had to help him conquer his doubts.

"It is not hopeless, Eoin," she said, "but we do not have much time. They are looking for the cross. They have come back for it. Tirell has realized his folly."

She brushed her thumb over the cross's brilliant emerald. "I must get out of here. Are there not any more men?" Her hands broke out in a sudden sweat. "Eoin!" she snapped when he did not answer her.

He ducked behind the tree and looked at her sharply. "No, milady. A call for aid was sent to Mithel, but it is said they will not reach us in time."

Finockt's heart dropped. It was up to her then.

"Wait here," she told him. She gave Eoin's hand a squeeze and sprang to her feet, but he pulled her back down.

"Where are you going?" Genuine fear filled his eyes, and his face crumpled, almost as if he might cry.

"Oh, Eoin," Finockt said, grasping his forearm. "It's the cross they're really after, but if they can they will kill the king as well." His eyes grew even bigger when she said this; she held onto his small hand. "I must get out of the camp, be a diversion for them. Perhaps they will follow me, and then my grandfather will have a chance, and you will, too."

She tossed another glance toward the pearl-white pavilion stained with streaks of heroes' blood. Yet Coinneach's soldiers had not relented. Though so few remained, they continued to strike hard, refusing to give the king up to an unjust death.

Finockt rose, determined to do what she could in order to save him and the others.

"Please, milady, do not leave me," Eoin blurted, looking up at her, a sob catching in his throat. At his confession, a look of shame crossed his face, and he bowed his head.

Finockt's heart melted. He had just voiced every emotion she had felt when Gwri left her: helpless, lost, frightened, and terrified of the outcome. She had been so angry, and angry was how she felt right now. She crouched beside him. "Do not fear, Eoin. By God's grace and mercy you will live. He is with you, and you shall be safe. I promise." She smoothed his hair. "You must be a brave lad. They will leave as soon as I do, so you must let me fly."

"Promise you will come back, Princess?"

Finockt regarded him solemnly, absorbing his hopeful gaze. "By God's will," she answered, "I will return. I cannot promise you anything more than that. Haí, remember, Eoin, you are not alone, should God be by your side." She held the young lad by the shoulders. "Now listen to me carefully. Do not move from this spot until the enemy has left. Promise me, Eoin. You will be safe here."

Bitter tears filled his eyes and slipped down his cheeks though he tried hard to keep them from falling. He did not move, and Finockt marveled that even at his age, pride prevented him from touching his hand to his face.

"I am a coward, milady, aren't I? I am everything Darce told me I should *not* be!" He shared the words with vehemence and hung his head in humiliation.

At Eoin's mention of Darce, an intense flush of anger washed over her at the turmoil this traitor had set upon a boy too young to bear it. "You are a servant to the King, Eoin," she said with conviction, "and are of more value than you can imagine. You must keep watch for the army of Mithel and direct them as need be when they come. I take it they know enough to come here when they arrive?"

Eoin nodded, his head still bowed.

"Then it is up to you to give them direction to save the rest of Thorlóthlon. I need you alive in order to do this, do you understand?"

Eoin barely gave her another nod, more tears falling pitifully to darken the dry earth near his feet.

"You saved my life, Eoin," Finockt said, lifting the boy's face to hers. "You are a brave lad, faithful and daring. Now stay alert that you may spare my life once again should I need it!"

A flicker of a smile shadowed his face, and he now ventured the back of his hand to his nose to wipe it. "Aye, milady," he sniffed. "Be careful."

Finockt smiled and kissed him gently on the forehead. "You, too," she said with a wink. "And God be with you. Trust me. When the time comes, He will give you both courage and victory."

Leaping over the tree's thick root, she headed back to the encampment by way of the wood. From the safety of the oak, Eoin watched her every step and then struck out from the oak's trunk to see her when the shadows and trees hid her from view.

No sooner had he distanced himself from his safe haven than blood red and gray caught his eye. Heart drumming, he scaled the oak's root and threw himself into a natural depression tucked between the base of the tree and a soft mound of grassy earth.

The soldier cantered along close beside him, his sharp eyes dutifully scanning the interior of the encampment. Eoin held his breath and prayed he would not be seen. Moments later, he heaved a sigh of relief, and his heart quieted, as the Dúnarian passed him without even a backward glance.

Meanwhile, Finockt dodged her way between widely spaced trees until she was as close to Tohr as she could possibly get without exiting the wood. Beyond him a small contingent of Dúnarian horsemen still fought the last few soldiers protecting Coinneach's tent, while the rest wreaked havoc on the camp, tearing down tents and rummaging through ironclad chests and trunks in search of the cross. The sight made Finockt's blood boil and withered away any remaining strands of fear.

Keeping a steady gaze on the Dúnarians, she stepped out from under the protection of the forest and then raced for the line of horses. So far, so good. She had been quick enough to reach them without attracting the Dúnarians' attention. She hoped the rest of her mission proved just as easy. One by one, she passed silently beneath the horses' heads in her pursuit of Tohr. However, her rapid approach and swift movements unnerved the sleek, muscled war horses. They danced and shied against their tethers, kicking up dust and stamping out a warning. Finockt reached up and placed a gentle hand on the soft, whiskered nose of each restless steed in turn in an attempt to quiet them, but her efforts failed. Disarmed by her urgency, they still jolted at her approach and rolled their eyes back in their heads. Tufts of dust continued to rise in soft plumes, signaling her unwanted presence, and frantic blasts of hot air fired from their nostrils. Finockt felt the heat from their breath hit the back of her neck and penetrate the sleeves of her gown as she slipped past them.

Only two steeds now separated her from her beloved companion. Her courage mounted. No one had spotted her yet. Three steps more and she was beside Tohr. She ran a hand down the side of his coal black neck, trying to calm him, but he would not settle. His blood raced, as Finockt's sharpening anxiety flowed through her into him, until his sides quivered under her touch. She kept her hands flat against him, relaxed her shoulders, and took a deep breath. But it was no use. He snorted, pawing the ground uneasily with his hooves, and then he whinnied.

The soldiers ceased their plundering and set an iron gaze on the row of horses. Finockt ducked, hoping Tohr would shield her from immediate detection. Then slowly, methodically, she moved toward the horizontal post. *You must ride hard,* she told herself. *They've seen you now. There's no turning back.*

The mounted soldiers advanced toward her, their horses half trotting, half walking. Finockt stooped beside Tohr's nose, and with one flick of her wrist, she flung the tether from around the post and threw the ends around his neck.

"Hey!" one of the soldiers shouted. "Hold there!"

Immediately Finockt pushed Tohr away from the post, and with a skip and a hop, she threw herself stomach-down across his broad, bare back as he skittered away from the other horses. His forward momentum helped Finockt easily right herself. She snatched up the makeshift reins and then pulled Tohr around to face the soldiers. They pressed toward her on all three sides, hemming her in, with the remaining horses creating a hedge behind. Several paces lay between each rider. Finockt tensed, and Tohr jerked and sidestepped beneath her, as the muscles in her legs tightened around his belly. The path to freedom was a small one, but it was a path nevertheless. Tohr fought her, anxious to run, and he tossed his nose against the rope.

"Hold, lassie," a soldier sneered. They smirked as they drew in around her; the challenge she posed appeared an easy victory for them.

Finockt glared at them. Mentally, she weighed the possibility of her escape and roughly calculated the distance needed to get her there. She readjusted her grip on the reins and tucked her heels against Tohr's belly to give him a command when the Dúnarian steed to her right suddenly bucked and reared, catapulting the soldier off his back. In rapid succession, the other two Dúnarian riders struggled to maintain their seated position as their horses bucked and shied before her. The gap between the soldiers gently widened, giving Finockt the advantage she needed. She jerked Tohr toward the narrow opening and dug her bare heels into his underbelly.

Spurred to action, Tohr doubled his pace, tossing up clods of dirt and grass behind them. One of the soldiers reached for her, but she clung to Tohr and leaned away from him, evading the man's grasp. In the same moment, the cross slipped into view, dangling beneath her palm to mingle with Tohr's black mane. Its emerald spit fire, snapping in the sunlight.

The soldier's sneer vanished. "After her!" he bellowed. "She has the cross!"

At the glen's far edge, Finockt looked back for Eoin and saw him stretched out over a thick oak branch, his sling in one hand and another smooth, round stone hanging at the ready in the other. It was as she predicted. He had saved her life once again. A grin caught at her, and hope sprang afresh. She leaned lower with Tohr. Soon Eoin was lost amongst the heavy brush and tree trunks. Half a minute more she ducked beneath a tree branch and lurched forward as Tohr cleaved the stream close to camp, dousing himself and her in a fine, tattered veil of water. To her relief, the diversion worked. The Dúnarians were not far behind. Most of them had followed suit, eager to catch their prey. Those six enemy soldiers left behind in the camp were vulnerable and alone. Seeing victory within their grasp, Valínthia's soldiers found their strength renewed; their strokes grew faster and sharper and fell heavier and with more precision. In that moment, a weight lifted off Finockt's shoulders, and she breathed easier. Eoin was safe, as was her grandfather.

From his perch in the oak, Eoin, too, breathed easier. He had hope the war may yet be won.

CHAPTER THIRTY

O NCE CLEAR OF the Glen of Farith, Finockt found no need to encourage Tohr's flight. Released from his posted prison, he flew across the land and beat the earth bare. And yet only the gentlest movement of Finockt's hand on the rein altered his course through the forest's thickly wooded breadth.

She now headed southeast in hopes of losing the Dúnarians somewhere along the way. But they were not deterred. They followed close behind, relentless in their pursuit, their horses fast, agile, and tireless.

Finockt glanced down at the sweat foaming on Tohr's neck, chest, and shoulders. Steady as he was, she wondered if he would be able to outlast them.

She rode a few minutes more before she realized she was never going to lose the enemy unless she made some transition. She trained her eyes on the wood ahead, hopeful of finding something useful to make her final escape. As if she had conjured it up, a partial view of a small clearing came into her line of sight, the whole of it hidden behind a copse of trees jetting out from the rest of the forest, creating a natural, un-gated entrance into the small glade.

Finockt crisscrossed through the forest in an attempt to throw the Dúnarians off their lead. To her surprise, it worked. The Dúnarians slowed their pace, as the trees and forest scrub marred their formerly clear view of her. She could hear them shouting orders to one another in an effort to determine her course. But the dual change in the wood and in Finockt's riding pattern forced their reliance on their other senses, and they slowed even more, now counting on their ears not just their eyes to guide them.

Finockt looked back and saw that the Dúnarians were fall-ing farther and farther behind. To her relief, the adjustment in both pace and direction had produced the advantage she needed. She gave another light pull on the reins and Tohr headed straight for the clearing. Once within its protective arms, she reined him in hard. He reared gently in protest.

Moments later, the sound of horses' hooves pounded inevi-tably nearer, overshadowing the blood rushing in her ears. Finockt forced her mind to calm. Then she combed the glade more thoroughly until she found what she had been looking for: a wedge of underbrush nearly behind her to her left. No trees stood behind it. She nudged Tohr in the side. He skipped forward a couple of steps. The wedge of wild growth grew higher than the usual brush, but she had no other choice.

The Dúnarians were close now. Finockt could see them filtering through the trees in search of her. She tapped Tohr lightly in the belly with her heel and led him across the clear-ing. Then she turned him around. "Haí," she said and clicked her tongue at him. He took off and headed straight for the wild hedge. She tapped him once more in the side, and he jumped it, leaving little sign they had passed there but for the place his back hoof caught the top of the underbrush. Dirt rose in a fine cloud of dust as he landed. Then suddenly he stumbled and bolted to the left. The unexpected change in direction unseated Finockt. She groped for Tohr's mane but grabbed air instead. Her arms braced for impact, she tumbled from his back and hit the ground like a rag doll, knocking her head and grazing her knuckles and the sides of her hands on the knobby forest floor. For a long while, she lay there in a daze, her mind fogged and confused. When she attempted to move, a groan erupted from her whole body. She felt everything, from the sharp little stones that bit into her skin through her clothes to the thick, fibrous tree roots digging into her bones. Her knees ached. Her hip was so tender even breathing made it twinge with pain, and her injured shoulder oozed more blood through the now filthy linen that held her wound together. Almost she did not care if the Dúnarians found her. She wanted to lie still until the forest darkened and her body gave way to the grave. Fatigue she had been holding back for months spread over her, licking up any bit of stamina she had left.

After a few minutes, she slowly rolled onto her back, wincing and struggling to inhale new breaths of air. Her chest hurt with the effort. She clutched the cross to her waist and tried not to think about the searing pain pulsing through her with every beat of her heart.

Ahead of her the Dúnarians drew closer. Finockt suffered another small groan, as she attempted to move again, then she pinched her mouth shut to keep herself from drawing the enemy's attention. Tohr wandered back to her side. The slow plodding of his hooves stopped next to her head, and he stood patiently over her. She glanced up at him through a head-pounding haze and swallowed hard, fighting off nausea with deep breaths of fresh air. He nuzzled her shoulder gently and grumbled at her, nibbling her hair, but he could not coax her up. She lay on the ground, unable to move. The sound of the soldiers' approach thundering against the earth resounded deafeningly in her ears through the forest floor. It was all she could do to stifle the moans threatening to disclose her. On the other side of the hedge, the grass swished, and the jangle and jostle of armor and saddle grew more distinct. Finockt drew faster and shallower breaths.

The Dúnarians had entered the glade.

The need for safety now dealt her a sharp blow, its impact overriding her misery. She knew she must find a better hiding place. Immediately. Clearly, staying where she was only left her more vulnerable and open to capture by the Dúnarians. She had to retreat and seek better coverage. Even a fool was wise enough to know that.

Wracked with pain, she clambered to her feet, her hand glued to her side. Tohr drew up beside her, and she leaned into him, thankful for his support. He led her limping farther into the wood, as if he, too, understood the danger upon them. When they had gained protection behind a nearly solid patch of underbrush and young yew trees, he automatically stopped. Finockt rested against him and listened for the Dúnarians. A stone's throw away from her, they continued to round the glade on horseback and glean its edges with a trained eye. She could see them through the forest scrub, their dark red and gray uniforms flashing tints of color between the fine spaces of tree and overgrowth and their polished helmets brandishing sunlight where it filtered down from the forest ceiling. Their movement was fluid and quick, without pause or any indication of dismounting.

Finockt closed her eyes. They would not enter this part of the forest then. The plan had worked. She exhaled gently. For the first time since leaving the Glen of Farith, her whole body relaxed, and the tension she harbored lifted from around her shoulders. Her weight shifted back onto her heels, and a twig snapped underfoot. The sound seemed overly amplified in the quiet forest. Her gaze flew to the glade. No longer certain of the Dúnarians' whereabouts, she crouched on the forest floor, tucking herself more deeply into its foliage, and watched for movement. She only hoped Tohr's black coat would not give them away.

The light thud of the Dúnarian horse's hooves suddenly fell heavier against the earth, and the creak of the Dúnarian's saddle rent the air, as he leaned forward to capture every detail of the dense wood. By slow measures, Finockt worked her eyes up from the animal's spindly legs to the Dúnarian's girded waist, but in the end, she could not raise her eyes any farther than his breastplate. He peered into the wood for so long Finockt was sure his keen eye had separated Tohr's dark coat from the shadows—even at this distance. She held her breath, afraid to move even a fraction of an inch. Unlike his comrades, this man was alert and vicious, determined to catch his prey. He remained beside the hedge, studying its form in detail and calculating the possibilities of Finockt's escape and disappearance. Then he stood in the stirrups and leaned forward, as if something had piqued his interest.

Sweat trickled down the side of Finockt's face, raced down her back, and peppered her upper lip. For once, Tohr stood quietly beside her, his ears flicking back and forth, intent on capturing every bit of sound the forest had to offer.

The Dúnarian shaded his eyes, his body gently swaying in the saddle, as he attempted to distinguish what lay beyond the wild hedge. Before he could make certain of his discovery, his companions hailed his return, and a fellow soldier rode up beside him and clapped a heavy hand on his back. "Come on," he barked. "Quit wasting your time!"

Reluctantly, the Dúnarian left his post and joined in their retreat, but not before taking one last sweep of the endless forest and spitting into the underbrush. The thick wood shut him out before the last of his steed's footfalls faded from her ears. Then all was silent.

Finockt heaved an audible sigh and sank onto the forest floor in relief. Moments later, at Tohr's prodding, she slowly pushed herself to her feet again. Dizziness flooded her. She leaned against a tree trunk, tipped her head back, and rested, until she regained some semblance of balance. The extent of her bruises had already begun to make their mark: dark purple almost green pools that slowly grew into large, irregular rings on her leg and hip. She could feel them deepening, reaching to the bone. Already her aching arm had turned stiff, the growing immobility reaching into her shoulder. She remounted Tohr with difficulty, and when she had attained her seating, her loyal companion took off at a fast trot. But he refused to go any faster, despite Finockt's insistency with her heel.

"I'm all right, boy," she soothed, patting his sweaty neck. He flicked his ears back. "I am not badly hurt. Come, we must fly."

Reassured by her tone, Tohr increased his gait. The wind rushed in their ears. Finockt tucked her head to avoid another tree branch and scanned the wood to either side before glancing over her shoulder. The forest lay empty at all points. They rode forward, Finockt reining Tohr to a trot every few minutes and straining her ears for some sound of the soldiers' continued pursuit. But silence ran a solid ring around her. Finally, she slumped on Tohr's back. Her legs tingled, cramped by the ride and the absence of a saddle. Soon she felt anxiety release its hold on her, like a breath of air held too long. The thought was nonsensical, but perhaps, just perhaps, she was getting used to these adventures—and to riding bareback.

She made a wide circle through the wood: first heading south and then southeast and then north until at last she turned northwest, back to the Glen of Farith. Time passed. Too much time. She should have reached the glen by now. She examined her surroundings for a second and third time and then searched for the direction of the sun. Nature's course had brought her round and about many different changes in wood and path, but she was certain her direction had remained a northwesterly one. She looked sharply for any sign of the Dúnarians. If she had fallen too far short of the encampment, she had to ensure she had not drawn near to the enemy. But everything was undisturbed. The birds gave no cry for attention, and the land was not flattened by boot or wagon.

Finockt looked again to the sky. The sun was low enough to gauge a clear eastern route, but the thought came to her that perhaps she had misjudged and the glen rested more to the northeast or a little behind her to the southwest. Her legs stiffened, and Tohr started beneath her. She turned on his back, alarm tightening its hand around her throat as she scanned all four corners of the wood. She had no idea how to get back.

The dread of falling into the hands of the Dúnarians

suppressed all growing weariness of heart and mind, and the quiet she once welcomed was now a grave unsettling thing that ceased to change, except for the occasional purring cluck of a squirrel. Her heart beat faster. For the first time in her life, she realized she was *lost*. Every escape, every venture through the wood had never unnerved her like this one. Then, she knew her way home: to the village or to Thorlóthlon. But this was different. These woods were unfamiliar, their breadth expansive and thick.

Tohr moved uneasily beneath her while Finockt struggled to keep her increasing panic at bay. A small stream gurgled to her right. Suddenly thirsty and in need of a distraction, she dismounted and knelt beside it. Sweat dripped from her chin, and her head ached fiercely. She dunked her hands beneath the flowing surface, intent on clearing her mind. The cold water pricked her skin and raised goose bumps on her arms, and when she doused her face with stinging cupfuls of it, she thought her aching head would split in half. She bent now and drank from the stream. After a moment, Tohr ambled forward and drank beside her. Water climbed the sleeves of her gown, making the fabric stick unbearably to her skin, and her stomach rumbled. How long had it been since she had eaten? Too long ago. Much like this diversion to save the king had taken—too long. She needed to return, to ensure her grandfather's safety.

She sat back and raised her eyes to the fading sky. There was not much daylight left to be had: four or five hours at most. Leaning forward again, she dunked her hand back into the cold water then stopped. A low dismal hum had invaded the quiet forest.

Rising from beside the stream, Finockt took Tohr by the

reins and led him a few paces closer to the murmur. It grew clearer and closer. She mounted with more ease this time and nudged Tohr into a walk. Before long, the far off clang of swords and an eerie, frightening noise she did not want to place brought chills to her spine and fresh goose bumps to her skin.

Finockt stopped Tohr and listened again. There was no mistaking it—battle was at hand.

CHAPTER THIRTY-ONE

O HER OWN surprise, Finockt did not rein Tohr in. Instead, she allowed him to keep his pace through the wood. And though everything in her told her to turn away and find a safe path back to camp, her heart told her to keep going.

The bitter sounds of battle increased the closer she drew to the ugly scene, and when she broke free from the wood into a fair clearing strewn with towering old trees, every muscle in her body contracted, and the color drained from her face.

Dúnarian and Valínthian were locked in arms, fighting to the death. Finockt's heart constricted anew, as metal struck hard against metal, and in the interest of self-preservation, she hung back. Wounded and dying soldiers lay everywhere: at her feet, over the clearing, even on the edge of the wood. With every second that passed, more joined their wounded or fallen comrades.

Finockt strove to ignore the bloody struggle before her,

but she could not; the mayhem was too much, and the only thought that made her sicker was the knowledge that somewhere out there Gwri was amongst this brutality. Her heart beat wildly. The whole of the Dúnahez was upon them. She strained her eyes, gleaning the chaos in hopes of finding him, but she could not separate him from the fighting.

Tohr skittered and sidestepped beneath her. She held the reins. Gwri had to be here. She would not resign him to death or dying amongst the others. She shuddered again. Awful cries and screams rang up into the air; the wild, excruciating sound pierced her to the core and made her hair stand on end. Then suddenly she started, the all too familiar whine of an arrow turning her heart to stone. The stray shot hissed through the air just above her head. Tohr jerked and half reared, whinnying in protest as Finockt clung to him and fought to maintain her seating. Her insides coiled then quivered at the nearly fatal shot, and she trembled almost as deeply as Tohr. His eyes were feral, his nerves shaken by the chaos of battle, and when she had calmed him, by some intuitive gesture, she lifted her eyes over the open field to Deverell. Her heart instantly pulsed with a new terror. He was set in the thickest part of the battle, mercilessly fending off one soldier only to face another. Fellow comrades in arms surrounded him and fought with equal brazenness and fervor. Colored banners bearing the symbols and strength of the Dúnahez and Thorlóthlon and her faithful allies stood tall and then fell, as the one who held them slumped under the enemy's strike, each one lost amongst a rhythmic rise and fall of ageless weapons. Thorlóthlon's army and that of her allies appeared so frail and vulnerable—a meager number set against so many—and yet, by some miracle, with each passing moment the Dúnarians seemed to suffer more.

Finockt watched the horrific scene with bated breath when suddenly she jerked upright, her legs clamping around Tohr, and her heart tightening into knots. "*No, no!*" she cried, her eyes tracking Deverell's every movement as well as the soldier moving swiftly behind him. She plunged her heels into Tohr's sides and urged him forward, but he resisted her command, shying and rearing at the blood and gore at his feet.

"*Deverell!*" Finockt screamed as she clung to Tohr's back. "*Deverell!*" But the distance between them was too great. Now, as with Gwri at Caldária, she could do nothing, except watch. Panic coursed through her. He had promised to guard himself well, for her sake…

Across the field, Deverell withdrew his sword from the enemy.

"Haí, Deverell! Behind you!" Strahan shouted across from him, his blue eyes bearing alarm as he knocked the enemy in front of him to the ground. Deverell turned sharply in the direction of Strahan's gaze and easily parried two of the Dúnarian's blows. Then he leveled his sword into his opponent's chest.

Finockt felt sick. The ground was saturated with blood, and amidst the continual screams and cries of agony, the foul odor of death and dying rent the air. Men with their eyes still open, others unrecognizable, and the wounded, some whimpering, some crying for their loved ones or sweethearts, turned her stomach and wrenched her heart. What now prevented her from turning away from this bloodshed?

A prolonged spectator on the battle's fringes, Finockt could find no thread of courage either to join the mayhem or to turn her back on it. And the one person who ultimately kept her there remained locked within the fray.

Deverell's hair was soaked with sweat. He slung it from his eyes with a toss of his head and beckoned his comrades and shouted orders, parrying blows in between, when Maegowan stepped forward, his broad sword dripping red with blood. His eye had been on his old friend since the start of battle, and only now had he been given the chance to stand before him.

Deverell wiped a heavy sheen of sweat from his brow. "Will it ease your conscience to kill me now in battle?"

Maegowan laughed. "I would have killed you before, old friend, had I the chance."

"As I recall you did have the chance."

"Yes, but then, had I shot straight and the arrow taken your life, the fight would not have been fair. Now I have the opportunity to make amends."

Deverell raised his blade. Maegowan smiled then lunged forward, and a side war began, its cacophonous tones of a deeper, more personal, and vengeful nature.

Tohr reared again, a banner falling before them, its colors fluttering in the wind before cascading into a heap on the blood-soaked ground. Finockt looked over and saw the lad who had borne it tumble to his knees, his lips mouthing a prayer, calling for his mother, the deep sleep of death closing his eyes. A lad. *A boy, hardly older than Eoin.*

Her breath tightened in her chest, and without realizing it, she had taken the reins and forced Tohr around the poor dead boy; she left Tohr no option of resistance. Death was real to her now, more real than it had been with Gawain. With Gawain, death had been nearly a façade, a watery dream that evoked pain but was hard to trust in either its form or consistency. Even now she believed Gawain was still alive, fighting at present amongst friend and enemy, while Deverell struggled to deflect each of

Maegowan's relentless and powerful blows. Her heart burned with the fear that Deverell's next strike would be his last.

A gleam of gold struck her periphery as she crossed the field, its color shimmering again and again in the setting sun. For a moment, she let Tohr pick his way over the clearing and focused instead on the soldier locked in combat not far from Deverell. His hair and tunic were familiar. At once she knew it was Gwri who fought steadily alongside Deverell, his blade darkened with blood. Pain marred his features, but his strength did not seem to have left him. He came to Deverell's rescue, once, twice. Others in Deverell's group lent him aid as well, but the Dúnarians were many, thus each man was quickly divided from his comrade a second, third, and fourth time. The scene was overwhelming.

Beside Deverell Gwri struck harder. But in the same moment he felled one enemy, another ran up on his side. With one turn on his heel, he met the challenger, struck him down, and then became separated from his friends once more.

Sending two more soldiers to their deaths, he looked up sharply again for Deverell. But in the increasing mayhem, he could not find his companion. He parried a death strike and sent his opponent to his knees, but before he could recover from defending himself from that soldier, another was on top of him, cutting his arm, the weight of the Dúnarian's sword easily slicing through his heavy tunic.

Finockt held Tohr in check. With every consecutive clash of their blades, she wrestled the issue of whether she should stay put or rush headlong into the fray and rescue Gwri first and foremost. Indecisive, she stayed where she was, watching him strike back with renewed vigor until a final blow felled the enemy.

In the open field, painful spasms shot through Gwri's arm. He grasped his wound tightly, gritting his teeth against the additional searing heat of it. But he had no time to consider his misery. Another soldier was upon him. Gwri stumbled aside, successfully blocking his adversary's blow. His arm collapsed across his chest after each attack, and his face grew whiter; the effects of Deverell's nostrum was wearing off. Blood seeped through the bandage around his waist, darkening his clothing and playing traitor to his life—by it the Dúnarian had found his enemy's weakness. The soldier pushed in sharply, flinging Gwri's strike aloft and kicking him hard in the side. Gwri hit the ground and rolled to stand, but the effort and the extent of his pain prevented him from achieving his goal.

The Dúnarian now stood over him, his feet rooted to the earth, his sword gripped tightly between his hands, and his great hulk casting shadows over Thorlóthlon's ally. He smirked and spit on the ground next to Gwri's head. Then suddenly the man fell, perishing before the ground could embrace him. Behind him Strahan appeared, his battle-ax steady in his hands. At his waist hung his sword. He stretched his hand out to Gwri and helped him to his feet.

Not far from them, Finockt's heart won over her mind, and without comprehending what she was doing, she clipped Tohr hard in the sides and spurred him across the battlefield. At the thunder of horse's hooves, Strahan started and looked up into her white face in surprise as she abruptly reined Tohr in beside them. By his reaction, it was obvious she was the last person he expected to see in the middle of this battle, but clearly he thought the better of reprimanding her presence.

"Take him out of here!" he shouted, hauling Gwri upright and throwing him up behind Finockt. Once astride Tohr,

Gwri immediately sagged forward. Finockt doubled over, her back bearing the brunt of his weight. She looked desperately at Strahan, who grabbed Gwri's sword from the ground and tossed it into her ready hands. "Go! Go!" he yelled, waving her onward. Then he wheeled to fight off the Dúnarians who rushed them.

"Gwri, hold tight," Finockt said.

Conscious enough to hear her, he loosely clasped her waist, while Finockt encouraged Tohr's retreat with her heels. They leaped forward, Tohr nimbly picking his way through the fray to open land. Once fresh earth was under their feet again, he sprinted for the wood.

Halfway across the battlefield, Deverell ducked again beneath a fatal strike and spun out of reach of Maegowan's sword. Ever since he saw Finockt enter this blood-filled conflict, his eye had been trained on her, his heart vying for her safety rather than his own. Now, as Tohr spanned the periphery of war in a sudden blur of activity, worry filled Deverell's gaze, his muscles tightened, and for a moment his attention was drawn to the mounted horseman in hot pursuit. Vibrant colors flapped in the wind—a noble's colors. Tirell's. With his sword drawn and his steed set at a full gallop, even distance could not mask the severe look of hatred chiseled upon his face. For the first time in Deverell's life, sheer panic overwhelmed him. Forgetting himself, he bolted for Finockt when Maegowan drew his sword down hard toward Deverell's middle.

Catching the glint of metal in the setting sun, and further alerted by the buffering of the blade against the air, Deverell narrowly managed to parry the blow and save himself from being cut through. Infuriated by his friend's counterattack, Maegowan pushed in hard, locking his sword over top of

Deverell's and pinning him against a tree. Like dry winter leaves skidding across ice, Deverell's blade slid in close to his own neck. He struggled against the increasing pressure and stretched his chin to keep his throat from being cut when Maegowan dug his heel into the earth and pushed harder. His weight knocked the air from Deverell's chest. Deverell grimaced, his back grinding into the tree's bark and his blade pressing close against his own flesh, pricking his skin and drawing blood. In the next instance, Maegowan tilted his head back to butt Deverell in the face when the Northerner pushed his arms forward with the last of his strength. At the same time, tucking his legs up close to his chest, he pressed his boots against Maegowan's massive bulk and, with considerable effort, used every last bit of force he had in him to throw Maegowan back far enough for him to drop free of the swords' blades and roll away.

At the Northerner's escape, Maegowan plunged forward, plowing into the tree's trunk and splitting his forehead. Blood seeped from his torn flesh and trickled in rivulets down his rough face. Dazed and furious, he shot a livid gaze over the battlefield for his rival, who patiently awaited him, sword supple in hand, no scratch upon him that had been made by Maegowan's sword.

Incensed, the Dúnarian sympathizer charged him, with sword swinging, and the two were locked deep in combat once again. Within moments, Deverell found himself with his back to the same tree once more, but this time he was not trapped against it. Sweat dripped from his face, his clothes were soaked with it, and the sword was falling heavy in his hand, his arm numbed by the relentless fighting. He ducked. Maegowan's ill-timed strike swung through thin air and chipped bark from

the tree, and then Deverell slashed upward. Maegowan stumbled back, his hand to his side. Deverell held steady, waiting,
anticipating, but curiously Maegowan only gently tipped back
on his heels.

The Northerner kept a sharp eye on him, his every muscle
tensed for a renewed attack, when a foot soldier under
Maegowan's command saw his wounded captain falter before
the enemy. At once, he took his vengeance on the Northerner.
Deverell fought him with difficulty. The lad's faster, sharper
strokes overwhelmed him compared to the slower, heavier
blows he had exchanged with Maegowan. His only advantage was the lad's inexperience, and soon the Dúnarian was
wounded beyond the ability to wage further battle. The lad
withdrew to the wood beside them and sank into the bracken.

Leaning against a tree, Deverell breathed heavily, fatigue
finally taking its course. It had been more than four hours
since the heaviest part of the battle had begun. He swiped his
hand across his face. His sweat burned his eyes and blurred
his vision. He shook his head to clear his sight and searched
the open field for Maegowan when his expression transcended
from one of utter fatigue to wounded surprise. Like lightening,
Maegowan had pulled a dagger from his boot and let it fly.
Deverell reeled back as it entered his upper chest, and upon
the knife's impact, his sword fell idle in his hand, its tip lodged
in the grass. He reached for the dagger's hilt then let his hand
fall back and gritted his teeth. Slowly, Maegowan threaded
his way through the grass, his face crimson with fury, and his
hand more determined than ever to stain his dull blade bright
once more. It pleased him only a little that he had finally given
Deverell a blow.

The Northerner now took hold of the jeweled hilt of the

dagger with both hands, and by slow, painful measures, he slid it free from his flesh. Blood oozed from his wound and drained down his chest and over his arm. A second later, Maegowan stood before him, his eyes narrowed and menacing, his sword tip resting on Deverell's chest.

"You've improved since the last time we fought," Maegowan said, his voice pinched. "You remember it well, don't you, in the Dúnahez? You were no more than a lad then. I've waited long for this day, and by your death, I'll have finally made amends: the last remnant of the Queen of Evanthia's people—dead." He laughed, a deep, heavy rumble, but clearly, Deverell's earlier wound had made an impact on him, for the pain was taking its toll in slow measures. "And you, my old friend." He paused for breath. "You may rest well in the grave knowing you fought with honor and gave me my fair share."

"Have I?" Deverell asked. "By whose standards is that made?"

"By only the best," Maegowan said, indicating himself. "Your last breath can, can be made with the knowledge of a compliment: you fought well and bravely, like, like a true Dúnarian." He smirked. "Now your end has come."

"Only God determines a man's end," Deverell said.

He shot his hand over the flat of Maegowan's blade, casting it aside, and sent the dagger hanging in his opposite hand into Maegowan's thick neck. Stunned, the Dúnarian stood motionless. Then the last blow was delivered with the captain's own sword, pulled from his own hand. His black heart severed, death darkened his face, and Maegowan collapsed to his knees, a defeated, sorry look in his eyes. He toppled over with a heavy thud and stirred no more.

Deverell stood before him, weary and exhausted. "And

so God determines your fate, old friend," he said with no ounce of pleasure. He flung Maegowan's sword from him and glanced down at his chest. Blood still flowed heartily from it, and a look of pain mixed with exasperation crossed his countenance. The bite of the knife was sharp, but the act of killing was sharper. He shifted his gaze to the scene spinning around him. Battle still waged strong, but for now, he seemed to have been forgotten, to have blended in with the trees.

His head throbbed with dehydration and worry, and his every thought returned to Finockt. What bothered him most was the fear that he was too late, that harm had been done, and he would arrive to find her fatally wounded or worse…already gone. This latter thought spurred him to action.

He wrapped his left shoulder and chest tightly with a strip of cloth torn from his tunic and used his teeth to help secure the ends when his affected arm gave out. Then snatching up his sword, he took off at a run, staving off more soldiers as he made his way through the fighting, his left arm cradled at his side.

CHAPTER THIRTY-TWO

INOCKT SLOWED TOHR to a canter when the sound of battle had dwindled to a distant murmur. She knew Gwri was fading without even looking at him. Already she felt his hands sliding away from her waist. Half a moment later his weight shifted. He was falling. She gripped the side of his tunic more tightly, but she could not keep hold of him. Urging Tohr toward the tree line, she then pulled in on the rein and called out for him to stop. He softly checked himself as his riders' weight grew more unbalanced. With a slow thump, Gwri landed in the long grasses at Tohr's feet.

Finockt slid off Tohr's back and fell to her knees beside Gwri. His breathing was labored, and his face was quite pale in the failing light, much paler than before. Above the trees the sky was gold and cream, and the first gentle sounds of evening had just begun to sing over the small, open field. With the crickets' song, a sudden coolness followed, creeping in over the land, its encroaching presence licking up what remained of the day's heat, and on the wake of its coming, Gwri broke out in a fresh sweat.

Finockt brushed his hair back from his face, and worry puckered her brow. "Gwri, can you move?" she asked him.

"Aye," he replied. His voice was weak and came out in a shuddered breath.

"Come on then, we've got to get you out of this clearing."

With Finockt's help, he stumbled to his feet and would have collapsed again had she not ducked under his arm and held him steady. He pressed a hand to his wounded side and leaned heavily on her as she led him through the willowy grasses to an old beech tree. When she had helped to settle him against it, she dropped onto the grass beside him. Gwri closed his eyes and set his jaw against the harrowing pain. "I should go back," he groaned.

"Don't be a fool!" Finockt snapped, her eyes bright with disbelief. "You're on the brink of death as it is."

"Am I?" He drew his breath in sharply through his teeth and dug his heel into the earth in an attempt to position himself more snugly against the beech's wide base.

"Let me see your arm." Finockt leaned forward to inspect his new wound. Her eyes narrowed when she drew back the edges of his torn tunic, and a frown pulled the corners of her mouth tight. It did not look good. The gash was quite wicked and deep, and blood flowed freely from it. She lifted the tattered folds of her light green skirt and tore a long piece from around the bottom of her once white underdress. This she wrapped firmly about his arm several times then tugged the fabric into a tight knot.

Gwri looked up into the depths of her hazel eyes. "You look as if you are ready to keen the dead," he said as she mopped the sweat away from his temples with a cleaner edge of her torn skirt.

Finockt avoided his gaze. "You might *have* died out there, Gwri, if I hadn't…" She broke off, her eyes brimming with tears, and she turned away so Gwri would not immediately see her torment.

"Is it so impossible to tell me the truth," she finally said, facing him, her cheeks stained with tears. She swallowed. The words took courage. "Tell me. Tell me what you would not tell me in times past—there must be some reason for your sudden avoidance of me. All your speech of dying and…"

Gwri closed his eyes. "Don't Finockt. Leave it lie." He licked his dry lips.

"Is there no hope of happiness between us then?" she asked. "Is that not what you sought at Thorlóthlon?"

His heart tore within him. "Some water, Finockt," he said instead. "Please, some water."

She looked upon him, her eyes like flint, but behind that grave stare, her spirit crumbled. Gwri easily saw it, but still he could not speak; the truth hurt too much.

Pushing herself to her feet, she walked away. Gwri watched her go, and when she was a safe distance from him, he fumbled in his pocket and brought forth a silver brooch bearing the wide, glaring eye of a polished amethyst stone. He stroked the oval cut jewel with his thumb. What was he doing? What had he done?

Trapped in the jewel's purple face was the truth of why he must sever his bond with Finockt. But he could not. Not yet. With a frustrated sigh, he drove the amethyst deep within his pocket once more, then tilted his head back against the beech, and closed his eyes. He wanted to tell her now, to reveal the truth. But he could not. The nagging thought would not let him be: perhaps there was still hope.

Finockt drew her skirt closer about her and trudged through the dense, browning grasses to Tohr. The light was fading quickly now, and the open field deepened to a greenish black with the coming night. A light, cool wind drifted over the meadow, sending autumn's first fall leaves skittering and wheeling freely over the changing grasses until they suddenly collected within a particularly thick clump of vegetation. Tohr lowered his head and nibbled at the ground, his thick lips picking over the tarnished blades.

"Haí, Tohr," Finockt said. She patted him on the neck in a weak attempt to draw some comfort from him. Her jumbled thoughts made her head ache, and a strange, sick feeling filled the pit of her stomach, as the content of her conversation with Gwri went round in her mind again. Why did he deny it so? He did love her, did he not? Was that not the point of their rendez-vous in the garden at Thorlóthlon? Or was it all a lie? Did he ever really love her? He had to because she loved him, did she not? Or was she just fooling herself as well? No—but yes. Her heart felt so completely shattered, she did not know *what* she felt anymore. Yet love could not possibly die in one day, if it were true. Could it? She reached for the waterskin and instantly felt awkward and foolish when she realized there was no saddle. She laid her head down in misery upon Tohr's back and felt his hide twitch beneath her cheek. Like the cloth she had torn from her dress, this was all pulling away from her, and nothing could be done to stop it or keep it within her grasp. She was losing Gwri in a way that was beyond recovery.

She *had* lost him, and the possibility of resurrecting anything between them was hopeless.

Lifting her head, she wiped her nose with the back of her hand. She did not want to shed tears over something that could not be changed no matter how much it hurt, but the result was not what she had imagined. In place of tears, the weight of a thousand years of sorrow oppressed her. She could feel her resolve breaking. One more brooding thought and the tears pricking her eyes would release in a salty torrent from which she would not be able to recover.

She closed her eyes in frustration, ignoring the few drops that leaked freely down her cheeks, and tried to shake off the inevitable: they should head back to the Glen of Farith—together—but how was she to get Gwri there? Wounded as he was, he could not ride any farther without water or something of sustenance to tide him over, both of which she did not have on her person. Had he a knife, she might fashion a type of sled to carry him back. Gelis had taught her how to weave the supple, sticky slivers of saplings together, if they were cut right. She might also be able to use a strip of cloth to tie each side of the sled to Tohr's makeshift reins. But would it even work? And how long would it take? She had to have the right wood and the right knife. It would take time. Shadows were already moving in, claiming their space, swallowing up the light. With them, a sudden eeriness swept over her, pinning her in place.

She was being watched.

His gaze chilled her, and goose bumps rose afresh on her skin. Her heart drummed in her chest. The silence was strained, and in it the tight stretch of a bowstring resonated. At the sound, Tohr raised his head, laid back his ears, and snorted. Finockt gasped softly. The threat was real. A rush of energy swept over her, immediately clearing her mind. She grabbed a fistful of Tohr's mane and jumped up in a frantic attempt to mount him when the black arrow sprang loose from the bow. A flash of pain thrust her forward, burning its way over her shoulder and down her arm, the intensity of it cramping every muscle, widening and spreading until it threaded the excruciating spasm into her left shoulder as well. Movement was impossible. In a daze, she felt her hands and legs slip from Tohr's satin back until she was face down in the supple grasses beside him. Spooked, he skittered away at her fall.

The grass was cool beneath her cheek, the heat of day already gone from it, and the long blades parted with a rustling murmur as the archer marched across the field, his stride quick and steady. Finockt looked for some point of reference. But the line between earth and sky could not be determined, and night's lengthening shadows pulled heavier shades over her eyes. Still he came. She clutched the grasses and attempted to crawl away from him, but the contraction of her muscles only inflicted more suffering upon herself to the amusement of the enemy. She froze. He stood beside her, stuck a boot beneath her rib, and tossed her onto her back. The arrow's fletching splintered and snapped under her weight, the pressure driving its tip more deeply into her flesh until it stood at a steep angle. Finockt screamed and gasped for breath. The pain was impossible now. Sobs racked her. She rolled onto her side to ease her torment and clamped a hand down on her shoulder with an iron grip—a desperate attempt to subdue the hellish, searing pain of her wound. But this endeavor only made things worse.

An amused murmur escaped her aggressor's lips. He kicked her feet out of the way, and kneeling beside her, pried her fingers open, removed the cross, and yanked the chain free from around her wrist. Finockt heard snatches of his speech as she drifted in and out of consciousness. The voice was harsh and venomous, full of malice and rage, typical of a Dúnarian; and yet, there was a gentle difference to it that was difficult to place.

"I should have done this long ago when I had the chance," the man said. "Finally I shall avenge myself and earn my place. I'll be free, as hopefully you will be. If there was another way, I promise you, I'd take it. But as it so stands, so must it then be: one life for another. Farewell, Cousin. May God show you the mercy I have begged from Him for myself. Know that the torment of us both ends here, this day, as I have yet hoped and prayed. My death and yours is inevitable. There is nothing we may do to redirect our fate."

Finockt made no effort to save herself. It took enough of her energy just to maintain consciousness. She heard his sword ring out from the sheath, followed by his blade buffeting the air. Her breath faded, and pain darkened her mind until she heard and understood no more.

Gwri's blade blocked the enemy's strike just before it pierced Finockt's flesh. With one excruciating push, he knocked the nobleman away from her.

The Dúnarian looked upon him and snickered through his helmet. "You have chosen the wrong man with whom to pick a fight, lad." His voice was deep and gruff, and he gripped his sword tightly with both hands.

"I think not, Tirell," Gwri replied, his blade ready.

The other just laughed heartily. "Tirell. Yes, of course." Gwri's eyes narrowed at the mocking tone in his voice. Eager to claim victory, Tirell lunged forward.

They fought for several minutes, blocking one another's blows and throwing each other off balance, but each man held firm. Tirell was like a dragon unleashed from his chains. His eyes flashed brilliantly the hatred and rage he felt within, and he struck with the strength and intensity of ten men. Equally vexed, Gwri fought back with all the strength he had left. His strikes were well-timed and well-placed, and he always stayed one step ahead of Tirell until Gwri gouged him in the arm. Surprised by the accuracy of the strike, Tirell paused in his sword play and stood strangely still. His grip on his sword tightened into a death-like vice. Little by little an incredible ferocity overcame him when the sting of his wound sharpened and he observed his gray tunic stain crimson. At the darkening stance of the enemy, Gwri stood on the defensive, his whole body tensed for Tirell's advance.

Now thoroughly enraged, Tirell leaped forward and thrust and struck, whipping his blade back and forth in such a manner that Gwri could not rightly anticipate his adversary's next move. The advantage lost, Gwri stumbled back, losing ground every second. The blade swung around again, this time toward the earth. The strike was parried. Incensed, Tirell drove down hard upon him. Gwri could smell the sweat beneath the helmet, and Tirell's breath sounded heavy against the silence and seethed in Gwri's ears. "You should have been wiser, lad, for now death is at your door," he snarled. With a twist of his arm, he jerked the pommel of his sword upward. Gwri's head snapped back, and the next thing he knew, he was lying on the ground with Tirell standing above him. He groped for his sword, but it was out of reach. His fingers kept searching for the hilt when the flash of metal split the evening light. Gwri tensed, waiting for the impact, pain, and draining weakness of death, when Tirell froze and horror crossed his concealed countenance. He looked up, his face full of suffering, but Gwri witnessed nothing more than the silver of Tirell's helmet, now dull gray by twilight, flipping backward toward the heavens. His back arched sharply, and he fell, knees first, onto the cool earth.

Chest heaving, Deverell stood behind him. "And you should always remember to watch your back, my friend."

Gwri released a sigh of relief when he saw Tirell drop face-down onto the ground and Deverell left standing in his stead.

"Are you all right?" Deverell asked, stepping around Tirell's dead body and extending his hand. His breath still came quickly. He leaned on his sword, and a look of deeper sorrow passed over his tired face.

"Aye," Gwri replied when he had regained his footing. He looked Tirell over slowly, his gaze holding steady beside Tirell's shoulder. Reaching beyond it, he plucked Finockt's necklace from the ground and looked with disgust upon the nobleman's lifeless body. A sudden rage shot through him. He knelt beside the dead man, his hands poised to remove the Dúnarian's helmet, but then, as if on second thought, he decided against the dishonoring action. He rose instead. "He has finally been given what he deserves."

"Don't speak so," Deverell reprimanded him. "Given time, he might have been a good man."

"A good man? When, Deverell? I believe your one weakness of seeing people how you want them to be, not how they are, has conquered you this day. Your attribution of goodness is impossible, for that man has only ever been—"

"Where's Finockt?" Deverell interrupted.

Gwri's eyes riveted on the wall of grasses which partially

hid Finockt's still body, and panic drew lines across his visage, too, as he and Deverell ran to her side. Deverell was the first to reach her. He dropped to his knees, and his face crinkled with concern when he saw her neck and the grasses around her red with blood. The black arrow's tri-barbed tip was still buried at an odd angle in her shoulder. He turned her gently in his arms and tucked her against his chest as he ran his hand over her wound. His heart tore within him. The arrow was deep. It butted up against the skin beneath her collar bone. He could feel the tip protruding under his finger.

Stabilizing the arrow at the site of her wound, he gently broke off as much of the shaft as he could. Once again, he inspected the area where the arrow had entered. Aside from all the heinous things he had ever witnessed in his life, the sight of the arrow buried in Finockt's flesh turned his stomach the most. The one thing he hated more was the fact that he had to remove it.

CHAPTER THIRTY-THREE

DEVERELL TORE BACK the yoke of Finockt's gown and positioned his fingers more artfully around the arrow's shaft. The arrowhead would not be easy to extract. Forbearance and nimble fingers were needed to free it. He looked up at Gwri who nodded, his white face blanching whiter. Deverell tamped her skin down and pushed. The arrow bulged, like a bull frog's throat, against its fleshy barrier before it broke through Finockt's skin and the jagged barbs slid free of her shoulder. She briefly woke and moaned pitifully before fainting again. Tears hung like glass rims upon Deverell's eyes at the appearance of her torn flesh. "Hold on, Finockt, hold on," he whispered, cradling her body against him and applying pressure to the wound.

He slipped his other hand into his tunic, and drawing some herbal concoction and a fine powder from it, he moistened both herb and powder with water poured from a small leather pouch hooked on his belt. These he made into a thick salve before carefully smearing the fragrant paste into her gaping wounds. Then he quickly bound her shoulder, lifted the unconscious girl up, and set her on Tohr's back. Gwri placed one arm tightly around her waist and pulled her to him, until her head naturally nestled in the crook of his neck.

"Take her back to camp. I'll meet up with you later," Deverell said.

"Aye," Gwri replied with a nod. "And thank you, Deverell."

Deverell nodded, Gwri squeezed Tohr gently in the sides, and Finockt's faithful companion lurched into a gentle canter. When they had gone, Deverell turned back with a troubled heart to bury Tirell.

When the last tuft of dirt had been laid, he knelt in the soft earth beside Tirell's simple grave, devoid of all pomp and noble adornments and sheltered only by the massive eaves of an old elm. "I'm sorry it ended this way," he said. "Yet unto me will you forever remain the man I once knew, and the man you could have been, Finain of Galóthlon."

Still kneeling beside the grave, Deverell lifted Finain's bloodstained sword from the ground and held it by the cross bar, its tapered point supported by the earth. Ambiguous feelings of relief and sorrow filled him. The war between them was over. It cost more lives than they could count, but it was finally over. For several minutes, he knelt in the thickening silence under a darkening night sky. There was something in him that did not want to leave. A greater sorrow filled him for a life lost. An irretrievable breath that would never stir again. All of it was gone. The sadness of a life unchanged—unwilling to change—and the consequences of that unchanged life reached to the core of him, touching him with a grief and sorrow so profound he nearly drowned in it. All his life he had hoped Finain would give himself up to the man he could truly be. And now, all that hope had been whisked away. No one could infuse his body with life again or bring back the hope of his soul one day being renewed. The unchanged was now permanent.

He laid Tirell's sword in the freshly broken dirt and pressed it hard into the upturned earth with his palms. For as long as it would remain, its presence was the only token and solemn mark of a lost warrior's marred and mangled past. His hand lingered on the crossbar, and for a moment, his eyes narrowed, taking in the intricate craftsmanship and the shape of the hilt and pommel. The sight was not what he expected.

He rose, shock illuminating his features. He needed Banain to confirm it. The faster they returned to Thorlóthlon, the better. He hoped what he surmised would remain untrue. For now, he would return to the Glen of Farith and warn Strahan, Cronan, Boynton, and the others.

"Farewell, brother," he said, looking one last time upon the hastily made grave.

Then he turned and made his way back to the others under the veil of night.

Upon reaching the encampment, Gwri gingerly passed Finockt off to the nearest member of Thorlóthlon's army, leaped down from Tohr, and followed them into an empty pavilion amidst a flurry of frenzied human activity. After she had been settled on a cot, he stayed and looked upon her a moment while the healers and servants redressed her wound; his heart ached within him. When he could stand the sight of her injury no longer, he left, silent and grim.

For four days, Finockt remained delirious. Deverell stayed fast by her side whenever the moment could spare him, administering his herbal nostrums as needed, while Gwri found himself beside her for as long as he could emotionally withstand, his heart and mind endlessly battling the tempest of love and duty.

His mind lay heavy, and his heart gravely burdened, as he sat beside Finockt on this fifth day. Her fever had finally broken, and her arrow wound did not look so red or so angry. Heat no longer emanated from it, and the skin around it had normalized. So it seemed she was finally on the mend. Deverell, feeling she was safe, had departed to attend the king, and the maidservants had disappeared. For the moment, Gwri was alone. He looked solemnly upon Finockt's still features and listened with an anxious ear to her slow, soft breathing. Privacy and solitude became his temptation. His heart burst, and words unprovoked, unchallenged, and unbridled sought wings upon his lips only to fall upon deaf ears. Finockt neither stirred nor shifted upon the tiny cot. And when he fully realized his error, a sudden relief overtook him, and he was at once glad she was not able to bear witness to such an untimely profession of love. In that merciful instant of grace, he knew what he must do: here he must now relinquish all thoughts of felt love toward her.

Removing the cross from his pocket, he pressed it into the palm of her hand and kissed her lovingly upon the forehead as he had previously done at Thorlóthlon on that fateful night when Darce had made an attempt on her life. His blond hair traced her cheek, its touch drawing her from lost memory and time as it had once before. Her eyes fluttered, and somewhere between wakeful consciousness and deep, insentient sleep, she perceived his kiss and felt him draw his lips from her forehead. All the while she was also aware of the solid press of the pendant in her hand. Scruples, however, led her to keep her wakefulness secret, and as she made no pretense at mindful consciousness, Gwri straightened, and with a clear conscience, he crossed the tent and thrust the tent flap out of his way.

A young woman reeled back as he exited.

"Forgive me, milady…" he mumbled with a bow of his head, and then he strode into the encampment without looking back.

The young maiden looked after him, a frown furrowing her brow, and she wondered what troubled him. But seeing he was in no mood to be stopped, and knowing by the lowered brow and hooded eyes she could most likely not fix what ailed him, she proceeded to enter the pavilion with a wide pewter basin balanced on her hip. Some of the water splashed over its side, darkening her skirt, as she crossed the tent space.

Finockt stirred on the cot and blinked, straining to familiarize herself with the stranger who approached. But disuse of her eyes for several days had produced a persistent haze that marred her vision, rendering her sightless, but for the dark outline of objects in the tent and persons who came and went, their darker forms overriding the warm blue blur that the colored pavilion manifested when the sun shone in full. Presently, she heard water flowing into a basin. Next she felt a cool cloth gently touch both her cheeks before it was draped over her eyes. A few minutes later, the young maiden removed it. Finockt blinked at the sudden transition from darkness to light. She opened her eyes, squinting and blinking repetitively. Finally, her vision cleared, and her gaze focused on the dark tresses of the girl who sat beside her.

"Welcome back, milady," a sweet voice said with a laugh.

"Liusaidh!" Finockt exclaimed amidst a sudden flux of tears and a heartbreaking sob.

"Aye, my sweet friend, I'm here." She took Finockt's hand and reached for her.

Finockt half rose to return her embrace, but the pain of her wound was sharper than she realized. "Ahh!" she moaned and violently arched her back.

"Forgive me." Liusaidh's face flushed with guilt. "I forgot about your shoulder."

"As did I," Finockt replied. "But it is best I sit up. I have lain for too long. Will you help me?"

Liusaidh willingly obliged. The act took so much energy Finockt only wanted to lie down again and stamp out the unbearable burn drawing across her skin. Her knife wound felt like a scratch compared to this new torment. She settled against the feather pillows Liusaidh propped up for her and then looked at her friend.

"I'm so glad you're here. Seeing you, I am greatly comforted."

"My heart's sentiments exactly," Liusaidh said and took Finockt's hand again.

"How long have I been here?"

"Five days. We were wont to believe you'd never wake up." A smile lighted her face now that Finockt had recovered enough to wake and talk. Her charge had escaped infection of both wounds so far; the skin had advanced well and started to knit itself back together. With time, Finockt would heal nicely but for a few scars and the memory of obtaining them.

"And Deverell and Gwri?" Finockt asked. "Are they safe?"

"Aye, they are quite well and recovering nicely from their

wounds. The war is over. Thorlóthlon's future—and ours—is bright."

Finockt sighed. "And you, Liusaidh? How's your mother?"

"She passed away nigh on three mornings ago—ah, there, there," she said at the increasing sorrow dampening Finockt's eyes. "She's in a far better place now and no longer suffering, and that brings comfort to my aching heart. She is well again. I have shed many a tear and will continue to do so, and yet, in some regard, I believe my grieving for her has been lifted but a little from my heart, and yet…and yet for…"

Liusaidh broke off. Her voice quivered, and fresh tears blurred her vision. Finockt tensed. She knew what Liusaidh was about to ask, and she did not want to answer her.

"My Gawain…is it true, Finockt, is he really dead? They say it was you who saw him die."

An onslaught of tears flooded Finockt's eyes, and she wrapped her hand more fully around Liusaidh's. "'Tis all my fault, Liusaidh. If it weren't for me, he never would have been caught up in all that has passed."

"It is true then," she said and rocked back on her heels in defeat. "My heart still held hope that perhaps it was not, but I think I knew. I think I just did not want to believe it."

"Oh, Liusaidh—"

"Don't Finockt, don't. You mustn't blame yourself for it. And do not believe I would ever blame you for what has come to pass. It was of his own free will that he came to your aid, not by staid promise begged from those of a higher service than he." Tears coursed unheeded down Liusaidh's face. She stifled a gut-wrenching sob and covered her face with her hands.

Finockt's heart broke all over again. "He saved my life, Liusaidh," she said. Her voice cracked with sorrow and guilt.

"Mine and Gwri's. If it weren't for him, we would never have escaped Caldária. I will forever be grateful to him and to you. His sacrifice is your sacrifice—he is Thorlóthlon's hero and mine. No one can ever strip him of that."

Liusaidh hugged Finockt so hard her shoulder burned, the pain of it bringing hot tears to her eyes and darkening her vision. She disregarded the galling misery of it as best she could and clung to Liusaidh. "His last thoughts were of you," Finockt added with a sob when they parted, "and his last words were to you. He wanted me to tell you that he loved you."

At this, her friend burst into happy yet bitter tears. The two girls tightly embraced once again, until Liusaidh broke away, tears still flowing down her cheeks. "You should rest now. I have stayed too long." She sniffed and wiped at her eyes.

"I'm so sorry, Liusaidh. Truly I am."

"Rest. I'll gather some cooler cloths." Liusaidh's face crumpled briefly under another mind-numbing rush of grief before she flawlessly composed herself again and rose. Meanwhile, Finockt lay back down and covered her face with both hands. Shame and guilt overwhelmed her, drowning out all thoughts and clarity of mind, when shouts suddenly issued forth from outside the tent and Eoin came running up fast, calamity written all over his small face. "Milady! milady!" he yelled, storming through the pavilion's entrance.

"Hush, Eoin!" Liusaidh scolded. "Your voice is loud enough to scare the devil himself! Thy Lady seeks repose!"

Scowling at Liusaidh, Eoin pushed past her and ran to Finockt. With a grimace, Finockt sat up taller, supported by her elbow.

"Milady! I have been looking for you everywhere!" he panted. "Are you any better?" he then asked.

Finockt smirked. "I'll manage," she said. "I saw you in the tree before I left the encampment. Thank you for saving my life."

"God gave me the courage when I needed it."

"So He did. And your action gave me the advantage I needed to escape. Perhaps you have a warrior's heart after all."

A glowing smile brushed the corners of his little mouth, and he bobbed a short, crisp bow. "You kept your promise as you said you would," he added.

"As did you." Finockt smiled back.

"But you must come quickly!" he now said, his tiny face mirroring her need for haste. Finockt drew up in alarm, and he briskly motioned for her to follow. "The king has called for you! Hurry, milady," he cried over his shoulder. "There's not much time!" Then he darted out amongst the tents and disappeared.

Grimacing again, Finockt rose with difficulty from the cot. Every minor use of her arm fanned white-hot flames of pain down into her hand and across her shoulders. Her arm was stiff from disuse, and she cradled it with her other hand as she hurried after Eoin. Liusaidh walked beside her and gently supported her as they crossed the camp and made their way to Coinneach. Worry puckered Finockt's brow. Her grandfather's urgent summons instantly filled her with dread; she did not like to think what his news might entail. For certain, she expected the worst.

CHAPTER THIRTY-FOUR

When Finockt reached her grandfather's tent, she was startled, despite her anticipation of it, to find a large crowd of Thorlóthlon's company and their allies all congregated there, somber and silent, as if already in mourning. She searched their faces for the truth behind their assembly as they parted before her. Slowly, she passed by them, Liusaidh still at her side. The more she searched the few women's faces that were present, the more dismal they grew, and tears glistened all the more brightly on their rough or young and flawless cheeks. King Aonghus of Anvelúth stood solemn, not far from the tent, and so did some of the other kings and clan nobles she had seen at Coinneach's banquet. Aonghus grimly nodded at her when their eyes met.

"Forgive me, Finockt," Liusaidh said softly beside her. "I should have warned you…" She stifled a sob and placed a hand to her mouth to staunch the tears rising in her throat.

At Liusaidh's distress, Finockt's heart jolted within her, and sensing the sudden, desperate urgency resonating throughout the crowd, she hastened toward the bloodstained entrance to her grandfather's tent. A soldier pulled back the flap, and she left Liusaidh behind.

Daylight illuminated almost too brightly the tent's interior. Then darkness snuffed the brilliant glare when the guard let the thin wedge of fabric fall back into place. Finockt's eyes quickly adjusted to the dim glow of candlelight near Coinneach's bedside. On the ornate, sturdy bed cushioned with eiderdown mattresses and pillows and yards of expensive and warm woolen covers lay Coinneach himself. Solemn and still, Uisdean stood opposite the bed in the shadowed recesses of the tent. Beside him stood Deverell. Finockt looked to her brother. His hands were clasped in front of him, his stance stoic and deferential—a mirror image of the Northerner—and upon her brother's downturned face, she saw he already wore an expression of grief and loss.

"Is he…?"

"No," Uisdean assured her. "He is but resting."

Slowly, Finockt turned her eyes upon her grandfather. With measured steps, she approached the ornately carved bed and knelt beside it. Coinneach was very still, and his face was wrinkled with pain. The family thus assembled, Deverell slipped out of the tent and left the three in peace.

"Sire?" Finockt called softly.

He coughed a deep, rough bark that gave her a start.

"What's wrong, Grandfather?" Finockt then questioned in earnest.

His face had turned bluish and was ashen now, which alarmed her gravely, and he worked to clear his throat.

"I'll not lie to you, Granddaughter," he said when he had

caught his breath. "I'm dying. I've been dying since before you arrived at the stone walls of Thorlóthlon. I've not much time left. God has granted it so. I can feel it in my bones." He ended with a series of more violent coughs.

"No, Grandfather!" Finockt said in a hushed voice, trying not to cry. "You'll regain your health again in no time. You'll see. The war is over. We've won! There is nothing more to fear. All you need is long rest and healing and the refreshing breeze of the Highland air."

"Finockt," he said, taking her hand in his cold one, the difference in temperature alarming her further. "It's too late for all of that, lass. No amount of healing or fresh air can cure a man's appointed time. A healing better than this world can give is coming. I hope you understand, and I hope you will forgive me one last time for the pain I have caused you. I tried my hardest to change my ways, but it seems that change is much harder than I thought it to be—even more so for me."

"But…"

"No. No buts now. I have talked to Malise and straightened my life out for sure. All will be well again soon. I just pray you can find it in your heart to forgive a cross old man for all the pain and misery he has so cruelly and heartlessly inflicted upon you."

"Of course, Grandfather, of course," Finockt cried, holding his hand to her cheek.

"You're right you know. The kingdom is safe now, my darling lassie. Your brother will be king in my stead. The people will embrace him when they realize his lineage and my choice. It is settled. I've told that young man of yours I hope he will serve well under Thorlóthlon's banner when it is needed, and

I've extended my highest apologizes to him for the way in which I treated him. I needed you to know that."

Finockt shook her head. A tear slipped from the inner corner of her eye, trickled down her nose, and dropped onto Coinneach's broad chest; she sniffed softly.

"You've made me proud, lassie," Coinneach whispered, his breathing slowing with each labored gasp for air. He fingered her cheek gently with his hand. "I love you, Finockt," he gently whispered. "Promise me…you will always follow your heart—for yours…like your father's…speaks truth…when all others'… fail."

Finockt gazed upon him in wonder, baffled by his assertion, and her heart warmed all the more toward him because he had accepted her, had approved of her; and all in the same moment, it collapsed with guilt. "You can't die, Grandfather, not now, not after all I've said and all I've done!" she cried in a dismal whisper.

"Haí, now, love," he said. "That's not…remembered. You're forgiven, lass…and were…and were…the moment you said it. My heart told me the same. Ah," he sighed and breathed deeply. "I…love you, Finockt. I love you."

"And I love you, Grandfather," she said, clasping his hand between both of hers and kissing it. Her tears fell to mingle with the cold, clammy wrinkles woven about the back of his hand.

Coinneach looked up at the top of the pavilion and sighed contentedly. "He's come to take me home," he said distantly, "as He promised." He closed his eyes, his hand went limp, and then a peaceful smile melted over his lips. He was gone.

Uisdean approached the bedside and laid a kind hand on Finockt's shoulder. "He asked us to bury him alongside our grandmother, Emanon, at Thorlóthlon," he said quietly. "We leave in the morning. You had best get some rest tonight. I'll come back for you in a while."

Finockt could not answer. It took all her strength to prevent an explosion of sobs and to quell the stifling rise of throat-numbing tears. The only sign of her anguish was the heave of her shoulders under the sorrows of death.

Vaguely, she heard Uisdean announce the King of Thorlóthlon's death to the people present. Broken sobs emitted from the women and the unleashing of swords came from the soldiers, as they showed the proper signs of respect upon the death of their king. And as expected, following these outward signs of respect, an inward turmoil grew amongst the people gathered there. Their hope had died. For, in their eyes, Thorlóthlon was now leaderless.

Finockt stayed beside her grandfather until the tall white candles sputtered and fought for further life and dimmed the tent so that it was nearly pitch-black within. Eventually sleep overtook her. The next thing she knew she was in Uisdean's arms, and he was carrying her to Liusaidh's tent where he placed her gently upon a cot and pulled a blanket up close around her. Then he left without a word while Liusaidh climbed into a cot on the other side of the pavilion and blew out the candle. Finockt heard Uisdean's boots swish against the grass as he strode away, and a tear rushed down her cheek. Tonight, there was something so incredibly mournful in the normal, everyday sound. Numbed by this additional grief, she rolled over and drifted into an exhausted sleep, still clutching her cross in the palm of her hand.

CHAPTER THIRTY-FIVE

FTER SEVERAL DAYS' journey slowed by rain, they returned to the castle, and Coinneach was finally laid to rest beside his wife beneath an ancient carved stone tablet in the tomb of kings. The site now lay wreathed, as tradition indicated, in the fragrance and color of many flowers. For Coinneach, it held what remained of Thorlóthlon's late summer blooms.

Uisdean stood long beside the grave, but as soon as the last of the long funeral rites and customs were behind her, Finockt sought comfort in the solitude of the oak forest where she had wandered so many times with Gwri. Her heart bled remorse at her grandfather's death and burned with his loss. So many things had been left unsaid. Knowing this compounded the already complicated torment of his death. She longed to escape it. He had forgiven her, but there was so much more she felt she needed to say, to ask his forgiveness for. It was for this very reason she had left his graveside early. But the garden did not provide the pleasant distraction she so believed it would. Nostalgia overwhelmed her when the first deeply earthy and dusty scent of the mini-woodland entered her nostrils. She pressed farther amongst the oaks, but she could not escape her sorrow. It clung to her, increasing in a new and manifold way, especially when she came upon the garden pool Gwri had shown her all those nights ago. Once vibrant and full of life and warmth, the growing cold of the early autumnal nights and the lingering heat of summer during the day had taken their toll. The flowers had all died, and the tiny waterfall, which had sung so gleefully in spring, now trickled dismally into the pool below. The water's surface no longer sparkled with light but lay still and dull and scattered with clumps of algae and faded lily pads. All had changed in less than a few months' time.

Finockt trailed her hand through a clean patch of frigid water and watched her reflection bob in muddled and distorted ripples. The scene was a confirmation—her walk had not given her the reprieve she sought. She exited the oak grove with less conviction regarding the reasons for Gwri's change of heart than when she had entered, and in leaving the mini-woodland behind, she felt as if she left her heart buried there as well. To her, it was a bad omen. She sat on a bench in the main stretch of the garden and absently rolled one of summer's last white flowers between restless fingers.

"May I join you?"

Finockt looked up at Uisdean and smiled faintly. "Aye, if you wish."

"Don't look so glum," he said, taking a seat beside her. "It's not the end of the world now is it? He hasn't even left yet." He nudged her gently with his elbow.

Finockt felt her mouth suddenly go dry. "He's leaving?" she said, trying to temper the tears that rushed her eyes.

Uisdean's face went blank with surprise. "You were not aware?"

Finockt's silence told him the truth of it. She sat a moment longer then said, "It seems I was not informed about a lot of things, and the list keeps growing."

Uisdean nodded. "I'm sorry you didn't know. He's leaving after my coronation." He leaned his elbows on his knees and pressed his fingers together. "He wants to say good-bye."

Finockt shook her head. "I don't. Let him leave if that is what he wishes. He's not beholden to me."

"I didn't expect that," Uisdean said at the touch of anger in her voice. "After everything he's done for you? And how he's always looked after you? At the very least you could say good-bye."

Finockt fidgeted beside him. She did not want any private encounters with Gwri. "I've given you my answer," she said, and rising from the bench, she took the longer way back to the castle.

Five days later when Finockt returned from riding Tohr, Uisdean met her in the main courtyard. She reined Tohr in near her brother, her cheeks bright and flushed from the wind and her hair wild and unbound. This past week was the first she had been so free since she had left the village. With the Dúnarians vanquished and Tirell dead, the need to remain imprisoned behind Thorlóthlon's high walls was no longer necessary. Finockt found she relished these moments of riding whenever she wanted and however far she wanted.

It was the only thing lifting her spirits since the pall that had fallen over them at Coinneach's death. She dismounted at Uisdean's approach.

"You rode long today."

Finockt handed the reins to the stable boy. "No longer than usual," she replied, twisting her hand lightly around her arm that sustained the knife injury at Caldária.

"Still sore?"

She nodded. "'Tis only an ache I feel alongside my shoulder after I ride."

"Seems you've returned just in time," Uisdean commented. He cast a glance above their heads and Thorlóthlon's high flanking towers. Finockt followed his gaze beyond the castle's gray stones to the dismal, even grayer sky threatening rain, and nodded again. In these last end-all days of summer, the daylight hours still stretched long with heat, but the evening air quickly turned cooler with the first turn of the seasons and often brought a soft rain or storm.

"Walk with me," Uisdean said.

She fell in step beside her brother.

"My coronation is tomorrow," he said when they rounded a bend and stepped into the garden.

"Aye, I know." Finockt waited for him to latch the door closed behind them. "Are you nervous? Is that why you've met with me this day?"

"No. But there is something I've been wanting to show you. We've waited long enough for you to come," he said and took her hand.

"We?"

But Uisdean kept his response secret and led her with increased speed down the garden path and up the balcony steps into the castle. She nearly had to run to keep up with him. "Why all the hurry?" she asked, panting a little as he pulled her up another flight of stairs and through a wide, arched doorway. When she saw the reason for his haste, she fell still in awe.

He had brought her to a meeting room, obvious by the size of the moderate fireplace and the deep gleam of dark wood found in a single large table, complete with long benches and king's chairs at either end. Crimson runners embroidered and edged in gold flowed over the table's rich dark surface and tumbled off each end in a marbled fall of dark red and golden splendor. But it was the tall, sweeping window that affected her. Light flowed strongly through its lattice panes, and its view afforded Finockt the ability to look down upon the lower, exterior walls of the castle and upon Thorlóthlon's eastern valley, whose green expanse was dotted with grazing sheep and long-haired cattle. As surely as the light flowed strongly, it all in the same moment dimmed with the lowering cloud cover, but not before Finockt's eyes enveloped the magnificent artistry laid out over the top of the window. From an elaborate painted frieze set just above the window's arched apex, the whole of her father's artwork extended, revealing the magnificence of a master's highly skilled hand—so very different from the amateur beginnings she had seen on her father's map. The width and breadth and height of this painted landscape dwarfed the remainder of the meeting hall and shut out every distraction around her, while simultaneously drawing her in as though she were a part of its world.

Uisdean stood silent beside her as she took in the free-flowing delineations of the painting. It had struck him, too, the first time he had entered this room, and had held him captive. There was no possibility of merely passing by it. Every inch dripped with color and intrigue and told fragments of a story that must be told again in its entirety by those who knew it.

His eyes followed hers, taking in again the Great Queen's tower rising out of a dewy fog to the west, its blue-white stones filling the soft, mounded land below in an otherworldly sheen of blue haze. Large, winding amethyst-colored trees, thickly foliaged with leaves of the same hue, gathered in competing circles at the foot of the Great Queen's tower, bent their heads together, and tossed dark purple branches above the silver froth and spittle of Evanthia's thundering shores. At the tower's farthest western edges and high above its tiled roofs, night lowered its brow, engrossing the boundaries of the painting in the gentlest wisps of purple-black shadows, while to the east, a warm spring sun broke the horizon, pushed back the sad, lonely shadows creeping in from the west, and gilded in golden bliss high mounds of morning clouds, which rose above the stately round towers and high stories of Thorlóthlon. Interlacing and thistles wove a delicate thread around the foundation stones of the high castle walls, and beyond the castle itself, Thorlóthlon's native trees grew in abundance, each humbly bowing beneath the gray-blue mountain peaks of the North, whose snow melt fed the clear mountain streams and lush green grasses below.

A subtle movement by Finockt stole Uisdean's attention from the scene above his head. She had stepped closer to the painting, a small frown settling over her face. She had come at last to the rendering of the south, where a blackness broiled and writhed, so thick it could nearly be felt, touching the skin with a palpable, eerie whisper. Its presence smothered the ghost of a lavender light, the purple shade meant to represent rolling fields of lavender and heather—flowers with healing powers—both a glimmer of what the Dúnahez might have been had their past been different.

Uisdean let his gaze momentarily linger on the red sheen of fire smoldering under the restless darkness of the Dúnahez, then his eye fell again on Finockt. Her frown had deepened, and by the tilt of her head, he could tell the scene troubled her. He knew what she was thinking: their defeat of the darkness seemed too easy, despite the growing loss of life that occurred, for the severely wounded still daily joined the ranks of those who had already died valiantly in battle. To think Tirell had been vanquished in that one large battle seemed impossible. But it had happened and yet not without lingering changes to Thorlóthlon and her people. Those remaining Dúnarians had given up their arms—some by force, others by choice—and returned to their homeland under the watchful eye of their northern neighbors. A partial military presence had been enforced near their borders to prevent further uprising, and those of Thorlóthlon separated from their loved ones habitually prayed for continued peace and their loved ones' safe return. Uisdean, too, prayed his coming reign as king would hold the kingdoms together and preserve the peace established through victory. But only God knew what was to come.

The light outside Thorlóthlon's walls grew in strength until a stray shaft of brilliant sunlight pierced a hole through the swollen evening sky. It streamed through the open window, illuminating the painting and drawing Finockt's attention to the vast night sky floating high above the entire scene. The dark expanse was perforated with tiny silver gleams and held a great four-pointed star, bright and almost tangible in all its painted glory—a guiding light.

Uisdean tucked his arms comfortably across his chest and smiled at both the change in the painting and his sister when she beheld it. She gasped as the stars and colors continued to brighten with the increasing natural light coming in through the window. Then she held out her arms in further surprise as dusty starlight swept over her skin and cast patterns over her face. Seconds later, outside the open window, dark clouds loomed over the sky, their bulk snuffing out the tawny beams of fading evening sunlight and simultaneously extinguishing the brilliancy of the stars. The patterns dropped from her face, and the cloud cover chased the starlight from her fingertips, until she was draped once more in twilight's shadows.

A touch from Uisdean's hand brought her eyes to his. She looked over his shoulder to find Malise standing in the room and Deverell entering from a side door.

"Grandfather!" She ran and threw her arms around his neck. "Ah, thank God, you're safe!"

"Good evening, lassie!" He wrapped his strong arms about her and lifted her slightly off the floor. "I'm glad to see you are faring well now." His blue eyes twinkled brightly in the twilight, and a happy smile nearly burst the tanned flood of wrinkles about his eyes and mouth.

"And I'm so glad you're here! I've sorely missed you." She clung to him, as if she would never let go, then she caught Gwri's eye over her grandfather's shoulder and gasped softly. She had not seen him enter with Deverell, nor had she seen him since they had first returned to Thorlóthlon to bury Coinneach. Gwri broke her gaze, but not before Deverell caught the discomforting interaction between the two.

"Are you all right? I didn't hurt you, did I?" Malise asked, gently pulling her away from him.

"No, I'm fine. Good eve to you, Deverell," she said when their eyes met a second time. She threw her arms around his neck as well. "I'm so very happy to see you, too."

"Shoulder's all better I trust?" he said with a wink. "You always were a quick healer."

"Aye." Finockt smiled. "Thanks to you it's almost back to normal."

He smiled in return before she turned away from him, her attention drawn by Uisdean's hand in hers.

"Finockt," he said, his eyes bright with excitement. "There's something very special you need to see."

CHAPTER THIRTY-SIX

ISDEAN'S HAND TIGHTENED around Finockt's as he drew her the short distance from the fireside to the large table that filled the center of the room. Its surface was no longer empty. A very long, dark box—much longer and larger and more beautiful than any of the boxes she had ever seen—sat upon the table's wide mahogany slabs and shone with all the familiarity and brilliance that had been etched on her father's lost box, save one thing: like the frieze above the window, this one bore in beautiful, intricate detail the union of the two kingdoms of the East and West: stately towers, amethyst-colored trees, star and sun, hill and sea, and crests of resplendent jade-green waves capped in the bright frothy gleam of fine white jewels. Emerald rivets marched around the top portion of the box, and in the middle of all the scroll work and beauty of the box's face was an exact replica of her golden cross. This time both halves were present and replete with a single, brilliant, round cut emerald set directly between the cross's arms. Below the glittering emerald and just to the left of it was an oddly shaped keyhole. It bore a half-moon that faced the right edge of the box and had tiny slits branching off from each end of the aperture like the head and tail of a star; its presence gently split the cross in half. This was exactly what Tirell had been searching for. No wonder he had so quickly dismissed the other box at Caldária. He had seen this one before, perhaps as a boy wandering these stone gray halls. He had recognized everything she had not. This very box had eluded them all but Uisdean. The more she studied it, the more Finockt marveled at the escutcheon. Eyes shining, she let her gaze travel to the box's lid, upon which lay the same ethereal dwellings of the Great Queen's silver-blue kingdom, its base chiseled with the same weathered, ancient words that lay penned upon Anwyl's version of the box. But now she recognized and understood them.

"Ra vo karantez Doue ganeoch'h, hag an Aotrou Doue da roi nerz da ho kalon," she read aloud, tracing the undulating words with her finger. *"May the love of God be with you, and may the Lord God of Heaven always give strength to your heart."*

It was far more beautiful and opulent in appearance than what her father had drawn on the map she had found at the chapel. On her own, she could never have envisioned anything so striking.

"Where did you get this, Uisdean?" she asked.

"I've had it since I was a lad. Father gave it to me when I was very young. He told me to keep it safe for it was of great value. It was so beautiful and so splendidly made that I kept true to his command and later buried it in a secret place. When you said you had come looking for a box, I knew immediately this was what you were searching for. But by the time

I returned, war had already broken out, and it was too late to do anything with it. Yet now the time has come."

It was true then. Uisdean *was* part of the mystery without even knowing it. The water-stained parchment was not a loss, for the mystery still unveiled itself even without the parchment's aid.

"Can you open it?" Finockt asked. Her voice trembled with excitement.

"We'll see." Uisdean gripped the sides of the lid and gave a slight tug upwards, but nothing happened. "Perhaps there is a secret trigger or something," he mumbled while examining the outside of the box.

"Did you not *ever* open it?" Finockt asked.

"No, never. Father told me it was not to be opened until the appointed time. This he said I would gradually come to know and recognize, for the times of the age would reveal it to me."

He leaned forward, and a gold chain slipped free of his loosely tied shirt. It swung down in front of him to reveal the solid form of a halved golden pendant.

"Uisdean!" Finockt cried out when she saw it. "You have a cross!"

"Ach, well, I've had it since childhood," he said nonchalantly, now fiddling more intensely with the chest.

"And it's plainly broken on its left-hand side."

"Aye?" Still fiddling with the box, Uisdean glanced up at her impatiently. "It always has been."

"As has mine." She pulled her halved cross up from below her neckline, quickly unfastened its newly mended chain, and held it flat in the palm of her hand to show him. "Do you not see? Tirell said that it was useless. That he had no desire for the necklace, for he claimed it was not that which had been bound to Arnorylja, the Great Queen!"

"For sure it was Arnorylja's," Deverell interjected, "even though it has been cloven in two. And as the prophecies and legends bespoke, its silver radiance has burned to that of gold."

"Uisdean, did Father ever say what the necklace was for?" Finockt now beseeched him.

"No," he answered softly in remembrance. "I do not recall ever asking him about it. I fear I was much too young to fully understand any of its significance."

"Do you not see it even now?" she asked, trying to contain her exhilaration.

Uisdean frowned at her. "No, I don't suppose I do."

"It's a key!" she exclaimed, shaking her head at him and laughing.

"A key?"

"Yes! May I see it? Oh, never mind! Just take it off! Take it off!" Finockt cried and madly reached for his half of the cross.

"All right! All right! Half a moment! Have some patience!" Uisdean almost laughed as he fumbled with the clasp.

No sooner had he extended his half of the cross toward his sister than she took it from his hand and attempted to join the two pieces together. But to her astonishment, one half rejected the other.

"It doesn't work!" she cried, holding the broken pieces aloft in her hands, her eyes wide with shock.

"Let me see." Uisdean, too, took a turn that produced the same result.

Finockt shook her head. "I thought for sure..." A grave sadness filled her. Tirell was dead, but to her great disappointment the kingdom still could not be fully claimed.

To have come so far, to have gone through so much, only to find the way remained blocked—even now. It tested her faith. She looked upon all those gathered around her with a sinking heart. "Maybe we're not to open the box," she said. "Everyone already knows that you are king anyway, Uisdean, for Thorlóthlon's law decrees it, as you are Anwyl's rightful heir."

Her brother paused his continued attempts to snap both halves of the cross together. "Then what use would we have for it?" he asked her. "There must be something in it which is important. Why else would Father tell me to keep it safe and guard it carefully?"

"I believe you're right, lad," Malise said. "Perhaps there is something on the box which will unlock it."

Uisdean set the halved portions of the cross aside and took hold of the box. For several minutes he scrutinized every edge of it and underneath it as well; Deverell helped him.

"There's nothing," Uisdean finally said with a shrug of his shoulders.

"Is it possible Tirell was actually right about something?" Finockt asked, almost under her breath.

"Put the thought behind you, Finockt," Uisdean returned. "There must be a way."

"Aye, your brother is right," Malise added. "We cannot have come this far just to face a dead-end."

Uisdean sighed. "It is a puzzle though. Father knew what he was doing." His fingers worked quickly as he talked, pressing jewels, sliding along the woodwork, avidly searching for a hidden spring or button with no luck. "Perhaps there is something we overlooked on the back, Deverell. Will you help me?"

Deverell nodded, and the two worked to set the box back

down and turn it when Uisdean's end slipped out of his hand and hit the table hard. The sudden impact sprang the jeweled half of the cross loose from the escutcheon, and it fell with a clatter onto the table. Finockt locked eyes with Uisdean. His gaze matched hers, both bright with surprise.

"Can it be?" Malise whispered. Beside him Gwri leaned forward from the shadows and watched Uisdean pick up his plain half of the cross and slowly bring the box's jeweled half toward it. A collective gasp filled the room when, with one soft *click*, the two halves snapped cleanly together. True to its course, the mystery continued to solve itself, a clue or solution always present when the mystery seemed the most impossible to elucidate.

Malise clapped Uisdean on the shoulder with pride. "Well done, lad," he said.

Uisdean looked over at his sister, a crazy grin running from ear to ear. "Well?" he asked. Finockt nodded her approval, while the others stepped closer, crowding around them both in anticipation as Uisdean fitted the end of the cross into the keyhole. In the moments that followed, a growing restlessness and exhilarating silence engulfed the room. Only the whipping fire and the thunk of Uisdean's thick chain when it met the edge of the table interrupted the quiet. With ease, he pushed the golden pendant all the way into the slit, so that the top bar of the cross was the only thing visible. Then he twisted it to the left, and with another gentle *click,* the lid sprang up.

Uisdean turned toward his sister, his face beaming. "Would you do the honors, Finockt?"

"Aye," she answered, the joy in her face mirroring his.

Uisdean moved aside so she could stand before the ancient relic. A silent power rushed her fingers as her hands hovered over each corner of the lid, but she did not sense from it a warning. Rather, she felt as if what she was about to do embraced a meaning more profound than she could imagine. Duty called her to it, and she was not afraid to answer.

She grasped the box and felt the emeralds and the carvings press back against her fingertips. The lid was heavy, and lifting it required more effort than she anticipated. By slow, even measures, she pushed it back. Firelight sparkled off the luminous colors, inlaid wood, and great drops of emeralds lining its edges. Then something strange happened. As Finockt worked to raise the lid higher, liquid silver rays of light streamed with greater intensity from the box and flooded the air, turning her skin an even paler, milky color and brightening her face. Now with the box's elements fully open to the room, Finockt and the others found its padded interior lined with deep blue velvet, and in its midst—on a soft blue velvet mound—lay one of Thorlóthlon's most valued treasures: Arnorylja's royal crown!

"Could that possibly be what I think it is?" Finockt asked, staring at the Great Queen's diadem.

"It could be no other," Deverell answered her, his countenance quietly reflective. "Evanthia's lost emblem."

"One of them anyway," Gwri added.

Uisdean shook his head in wonder at the box's revelation, and a warm giddiness suffused them all. Yet no sooner had the lid been raised and Thorlóthlon's night air touched the royal ensign than a blinding flash of silver light burst forth from the chest, forcing them to shield their eyes from the sudden magnificent, effulgent light. Seconds later, the radiant silver beams vanished, and when their eyes adjusted once more to the dimly lighted room, each drew a breathless gasp, for Arnorylja's once silver crown had deepened to that of brilliant gold, its resplendent state more easily revealing its complex intricacy.

For all around the base of the crown, enclosed in a thin frame, was an intricate golden inlay of scrolling ivy, interlacing, trisceles, heather and thistles, and small seabirds. Above this, rough waves capped with sea foam crested and broke, and rising up between the heads of two larger waves was a sable-blue sword—Brionglóid—bright and flaming—upon the crown's forward curve. Just above these storm-tossed waves, the hot, lucid glow of emeralds upheld the teeth of the crown, each of which gently rose to embrace an elaborate four-pointed star.

The beauty of the crown glowed hot in the firelight. Deverell stood in awe, for though an Evanthian himself, he had never once laid eyes upon the imposing splendor of his people. His gaze now followed Finockt's hands as she reached beyond Arnorylja's crown into a narrow depression for Evanthia's second emblem.

With reverence, she lifted the silver scepter free from the box. She had not even held it long enough to absorb the heat from her hand when veins of gold rippled up from the scepter's rounded base and extended from every angle beneath her curled fingers. Then the scepter, like Arnorylja's crown, glowed a molten silver under the swirling gold, and dazzling beams of light burst forth from the miniature shining stars caught within a fine web of ivy interlacing twisting around the scepter's shaft. With the light, a delicious warmth spread through Finockt's hand and crept up her arm. Yet neither the light nor the warmth harmed her in any way. The only thing she felt was protected, comforted, and reassured. It seemed to work its way inside her, calm her mind, and temper her doubts.

Like the crown, so brilliant was the combination of white and golden light that Finockt was again forced to shield her eyes from its rising glare, as the golden veins intercepted one another until they fused as one and slowly climbed the height of the scepter's shaft in mesmerizing turns. At its summit, the gold continued to swirl, wrapping around the commanding presence of a seabird in mid-flight, its wings outstretched, its underbelly brushing the salt spray of a beautifully curving wave; and set back under the artistic arch of this wave, at its base, was an exquisite arrangement of silver shells, their presence overshadowed by the wave and seabird above them. An instant later, the light was gone. Finockt lowered her arm and looked in surprise upon the scepter to find it was now solid gold, its details emerging with renewed clarity.

Deverell now stood stupefied. Never in all his life had he imagined the box contained anything so beautiful. Nor had the others. They stood around him in a similar manner—all eyes fastened on Finockt in whose hand the scepter shimmered and sparkled—each in the company completely enchanted and unable to speak. The magnificence of the gleaming riches once sheltered by the Great Queen was at the very least astonishing. Both scepter and crown gave silence its full and rightful reign, for in them lay the strength of a quiet force which had, since their inception, incited war amongst those peoples who sought their powers, peace amongst those who lived in their shadow, and power and victory for those in whose hands they lay.

Finockt held the scepter flat in both hands and with pride extended it toward her brother with a sweeping bow. He hesitated then reached for Arnorylja's golden scepter. The grave realization of his duty to kingdom and country was written all over his face when he touched it, and a responsibility such as he had never been given before now settled over his shoulders. He felt its weight fall heavier upon him when he fully accepted Evanthia's second emblem from his sister's outstretched hands.

"My lord," she said with a smile and dipped lower to the flagstone floor. Following her lead, the men also knelt and bowed their heads before him.

At first, Uisdean swelled with an immense pride and a profound sense of obligation, but it did not take him long to understand what the crown would cost him. "Enough! Enough! Stop! I beg of you! Please! Do not bow before me," he urged them, flustered by their attention. "You embarrass me by such honors. I am not king yet, nor did I know I would truly bear such a title until recently. I shall not have my dearest friends, or my sister, bow in subjection to one of their own!"

The men rose, smiles still lighting their faces, and they congratulated Uisdean with hearty handshakes and roughhousing. But something of greater interest snagged Finockt's attention. She lifted a small scroll from the interior of the beautiful box. It was sealed with red wax.

"Uisdean," she said, "there is something written on this."

She handed the parchment to her brother who swiftly laid the scepter on the table and, with a shaking hand, cracked the wax seal. He recognized the writing. With haste he unrolled it and silently began to read words his father had meant only for him:

Dearest Uisdean,

The appointed time has come, my son, if these words are being read. Long years have passed since I bestowed such responsibility into your hands without your knowing it. You were a boy then, and now you have become a man. I am proud of you, for I know you have endured much. If all has come to pass as I so believe it will, your sister lives still and reads this letter at your side. Take care of her, Uisdean, for she is your flesh and blood.

Ah, how my heart breaks within me in this moment! Time can heal, but it can also curse. For every choice made, there is a consequence. Never have I understood this more profoundly until now. I believed my flight from Thorlóthlon would secure my happiness and would ultimately be the path to overcoming Tirell and the key to saving you, your mother, and your sister, as well as be the means to rectifying our future. But I now see the selfish act was committed out of anger and the wisdom of men. My error as king has cost me everything; I cannot protect you. Do not stand alone, Uisdean; there is no power in it. And do not seek the approval of man; it will only lead to ruin. Rather, live your life to please God Who really matters.

Though I do not regret my marriage to your mother or the birth of you and your sister, my only regret lies at the feet of Thorlóthlon and my inability to reconcile with my father. My deepest longing was my downfall, and I have yet to achieve the purpose of my flight: the acceptance of a king—your grandfather—and the defeat of my own cousin. My past actions now threaten your very lives. My only hope is that God will see that you live to fulfill your destiny, as I have hoped and prayed for since your birth. Thorlóthlon's victory will no longer be realized through me, and to my shame, I fear I have left my homeland to fall into ruin and disarray if this meeting with the clan nobles bears no fruit. On my knees I beg forgiveness for it, for there is little hope it will be received warmly. My end has come—and death on fleeting wings behind it; it is a knowledge I have sensed for some time now.

It grieves me to know that, despite my best intentions, I have left naught but a wake of turmoil for you to sift through and perilous roads for you to wander until you inherit the crown—all because I now realize selfish gains and pride drove my life. For this, have I tried hard to set the past aright—to ensure your future—but I have gravely failed. Do not follow my path or my example. Be mindful that only you have the power to forge what I envisioned for you, now that you are free to be Thorlóthlon's king. Follow your heart, my son, and fear nothing, for with God as your Sovereign, Shield, and Defender, you cannot fail nor be shamed.

You are a son of kings, and although I do not know what choice you will make, for over such matters doth my will have little power, in my heart I do know that because of Malise's guidance you will know well in what manner to lead your life. Through wisdom and prayer, I do not doubt you will make the right choices. This comforts me above all else.

Therefore, by my power as King of Thorlóthlon, I hereby declare under God that Uisdean, my only son, is to be coronated as regent in my rightful stead, upon my death, according to the laws and decrees of Thorlóthlon. It is my wish that he rule in my place until old age or death claims his life or until his heir or that of his sister's comes of age to claim the throne as his own. In the event no heir is apparent, he shall choose the man who is most worthy to hold the title of regent.

Know always, my dear son, that I love you.

Signed, Anwyl Toran, Son of Coinneach,

King of Thorlóthlon.

Uisdean looked upon the parchment in silence, his heart breaking.

Finockt studied his countenance but could glean nothing from it "Well?" she finally asked. "What does it say?"

"It formally announces my right to reign as King of Thorlóthlon. These are the official papers which bear the crest of Thorlóthlon as well as the mark of the king. It is done."

"'Tis a humbling honor, my boy!" Malise said, roughly hugging him and then clapping him on the back. "You are definitely most worthy to hold it."

Unknowingly, Finockt felt the same fear and despair Uisdean did. She stood looking at her half of the cross and fingered it gently, watching it glisten in the candlelight. Deverell came and stood beside her, while Gwri and Malise congratulated Uisdean all over again. Yet Gwri discreetly watched and listened more intently to what Finockt was doing and saying than to Malise's hearty conversation with Uisdean.

She picked at the other half of the cross on the box until it popped out as well. Mechanically, she swept it up from the table, snapped both halves together, and gazed at its completed form without much surprise. "I have no use for it now," she said, a bit saddened. "To think each of us had the key, but we couldn't piece together the puzzle until all circumstances were aligned and fate had had its way. We needed each other in order for it all to work. It's strange now to think that all this was for a piece of metal—all the fear, danger, and death. And now…now it's all over."

"And yet it will always be a reminder of what you went through to get to this moment," Deverell replied.

She half smiled and looked up at him. His blue eyes shone even brighter in the firelight, and she felt a sudden comfort in that lingering gaze that she had not felt for a long time.

"The day I first met you seems so very long ago," she said, "but I am strangely glad it has all come to pass."

"Aye, that it does. Though all is well now," he said softly.

"Not quite," Finockt murmured and glanced at Gwri. He started when he met her gaze across the room, but he gave her no vision of hope. Instead, he focused on Uisdean and forced a laugh.

Finockt unsnapped her half of the cross and laid it on the table. Then she placed its other half in its grooved niche about the keyhole. It clicked into place quietly. "I believe I shall retire now," she said abruptly to Deverell. "It has been an eventful day, and I do not feel myself at this moment. I should bid you good-night."

"Aye, milady," Deverell said, bowing his head slightly, his dark hair rushing forward. "I pray you find repose and solitude this night. Rest well."

"And you," Finockt returned, her emotions beginning to get the better of her. She mumbled her excuses to Uisdean and Malise, both of whom bowed slightly and offered their own farewells for the night then resumed their causerie while Finockt headed for the door Deverell held open for her. Gwri stiffened as she left the room, and then he relaxed in the hope no one had noticed his unease. Shortly after her departure, Deverell bid them all goodnight, and then Malise did the same, leaving Gwri and Uisdean alone.

"I've been wanting to talk to you," Uisdean said quietly. He set the golden scepter back beside the crown, closed the lid, and relocked the box. "You seem preoccupied by something. Do you mind telling me what it is?" He withdrew the pendant from the keyhole and put everything back as it was.

Gwri did not respond.

"You're in love with my sister, aren't you? I have seen a change in you. You haven't been the same these past few months…"

"I am betrothed to another," Gwri said in a low voice.

"Betrothed?" Uisdean said in surprise, believing it was for some other reason Gwri reacted so coldly.

"Aye, that's why I'm leaving. It is an oath that cannot be broken, one made long ago by my father. My refusal would only bring shame and dishonor to my family. I see that now. You know I cannot break this vow either, and it is…for other reasons that I leave."

"Does my sister know and understand this?"

"Aye, she does. She knows we cannot be together, though she is not aware of the particulars. I could not tell her, but I believe she understands though she does not want to."

There was silence a moment as Uisdean nodded his head thoughtfully.

"I won't be attending the coronation, Uisdean. I'll be leaving in the morning. It will be better if I go then, for I will not be missed until late."

"Aye, that would be wise." Regret filled his voice.

"I shall retire then, my king," Gwri said, kneeling before him.

"Do not kneel before me, Gwri. You are my friend and like a brother to me, and you are a prince as well. If you are to kneel before me then I shall have to kneel before you."

Gwri rose, smiling faintly, then he clasped Uisdean in a rough hug, and it was with great reluctance that he released him. He gave him a troubled smile and then headed for the door.

"Gwri," Uisdean called.

He stopped in his tracks by the table.

"Where will you go?"

"To Mithel, where my father's people live. I will take his place as king in time, as you are doing now."

"Do not keep the time long between us before we meet again, brother."

"Aye, I will return."

"Until the morrow?"

"Aye, until the morrow."

With that, Gwri turned to leave, and as he did so, his eye caught the enticing glow of Finockt's cross lying next to the box. On impulse, he snatched it up then strode out into the dimly lighted corridor. Uisdean said nothing as he disappeared, but in his heart he grieved for Finockt.

CHAPTER THIRTY-SEVEN

THE HALL WAS quiet. No clink of metal or tread of footsteps echoed throughout the deadly silent castle. In the wee hours of the night, no one was about. Only the dusty blue light of a half-moon filtering down through every crevice, hole, and window of Thorlóthlon kept Finockt company. For some hours, unable to rest, she had wandered the castle at great length before curling up in a lattice window seat that overlooked a starlit garden. But now the draw of sleep led her back to her chamber. Intense nostalgia overwhelmed her as she leaned back against the heavy wooden door and surveyed her room. It was dark, but the moonlight spilling through the arches somehow rendered everything more acutely visible. Her eye moved from the wolfskins and the richly carved bed with its frosty curtained veil and pure white sheets to the warmth of the embers in the fireplace only to return to the peacefulness of the open arches.

The wind blew swiftly through the oak trees beyond the

balcony railing, their movement and sound calling for her. She swept aside the arches' filmy curtains. Without, the September night air was already cool: a welcome relief that foretold of upcoming changes. Many changes. Some of which could not be so easily predicted. The more she realized her future lay fraught with the uncertainty of what would happen next, the more Finockt found she was not ready for it. Another chapter of her life was ending, and she was not convinced she wanted to see it close, despite how painful some of its memories had been and still were. The quest for Evanthia's emblems and the battle to save her father's throne had consumed her, and she now found herself empty, without meaning or a plan for her next step in life. What would happen tomorrow was evident: Uisdean would be crowned king. The people would rejoice, and Thorlóthlon would be saved, as well as the whole of Valínthia and those allied realms adjoining her. She even knew her role: Princess of Thorlóthlon and advisor to her brother should he ever request it. But what truly dedicated purpose would she serve the days and weeks following Uisdean's coronation? And what contribution would she have to Thorlóthlon while in Uisdean's shadow? Nothing could comfort the loss she felt at this vast turning point in her life, and what was worse, Gwri would not be there to help her through it. All her troubled fears and doubts she must face alone. His absence at Thorlóthlon would be keenly felt.

Curling up in bed, Finockt pressed her head into her pillow and stared out the arches. The soft night breezes flowed in gently from the balcony to play with the curtains and lay filled with the sweet, symphonic hum of crickets and the tree frogs' lazy hiccups. But tonight their song seemed unusually sorrowful. It was as if they knew all that Finockt felt and thought, and they refused to let her be. Their chanting drowned her ears with a deep sadness her heart already sang. Soon Gwri would be gone. His mark on her life would be lost forever, and this current chapter she tried hard to hold onto would inevitably close, never to reopen. She was not ready for that. But then she would never be prepared for its ending. Because of this, she could not help but wish that tomorrow would never come. For then time would not change, and Gwri would not leave.

Finockt woke suddenly from her restive slumber. The sun was high in its daily trek across the sky, and a soft wind still blew gently through the trees, rustling their branches, turning over their leaves, and pushing the high, fluffy clouds through the heavens, like a ship in full sail. Finockt raised up on her pillows and stared at the door through blurry eyes. Something drew her from her troubled repose, but what was it?

The answer came when the door opened without a sound and Liusaidh appeared. In the next instant, she heard Liusaidh gasp and saw her reach for the door. But she was too late! Caught in the cross-breeze flowing in through the balcony arches, the door slammed shut with a *creak* and a *bang!* Liusaidh cringed. Slowly, she turned and faced Finockt, guilt still pinching her fair features. "Forgive me, Finockt."

Finockt smiled and wiped the last veil of sleep from her eyes. Then she winced as she shifted her weight and her injured shoulder bore the brunt of her movement. It was still quite tender.

"I was awake before you entered," Finockt reassured her. "What falls the hour?"

"It goes nigh on three o'clock, milady," Liusaidh replied, opening the armoire and pulling from it a silky overlaid gown.

"So late!" Finockt cried, thrusting her feet to the floor.

"Haí, there's no need to rush. Your brother insisted no one was to disturb you until you had arisen on your own. I only come now because the coronation service is about to take place in no less than two hours. Otherwise I would have let you sleep much longer."

Tension turned to fretfulness. Finockt curled her toes into the wolfskin on the floor beside her bed. "Is he already gone?" she asked, rubbing at her arms as if she were cold.

"Is who gone?" Liusaidh asked, hurrying to finish assembling Finockt's dress.

"Uisdean just said…never mind. It's nothing."

Liusaidh gave her a sly smile. "You don't have to keep playing games with me, Finockt. I've known your secret for a long time." She held Finockt's dress up to herself and examined it for wrinkles.

"No…I" A fine blush crept over Finockt's cheeks. She tucked a lock of hair behind her ear, and her eyes grew large and expressive. "How? How do you know such things?" she asked.

"You forget I haven't been gone that long. I could see it in your eyes every time he came around, and I knew he loved you, too, because of his desire to make you happy. Most importantly, I saw it on his countenance when he cared for you in the tent, wounded as you were. His face was a constant mask of concern and worry. No man could love a woman more than he loves you."

Finockt fought back tears. "You believe he loves me that much?" She had not felt that kind of love from another human being since Gelis…or Caslon. Murron's love was like that of a sister: constant and true, even when things grew sour. But love from a man she loved in return, she had never truly felt.

"Aye, I do. Gawain used to look at me the same way."

"Will he come to the coronation do you think?"

Liusaidh almost laughed out loud. "Aye, he should." She laid Finockt's dress at the foot of her bed. "Now come, your bath is ready," she said, her eyes still bright with joy and laughter.

With her bath taken and her hair washed, Finockt slipped into a beautiful emerald green dress. Liusaidh's fingers moved quickly, securing the tiny buttons and the fine lacing at its back, while Finockt smoothed the delicate silver belt around her waist and adjusted it until it hung perfectly centered. Its length reached to the tops of her silver slippers, decoratively stitched with green threads and bits of emeralds to create a delicate weave of thistles, complete with tufts of light purple stitching. The servant girls had gathered dog roses and blue forget-me-nots from the meadow and woods. These they pieced together in tiny bundles, which Liusaidh used in a half-crown to accent the back of Finockt's hair. With the placement of the last flower, Liusaidh then helped Finockt slip into a beautiful sleeveless emerald green coronation robe and tucked Finockt's flowing tresses back over the reddish fox fur collar. The outside of the robe shone with bright, sparkling, four-pointed silver stars; each star's head and tail connected one to the other, all in a line, and marched in perfect order down the length of the sweeping full train.

A last, finishing touch, Finockt donned ornate silver chandelier earrings fitted with emeralds of various sizes. Liusaidh stood glowing behind her. The long preparation for Uisdean's coronation had finally drawn to a very satisfying close on her part.

"You look like a Princess, Finockt! Absolutely beautiful," she whispered as she lightly pulled Finockt's hair back from her shoulders.

"Thank you, Liusaidh. 'Tis you who has worked such magic."

Blushing, Liusaidh proudly touched up Finockt's coppery-red hair and twisted a stray curl or two into final submission. "What? What is it?" she then asked when she looked up and saw the color draining rapidly from Finockt's face.

"My necklace," Finockt said. She reached forward and touched the bare spot on her dressing table. "It's not here. Have you seen it?"

"No, milady. You're sure you didn't move it?" Liusaidh briskly looked over the room, flipped over pillows, and turned back the edges of the wolfskin rugs.

"I could have sworn I left it here this past evening," Finockt murmured. Her mind worked feverishly, trying to identify where she had last placed it.

"Don't worry. It cannot be far. Perhaps it is in the small chest?"

"I don't think so…"

A soft knock stole their attention. Liusaidh hurried to the door. "Wonder who that could be," she said with a grin.

Finockt looked up expectantly as Liusaidh whisked open the door and greeted Malise with a warm smile.

"And how doth thee fare, Liusaidh?" Malise asked her, his voice jolly and bright.

"Well, my lord," she said with a little bow of her head. Her radiant smile never dulled. She shut the door behind him and gestured to the side. "Finockt awaits you."

"Ah, you look beautiful, lassie." Malise beamed when he saw his granddaughter.

His open praise warmed her, and at the same time, his arrival suddenly woke her to the inevitable. She felt her hands grow clammy. "Is it almost time then?" she asked him.

"Almost," Malise answered.

"We need not leave just yet," Liusaidh informed them as she tidied up the room.

"Ah, there is time then for a gift." Malise winked and drew from his pocket a round silver object.

"A gift? For me?" Finockt asked.

"It was your mother's," he replied, laying the warm band of silver in her hand. It was broad and thick and big enough for a man's finger to fit through and engraved on it was a knotted pattern of interlacing and shields, each shield nested in an artistic weaving of ivy.

"My mother's?" Finockt said, marveling at its size and craftsmanship. "But it's so grand!" She slipped it onto her thumb. Even there it was too big. "Did my mother actually wear this?"

Malise burst out laughing. "Heaven's no, child," he said, visibly amused. "It was a gift from your mother to your father. 'Tis a posy ring, given to another in friendship or in the name of love. Look inside."

"*A wir galon,*" Finockt read slowly. "*With a true heart.*" She looked up at him again. "But how did you come to have it? I should have thought it would have been lost alongside them."

"I found it in the wood after the raid. I almost did not see it at first. It was so small next to the charred timber and ash from the caravan. How it survived I know not. Your father was never without it. It was clean and untouched when I came across it half hidden under some blackened floorboards and part of a wheel. Feeling it was an earthly gift of grace from the Lord, I took it up and have kept it with me since that day, waiting for such a moment to give it to you. It is yours now." He kissed her sweetly atop the head.

"Thank you, Malise. Truly. 'Tis an honor to have something that belonged to them."

"Your mother and father had a bond I've not seen in my lifetime, and I doubt I will ever see it again."

Finockt looked at him thoughtfully. "And yet I hope to have that some day."

"Maybe you will, lassie. I can only hope and pray the same will exist for you and Uisdean."

A gentle look from Liusaidh redirected his discourse.

"Ah, speaking of which, the ceremony is about to start. We mustn't keep your brother waiting," he said cheerfully.

Finockt half smiled and rose to follow him when a sudden flux of emotion gripped her. She stopped midway across the room, her heart quickening. The first step she took through that doorway would change her life forever. There would be no going back to reclaim everything that had passed before. Such knowledge both thrilled and petrified her. It was like reliving her first visit to Thorlóthlon. Only then she had felt significantly more apprehension than excitement.

"Malise, I don't know if I can do this," she stammered.

He read the fear and distress abounding in her eyes. "Ah, I see now why you are troubled. Take courage, lass. God will show you what you must do with the time to come. But right now, in this moment, He wants you beside your brother. Your parents would want the same. Rest at present. Tomorrow will bring plenty of its own worry. Don't let this unknown future of yours steal your joy today."

"I agree with him," Liusaidh said, coming alongside her. "You both need each other."

Finockt threw her arms around her friend, who enthusiastically returned her embrace. "Promise me, Liusaidh, no matter what events waylay our lives, our friendship will not wear away. Promise me it won't change?"

"Aye, my dear, sweet Finockt. Stay thy mind to thoughts of peace. Nothing can break the bond we have established. I think we've both seen to that. Now go, your brother is waiting. I will meet you here when all is over." She wiped a tear from the corner of her eye and laughed. "Ah, I think tears are bad luck on a coronation day!"

Finockt squeezed Liusaidh's hand tightly. "I'll look for you in the crowd. Don't be late."

Liusaidh shook her head. "No. I won't be. Promise. Enjoy it. 'Tis a grand day for all of us!"

Finockt nodded and hurried to join her grandfather who still waited by the door. Once they entered the corridor, she felt the vibrant force of change draw her forward. There was no turning back.

CHAPTER THIRTY-EIGHT

ELOW, THE CASTLE thronged with guests and relatives—twice, thrice, even four times removed—who had come from afar to bear witness to the crowning of their new king: relatives of their parents whom Uisdean and Finockt had never known existed before this day and whose relation was confirmed only by those who had been close to Coinneach and knew the family line. Even those of the House of Eilthárion—their mother's family—more specifically their aunt Arnarlwyn—were there. To Finockt's grief and delight, she was able to personally meet with each one of them and thank them for their pledged service to Thorlóthlon and for the gift of knowing their daughter—her dear sweet cousin, Eilidh—whose personal sacrifice and service saved Finockt in a way the House of Eilthárion would never be able to fully appreciate. Eilidh had been Finockt's anchor and spiritual encourager when she needed it most, and her legacy lived on in a way that impacted Thorlóthlon more profoundly than her dedicated service ever could. Finockt would always feel deeply indebted to her. She knew Eilidh would have loved this day. Everywhere Finockt looked she seemed to catch the brightness and quiet vivaciousness of her cousin's bewitching personality.

All throughout Thorlóthlon, garlands of fresh greenery and bright autumn flowers crept over the doors and dangled from the iron torch holders that clung to the castle walls. And representing the final peace accord established by the Great Queen Arnorylja, colorful banners hung all over the castle. Symbols of unity and brotherhood, they bore the crests of all the clans and those of their neighbors and allies—the northern kingdoms and Evanthia. The Great Hall itself was already bursting with color and with scores of people awaiting the much-delayed coronation of their next king.

Malise and Finockt hung back, waiting for the rest of the attendees to enter. Several paused and bowed slightly to both her and Malise before threading their way into the hall itself. Close beside the door, a double row of men stood ready, each one with the smooth, carved arch of a ram's horn in his hand. From where she stood, Finockt could glimpse the farthest end of the Great Hall. The crest of the Gwrithlís and that of Evanthia shimmered boldly upon the lengthy banners that swung free from the ceiling's great rafters—each a symbol of the merging of the old and new Evanthia and the ever-enduring alliance between Evanthia and Thorlóthlon. More banners hung from the walls on either side of the Great Hall, while a deep blue runner, as soft as a bird's wing, flowed down the middle and separated into two large groups those attending Uisdean's coronation.

Finockt leaned forward, searching the hall's interior for anyone she knew, searching mainly for Gwri. But the guests and king's subjects milled too densely for her to see much of anything aside from elegant gowns, braided hair, and men and women of all shapes and sizes; some of the men she recognized from the Glen of Farith.

Malise patted her hand now and again as she periodically stood on tiptoe to see over the assembly. "Be patient, Finockt, he'll come," he encouraged.

She blushed, her temperature fluctuating intensely. First hot and then cold and then unbearably hot again. Did her grandfather know? She did not dare ask him to whom he referred. Instead she nodded and half smiled, her eyes still straining to cover the hive of activity bustling within the Great Hall.

Once or twice, the crowd thinned, and she saw the dais where Uisdean would be given his rights to become king—the same dais where she had first seen Coinneach. But this time, at its summit sat a wide square box instead of Coinneach's high back chair. Thorlóthlon's royal seat stood at the end of the blue runner that climbed three simple steps. It was Valínthian tradition to utilize the very seat that had been used to crown Thorlóthlon's first king, Gaothaire, after the death of his father, Egil, some six hundred years earlier. Carved lion heads guarded its four top corners and at its four bottom corners a clawed paw stretched its toes over the flagstone floor. Filling the gap between each ferocious head and restless ancient foot, threads of carefully wrought gold and silver crisscrossed around each corner post, while in continuous unrivaled craftsmanship, every paneled side of the simple, royal chair displayed the alignment of the two kingdoms: East and West. Glorious gray mountain peaks, flowing green valleys, and the emerald glow of fertile land and wooded plains represented in rich imagery the whole of Valínthia—the kingdom of the East. Crests of waves—some billowing out from the sable-blue sword, Brionglóid and others reaching for the majestic, soaring forms of bright seabirds—represented the kingdom of the West—Arnorylja's haven. Each Evanthian symbol was the Valínthians' tribute to the Great Queen for everything she had done to save them during the reign of Egil and represented the unity and alliance the two kingdoms had forged centuries ago to save Evanthia and her people and to spare all those in the east from suffering the same death, loss, and destruction Evanthia had at the hands of the Úlga-daveen.

Atop the primitive royal throne, a dark sapphire velvet pillow softened the throne's wooden seat. Gold and silver stitching and braiding embellished the pillow's borders, and tassels of the same hues hung from each corner. In like manner, the same gold and silver stitching created a magnificently graceful V in the center of the pillow itself. Directly behind the age-old throne spilled an ancient white banner embroidered with an elaborate four-pointed star delicately surrounded by ivy and interlacing. It cascaded from the lofty blackened ceiling beams and hung between two banners bearing Thorlóthlon's crest: a standing lion whose form represented Christ as the Lion of Judah. The lion's powerful frame was ensconced in a familiar, large V, embellished with interlacing and threaded with vines, heather, and thistles, with Thorlóthlon's motto beneath it—*Mevelien Doue, Mevelien an oll dud. Servants of God, servants to all.* Above this four-pointed star was a letter G: a homage to the Gwrithlís, whose clan now ruled the land of Evanthia and still watched over Valínthia and her people, and expertly anchored below the tail of the star was the letter V. While the exquisite four-pointed star signified Evanthia, the two letters—more recently embroidered over the centuries evident by their more vivid colors—served as another symbol of East and West standing in unification.

The banner sagged gently in some places and now showed signs of wear after centuries of use; of further note, the light, clean creases of a life spent too long beneath the oak slabs of some ancient chest had not yet fallen free. At first glance, turmoil seemed fraught within the banner's weaving, but upon a closer look, its stitching seemed to brighten with hope at the freedom to list in a fresh breeze. Its time had finally come again.

"Look! There he is!" Malise pointed down the corridor.

Finockt's face flushed brighter at the prospect of seeing Gwri when she realized Malise was most likely referring to her brother. She scanned the crowd still funneling into the hall and gleaned the corridors for Uisdean, but there was no sign of him or Deverell.

Malise patted her on the arm and smiled. "Did you miss him, my dear? Ah, don't fret. You'll see him then before long. It shall be our turn to go soon enough." He covered her cold fingers with a warm hand. "You must calm your nerves, lassie. Enjoy yourself! This is your brother's day. And your day as well, for 'tis you who have helped to see him crowned king."

Finockt feigned a smile. The anxiety she felt was not for the coronation ceremony. If only she could see him! She jumped as Malise caught her gently by the arm. "Come, lassie, it's our turn."

Slowly, he walked her onto the long deep blue runner. She felt its softness even through her slippered feet. In five more strides, they passed through the double doors and the short enclosed passage into the hall itself and trod the deep blue path to the coronation site. Ahead of her the assembly's voices softened to a low murmur. Finockt's eyes flew over the crowd, searching and hoping for…A glimpse of fair hair rushed her vision. Her heart beat madly in her chest. It was him! He *had* stayed! But his eyes were not upon her. He was not looking for her as she had been for him. He was too deeply engaged with the young woman beside him. Finockt felt her head spin and her heart snag with a million different emotions, all while silently begging him to look her way. Then the pounding in her ears stopped, and her heart convulsed with fear. Only two more paces and she would leave him behind. The realization made her frantic. She had to speak with him again, before he left, before it was too late. Beside her Malise watched the changes in her face and followed her gaze to the young man. He patted her hand again, and Malise felt her grip inadvertently tighten on his forearm. Just before they had passed him by completely, the young man lifted his face and locked eyes with Finockt. Her heart ascended to the heights of the castle, only to plummet back down when his moss green eyes met hers and the blond hair gave way to dark brown. At her gaze, the stranger respectfully inclined his head.

Finockt quickly averted her eyes. All the color drained from her face, and she stiffened sharply. At the tug on his sleeve, Malise looked down again at his granddaughter, but she would not meet his gaze. Her own lay straight ahead, fastened on the throne, her procession beside him rigid and stone-like. Before he looked away, he thought he saw the shimmer of a tear in her eye.

"Are you all right, my dear?" he whispered. He felt her slump a little.

"Aye, Grandfather, I'm fine."

When they reached the end of the runner, they stepped to the side of the small flight of steps that knelt before the simple throne. Inwardly, Finockt cursed herself as she took her place. She had wanted so badly for Gwri to be in the crowd, she had virtually made him appear. Such foolishness irritated her. Was she *so* desperate for his love she had reduced herself to this? Perhaps. She knew he loved her, *had* loved her, and nothing except his own stubbornness to attend to his sudden obligations led her to believe he no longer did. She needed closure from him, not excuses. She needed the truth in its entirety.

Now threatened by an overwhelming urge to cry, Finockt tapped restless fingers against her skirt and shifted her gaze to the main door. She and Malise stood painfully erect as they patiently, or, for Finockt, impatiently, awaited the others—those of Deverell's men—to join them at their rightful places on either side of the deep blue runner.

Soon Deverell entered, looking handsome in his new attire: a high-collared damask tunic and finely woven breeches. He took his place directly across from her and gave her a quick wink in hopes of cheering her gloomy heart. A faint smile lit her face, and then her attention snapped to the other end of the hall, as the deep, throaty blast of the rams' horns filled the entire room and glaringly announced the arrival of Thorlóthlon's new king.

Uisdean strode down the dark runner. A fine blue velvet cape edged in white-silver and gold flowed from his shoulders. It fit him perfectly. His eyes shone brightly but contained no hint of haughtiness. He was most definitely Anwyl's heir: given great title, he bore no stain of pride or contempt, nor did he chance to believe his new title and rank gave him liberty to disdain others and exalt himself. Finockt was honored to be his sister.

The lengthy coronation itself was magnificent but over all

too quickly. Finockt felt such pride for her brother, who after having declared his allegiance to God first and country second had then been officially crowned King of Thorlóthlon. The emotion of it left her grinning widely. For upon the ceremony's completion, a great cheer had risen to the castle's rafters the moment the Great Queen Arnorylja's crown was placed firmly on his head and her scepter was pressed into his palm.

During the ceremony, Uisdean smiled frequently at Finockt, but now he seemed a little on edge, as if something grave was about to happen. Finockt did not take these changes in mood to heart, as Uisdean had told her a day or so before the coronation he was afraid all the attention would leave him drained and fatigued. He was used to the Highlands and Malise's way of living. The pomp and circumstance of their grandfather's kingdom was a burden he would have to work around the rest of his life. She watched as he was led to another hall—Thorlóthlon's Main Hall—a room three-quarters the size of the one present, and in which there was to be held a great celebration. His transition was quick, and when he left, those who had come to give testimony to his coronation followed immediately after, eager to find the best seating. Finockt easily became lost in the crowd and even lost sight of Deverell, Malise, Strahan, and Deverell's other men who had fought so bravely alongside him, for the endless waves of foot traffic bore them away.

Suddenly Aonghus, the King of Anvelúth, approached her. Taking her hand in his, he warmly congratulated her on Thorlóthlon's victory and Uisdean's coronation. "We were proud to stand beside you, lassie," he said. "A common enemy is dead, their country defeated, for now. I pray this helps you sleep better, knowing Valínthia is free."

Finockt gave him a brisk nod though she had yet to pass a peaceful night's sleep.

"You may rest assured, Princess," he added, "that you will always have our kingdom at hand in future, should you and your brother ever need our services again. I will extend the same offer to Uisdean when I speak with him." He kissed the back of her hand and gave her a winsome wink before leaving her and wending his way through the crowd to find and personally congratulate Uisdean himself. Finockt watched him go and felt relieved to have such an ally in this strange, confident man.

She stumbled aside as two tittering young ladies forcibly brushed past her, ignorant of who she was, their focus bent on finding the young and handsome new king. Finockt rolled her eyes and pressed forward. This unexpected example of the changes at Thorlóthlon since Uisdean's new undertaking as king was one she had not anticipated nor was she prepared for. She was out of her element amongst all these people, and the open flirtation of the young women with regard to her brother—their king—was almost more than she could stand. She did not look forward to witnessing it again.

When she finally reached the adjoining hall, it was so over-crowded she could barely enter. Those guests who could not find seating stood, too eager to see the proceedings to regard the absence of a seat as a bother. Such a mass of people wilted any desire Finockt had to attempt to finagle her way in for a better position to see Uisdean. Standing on her tiptoes, she rocked this way and that in order to see her brother through and above the sea of necks and ladies' elaborate headdresses and hairstyles. Finally, she spotted him at the head of the assembly, readying himself to address the crowd. He gave a short speech, proclaiming victory and long-sought peace, and when he had finished, another great cry of joy sprang up from the people.

Unable to see anything more, or find Liusaidh amongst the tight press of bodies, Finockt shed her coronation robe, passing it off to one of the servant girls before she withdrew to the solitude of the castle's far, empty corridors. Here she could breathe freely. The air flowed light and cool, unlike the hot, heavy, stale air of the Main Hall with its over abundance of people and scents and perfumes. The farther she walked, the more the din of the castle's merrymaking hung lower and more muffled.

Finding a quiet, empty window seat, she sat upon it and tucked the shiny silken folds of her gown over her knees and feet. Now all was too quiet. Her thoughts drifted to Gwri. Liusaidh had been wrong. He had not attended, as she said he would. Finockt shook her head and wondered what she would have said if she *had* met with him today before he left. Would she ever have been able to express herself the way she needed to? Would she ever be able to convince him they should be together? Initially she had avoided his wish to say good-bye when Uisdean offered it, but now that she wanted it, something stood in their way. She was sorry she had not taken advantage of her opportunity. Now that she was eager to meet with him, it seemed too late. He avoided her, but why? Clearly, a deeper concern kept him separated from her, despite the truth of how they both felt about each other. Love was not enough to conquer his doubts. If it were, he would be here, beside her, and she would not be facing the events of this evening alone. This assumption convicted her of the potential truth between them, and she could not help but consider that what they both felt for each other might be false, seeing that something beyond both their powers prevented their alliance. A troubled sigh escaped her lips. She drew the ring Malise had given her from the folds of her gown and spun it around with her fingers when a man's tread across the flagstones interrupted her thoughts, the direction of his gait clearly intended for her. She straightened at the sound and slipped off the window seat to face Deverell.

"Not the one for whom you were waiting?" he asked, reading the surprise and disappointment dampening her features.

Finockt flushed. "No, Deverell, it's not that," she said, unusually embarrassed. "I...I only thought you would be Uisdean. We were to dine together in the Main Hall. He promised me I wouldn't get lost. I guess he has forgotten." She toyed with her mother's ring and then put it away.

"No, he hasn't forgotten," Deverell said. "It is why I have come."

Finockt half smiled. "In truth, you are the only one who is ever able to find me." She gazed out the window that looked across the way and through another window where the celebration could yet be viewed. Her eyes kept pace with the frequent movement of Thorlóthlon's guests, their constant chatter, and their open mouths ringing with laughter. "It was a grand coronation, wasn't it?" she said, but surprisingly she could remember little of all that took place; it was all a blur in her mind.

Awkward silence spread over them. Finockt felt it keenly because it was the first time it had ever truly been so between them. Deverell shifted beside her, and she sensed he would speak even before he said anything. But she did not look at him.

"He loves you, Finockt."

Her eyes locked with his, and a deep blush brightened her cheeks and illuminated her eyes.

"It's true," Deverell said. "He told me long ago."

Finockt looked down at her hands and rallied her strength. "I rather thought it was," she said, her throat dry. Deverell raised his eyebrows in surprise. "I heard you, in the garden," she explained, "that night…but he is gone now, and it matters little—I think we should adjourn to the Main Hall. Uisdean will be wanting to know what has kept us."

She gathered her skirts and headed past him when Deverell shot out his hand and stopped her. His face was troubled, and at the uncertainty reflecting in her eyes and the abruptness of his own action, he released her. "He's not far, Finockt. I know where he has gone. If you go now, you may still be able to catch him."

Tears stung her eyes. She glanced down the corridor behind them and sniffed softly. "Even should I go," she said, struggling with his suggestion, "there are too many people to sift through. I cannot make it to Tohr."

"Follow me," he said quietly and held out his hand.

Finockt hesitated, then she fit her hand into his, and he took off down the corridor with her in tow. She had to trot briskly behind him so long were his strides. Within moments, he had pulled her down several side corridors that led to short, narrow passageways—more unknown secrets of Thorlóthlon— and then down an enclosed passage toward the open quarters of a small side courtyard. Before the courtyard's entrance, he felt her hand trembling in his own and mistook it for excitement. He did not realize she was not sure she had made the right decision in following him.

CHAPTER THIRTY-NINE

"My horse Ivar is waiting for you," Deverell said, opening the heavy door for her. "Wait here. I'll bring him to you."

Finockt's heart raced as Deverell ducked under the rounded lintel and headed across the courtyard. She watched him go then spun around and paced along the darkened passage. This was madness! Complete madness to pursue a boy who had already indicated he wanted nothing to do with her, despite his declaration of how he obviously felt to everyone—but her. She wanted closure, yes, but to do all this on a whim? It was not like her. And why would Deverell of all people encourage her? His support baffled her and caused her to hesitate, striking more doubt in her mind and encouraging her to reconsider the outcome of what she was doing. The very next moment, she determined everything she had just thought did not make perfect sense. Her spirits then soared at the prospect of seeing Gwri, only to tumble a second time when she paused to reflect on one very important thing—Deverell *never* openly agreed with her. His agreement with her now eroded any burgeoning confidence in her decision and only served to deepen her reservation in leaving. Deverell's pursuit had been and always would be a quest for duty and honor. It was beyond strange that now of all occasions he advocated for her departure. For once in his life, had he given up his stoicism for matters of the heart?

She faltered at the rush of boots falling heavily along the corridor behind her.

"Finockt! You're still here!" Uisdean cried out, practically skidding to a stop. He wiped a light sheen of sweat off his brow. He was winded, and his robe and newly placed crown were both missing. "I've been looking everywhere for you. I didn't know if I'd make it."

Finockt frowned, even more confused. "Make it for what? To see me off?" she asked, wringing her hands. She glanced at the partially closed door, and a dreadful tension tightened its hold on her. She rubbed her fingers across her forehead. "I don't know, Uisdean. Perhaps this is a mistake."

"No, no," Uisdean said, drawing her aside even as she bristled with skepticism. "You'll see how wrong you are when you read this."

He handed her a folded piece of crinkled parchment. The initials *F.A.* were faintly scrolled with an elegant grace upon its creamy, faded top. "I found it late last night," he said. "I know you would have wished me to bring it to you immediately, but it seemed wrong to wake you as it was so late. And after so many years locked away, another few hours didn't seem worth the trouble of wresting you from your slumber. I pray you're not cross with me?"

"No, of course not. I do not believe I could ever be cross with you," Finockt murmured. She eyed the once ivory sheet of parchment, now tarnished light brown by the years and much handling, and took it from him with reluctant hands, a look of wonder upon her face as she caressed the fancy, blurred lettering. "What is it?" she asked.

"I don't know. I meant to give it to you earlier this morning, but other duties prevented me from carrying out my intention. I pray that it is not too late." Uisdean looked at her expectantly.

"Too late?" Finockt asked, worry upending her. "But… how do you know this was even meant for me?"

"Just open it," he urged her.

She flipped over the parchment. It shook lightly between her white hands, and her eyes widened when she recognized Thorlóthlon's coat of arms set snug within the seal's thick mold. Breaking its rubbery contours, she quickly skimmed the long, flowing script, then she looked up at Uisdean, her eyes emanating a mixture of both joy and uncertain dismay at the letter's brief content.

"What does it say?" he pressed.

"I don't know. It's hard to decipher. Some of the letters are missing and most of the words are marred."

"Missing?" Uisdean asked.

Finockt closed her eyes a brief moment. "But should it even say what I believe it does, how can I know it holds true? That the letter speaks of myself?"

"What's true? Let me see!"

Uisdean tore the parchment from Finockt's hands and moved to the nearest wedge of daylight streaming into the dark corridor. His eyes flashed over the script. Finockt edged closer to him and peered over his shoulder, rereading its contents once more alongside him in the dim lighting.

"Well?" she asked, her heart bursting within her when he lowered the parchment a tad and looked over at her. "Do you believe it says the same? Is it true?"

"It is true that the letters are marred. Therefore, it is quite difficult to understand. But it must speak of yourself, as there is none other with these same initials." He handed the parchment back to her. She reached for it and scanned it once more.

"Furthermore, what can be read finds itself clear in both meaning and understanding, as I so anticipated," her brother continued. "I can only pray for your sake that the words written here so long ago hold true to their meaning. There's only one way to find out…but it all makes sense based on what—"

"Only one way to find out?"

"Yes—one way—by meeting with Gwri."

Meeting with Gwri. Uisdean said it so easily, as if it was a simple request to drop everything and take a stroll with him.

Her heart beat faster in her attempt to sort it all out. "Where did you find this?" she asked. Her hands shook, but she could not quite decide whether they shook from excitement and anticipation or a feverish reluctance to accept her fate. She could not help but admit it was different now that it was a mandate rather than a decision of the heart. Maybe this was what Gwri feared? That she would not agree. Would this knowledge sway him, or would he still refuse her, despite the possibility of a happy union?

She refocused on Uisdean when he started talking. "I actually found it stuck amongst some parchments when going through those documents you gave Deverell for safekeeping at the Glen of Farith," he said. "That the parchment came from Father's most important papers furthers the truth of its message and encourages my heart, for of whom else could the parchment speak? There are no other kin of whom I am aware who bear these same initials," he concluded, hope for her rising within him. He paused a moment before setting his hand upon hers. "It seems the tides are definitely turning for you, dear sister, and the winds of change are blowing ever strong. It seems your hour has come." He smiled, then suddenly, a great agitation overtook him the longer she remained silent and still. But she could not speak nor could she move. Incredulity rooted her in place. The news was too perfect for her, too wonderful to be real. It scared her, and yet the more she considered the challenge of finding him, the more eager she was to depart. She strove to temper the thrill running through her.

"I am sorry I did not bring this to you sooner," Uisdean said, fearing her silence proceeded from a lingering hopelessness and disappointment in him.

Finockt began to reread the parchment a fourth time. Instead, she looked over at her brother. "I do not begrudge you anything," she said, the ache in her heart growing stronger. How could she tell him? Did she have the courage to reveal her innermost secret? She sought the words to express herself, but nothing reached her lips.

Uisdean studied her quietly, impatiently restraining himself and gently attempting to quell his frustration at her lack of action. When his heart could stand it no more, his tongue unloosed. "Well, what are you waiting for, Finockt? Go!" he cried. "Deverell has been waiting for you for some time now!"

Finockt started. Surprise widened her eyes, and the clarity of her gaze clouded over with hurt. But at her brother's continued cry, she gathered her skirts about her and moved quickly to the door, bodily forced there by the harshness of his commands.

"Go...go on!" he admonished, batting her away. "Time spends itself while you linger."

Through the crack in the door, she saw Deverell soothing Ivar and patiently awaiting her arrival. Every now and again, he looked to the side passage. How he knew Uisdean kept her and that the conversation between them was private, she did not know. She did not remember his returning to fetch her or interrupting their discourse at any given time to announce Ivar waited for her. She reached for the edge of the door then halted at the sadness coloring Uisdean's voice.

"I'm sorry to lose you, sister."

Tears trembled on the banks of her eyes. Rushing up to him, she threw her arms around his neck and embraced him warmly. "I love you, Uisdean. I know you must think I'm mad. I hardly know you, but I feel as though I've known you all my life. You don't know how happy I am that you're forever my brother and now my king."

Uisdean smiled and clasped her in another rough hug. "You have a good heart, little sister. I pray happiness will always find itself in your house," he whispered, holding her tightly, his eyes veiled with tears. "Now go! I bid you Godspeed. Go! He waits for you!" His voice was soft and gentle and full of brotherly love.

Finockt bestowed on him a grateful smile. Then she pressed his hand in a reluctant farewell before she ducked beneath the lintel and hurried across the courtyard to Deverell. Within the doorway, Uisdean lingered, watching her, a tear shimmering in his eye and a hopeful smile on his face. Pleased with his success, he then turned on his heel and strode back to the Main Hall.

Meanwhile, in the courtyard, Deverell helped Finockt up into the saddle then stepped back. She looked down at him. "You will not take me?" she asked, unable to hide her disappointment. He had always been her guide. Going without him seemed impossible. He gave her courage when no one else could.

"No," he said. "On this quest you must go alone."

She fingered the reins and collected her thoughts. "How do I find him?" she asked with more determination in her voice.

"If he has not yet gone, he rests to the northeast of MacPherson's Crag. You may reach it before sundown. Ivar knows the way. He will take care of you. Now go, time wanes while you linger."

He sounded like her brother. She gathered the reins and nudged Ivar. He skipped forward, but she held him in check and turned him around to face Deverell. The scene was all too familiar in her mind. It reminded her of another man, a boy really, she had loved and reluctantly left behind. A thread of dismay and caution entered her heart, and the realization that the same scene was repeating itself with Deverell of all men startled her. She felt unable to process it all or turn her back on it as she had in the village. What did it mean? Was she so superstitious? Or was there something more to all this? Something she did not want to admit even to herself? It struck her as another bad omen.

"It's all right, lass. The time is right. Go to him now! God bestows the gift upon you," Deverell exhorted her, his eyes misting with tears. He paused a moment. "Why do you stay?"

"Suddenly I'm afraid," Finockt replied, unable to tell him the truth.

"Afraid?" Deverell said. "Is it worth your leaving then?"

She looked over her shoulder toward the gate. "Yes—because…"

Deverell's heart constricted. "Then go. He deserves to know it," he said before she had finished.

She held his gaze. Ivar chomped at the bit and grew restless, but she kept a steady hand on him. "Do you approve, Deverell?" she asked, although she did not know why she asked it.

"I have approved of your heart's happiness since the beginning. I just did not want to see you hurt before the time was right," he gently replied.

He expected her departure, but still she did not release Ivar. "You'll be leaving soon, won't you?" she asked him, somehow sensing the time left between them was short. She studied him carefully.

"Aye, I'm called to other regions…other kingdoms…"

"To other places where you are needed most," she joked.

"Aye," he said, his answer accompanied by a short laugh.

"Promise me you will not stay away forever."

"No, I shall abide with the new king a while longer."

"Thorlóthlon will not be the same when you have gone."

Deverell's heart melted within him. "I shall miss you, Finockt. You are…" His voice trailed off, and his eyes clouded over in pain. "You are unlike any maiden I have ever met," he said in defeat, meeting her troubled eyes with the same saddened expression.

At these words, Finockt felt an unexpected twinge of disappointment flare within her—a strange, foreign, irritable feeling she could not rationalize. What had she hoped for him to say? She wanted to be with Gwri, did she not? Why was Deverell making her doubt everything and stripping away her clarity of mind, like he always did?

Behind her the soldiers opened the gates. Deverell stood still.

"I shall always remember your kindness," she told him. "For with you, have I always known that all lies safe."

"Aye, and I shall always remember your courage and your passionate heart. Now be gone with you," he scolded, laughing a little, as he swatted Ivar on the rump. The horse skittered, and Finockt guided him in a fast trot toward the gate. Before they passed beneath the portal, she looked back. Deverell's blue eyes shone brightly against the cloak of evening that had settled within the courtyard, and they emanated something she did not quite comprehend. She adjusted the reins within her hand as Ivar clattered across the dirt and cobblestones and kicked up dust on the thin track leading away from Thorlóthlon. Just before she gained the valley beyond the courtyard gates, she checked a prancing Ivar once again and looked upon Deverell long. Her distress increased, and her heart nearly strangled her. She did not want to leave, and she wrestled with the cumbersome notion of why. "I love you, Deverell," she whispered. The words bounded off her tongue—unforeseen and unbidden—as they had once before with Caslon at a time and place that now seemed so very long ago; they startled her as much then as they did now. She stiffened in the saddle and waited. For what, she did not know? An answer from him, a gesture? A request for her to stay?

He read the words on her lips, and they seemed to trouble him. His silence eliminated any further doubts she harbored and sealed her mission. She clamped her heels down on Ivar's sides. Spurred to action, he bolted down into the valley.

A dog rose knocked free from her hair floated back on the breeze and settled on the path near the gates where Deverell now stood. He watched it fall then plucked it from the ground and lifted his gaze once more to the open valley. "And I love you…Finockt Adaria."

The words spilled freely and tenderly from his lips when the last glimpse of her emerald green train disappeared below the slope of the land. In the same moment he spoke those words, deep within his heart, something broke, and a flood of emotion he had been holding back for years overwhelmed him. He crushed the dog rose in his hand and, with a heavy spirit, dropped the flower into the dust at his feet. It rolled and flopped in the wind, its creamy white edges already brown and curling in the wake of death, its lonely form the delicate symbol of an utterly vanquished heart.

For Deverell, the worst of this day was behind him, the anticipation of it fulfilled. Tomorrow he would wake to an ever-predictable future. His service to the king was not quite over, and justice for Banain still needed addressed. But this time even duty could not staunch the pain lancing his heart.

With the loss of Thorlóthlon's princess weighing on him more deeply than ever before, he turned, crossed the court-yard, and reentered Thorlóthlon, alone.

NAMES

Some pronunciations of the Welsh, Breton, Irish Gaelic, and Scottish Gaelic names listed below were reviewed by a linguistics friend, who is one of the few Breton speakers left in all of Brittany. I extend my warmest and most sincere thanks and appreciation for the time he has taken to help me make this book unique.

I would also like to give a special thanks to Ian, a Scotsman from Glasgow, whom I randomly met one day. His kindness, generosity, and patience with my myriad of requests regarding characters' names allowed me to have a more correct pronunciation of a lot of the Celtic/Irish names I have used for this book. Wherever you are, Ian, thank you.

Female Characters:

****Adaria** (Scottish/Irish; A-DAR-e-ah)—From the oak tree ford; *allthingsbabynames.com* (accessed on November 1, 2023) stated the oak tree symbolizes "strength, endurance, and wisdom" for the Celts; the core part of the name (Adara) is also of Hebrew origin and means "fire" and "noble;" I altered the spelling a little to fit my taste and added the "i;" this is Finockt's middle name.

****Annwn** (Middle Welsh; AN-win; when pronounced, sounds more like AND-WIN, though there is actually no "d" present)—Otherworld.

****Arnarlwyn** (Welsh; AR-NARL-wyn)—Finockt's mother's sister; Eilidh's mother; fictitious name and origin of the name I created especially for this book; meaning unknown.

****Arnorylja** (AR-nor-eel-YAH)—Name of the Great Queen of the West, aka the Queen of Evanthia; this is a made-up combination of two names—Anora (Ah-nora), which is Old Norse for Light eagle—and Ylja (eel-yah), which is an unknown female Icelandic name. Some have also said that the name together could mean Arnor (Ar-nor)—a Norse male name—meaning Land of the King, and Ilja (eel-yah)—a Hebrew male name—meaning Jehovah is God. Personally, I liked either one, but preferred the latter meaning. So I leave it up to you, the reader, to determine which description you like best.

Careen (English; KA-reen)—Little, womanly one; variant of Caroline; Liusaidh's attendant who sometimes sees also to Finockt. Darce's sweetheart.

Donia (Scottish Gaelic; DON-yah)—World Ruler. Donia is the English variant of the Scottish Gaelic Donalda; one of Liusaidh's loyal attendants at Thorlóthlon who also attends Finockt.

Eideann (Scottish Gaelic; E-den)—Fiery; Finockt's mother.

Eilidh (Scottish Gaelic; AY-leh; technically pronounced AY-lee, however, with the Scottish brogue it rather sounds like AY-leh)—Light; Eilidh is another name for Helen; of the House of Eilthárion; Finockt's maternal cousin.

Emanon (Scottish Gaelic; EMMA-non)—Unknown; Finockt's paternal grandmother.

Finockt (Irish Gaelic; FINN-icht)—Princess; also known as a Princess of Meath. In a recent search, I found the meaning of Finockt is "generous, kindhearted, humane and philanthropic." Those named Finockt "desire love and independence, love arts and music, and are bold, broad-minded and spiritual." They "have will power and are determined, but are impulsive, contentious, ill-tempered, rebellious and impatient, too." They "are very romantic and very loyal and idealistic." They place those they love "at the forefront of life." They are also "responsible, self-sacrificing, compassionate, creative, know where the moral high ground is and always try to take it, and have a strong instinct about matters of the heart." Descriptive meanings for Finockt were all gathered from *www.babynology.com/name/finockt-f.html* on September 21, 2018.

Gelis (Irish Gaelic; GA-less)—Unknown—could be Old Irish for bright swan; Finockt's guardian and "mother."

Lánorlidh (Irish Gaelic; LAN-or-leh)—Eideann and Arnarlwyn's sister; Finockt's maternal aunt; fictitious name and origin of the name I created especially for this book; meaning unknown.

Liusaidh (Scottish Gaelic; LOO-shade)—Warrior woman; Finockt's attendant and friend at Thorlóthlon. Gawain's fiancé.

Murron (Scottish Gaelic; MUR-en)—Sea or White/Fair; Finockt's best friend from the village.

Proinnseas (Irish Gaelic; PRON-cious)—this is actually a boy's name meaning Frenchman, or is an English version of Francis, said to be connected to St. Francis of Assisi. Proincias is the normal Irish spelling, but in my book I chose to make it a unisex name and give it to a girl; the young serving girl at Pennarn Cottage.

Talínnith (Irish Gaelic; TA-LIN-nith)—One of many talents; fictitious name, meaning of the name, and origin of the name for the purposes of this book alone; Acair's sweetheart.

Male Characters:

Acair (Scottish Gaelic; A-care)—Anchor; soldier of Thorlóthlon and at Pennarn Cottage; Talínnith's sweetheart.

Aonghus (Scottish Gaelic; AN-gus)—Unique strength, one choice; Aonghus is an old spelling of the more traditionally known name Angus; King of Anvelúth; Valínthia's ally.

Anwyl (Welsh; AN-will)—Beloved; the Lost King of Thorlóthlon; Finockt and Uisdean's father.

****Banain** (Irish Gaelic; BAN-IN)—Little blond one; one of Deverell's men; Darce's brother; Tirell's son.

****Boynton** (English/Irish Gaelic; BOYN-ton)—From the white river. This name appears to have both an Irish and an English origin. The River Boyne in Ireland is a famous river where some of the oldest megaliths in Ireland (Newgrange) are found and near Tara, one of the most important ritual sites in all of Ireland. Boyne is an English version of the Gaelic Boinn or Boann. The earliest form of the name is Bouinda meaning the "White cow" in Old Irish. It is also the name of the mythological Irish goddess/queen Boinn/Boann. The "ton" part of the name makes it English; one of Deverell's men.

****Bráthain** (Irish Gaelic; BRA-thane)—Doubtful one; fictitious name, meaning of the name, and origin of the name I created especially for this book. The one who challenged Coinneach when he presented Finockt before Thorlóthlon at a banquet held in her honor to celebrate her return to Thorlóthlon and to her family.

****Carynton** (KARYN-ton)—Unknown; could be a variant of Carrington or Charlestown; one of Deverell's men who died in a skirmish with the Dúnarians not long after they rescued Finockt from the village.

****Caslon** (KAZ-lon)—Unknown; Finockt's other best friend from the village.

****Coinneach** (Scottish Gaelic; KONE-eek)—Handsome; Finockt's paternal grandfather; regent of Thorlóthlon.

****Creighton** (Old English; KRAY-ton)—Hill. This "English" place name is an Old English borrowing from Brittonic/Brythonic (not Gaelic) and means "hill." It is still used today in Breton under the form of "Creac'h" (as spelled in many place names [in Brittany]). One of Tirell's men.

Cronan (Gaelic; KRONE-in)—Dark-skinned one or dark brown one; one of Deverell's men.

Cullom (Irish Gaelic; CUL-um)—Dove. Colm in Irish means dove; the miller's son who died during the skirmish in Finockt's village when she was ultimately saved by Deverell.

Darce (Irish Gaelic; DAR-ce)—Dark-haired one. The corresponding Irish spelling is Dorchaidh. Darcy is the English version of it; Banain's brother; Tirell's son.

Deverell (Old Welsh; DEV-er-ell)—From the riverbank; The name also comes from older Welsh *dwfrial* "river of the lal" or "fertile upland region." The modern Welsh rendering of this Old Welsh name has its source in Wiltshire, England, not Wales; he grew up in the North Country and descended from the Old Evanthians; the Northerner's true name. "The Northerner" is frequently used interchangeably through this book with Deverell.

Egan (Irish Gaelic; E-gan)—Ardent, fiery one; one of the clan nobles and a cynical, cautious ally of Thorlóthlon.

Eoin (Scottish Gaelic; E-in)—God is gracious; Celtic form of John; page to the king.

Finain (Celtic; FINN-in)—Poison-tongued; Tirell's name before he adopted the Dúnarian customs and culture as his own; Coinneach's nephew; Anwyl's first cousin.

Galówen (Welsh; GA-LOW-en)—Newcomer; Fictitious name, meaning of the name, and origin of the name I created especially for this book. The young soldier whom Darce rendered unconscious upon his escape from Thorlóthlon.

Gawain (Welsh; GA-wayne)—Battle hawk. The traditional Welsh form is Gwalchmei and the root of the word is "gwalch" which means hawk; Liusaidh's fiancé.

****Glynarwyth**—(Welsh; Glyn-AR-wyth)—one of the old kings of Valínthia. Fictitious name and origin of the name I created especially for this book; meaning unknown. His image was on a tapestry on the eastern side of Thorlóthlon.

****Gwri** (Celtic; GUR-E)—Of the golden hair; descendent of Royd Annar and the Gwrithlís clan; Prince of Mithel; one of Deverell's men.

****Maegowan** (Scottish Gaelic; May-GOW-an)—Son of metalworker; Tirell's captain.

****Malise** (Scottish Gaelic; MA-lease)—Servant of God; Anwyl's mentor; Finockt and Uisdean's maternal grandfather.

****Morvan** (Breton; MOHR-vin)—Great in the ferocious attack/assault; Morvan is a common Breton name, even today. There were Celts in Scotland who also bore this name, but they were most likely Brythons (like Bretons). The oldest form of Morvan is Moruuan (9th Century); one of Deverell's allies; keeper/leader of the Deogal Cliffs.

****The Northerner**—Alternate name for Deverell, who spent much of his formative training in the North Country. Used synonymously with Deverell throughout this book.

****Rognvaldr** (Old High German or Norse; ROGEN-vall-der)—advice of the sovereign; servant boy/messenger at Pennarn Cottage in service to the king; in this case, Coinneach; there is a bit of a guttural rolling of the "r" at the beginning of the name; pronunciation gleaned from University of Colorado professor, Dr. Jackson Crawford's Youtube channel in 2023.

****Royd Annar**—This is a compound name. Royd (ROY-t), which is Norse for "Dwells in the clearing in the forest;" and Annar (AN-AR), which is Old Norse for either Second or Father of the world; he is the Great Queen of Evanthia's humble charge who she named as King of Evanthia upon her death because she had no heir. Royd Annar later changed the title of Evanthia's kingdom to Mithel; the two—Mithel and Evanthia—are frequently used interchangeably throughout this trilogy. Gwri is a descendent of this king.

****Strahan** (Scottish Gaelic; STRAY-in)—Valley of the horses; The meaning of the name is based on the local Scottish lands of Strachan (pronounced "Strawn"). The Gaelic root of the word "stath" means valley and "eachain" means "each horse." Hence, the completed translation of "the valley of the horses;" one of Deverell's men.

****Tirell** (Old English; TYR-ell)—Thunder-ruler; Coinneach's nephew; Anwyl's cousin; Finockt's second cousin and enemy; father of Banain and Darce.

****Toran** (Scottish Gaelic; TOR-an)—From the craggy hilltop; Anwyl's middle name.

****Trythwyn** (Welsh; TRYTH-win)—Sage; fictitious name, origin, and meaning of the name I created especially for this book; Thorlóthlon's scribe and keeper of Thorlóthlon's records, annals, and maps.

****Uisdean** (Gaelic; ISH-jun or OOSH-jun or OO-iz-dean)—Intelligent; Finockt's brother; Anwyl's son and Thorlóthlon's rightful heir. Malise and Coinneach's grand-son; there are obviously a few ways to pronounce Uisdean's name. I prefer OOSH-jun myself, but you are welcome to utilize whichever pronunciation suits you best.

Horses:

****Asmund** (Old Norse; AZ-munt)—God is protector; Finockt's borrowed horse that died during the skirmish with Tirell in the woods in *The Lost King's Daughter.*

****Fàlite** (Irish Gaelic; FOUL-chey)—Welcome; Gwri's horse.

****Ivar** (Scottish Gaelic; I-var)—Archer, bowman; Deverell's horse.

****Mónwyn** (Welsh; MON-wyn)—White Mount; Finockt's horse she rode from Thorlóthlon to Pennarn and then from Pennarn to the Highlands to see Malise; fictitious name, origin, and meaning of the name that I created especially for this book.

****Tohr** (Old Norse; TOR)—Thunder; Tohr is a spelling variation of Thor; Finockt's horse from the village.

Main kingdoms/countries:

****Dúnahez** (DUNA-hez)—The southern coastal lands, where Dubhloach, King of Ruminthness, was banished for slaying his brother Egil. Fictitious name I made for the southlands. Dubhloach means 'dark hero.'

****Evanthia** (E-VAN-thia)—The western coastal lands; the Great Queen's kingdom. Fictitious land name I made for the Great Queen, however, it seems from a recent Google search that Evanthia is actually a girl's name and is a Romanitization of Euanthe which is a Greek word meaning 'Good Blossom/ Flower.' On May 30, 2019, Babynamewizard.com described its full meaning as "a white evening blossoming flower that is pure and very fragrant." It is also tied to three saints—and here I'd thought I'd just made up the neatest name possible. Who knew? Fits well with my intended creation, so I'll take it, regardless!

****Mithel** (MITH-el)—A made-up name that means Starlight; the Great Queen of Evanthia's kingdom renamed Mithel by Royd Annar. Mithel and Evanthia are used interchangeably throughout this trilogy; fictitious name I created for this book.

****Thorlóthlon** (THOR-LOTH-lon)—the Lost King's stronghold and the stronghold currently presided over by the Lost King's father, Coinneach, until the true heir is determined; fictitious name I created for this book.

****Valínthia** (VA-LIN-thia)—Kingdom to the east of Evanthia. A made-up name for King Egil's kingdom, which is also Finockt's ancestral home; fictitious name I created for this book.

Minor kingdoms to the North:

****Anvelúth** (AN-vuh-LUTH)—smaller kingdom to the north, northeast of Valínthia; King Aonghus's kingdom; fictitious name I created especially for this book.

****Brúngélon** (BRUN-GELL-on)—small kingdom to the north, northwest of Valínthia; fictitious name I created especially for this book.

****Galóthlon** (GA-LOTH-lan)—Tirell's father's lands near Thorlóthlon; the kingdom Tirell would have been heir to by birthright; fictitious name I created for this book.

****Glynfinnín** (GLYN-finn-IN)—small kingdom to the north of Valínthia and south, southwest of Brúngélon; fictitious name I created especially for this book.

****Ruminthness** (RU-MINTH-ness)—Kingdom to the north, northeast of Evanthia. A made-up name for Dubhloach's kingdom, Egil's brother and murderer; fictitious name I created for this book.

Peoples:

Dúnarians (DUN-arians)—the people of the Dúnahez;
King Dubhloach's descendants; Tirell's mother's people;
fictitious name I created for this book.

Evanthians (E-VAN-thians)—the people of Evanthia; the
Great Queen's people and descendants; fictitious name I
created for this book.

Gwrithlís (GUR-ith-LESS)—Royd Annar's people/descen-
dants; those who renamed the Great Queen's citadel Mithel
after Royd Annar's ascension to the Great Queen's throne;
fictitious name I created for this book.

Halvarnathness (HAL-var-NATH-ness)—Shepherds of the
East and border guards to the distant Dúnahez; fictitious
name I created for this book.

Valínthians (VA-LIN-thians)—the people of Valínthia;
King Egil's descendants

Minor Locations:

Aedre River (Norse; AIR-drah—the 'h' is almost silent)—
"stream." The river that flows before the Deogal Cliffs.

Bricriu Forest (Bree-CREE-U)—the black forest where
Deverell and Annwn meet; name means 'poison-tongued;'
fictitious name and pronunciation I created for this book.

Caldária (Cal-DAR-ia)—Tirell's usurped Valínthian stronghold to the northeast of the Dúnahez and the southeast of
Thorlóthlon; fictitious name I created for this book.

Deogal Cliffs (Anglo-Saxon; DAY-O-gall)—Deogal, literally means "secret." Thus, these are the secret cliffs where
Morvan and his men hide out, and the place where

Deverell takes Coinneach and the others for protection after the attack on Pennarn Cottage.

Elwynna Woodland (Anglo-Saxon; EL-WYN-na)—"friend of the elves." The woodland in which lies the Deogal Cliffs and through which flows the Aedre River. I changed the spelling a little to fit my taste. The original spelling is with only one "n."

Émaron Grasses (E-mare-on)—the thick, verdant grassland Tirell took Finockt and Gwri through to get to Caldária; fictitious name I created for this book.

Glen of Farith (FA-RITH)—the encampment where Deverell takes Finockt after rescuing her outside Caldária and where Thorlóthlon's reduced army met to prepare for the big battle against Tirell; fictitious name and pronunciation I created for this book.

Palíthmar Mountains (PA-LITH-mar)—mountain range to the north, northwest of Thorlóthlon; fictitious name created especially for this book.

Pennarn Cottage (PENN-arn)—Coinneach's hunting lodge/cottage to the north, northeast of Thorlóthlon; fictitious name created especially for this book.

House of Eilthárion (ILL-THAR-ion)—Eilidh's family line; fictitious name created especially for this book.

Miscellaneous Names:

Brionglóid (Irish Gaelic; BRING-lode)—Dream, reverie; the name of the Great Queen's sword.

GLOSSARY

The Heir—Book II

Aye (pronounced "eye")—Scottish equivalent of "yes."

Haí (pronounced "hi")—believed to be an Egyptian word used to bring emphasis to a statement; also has a Japanese origin and brings emphasis to a question before it is asked. This word is used in this book to bring emphasis and attention to an important statement or declaration and/or to advice or an admonition to which the speaker wishes the receiver to adhere; sometimes it is used for consolation. I added the accent aigu (or if the Irish is preferred, the fadda) on the "i" for aesthetics and emphasis during pronunciation.

Hoarding—an exterior, sheltered gallery constructed on the side of a rampart or curtained wall of a castle built for defensive purposes. It typically contained a murder hole—a round hole in the floor of the structure—through which soldiers would throw stones, pour oil, etc. onto the advancing enemy. A big thank you to my younger brother, Zachary, for making me aware this type of medieval defense system even existed when I was writing my book and wanted something cool for my characters to escape through.

Breton words used in *The Heir* continue to act here in this second installment of *In the Shadow of Emerald Fire* as the "old language" of Evanthia and Valínthia and Finockt's ancestors. To reiterate, Breton is a very old—and real—Celtic language. It is one of the "dying languages" of my ancestors and is currently rarely spoken within the land of Brittany, a Celtic region located in the western arm of France; there are very few remaining Breton speakers who are fluent in this ancient language. All translations of the Breton language into English and vice-a-versa were completed by one of the few Breton speakers left in all of Brittany.

BRETON WORDS

The Heir

Mond a ra mat ar bed ganeoc'h?—literally, "Go that does
  well the world with ye?"
Mond—go
A—that
Ra—does
Mat—well
Ar—the
Bed—world
Ganeoc'h—with ye

Mond a ra—literally means "go does (it)?" This is a short-
  ened version of "Mond a ra mat ar bed ganeoc'h?" This
  latter phrase means "Go does (it) well with ye?" Update on
  this from Book 1: *The Lost King's Daughter:* "Mond a ra"
  would actually be closer to carrying the same connotation
  as "ça va?" in French, which literally means "it's going?"
  The response following someone asking you this is typically, "Oui, ça va," meaning "yes, it's going." It would *not*
  carry the Old English idea of "same to you" as I described
  in Book 1. I wanted to make sure I clarified this for you
  here in Book 2, as I don't feel my initial explanation of it

was accurate in *The Lost King's Daughter.* But I'm happy to have this opportunity to update you on my error and provide you (and myself!) with a better understanding of the Breton language.

Mond—go
A—that
Ra—does

❧

Ha c'hwi, ma breur—and ye, my brother
Ha—and
C'hwi—ye
Ma—my
Breur—brother

❧

Trugarez, ma breur—thank you, my brother
Trugarez—thank you
Ma—my
Breur—brother

❧

Ne oan ket gouest da skoazellañ ma zud—was I not able to help shoulder my people/folks/kinsmen
Ne oan ket—Was I not
Gouest—able
Da—to
Skoazellañ—help shoulder
Ma—my

Zud—people/folks/kinsmen; different than 'dud' found elsewhere in Breton secondary to the possessive 'my' before
the noun 'people/folks/kinsmen,' which changes 'dud' to
'zud.' In this case, it is pronounced 'zut.'

❦

Ra Doue ho pardono evit an droug ho-peus gwraet—may
God forgive you for the evil you have done
Ra—may
Doue—God
Ho—ye
Pardono—forgive
Evit—for
An droug—the evil/hurt
Ho-peus—ye have
Gwraet—done

❦

***Ra vo karantez Doue ganeoc'h, hag an Aotrou Doue da roi
nerz da ho kalon***—may the love (of) God be with you,
and may God strengthen your heart
Ra—may
Vo—be
Karantez—love
Doue—(of) God
Ganeoc'h—with you
Hag—and
An—the
Aotrou—Lord
Doue—God

Da—to
Roi—give
Nerz—strength
Da—to
Ho—your
Kalon—heart

❧

*A **wir galon***—with a true heart
A—That
Wir—with true
Galon—heart

Dear Reader:

Because of you, I am able to sit at my kitchen table and, with deep happiness of heart, write this missive to you. If it weren't for your enduring support, encouragement, and belief in Finockt's story, there may not be another one to tell—at least not in print anyway. A writer's job is in large part a solo effort, but in essence, that's where it stops—in writing the story. From there, it blossoms into something that involves so many lives there's probably not enough space to really include and thank everyone I would like to.

It was always my hope (a dream, really) to see Finockt's story in print, and I'd really hoped beyond measure there'd be at least *one* person who would actually be interested in *The Lost King's Daughter.* But you all have well exceeded my expectations. Your enthusiasm and genuine excitement for the next installment of Finockt's story, *The Heir,* which you are now holding in your hands, was a great motivator and served, in the vein of Anne from *Anne of Green Gables,* as a "delicious inspiration" during the process of editing and finalizing this next "chapter" of my series, *In the Shadow of Emerald Fire.*

I am so grateful for this opportunity to (hopefully!) entertain you yet again with the ongoing saga of Finockt's journey! Thank you for taking the time out of your day or evening or both to delve into *The Heir* and discover what happens next! I hope this installment transports you in the same way so many have said *The Lost King's Daughter* did.

Thank you for letting me serve you through my writing! If you'd like to connect with me, please check out my website at **www.adgermanbooks.com** or my Instagram page @adgermanbooks. If you'd also like to be one of the first to know what's happening with me and my books, subscribe to my monthly newsletter via the Home page on my website!

I'd love to get to know you better as well. So, please always feel free to email me at contact@adgermanbooks.com or hit reply to my newsletter, and I'll look forward to corresponding with you there!

God bless you for taking the time to read *The Heir!* I hope you have thoroughly enjoyed it, and are looking forward to the third and final installment of my trilogy *In the Shadow of Emerald Fire*. Again God bless, and wishing you many hours of exciting, thrilling, heart-pounding reading!!

~A.D. German

ACKNOWLEDGEMENTS

The best thing about being an independent publisher is the fact that I only have to answer to myself! Meaning, I get to acknowledge literally *everyone* I want to without anyone telling me to limit my outpouring of gratitude, in order "to save paper" or because it's "so much cheaper!" That being said, if you touched my life in any way, and I know your name, you'll find yours here! Thank you for all the love, support, and encouragement you have brought to my life. It's my prayer that through my books that you so faithfully share with others, I will be able to touch many more lives in turn. Thank you for making an author's dream come true!

Please also note that it is my intention to acknowledge and thank those who have touched my life in order of how they actually *came* into my life, not in terms of who is most important! Everyone is important and special to me, and I am very grateful for your presence in my life—except my mom! Sorry, she does take precedence! haha. So, without further ado...

To my mom: you've heard this already, but I'll say it again: Words cannot express my thanks for all that you've done to make my books shine! Literally. Figuratively. Without you, readers would never be able to enjoy my books in the same way. You know me better than I know myself—particularly when it comes to writing. Thank you for your enduring patience, your understanding, your innate ability to discern what I mean, even when I haven't conveyed it well on paper, and thank you, most of all, for the insane amount of *time* you devoted to reading/editing, rereading/reediting, and reading/editing again this second book! Thank you for truly loving the story and for your sincere concern and investment in all my characters and what happens to them! And a bigger thank you for your honest expression of and deep, heartfelt concern over what would happen to your favorite male character—Deverell! And last of all, thank you for always making me as "giddy as a schoolgirl" each time you shared how much you *loved* the continuation of Finockt's story. Your timing in that regard was consistently a Godsend because you literally always happened to share this with me on the days I needed the most encouragement! I love you so much, Mom, and am so incredibly grateful you've stuck this out with me and seen me through *The Lost King's Daughter* and now *The Heir!* Here's to Book 3! Hope you love it even more than the other two!

To my dad: thank you for helping me with the Great Homeschool Convention in Cincinnati! My first convention ever. That was a whirlwind experience! Thank you for traveling there and back as many times as you did and helping me unload and load, as well as helping me man my booth, assist book lovers with *The Lost King's Daughter,* and even wrap a book or two! Here's to the Great Homeschool Convention in 2024! Love you!

To Jason—my loving brother-in-law—the first one who said, before it was even published, "I'll buy your book!" You more than delivered on your promise! Thank you so much for your eagerness to encourage me and support my attempt to be an author through your purchase of *four* copies of *The*

Lost King's Daughter for your family! You are seriously the best brother-in-law a girl could have. Thank you for always being there for me, no matter what! For sharing *The Lost King's Daughter* with so many friends and for promoting it any and every way you can! What a blessing! I'm so glad you're a part of the family, and I really appreciate your always having my back throughout the years! Love you!

To my super supportive sister-in-law, Kim—thank you so much for advocating for clean fantasy in your local public library in Wabash, Indiana, and for believing my story fits that bill and is something young girls can read without hesitation! I'm so grateful for such an unexpected, but welcomed, gesture of love, support, and encouragement! You made my day when you shared with me proof that Wabash Public Library actually had *my* book on their shelves! I still can't get over that. You didn't know it then, but God allowed your act of kindness to pave the way for other local libraries to join in on the action! So, thank you! Hope you enjoy *The Heir* as much as *The Lost King's Daughter!* Love you!

To my older brother, Brandon—thank you for supporting this endeavor of mine through your purchase of *The Lost King's Daughter* for *your* daughters, my nieces! Your belief in my ability as a writer is touching. I loved that you believed in me and my book so much that you wanted your girls to have a story written by their aunt. Hope you enjoy *The Heir* just as much! I love you!

To my younger brother, Zach—thank you for your artistic eye and for helping me with my beautiful set-up at the Great Homeschool Convention! You always have my back, too, and I'm so grateful for your love and support! I love you!

To my younger sister, Caitlin—thank you for all your

support in finding *The Lost King's Daughter* some amazingly excited ARC reviewers! You are what helped me achieve everything I needed to promote *The Lost King's Daughter* at the Great Homeschool Convention! Thank you, too, for the time you've given to helping me find other places to promote *The Lost King's Daughter!* Because of you, now I have more avenues to pursue than I previously thought possible. Thank you for your love and encouragement and for always being there for me! I love you!

To my youngest sister, Marissa—thank you for your support and purchase of a copy of *The Lost King's Daughter* "just because I'm your sister!" Haha! You were also one of my very first print sales on Amazon! Thank you for making me legit! Thank you, too, for your support in sharing ARCs of my book with your friends! Because of you and Cait, I had a good number of readers interested in being ARC reviewers when I thought I'd have none. Thank you! I love you so much!

To Meredith G.—my very first purchaser! Thank you so much for purchasing my ebook! You were truly my very *first* sale! I was literally over the moon!! Wish you could have seen my face! Thank you, too, for further supporting me through your purchase of my print book. Your generosity well exceeded any expectations I might have had (I had none btw! I just appreciated you and your daughter joining my ARC team!). So, thank you so much for your support and kindness! You're what got me thinking, "Okay, maybe I can really do this!" So, thank you, thank you! And thank you for allowing your daughter, Logan, to participate in reviewing an ARC! Also, thank you for all your ideas regarding what to bring to my very first convention! That was a Godsend, and I'm so grateful!

To Katie H.—thank you so much for allowing your

daughter, Madalyn, to be an ARC reviewer and for leaving me a review on Amazon! I'm so glad you also really enjoyed reading *The Lost King's Daughter* yourself! I hope you are intrigued by *The Heir* and find it as entertaining as Book 1!

To Madalyn—a "writer in training" (you go, girl!) and one of my best and first supporters! Thank you for loving *The Lost King's Daughter* as much as you have! Thank you for your candid review and for sharing via my sister, Caitlin, how excited you were about Book 2's forthcoming publication! Your encouragement was a Godsend, and I'm so grateful that you enjoyed Book 1 to the extent that you have. Your feedback was especially encouraging because you are literally one of the readers for whom I wrote *The Lost King's Daughter!* As I mentioned elsewhere in this acknowledgements section, God allowed your encouragement to truly inspire me to keep pursuing the course, despite all the doubts that arose in the process. You always sent a message of encouragement and hope through my sister at the perfect time, and that is something that will always remain near and dear to my heart. Thank you! I hope *The Heir* surpasses your expectations and leaves you stoked for Book 3!

To Logan—allies in advocacy with Madalyn and also one of my staunchest supporters! Thank you so much for loving *The Lost King's Daughter* and for even loving the Glossary and Names section! I was thrilled that resonated with you, and your love for these two sections made me even happier I had included it! Your ongoing enthusiasm and encouragement for Book 1 is something I shall always treasure! You helped inspire me to throw everything I have into Book 2 and make it the best it could be! Thank you for your sincere excitement and anticipation of *The Heir* and for insisting that I be aware of how much you were looking forward to its release! To an author, this is indescribable—a type of encouragement that puts more meaning into every aspect of what I'm doing. I truly hope you enjoyed every page of Book 2 and can't wait for Book 3!

To Ginny—Thank you so much for all your wonderful encouragement and sincere compliments concerning *The Lost King's Daughter!* Thank you for being an ARC reviewer! You made my heart sing when you described *The Lost King's Daughter* as "transportive" and "a good escape" and reprieve from the rampant evil of this present world. Your description of my story was exactly everything I wanted readers to experience. Thank you for sharing how much you enjoyed my book and are looking forward to Book 2's publication! I hope *The Heir* exceeded your expectations as well!

To Ellen—You made my day when your mother shared with me via my sister, Marissa, how much you were talking to her about *The Lost King's Daughter* and everything that was happening in the story! I wish I could have been there to hear it first-hand! I was thrilled to know that you enjoyed it so much that you wanted to talk about it with your mom! That thrilled me to the core! I was so happy to hear that my story resonated with you in such a way as to make you want to discuss it with someone close to you. Thank you for being my ARC reviewer again! I hope you loved *The Heir* as much as *The Lost King's Daughter!*

To Don Gates: Thank you *so very much* for your incredible support of my fledgling attempt to be a "real" author! Ever since you discovered I had written a book, you've been one of my best and staunchest advocates. Thank you, thank you for your sincere love for my book (especially my Prologue!)! Your belief in me as a writer and your belief in my story have been both empowering and encouraging. Thank you for loving *The Lost King's Daughter* as much as you have! You always lifted me up with your genuine encouragement regarding my writing and my book right when I needed it most. You are a testimony that God is always watching out for me! I'm so grateful for your generosity and kindness, for your consistent promotion of *The Lost King's Daughter,* and for again believing in me so much that you bought copies of *The Lost King's Daughter* for your own granddaughters! Thank you, too, for sharing my book with other young girls you know and for your innate belief that they will love it as much as you do! I hope you enjoy *The Heir* as much as you did *The Lost King's Daughter!*

To Sharon Dickhaus: another super advocate of me and *The Lost King's Daughter!* Thank you for all your kind words regarding my story, the beauty of its weaving, and how much you loved every aspect of Finockt's first adventure! Thank you, too, for loving the cover art as much as you do and the symbolism and meaning found within it! That was thrilling to hear! You have been so kind and so incredibly supportive. I've been floored by your generosity and deep-seated belief in my writing and my story by sharing *The Lost King's Daughter* with so many friends and family! Thanks to you and Don Gates, you've helped make my publishing venture legit! Thank you so much! I hope you are looking forward to *The Heir* and have enjoyed reading it as much as you did *The Lost King's Daughter!*

To Lisa Helen Esselstein—my *amazing* work friend and the "sunshine" in my life! Thank you for everything! From your beautiful encouragement regarding Finockt's story to your belief that I actually do truly possess talent as a writer, thank you, thank you, thank you! God always led you to contact me when my confidence in my writing was flagging and my doubts about "doing this" rose above my head. You always called or texted to share your heartfelt encouragement and sincere compliments at the exact moment I needed it. Through you, God gave me the boost I had prayed for and the inspiration I needed to keep going! Thank you, too, for so lovingly reading *The Lost King's Daughter* and savoring the story by finding quotes and passages you thoroughly enjoyed! That was extra special to me and showed me we're even more kindred spirits than I believed because you always picked the same quotes and passages I actually enjoyed writing the most! So, thank you so very much for your loving and generous support of me! I miss you at work, but I'm so glad to know you're loving retirement. You deserve it! I hope *The Heir* transports you as much as *The Lost King's Daughter* has!

To N.C.—one of my newsletter subscribers and the very first to reply to inquiries I made in one of my monthly newsletters! Thank you for writing me and making my day brighter! It was so great to hear from a reader of *The Lost King's Daughter!* Thank you for your encouragement regarding how much you enjoyed Finockt's story and are looking forward to what happens next! This is always an author's dream come true! I hope *The Heir* kept you wanting to turn more pages!

To M.C.—another one of my newsletter subscribers and one of the first to reply to inquiries I made in my September newsletter! Thank you for writing me and sharing how much you enjoyed *The Lost King's Daughter* and how much you were looking forward to Book 2's release. It was so exciting to hear from a reader! You very much made my day! So thank you for taking the time to reach out and correspond with me. I've loved the fact that we've kept up correspondence since then, and I still always look forward to each and every email I receive from you. Here's to many more! I truly hope you enjoyed *The Heir* as much as Book 1!

And to my Lord and Savior Jesus Christ—thank You for even enabling me to start this adventure in the first place! It's always difficult for me to determine where to praise You! At the very beginning of the acknowledgements section or the end. I erred on the side of saving the absolute best for last! I decided that, by acknowledging You here, any reader of this section will end where all eyes ought to be: on Jesus! You have been my Advocate for life, even when I believed there was no reason to move forward. You shone Your Light into my life through countless others in the Body of Christ. You gave me encouragement through friends, family, and most of all, Your Word. When doubts arose that were so swift and fast, I felt I'd be swept under by the current, You showed me Your promises last, and You gave me the Strength to keep going. You gave me Peace and Comfort every time I prayed for it. My hope is that You are glorified through everything I write. You are the Giver of creativity and the Master Wordsmith. As I shared in *The Lost King's Daughter*, if there be any goodness, any wit, any vivacity, any talent of any kind that repeats itself in *The Heir*, it all stems from Christ—Who bestows all manner of goodness and blessing on His people as He sees fit. Without Him, my work would be nothing. It is He Who inspires and gives rise to creativity, and it is He Who is the Giver of words. To Him be all the glory. You are holding *The Heir* in your hands only because of Him.

Likewise, if there be anything of ill-repute or anything distasteful or unedifying or anything unsatisfactory, I claim the errancy and disappointment all as my own. If the latter be the case, I also pray Christ's forgiveness for not having lived up to the life He has called me to lead. My only consolation in that regard is that Christ is merciful and forgiving and His grace and love cover over a multitude of sins. May that be so here, as I strive only to live and serve Christ alone, forever.

ABOUT THE AUTHOR

A.D. German lives in the heart of the Midwest. She has loved fairy tales, a happy ending, and all things medieval since early childhood. When she was asked what she would like to do when she grew up, her mind would literally go blank—the only thing she envisioned was living in her imagination.

She never thought this possible until one day a daydream became a storyline, and a storyline became an actual, real, full-fledged book.

She hopes readers will enjoy this second installment of her debut, YA medieval Christian fantasy series *In the Shadow of Emerald Fire,* as much as she enjoyed writing it.